CW00524172

OBEDIENCE

TIES THAT BIND

BOOK ONE

LIZA SNOW

Book Cover and interior layout by: MiblArt.com
Edited by: Mads Arlow
Full-Cast Audiobook Narrated by: Daniel Zbel and Rapunzaroo. Additional Characters Voiced by Isabel Salazar, Lisa Graham and Pippa Ryder.

Acknowledgements

I had to think long and hard about the acknowledgements for this book. These one hundred and fifty thousand words are truly the reflection of my author journey the last seven years. They represent so many hours of time I dedicated, so many hurdles I've jumped through, so many times I have struggled and forced myself not to give up. They are truly my magnum opus, up to this point in my career.

I believe so strongly in the story on these pages, and feel it resound so profoundly within me, that I don't even think I have the capacity to truly thank every single person, every single event in my life, that has inspired this beautiful book of mine.

But I'm going to try.

First and foremost, the man who deserves to be at the top of this list. My husband, Thomas. A lot of the words on these pages pay homage to you, for every nudge you've given me toward this career, the countless hours you spent listening to me talk nonstop about my books, and for knowing as strongly as I did this is the reason I was put on this Earth, and kept me facing it.

To Cassandra, my heroines namesake, who I met at the Ringling Museum in Sarasota, Florida back shortly after I moved to Florida. I went and wrote there many times, and it was your and my conversation that inspired this book. You told me to name a character after you, and I am giving you the best one I have. Thank you for inspiring me with your stories about being an aerialist.

To Charity and Kevin, and Fadela. The first three people in my life, besides Thomas, who found out I wrote romance for a living. Who were all so supportive and encouraging, that I don't think I'd still be standing here without it. And I certainly wouldn't have had the courage to start shouting it from the rooftops now. Thank you.

To my entire family, my blood family, my extended family, my made family. My family that still talks to me, the ones that don't, and the ones that have passed on. The huge, overarching theme in this book is about family, and I feel like that's for a reason. Mostly because I have so much to say about it. Thought so long, went to many therapy sessions, experienced every emotion on the spectrum about it. But you're all my family. You've all shaped me. Made me who I am. Which, if I'm at this point right now, having put this book into the world, then you all did a hell of a job and I am incredibly grateful for all of you.

Joshua, I think about you a lot my friend. I miss you terribly. And I really wish you were still here, because I can imagine all the shit you'd give me for being a romance writer and I would have loved every minute of it. The world is a little darker without you in it.

To Margaret, who I also miss beyond measure. I would probably never have dared telling you I write romance for a living, but you too, told me so many times, to pursue writing. And the day you died, I published my very first story. Every time I have since, I always think of you.

To Mads, the best beta reader, editor and someone I now call my friend, in the entire universe, who chatted with me for so long about the book and helped me with it in so many ways. Who loves my book babies as much as I do. To Nina, my newsletter ninja. To all the betas who helped me and who I took every single one of your words into consideration.

Writing is a team sport, and you made me see that. I wouldn't have gotten here without you.

To Daniel, who took a chance and decided to voice my favorite character I've ever written. You were the only person meant to be Chandler, and I am forever grateful to you that you leapt with me. To Taylor, who was the only one meant to voice Cassandra. I knew it the instant I heard you. I love your beautiful voice, and there was no better person to take on the role. And the way you two sound together... Hot damn, couldn't have asked for anything better!

And last, but certainly not least, I cannot ever go without thanking my readers. All those who pick up my books and give them a chance. I still get chills to this day that there are people out there reading my words, who love my characters as much as I do, who take hours of their life to immerse themselves in my stories. For you, I am the most grateful, because I wouldn't be here without you. And I hope, beyond measure, that this book does justice in expressing how much that matters to me, and how much I care about giving you the absolute best I have to give.

Get the unforgettable full-cast narrated audiobook.
Let Chandler and Cassandra voice their story.

Available now.

In addition to the novel and paperback release, Obedience is also available in a full-cast narrated audiobook, starring Daniel Zbel and Rapunzaroo, along with a cast of additional voice over actresses. It is how the story was meant to be told, and it will be the best audiobook you listen to this year—possibly for a very long time. You'll love listening to the two voices of these iconic characters. Read along with them and enjoy a fantastic, immersive experience.

And don't forget **a paperback copy**. You'll need it to fan yourself off from some of the narration!

Get the audiobook on Audible.

PROLOGUE

CASSANDRA

The rope smelled like honey.

Not cheap, overly processed honey, lifeless and left with no aromatics. This was a special smell I imagined apiarists lived for. Pungent. It made you feel like you were walking through a meadow in springtime, soothing and warm.

The sensation was a sharp contrast to what I felt minutes earlier—the pounding of my heart, threatening to rip from my body at any moment, and the rapid succession of my breaths. Somehow, I managed to stay conscious.

"Yes. Breathe, little papillon." *Little butterfly.*

I heard his voice in my ear, a coarse, gravelly whisper with hints of an accent. If we were alone in a dark alley, I might have thought he was there to kill me. But there was something comforting about his disembodied tone. It felt like he was reaching out in a dream to guide me someplace safe. The idea was slightly amusing, given the fact he had tightened a rope against my skin. My arms were bound behind my back so firmly it was as if they no longer existed on my body.

Lengths of twisted red jute stretched around my chest, my flesh completely exposed aside from the blue, cotton undergarments I wore. It felt smooth yet firm against me. I had no understanding of what was being done; I only experienced the sensations of being bound by him. The gentle yanks when the rope was knotted, the drag of it across my bare skin. After a while, the pressure around me became almost comforting. I sank into it, my breaths deep and slow.

Time suspended while he worked. I found myself so transfixed that it seemed as if I'd gone to some ethereal place, far from the room we were in. There were times I'd forgotten there was an audience in front of us, the sounds of the audience fading. It was only him and me, sharing an experience I'd never imagined having.

"And, *fini*."

This time, his whisper bloomed, extending across the room. My mind came back into focus, noticing all of the eyes watching me. It was difficult to remain focused on anything other than the sensation of the ropes against my skin. While the lower half of my body remained free, my upper body was stationary. The only thing I could do was surrender; I had no choice, which made being watched the least of my concerns. Instead, it was the idea of my mercilessness. One of the most deliriously submissive feelings I'd ever felt in my life.

"How does it feel, little papillon?" I felt the warmth of his voice against the flesh of my ear, and it sent a small shiver down my spine.

"I feel alive."

CHAPTER 1

CHANDLER

Six Months Earlier...

One sentence, one string of words, could be enough to destroy a person. Another could save them. I never believed those words would be one and the same and come from a man like my father.

"You'll be attending the auditions."

Gabriel Moreau loomed opposite me at my office desk. I was the spitting image of my father, as much as I hated to admit it, given his thick, dark brown hair—mostly gray now, green eyes, and booming height. A sharp jawline with an intense personality to complement it. The Moreaus were something to behold. I gave them that much.

"Absolutely not." My voice rang across the length of my office, far more pronounced than I had intended. It was nestled in the corner of a hallway of the academy, where I occasionally assisted with teaching and other academic duties. Given my father owned the establishment, the position came with the territory.

It was clear by how empty the room was that I spent little time there. There was nothing outside of a handful of old, worn furniture and a bookshelf with a few books inside. And the atrocious artwork that had come permanently affixed in the space. Several pictures of clowns in the most obscure poses and jarring colors. I fucking hated clowns.

"It wasn't a question," my father said, his gaze unwavering. He leaned forward, his green eyes locked onto mine. "You're well aware of the responsibilities you have to this school. And to me. There's no discussion here."

The last bit was said in a sinister manner. The man knew what kind of hold he had on me and used it to his every advantage.

"I—" My voice started off loud, but I managed to calm myself. My head was thudding, the room spinning and a bit too bright for my liking. The annoying flicker of the fluorescent lighting above was starting to get to me. "I haven't helped with student auditions in years. I wouldn't have any idea what I was doing."

"Your colleague Thomas has fallen ill," my father explained. I knew who he was referring to. Thomas Little was one of my oldest friends, a fellow performer, and a teacher at the academy.

And I had known he had fallen ill. His wife Abigail had taken him to the hospital a few days prior for a bad case of meningitis. There had been a day or two we were worried he wasn't going to pull out of it, but luckily he had. It left him unable to resume his regular duties. What I hadn't expected was my father finding it necessary to make me his replacement.

"Why are you so hell-bent on *me* being there? There's a slew of qualified professionals at this school who would be willing to be on the committee. Hell, couldn't you do it with three people?"

"There has always been a four-person committee. You're familiar with Abigail, Sebastian, and Jeanne." My father replied, and the instant I heard Jeanne, I scowled. I had heard enough of the damn woman's name the last few months, and I was hoping to get a break from it after finalizing our divorce yesterday. "Besides, it would be good to have someone with your specific—ah—skillset, to be involved."

"Jeanne," I felt sick saying her name out loud, "is a silk aerialist, too. And as much as I hate to admit it, a gifted one. She's equally qualified to be on the committee, maybe more so, since she has been for years, unlike me." Talking about her sent further shooting pains through my skull. I regretted all the drinks I'd consumed last night after I left the lawyer's office. It had been a bittersweet celebration. Relieved the months of hell were finally over, but still saddened after everything we'd been through.

"True," my father replied. I hated that he hadn't once looked away from me. He was locked in on me like a laser, watching my every move. The man analyzed everything I said and did like I was a rat in a cage. I had been a rat in a cage my entire life. "But let's say I'd like you to be my personal eyes and ears. You'd be doing me a favor."

"What is that supposed to mean?" I asked, feeling somewhat confused by what he'd said. My father shifted his stance a bit, leaning so he could put his hands on my desk, coming closer to me. So much so that I rolled the chair backward. I leaned back a bit, uncomfortable with his proximity.

"I have a vested interest in the audition process this year," he replied matter-of-factly. "That's all you need to concern yourself with. That and being prompt to the auditions next week. Don't show up reeking of sweaty bourbon like you do right now." The man wasn't wrong. I probably looked and smelled like shit. But he was one to talk, wafting in a nasty odor of cigar smoke. I hated the smell of it ever since I was a little kid. It always made me nauseous, which wasn't helping my hangover presently.

"I realize you may have some unresolved issues with Jeanne as of late, which may be part of your little act of defiance right now." He leaned in again. I tried to stay stationary this time, holding my ground. I didn't want to move much more because every time I did, my head spun, and my stomach churned. "But I'll tell you something your grandfather used to tell me."

The mention of Elliott Moreau sent another wave of nausea through me. If there was one person I despised more than my father, it was my grandfather. I hadn't seen my grandfather since I was a teenager, but I was grateful when I heard he had passed away several years ago. Even still, he left catastrophic damage in his wake. I knew the words coming next.

"Mieux vaut plier que rompre." Adapt and survive. Despite my heritage, my knowledge of the French language had slipped over the last decade or two, but I would never forget that saying. My grandfather had said it for as long as I could remember.

My heart was racing, and my fist lay clenched underneath the desk. It was all I could do not to act. To not fight him. To an outsider, it would seem ridiculous. I was faculty at the school, and I had responsibilities. Attending an audition wasn't anything different than being forced to monitor a school function. It was typical of the employees who worked there.

But this favor, what he was asking of me, was more than that. Gabriel knew it. I knew it.

"Fine," I said after a few long breaths. "I'll be at the auditions."

The moment the words left my mouth, my father's gaze left me. He drummed his fingers on the desk for a second, turned, opened my office door, and shut it behind him. The moment he left, I fell back into the chair I'd been sitting in, breathing a sigh of relief. I collapsed beside my desk, barely making it to my garbage as a wave of nausea hit me.

My head pounded relentlessly until I managed to catch my breath again. I sat back, leaning against my desk, legs sprawled across the floor.

I stared at one of the hideous pictures of the clown on my wall. It was befitting art for Le Rêveur Académie, as it had first been dubbed when it opened fifty years ago. It was now referred to as the Dreamers Academy, the world-class institution for circus arts. The French name my grandfather had chosen had become a distant memory, only recognized by those more immersed in its history.

The eyes of the clown on the opposite wall stared down at me, haunting and hollow. His face twisted in a smile some might have found endearing or entertaining, but it only seemed sinister to me. All these pictures in my office were like mirages of the many faces of Gabriel Moreau. A clown disguised in paint, putting on a performance for the world. No one truly knew what lay underneath the façade.

"What the fuck did I agree to?" I whispered to no one, burying my face in my hands.

Tremblay Hall sat in the center of the Dreamers Academy campus in the small northeastern town of Acrefort, New York. The building was the centerpiece of the entire school and the oldest structure built almost a century ago. The establishments surrounding it were constructed later.

The original building had been purchased by Elliott Moreau based on its French Gothic architectural style. The vaulted ceilings, flying buttresses, infamous gargoyles, and ornate decorations were all part of the aesthetic. The other facilities had been built following the same example, so the entire academy seemed like you were stepping into mid-16th century France.

While I had always admired the architecture and the lush, tree-filled grounds the school sat on, my favorite part of the academy was the room in the center of the cross-shaped Tremblay Hall. Soleil Theater, or the Sun Theater, was a "theater in the round" where the entire audience surrounded the stage. The style was chosen to resemble most traditional circus theater setups.

Though I had spent the last two decades of my life performing underneath the canopies of circus tents, Soleil Theater had a charm like no other performance arena I had ever been in. Stained glass windows wrapped around four sections of the walls. Beautiful arches and towering ceilings were sunken and tiled with intricate pastel patterns. You could spend hours staring at the room, taking it all in. I'd done it so many times over the years. It was the perfect place to showcase some of the world's most prestigious circus talent.

Today, however, had been an exception. Out of the few dozen students who had already auditioned, hardly any had shown enough talent to inspire me. They'd been average. Cut out for state fair shows or small city performances. Nothing elite. Nothing our academy stood for. We were the eyes of the circus world. The premiere academy for performing arts.

Many students flocked to the Dreamers Academy purely because it housed some of the best instructors in the country, most of whom also worked at the neighboring Cirque du Lys. Including the colleagues sitting with me on the audition panel that morning. An elite group of four world-renowned circus performers. This meant we couldn't take anyone, and certainly, none of these marginally acceptable students auditioning.

"What moron was reviewing these applications?" I muttered under my breath, thumbing through a stack of paperwork from the latest student to leave the theater. Today we had been focused on two specialties—acrobatics and aerial arts. The acrobatics had been the earlier part of the day, leaving the aerialists for the afternoon. After our lunch break, the theater staff switched out the equipment for the aerialists. Poles, the Lyra, otherwise known as aerial hoops, hammocks, straps, and my personal favorite and specialty—the silks, had been stationed in the center of the stage, along with protective mats along the floor.

The last gentleman, who had performed primarily with the silks, had been somewhat decent. Still, it was nothing I couldn't teach a freshman high schooler with an ounce of athletic ability in a few lessons. It was far from exceptional. Far from what I was looking for.

"That moron was me," a voice said from beside me, apparently having heard my muttering. Sebastian Taylor was presently looking down at his own paperwork from the last audition, scrutinizing something in his resume. His short, brownish-blonde hair was styled a bit messily, and his warm brown eyes were flitting back and forth behind a pair of forest green reader glasses hanging off his nose. "I liked him. Jonathan James. Catchy name, too. He had some promise, I think. Just needs a bit of coaching."

Sebastian had been assisting at the Dreamers Academy and a ringmaster with my grandmother Lily's circus since I'd started performing decades ago. He'd been around for so long that he had been great friends with my grandmother while she'd still been alive.

I frowned. "I don't think we're letting students in based on your affinity with their names, Sebastian." I stacked the kid's paperwork to my right in the large pile of those who had already attended today. I had written a resounding NO on the top with a red pen.

A disappointed sigh came from the other side of me. When I glanced over, the curly red-haired woman with light blue eyes was smiling, shaking her head. "Sebastian's right, you know," Abigail Little replied with her usual warm tone. "You're being a little too harsh on all these poor kids. They're nervous as can be. Don't you remember how nervous you were when you first started out?"

"Or was it too long ago?" Sebastian chimed in. There was a laugh on the other side of Abigail, and I noticed my ex-wife, Jeanne Tremblay, was laughing and shaking her head. I shot Sebastian a look, knowing full well he was aware I didn't like people mentioning my age. A fact I'm sure Jeanne was taking pleasure in.

I was well aware I had gotten into my forties. I didn't need further reminding.

"Oh, I hit a nerve." Sebastian grinned at me. "You're never going to shake this foul mood about having to fill in for Thomas, are you?" The mention of Thomas, and my required attendance at this event, brought my mind back to my father and our conversation the previous week. He said I was supposed to be his "eyes and ears." I'd been so focused on trying to do the task at hand, selecting worthy talent, I'd almost forgotten my father's desire to have me here. It had likely been for a larger purpose than just to replace Thomas.

"How is Thomas doing?" I decided not to dwell on my thoughts for too long, turning my attention to his wife, Abigail, sitting beside me. She was busy finishing a few notes on her papers before putting them into her organized stack.

Abigail glanced at me, frowning a bit. "Still not feeling the best, I'm afraid. I feel so bad for him. It's been almost two weeks now." Thomas had made it home from the hospital, able to be in his own bed and familiar surroundings. I hadn't been able to visit him since he'd made it home. "He's on the mend, at least. The doctor says another week or so, and he should be back to normal. He's already a mess. You all know how he is, wanting to get back on his feet. Always trying to keep up with you." Abigail smiled at me.

Thomas, Abigail and I had been friends for over a decade now. They'd come from Las Vegas, Nevada, to work for Cirque du Lys and teach at the academy. The pair were two of the nicest, gentlest souls on the face of the planet. Not the types you'd expect to perform fire and danger acts for a living. A fact which generally blew minds. Even with Thomas and I having wildly different career choices, we still competed with one another anyway, over something or other. It was a friendly competition, of course, but a death match nonetheless.

Abigail pulled another stack of papers forward, and I noticed when she did, much to my relief, it was the final set of paperwork in the pile we'd gone through. At least after this, we'd be through for the day. Only to do it again for the next two days.

"Oh! I know this act!" Abigail exclaimed, and I watched her eyes grow wide, and a smile spread across her face. "I thought she was auditioning today. Thomas will be sad he doesn't get to see her." Abby turned her focus on me, still beaming. "You're going to love her, Chandler. She's been a big fan of yours since she was little."

I turned my focus back to the final paperwork in front of me, pulling it into view. Sebastian had done the same beside me, and at the far end of the table, so had Jeanne. I thumbed through the pages, glancing over her resume, educational background, and some performances and shows she'd been in over the last few years. Truthfully, it was nothing spectacular. She'd attended a state school in Nevada for her undergraduate degree and participated in a handful of off-the-strip performances near Las Vegas. Nothing memorable.

For a moment, I thought to question Abigail. I assumed her familiarity with the applicant had swayed her judgment a little. Still, her performance, not the words on these pages, would be the deciding factor.

As I was about to turn and call for the last auditioner to enter, I noticed someone walk straight past the desks set up in the audience, facing the aerial equipment.

A young woman, in her twenties. She focused straight ahead and was making every effort to look calm and composed, but it was clear to see she was trying *very* hard.

I could see her breathing and bits of perspiration on her face. She had likely been pacing up and down the halls outside. The woman's honey-brown hair had been pulled up in a neat ponytail. She walked up the steps onto the stage, taking her place in front of the equipment and turning to face us.

Abigail gave a friendly wave, and the young woman's stoic, rigid demeanor softened. She gave a little wave back and shook her body a bit, likely trying to relieve herself of some of the nerves she was feeling.

"Go ahead and tell us your name and a little about yourself." Jeanne had been the one to speak, and I glanced at her. She had tucked some of her blonde hair behind her ear, and her blue eyes honed in on the young woman on the stage.

Like myself, Jeanne had taken a vested interest in the auditions as she was also a silk aerialist. She would teach these students in the fall.

"My name is Cassandra. Cassandra Blackstone," the woman replied, nodding at my ex-wife. "I'm twenty-five years old, from Las Vegas, Nevada. I graduated this spring with honors. I'm here to audition for the aerialist program."

Blackstone. The name sounded familiar. When I thought about it, I realized it was the famous Blackstone Magician act. A show I'd seen several times over the years and admired. I wondered if she was somehow related to the husband and wife duo.

"Why do you want to become an aerialist?" Jeanne asked, placing her arms on the desk and leaning forward. I focused back on Cassandra in time to see her eyes shift to look straight at me. Though I couldn't make them out distinctly, they appeared hazel and were big and wide, accentuating her face.

"Because of Chandler Moreau," she replied simply. The way she was looking at me was terribly distracting. I found I couldn't look away from her, a little chill washing over me. "I've followed your performances since I was in middle school. Ever since I saw you do a Kamikaze drop at your traveling show in San Francisco, it's all I ever wanted to do. To perform the move as flawlessly as you did in the show you did it with."

I realized she mentioned the circus I'd been a part of for the last two decades. My grandfather Elliott bought the circus for my grandmother Lily short after he'd acquired the Dreamers Academy. "Cirque du Lys?" I found myself asking Cassandra, and she nodded.

The Kamikaze drop she had been referring to, and the specific show it had occurred at, had been interesting, to say the least. My ability to do one of the most difficult aerial silk drops was well known. But that particular show had been a special case.

At the last minute, Sebastian and I decided to change up some of the choreography. The entire sequence had been different for that one case. Not everyone knew that information, nor cared to.

She'd surprised me, to say the least. I wasn't quite sure how it made me feel.

"Anyway, that's why I'm here," Cassandra said, her voice a little shaky. She was clearly still nervous, and talking to me had made her more so. She turned her focus from me, looking beside me at Abigail. "How is Thomas doing?"

"He's on the mend," Abigail replied, smiling softly at her. "He's so sorry to have missed this. We'll tell him about it later when you're over." Cassandra nodded, smiling back at her softly. It was the first time I'd seen her smile since she arrived, and it was hard to look away. Even with how small it had been, it lit up her face. Gave a warmth I found myself compelled by for some reason.

Her smile disappeared quickly when Jeanne spoke again."You can start whenever you'd like," she told her, and Jeanne leaned back in her seat when I glanced over. The rest of my colleagues had settled in, too. I turned back to the stage, watching Cassandra nod and head to the silks.

There had been several pairs to choose from, but Cassandra selected a set of deep maroon-colored silks. They hung about seventy feet into the air. I watched the young woman's complete focus hone in on the fabric, and her entire being settled.

There was something about how her stance had changed, the way her movements became more fluid and relaxed, that said she had shifted into performance mode. The fear she'd shown vanished. There was no one else in the room with her. Nothing but her and the fabric.

Music began in the background, started by one of the stagehands through the room's speakers. Acoustically, the Soleil Theater was built for music in addition to its mesmerizing aesthetics. The sounds reverberated in every direction from the speakers set up around the theater, allowing complete immersion in the song.

After a few measures of the light classical piece, the beautiful string notes dancing into the room, I realized I recognized the work. A song I knew from many years ago. Composed by George Frideric Handel, it was the opening aria from the opera *Serse*. While I'd never been particularly fond of the opera, it was something Jeanne and I had gone to several times a year throughout our two-decade-long relationship because her mother had been an opera singer.

It was the reason I recognized the song. A choice made by Jeanne for a show we performed in our early twenties, if memory served me right. One of Cirque du Lys' summer showcases. While it had been Jeanne's choice of song, the entire act had been composed by us together, and to this day, it was perhaps one of my favorite performances.

When Cassandra began, every single reason why it had been flooded back to me. The young woman circled the silks for a moment, and then began her ascent on the fabrics. Twisting herself up them, as the last few measures of the song played, before the famous Cecilia Bartoli's beautiful mezzo-soprano voice joined the orchestra.

As the lyrics called out into the theater, circling around us, so did Cassandra from high above. I watched as she executed the first drop with absolute precision. Like I'd been in a dream, watching the performance from all those years ago, all over again. Watched her twist and circle, dropping down into a movement known as the Rainbow Marchenko, similar to an upside-down split, something Jeanne was famous for.

While I was so used to technicalities, having lived and breathed them for decades, something shifted inside me. The names, the little nuances of each of the steps to execute Cassandra's routine, disappeared in my mind.

Replaced by feelings of warmth, genuine excitement, and longing. That rush, those all-consuming emotions. While I could have focused more on all the subtle things she was doing differently—things only a genuinely seasoned artist would have the capacity to do—I found myself more wrapped up in the way it was making me feel so much adoration.

Cassandra ascended again as the opera singer's voice drew into the higher registers, preparing for the last sequence. The performance was crescendoing, and while I knew what was coming, I was excited to see how she'd do it differently. The dramatic set of falls and twists that would bring her back to the stage.

I was waiting for the double forward roll, which was one of my favorite aerial silk moves. The performer dived through the fabric as they rolled. It was a breathtaking spectacle if performed right.

All four of us in the audience held our breath, watching her as she prepared. My attention never left her, listening to the lyrics, waiting for the one moment when the singing dropped out for a second, only to triumphantly bellow again. Her cue.

Cassandra was high up in the silks, waiting. She had been looking out into the audience. Looking at me, specifically, or perhaps I imagined things. Something flickered across her face, her concentration dissipating.

I immediately stood up from my seat. As I straightened, I received an unpleasant reminder of the previous weekend rehearsals at Cirque du Lys. Pain shot up and down my left leg, radiating from my knee. I felt the throbbing from underneath the brace I'd been wearing around it, which hadn't done a damn bit of good helping with the pain.

My attention drew away from the throbbing, having very few seconds to spare before Cassandra would act. I shouted into the room, clapping my hands together. "Stop the music!"

When I called, the ache in my ribs reminded me of the fact they, too, were bruised, and it hurt quite a bit. I ignored it, waving at Sebastian to get out of my way. My friend shifted from his seat, allowing me to slip out around the desk we'd been sitting at. I made my way into the aisle leading up to the stage.

"Chandler, what on earth—" I heard Jeanne call out, but I disregarded her.

Meanwhile, the music had stopped, and when my attention focused on the silks, I watched Cassandra slowly descend the fabrics and back to the floor. By the time I had hobbled my way down the aisle and up the steps to meet her, she'd gotten down and was waiting for me. The walking I had done had been a painful reminder of how much I likely needed to rest my knee at this point, but I hadn't cared.

"You hesitated," I said as I walked across the stage toward Cassandra. The closer I got to her, the more distinct her eyes became. They were, in fact, a fascinating shade of hazel, favoring more on the green side, with flecks of brown and grays that became very predominant by the time I'd gotten in front of her. "Right before the final sequence, I saw it. The salto. You left the room. Why?"

Cassandra's big, bright eyes met mine head-on.

"I—" She looked at a loss for words, somewhat embarrassed. I waited, letting her try to formulate what she wanted to say. Still, nothing came, and eventually, she turned away from me.

I moved closer to her, closing some of the distance between us. "I'm not trying to embarrass you," I explained. I took hold of one of the two maroon silks flapping lightly with the breeze of the air conditioning in the room, wrapping it around my hand. Of course, the state of my knee made it impossible for me to do anything like she'd done in those last few minutes of her performance. Still, I could at least coach her.

"I want to know what you were thinking. You left the room. All the confidence you had the entire performance vanished. It can't happen, Cassandra, not in moments like that, when you're up in the silks. Not ever."

I'd surprised myself by calling her by her name. It fell from my lips effortlessly, sounding as beautiful as the singer's voice had when it rang through the theater a minute earlier. I didn't focus on it for long—too concerned about bringing her attention to the danger of her mishap.

My knee was a painful reminder, still throbbing in the brace. I glanced down at it for a second, trying to refrain from wincing, though it had become quite painful. Instead, I returned my focus to Cassandra. Gave her every ounce of my attention. She followed my gaze, looking down at my knee, then back up at me.

"Did that happen to you?" She asked in a candid way. Like we were friends, and she was genuinely curious about what had happened to me. It was strange to hear her ask me such a thing and had she been any other student auditioning today, I likely would have told her it was none of her business. Her head tilted a little, in a distractingly endearing way.

Instead, I surprised myself.

"Yes," I replied, nodding. Cassandra's gaze softened, somewhat empathetic. While I was aware my colleagues could hear everything I was saying, I was still wholly focused on Cassandra. The conversation was meant for her and me. We were the only two in the room at the moment. We were the only two who mattered.

"I, unfortunately, let my thoughts get the best of me," I replied honestly. "And it's not something you do. Not when you're in that kind of position. Understand?"

Cassandra nodded, and I watched her bite the edge of her lip for a moment. Felt the strangest lurch in my stomach at the sight of it. I didn't focus on it long, trying to pay attention to what she said next.

"I lost my nerve," she admitted, again sounding embarrassed. "The salto, the double forward roll... It's something I'm still trying to perfect, honestly. I've practiced it a million times. I had it down. But—the move is one of your favorite moves...."

The comment made me smile a fraction. I nodded, waiting for her to continue. "I wasn't expecting you to be here. Wasn't expecting to have to perform it in front of you..." Cassandra shook her head.

The slight smile of mine widened a bit, unable to help myself be a little flattered, and I let out a laugh. "Well, if it is any consolation, I wasn't planning on being here. I happened to be forced into it."

"He's been bitching all day long," Jeanne called out across the theater, and for a half-second, I remembered there were other people in the room watching us. I waved her off, still focused on Cassandra.

"We shouldn't matter," I told her flatly. "Your only concern right now is your performance. Not your audience. Forget your audience. Forget me. It's only you and those silks."

"You are hard to forget,"Cassandra replied almost instantly, those hazel eyes piercing into mine. That same strange feeling that had overcome me several times in the minutes since she entered this theater washed over me again. It felt foreign, like nothing I'd felt in an extraordinarily long time. I wasn't sure what she meant."It was my favorite silk performance of yours and Jeanne's I ever witnessed. I didn't want to disappoint either of you."

I took another step closer to her. There was only a few feet of distance between us now. I could have almost reached out and touched her, had I wanted. All of a sudden I was greeted with a very distinct smell. It took me a moment to place, but there had been no mistaking it. Citrus. Oranges. It was alluring. I wanted to draw closer.

Instead, I stopped abruptly, holding myself in place, my hand still wrapped around the silk. While I was flattered by the sentiment of her words, I was also concerned about her nerves. It wasn't a favorable sign at an audition. Natural for some, but this amount was concerning. And there was absolutely no room for it when you were sixty feet in the air, dangling by a single piece of fabric.

For a minute, I found myself scratching at the scruff on my face, lost in thought. My attention drifted away from her, looking up into the silks again. Trying to figure out how to help her. I could feel her eyes on me.

Eventually, the idea came to me, and I stared back at her. "Tell me the name of your best friend. The person you trust more than anyone."

Cassandra studied me, looking slightly confused, but she answered. "Alexandra."

"Ah—well—let's go with Alexander." My words seemed to puzzle her more, but I continued my thought. "Just think of Alexandra when you find yourself focused on me. She's here with you instead. Maybe a little more facial hair, a bit taller...."

A smile broke on Cassandra's face, and she let out a laugh. Once again, I was caught off guard, this time, completely wrapped up in the sound. It was hard to break away from, but when I heard it, I felt satisfied. Like I'd found a way to get through to her and break off her nerves.

"You're definitely *much* taller," she agreed.

"Okay," I nodded, taking a step back, unraveling my hand from the fabric I'd been holding on to. Trying to ignore the incessant throbbing of my knee was a reminder of how meaningful this conversation was with her. She needed one hundred percent focus. "In any case, you're performing for her right now. That's all. Don't worry about me anymore."

Cassandra nodded, looking far more relaxed than she had been. The smile still lingered a little on her face. She'd taken hold of the silk I'd let go of, wrapping it around her other hand so she was locked in.

"Are you ready to try again?" I asked, and Cassandra's eyes fell on me once more. She nodded. "Good. Remember the key to the salto. You'll have all the momentum you need, focus on the fluidity of the motion."

Cassandra nodded, and I felt satisfied. I glanced at her for a second before I turned away, walking across the stage. Instead of leaving it entirely, I only walked to the steps and turned back around. Meanwhile, Cassandra resumed her place back at the silks.

A few moments later, whoever had been in charge of the music, had brought it back enough measures to allow Cassandra to resume her ascent up the silks before the final set of movements. When she reached the height she had been at before, nearly sixty feet into the air, I watched her take slow, steady breaths. Waiting, calmly, for her cue. I knew without a shadow of a doubt she'd returned to the mindset she'd started in. Entirely in tune with what she was doing.

Cecile's voice boomed into the room, and Cassandra let go. I watched her fly down, diving into the fabric, rolling in beautiful loops that appeared far more effortless than they actually were. She captured the material after the salto, twisting into the last few drops and spins before her feet hit the floor as the song faded from the room.

My colleagues immediately rose to their feet, all three clapping. I'd joined in alongside them, and I couldn't help but offer a small smile and a nod when Cassandra glanced at me again. I took in the delighted look on her face, unable to help myself but take satisfaction in it, too.

"Thank you,"Cassandra called out before I walked back down the stage steps and resumed my place at the desk among my fellow colleagues. All were busy taking notes while Cassandra waited patiently on the stage. I had yet to bother to look back at her paperwork. My entire attention focused on her. I waited until the others had finished, and Sebastian spoke.

"Did you have anything else you wanted to ask?" After a beat, I realized he had been talking to me. I glanced at him a moment and shook my head.

"We've seen everything we need to see," I said, looking back at Cassandra, speaking to her. I tried my best to keep my tone calm and neutral, despite how my heart had picked up a little in my chest. I was doing my best to steady my excited breathing. Cassandra nodded at my response.

"Thank you all," she said, bowing her head a little before she walked off the stage. She paused momentarily as she made her way past the desk we'd been sitting at. I watched her as she locked on Abigail, offering a small smile. "See you in a few hours?"

"See you soon, sweetheart," Abigail replied, nodding. Cassandra's eyes flitted for one brief second, past Abigail, to me again. We looked at each other, a fleeting moment which felt like it lasted much longer than it actually had. She broke away, walking out of the room without another word.

The moment she left, I felt my breathing start to steady. I leaned back into my chair, glancing at each of my colleagues, who all seemed lost in thought.

"She did well," Jeanne said from the far end of the table. "Some of those movements were impressive. I feel like she got them from somewhere...."

I had done my best to avoid interacting with Jeanne for the better part of the day, but I couldn't help myself. "Jeanne, it was from our tour decades ago. It's been my favorite performance for years. We practiced the routine for months. Hell, you—you picked out the damn song. The aria from your favorite opera...."

Jeanne stared at me quizzically for a moment. "I picked it?" I nodded. "Funny, I don't really remember it."

I sighed, shaking my head. "I promise you." While I was annoyed with her, I didn't feel like arguing, still too wound up by the last audition to care.

"Okay, you two. Let's not get into it right now," Sebastian reminded us, bringing me back to the room and to the matter. "What do we think? Yay or nay?"

I got up from my seat, trying my best to ignore the shooting pains in my knee. I managed to get around Sebastian without him moving and made my way in front to face the rest of them. My hands fell down on the desk, and I stared Sebastian directly in the eyes, unwavering. "If she isn't here in the fall, I'll quit. This program, the circus. My career will be a joke."

"Liked her that much, eh?" Sebastian said, raising a brow at me.

"She's very talented," Abigail agreed, smiling at me. "See, I knew you'd like her. I've known her since she was little. Thomas and I were great friends with her parents. She's always had an affinity for the silks. I think she'd do really well here."

"Chandler has always had a thing for brunettes," Jeanne retorted, rolling her eyes. I glanced at her, feeling annoyed. "But if I'll be teaching her, I agree. She has potential. I think she'd do well. She just has to get over her nerves."

"It's settled then," I replied, looking back down at the paperwork on the desk and then back to each of my colleagues, landing on Sebastian last. "Cassandra Blackstone will be attending in the fall."

CHAPTER 2

CASSANDRA

Present Day...

The rhythmic sound of rain against a window woke me from a pleasant dream I'd been having. The instant my eyes began to flutter, it was fading. It must have been a good dream because I could still feel the warmth washing over me. Good dreams didn't happen often for me, not in a long time. So I laid there and enjoyed it for a minute.

I stared up at the white popcorn ceiling, at the seen-better-days ceiling fan wobbling a bit too much for comfort as it spun. Watching the blades go round and round for a few moments as I tried to get my bearings. When I looked over, glancing around the small bedroom, my eyes began to focus. The room was smaller than some people's closets, I imagined, and almost so sparse you'd think no one lived there.

A twin mattress sat on the hardwood floor, one I'd found at a yardsale close by. A small selection of clothes hung on a metal shower curtain rod I'd extended across the adjacent wall, by the window. A well-loved laptop and a collection of textbooks sat near the clothes, along with a shabby brown canvas sling bag. Beside the bed was a phone charger taped up a few times since its purchase, to prevent the wires from coming apart, and a phone attached to it that probably was around before I'd started high school.

The tapping sound caught my focus again. When I looked outside the singular window across from me, I noticed it was raining heavily and looked ominous and gloomy. The branches of a tall oak tree were obscuring much of the view, but I made out enough of it.

I looked back down at my phone. Beside it, there were two frames, as worn and as aged as pretty much every single thing in this room. But, outside of perhaps the contents in my sling bag, they were the most important possessions of mine.

In one frame was an old photo of my parents, Oliver and Katherine Blackstone, in front of the theater that showcased their magic show for decades. I was three or four in the picture, my hair still a mess of curls which hadn't loosened yet. Perched on my father's shoulders, looking as content as could be. My parents, smiling at each other. It was the one photo I had left of them.

Beside the old photo of my family was another keepsake held dear for over a decade now. An old, yellowing playbill with an autograph scribbled across it. Attached to a photo of me, in eighth grade, standing in front of a giant circus tent, my arms stretched in the air, smiling broadly.

To my left, a short, raven haired girl with her arm wrapped around my waist, smiling too. Alexandra Ledger, who adamantly insisted on being called Alex, and I had been friends since elementary school. The picture had been the last time I'd seen her until college years later. The last day we'd spent together, the day before my thirteenth birthday.

The day before my parents died.

The day I saw Chandler Moreau in the flesh.

I had shaken his hand after he had signed a copy of the playbill. I still remembered how excited I had been, looking up at him as he towered over me. Mesmerized by the talent pouring from him with everything he did. He was the master of his craft, in every sense of the word.

Chandler had performed on the traveling stage for his circus, Cirque du Lys, alongside his wife, Jeanne Tremblay. That performance had been when I decided, without a shadow of a doubt, I would perform beside him one day. Someday, he would be my teacher.

Though my confidence had wavered from time to time over the decade I waited for those days to come, they had finally arrived. Somehow, the audition committee had liked me so much, they'd given me a full scholarship. Soon, I'd be able to work alongside the one person I'd dreamed about performing with for over half my life.

Before my parents passed away, whenever things were particularly difficult, my mother would always quote her favorite author, Pema Chödrön, to me. In my mind, to this day, I could still hear every word as clearly as if she had been speaking them in front of me.

Nothing ever goes away, until it teaches us what we need to know.

Staring at the playbill, I lost myself in the daydream of the happy day with my parents, with Alex, watching that amazing man who I'd been lucky enough to meet again at my audition six months prior. I was jerked back to reality when my phone chirped from the floor. I looked down, noticing a text message flash across the beat-up screen.

Good luck today! See ya tonight! It was from Alex. I'd barely registered what she said before I noticed the time on my phone and felt all the blood drain from my face. I dashed to my feet in a mad panic; there was only twenty minutes until I was expected at Tremblay Hall, at the Dreamers Academy.

There was no way I'd make it the several blocks to campus and to the Circus History class where I'd be Jeanne Tremblay's teaching assistant in so little time. But I would try like hell anyway. The last person I'd want to make a bad impression on was the woman who would be my mentor for the semester. A woman who, while not as talented as Chandler Moreau was, wasn't far behind. She had been his partner for decades. I wanted her to like me. I had a bad feeling that if I was late, it would be more difficult.

Somehow I managed to throw on one of the three blouses I owned, a pair of slacks, and some slip-on shoes, pulling my hair into the neatest ponytail I could manage while gathering my things. I made it out the door, sling bag thrown over my shoulder, with ten minutes to spare before the class began.

Under the small awning of the apartment building, I stared out into the torrential downpour, opening the umbrella I'd had since early high school. It rattled in the wind as I lifted it over my head, and I stepped out onto the sidewalk, heading swiftly down the road. My neighbor, an older man with gray hair and beady brown eyes, watched me intently while he smoked on his porch. He reminded me of someone I didn't want to think about, so I tried not to look at him for long.

The small stretch of Acrefort I lived in, in what was mostly a pleasant little town in upstate New York, just happened to be the shadiest part. But it had been all I could afford, that tiny studio apartment.

As luck would have it, I managed to make good time cutting across the roads leading up to the Dreamers Academy. The green lights seemed to be in my favor, and when I checked my phone, it seemed like I was still going to make it.

Then I heard a snap. I watched as the six or seven-year-old, ratty-as-hell umbrella ripped upward, shredding into several pieces at once. The rain pelted over me in sheets. Drenched me within seconds. I was only two or three minutes away from getting inside Tremblay Hall and out of this mess of a morning.

Of course. Out of all the days for this to happen, it had to be *today*.

I sprinted as fast as I could across the outskirts of the academy campus, dodging other students and faculty walking around, sheltered by their non-shitty umbrellas. Feeling like a sponge drowning in a full sink of water.

Tremblay Hall towered in front of me, a beautiful old building. I'd read all about it in textbooks, and I'd seen it at my auditions months before. In my mad dash through the rain, I couldn't help but admire it, taking in all the intricacies. Several of the signature gargoyles loomed over the corners of the buildings, watching over the campus.

The minute I stumbled into the building behind a small group of other students, the cold indoor air greeted me, and I realized how absolutely drenched I was. Every single inch of me dripped all over the elegant tiled floors. Next to the doors I'd entered was a large garbage can, into which I aggressively tossed the shitty and now broken umbrella. After, I fumbled in my sling bag, which luckily was waterproofed enough to protect my belongings inside, grabbing my phone. I was five minutes late.

Not enough time to go to the bathroom and try to make myself the least bit presentable. So much for a good impression. I took off again down the hallway, admiring the variety of art hanging on the walls as I ran. Beautiful paintings and artwork on display, depicting various places in Acrefort, and many old photographs and trinkets from circus shows from all over the world.

A person could spend hours looking at everything in this building. Whoever had designed it had taken great care in making it stunning. Unfortunately, I didn't have hours. I skidded to a stop outside the doors to the classroom I was supposed to be in.

I took a deep breath, deciding to not waste any more time. Tugged the heavy wooden, windowless door to the classroom open. It was quiet when I entered. I released the door and someone slipped behind me, catching it.

"That thing will slam so loud, you'll scare the kids in Rosewood Commons." Rosewood was a student building on one end of the Dreamers Academy campus, opposite the direction I'd come from. The cafeteria and the student union were housed there.

When I turned my gaze toward the voice talking softly to me, I met the brown eyes of a lanky looking kid with brown, wavy hair, a little on the longer side. He was smiling at me, a curious expression on his face. "I am notoriously late for everything. I learned about the door the hard way."

"Thank you," I whispered back to him. He had a charming smile, warm and inviting. My voice stayed low, doing my best to not distract Jeanne at the other side of the room. She was my supervisor after all, and my mentor for the semester.

"I'm Henry," he said, holding out his hand.

"Cassie," I replied, taking his hand and returning his smile.

"Looks like it started raining pretty hard out there," Henry noted, eyeing me up and down. I watched him reach over and snag a jacket that had been laying across the arm of the chair he'd been sitting in. "Take this. It gets chilly in there."

"Thanks," I said, taking his jacket, graciously. "I better get down there, she's expecting me. I'm the teaching assistant this sem—"

Henry looked confused for a second but before I had an opportunity to inquire as to why, there was a loud clearing of a throat from down the aisle of the classroom interrupting me. When it stopped, I noticed it had become eerily quiet. Eventually, I turned toward the direction the sound had come from and nearly fell flat on my face in surprise.

Standing at the front of the room, dressed in a fitted deep green button down matching the color of his eyes, looking dead at me, was Chandler Moreau. *Professor Moreau,* I supposed he was called here, but in my mind, he'd always be the performer with Cirque du Lys I'd followed half my life.

He was certainly not Jeanne Tremblay, who I had been expecting.

His thick brown hair was styled neatly, his tall frame looming. The expression on his face was fierce and piercing straight into me. He was clearly annoyed, a drastic change from his demeanor the last time I'd interacted with him at my audition.

"Can I help you?" I remembered the sound of his voice when he spoke, a calm, slightly coarse and deep sound, with just a hint of an accent I couldn't place. The type of voice demanding your entire attention. I swallowed deeply, holding my eye contact with him.

"I—I think I might be in the wrong classroom," I realized the minute I said it. It had to have been what happened. "I'm supposed to be with Professor Tremblay. History of the Circus. I'm sorry, I didn't mean to inter—"

"Professor Tremblay is taking a leave of absence,"Chandler said, his facial expression and tone filled with annoyance. "You're in the right classroom. I'll be teaching History this semester. However, I suggest you make it a habit of not arriving late. Your peers aren't paying good money to listen to me lecture on tardiness."

"I'm sorry," I replied, starting to take steps forward, as difficult as it was due to the distracting nature of his gaze on me. I adjusted my sling bag on my damp shoulder, still clutching Henry's jacket he'd let me borrow. It was starting to feel cold and uncomfortable, and I didn't think I could be more gracious to Henry for his kindness to me. I looked back over my shoulder at him briefly, both to force myself to stop staring at Chandler, and also to try to silently thank him.

"—As I was saying," Chandler started speaking again, just as I'd made it to the end of the aisleway. As soon as I set my bag on the desk at the front of the room, he stopped speaking again.

When I looked over, Chandler's intense green eyes were zeroed in on me. His nostrils flared in annoyance, eyes narrowed."Have you not garnered enough attention this morning, Ms—"

"Blackstone," I said, trying to disregard his snide comment. "Cassandra Blackstone. I'm the teaching assistant for this class.

Jeanne's teaching assistant. I guess your assistant now..." I'd started rambling, trying to catch myself. "I'm sorry. I didn't know where you wanted me to go exactly."

I noticed a flicker on Chandler's face for a second. His disgruntled look softened like he'd come to some sort of realization. I wondered if he remembered who I was. When it disappeared seconds later, I assumed he didn't. I didn't really have a chance to ponder on it as Chandler continued to glare at me for whatever reason.

At that point, I'd started to feel my own little surge of annoyance with the man. Even if I had interrupted him, there hadn't been a need for him to act the way he was. Like he was deriving some small bit of pleasure by trying to torment me a little.

Chandler returned to his lecture, and I wrapped myself in Henry's jacket. It was entirely too big for me, but I didn't care. I turned my ponytail into a bun on top of my head. Then, before I got too far behind, I darted over to the whiteboard Chandler had been standing in front of. Most college professors were using Powerpoint presentations, but it seemed Chandler was old-fashioned. I didn't question him, uncapping a marker and drawing my focus to his voice.

"Circus Maximus will be our topic of discussion this week." When I looked over my shoulder, I watched Chandler stroll across the length of the classroom. I couldn't help but notice the injury he'd been suffering from at my audition had to have healed because he moved uninhibited and gracefully. "I could teach an entire class on Circus Maximus, but for the purpose of this introductory course, we'll be doing a brief overview."

I scribbled Circus Maximus across the blank whiteboard, just before he spoke again. "Can anyone tell me where the stadium was built and in what era?"

The room was dead quiet, the roughly two dozen students within it all unmoving. A hand shot into the air, and I realized it had been Henry's. Chandler nodded to him, and Henry said confidently, projecting into the room,"it was built in Ancient Rome, in the Old Kingdom era. The largest stadium ever built there."

Chandler nodded again, not looking the least bit fazed. Didn't compliment him when he'd known the answer. I wrote Henry's response across the whiteboard. I had learned this information in my undergraduate coursework. All of the students in this classroom were mostly freshmen and sophomores, so it was new to them. While Chandler might not have been impressed with Henry's knowledge the first day of class, I was proud of him.

"The ancient city of Rome was built on seven hills. Between two of those hills, Aventine and Palatine, was the Valley of Murica, where horse races were held. Circus Maximus started there as a simple hippodrome." When Chandler didn't elaborate on the term he used, I decided to put it on the whiteboard anyway. *A theater or performance venue.*

"I remember learning about Circus Maximus for the first time from one of my grandmother's books on circus history. Far more accurate and less drab than your textbooks now." I paused taking notes then, realizing he'd started drifting off into his own little world on a completely irrelevant tangent. Somehow, the next forty minutes of the class were filled with meaningless anecdotes and stories about Chandler and his experiences. Practically nothing relevant to the actual lecture, Circus Maximus.

The bell rang, and by the rush of students getting up from their seats, it signaled the end of the class. When I looked back at the whiteboard behind me, I realized I hadn't written a single thing since Henry had answered Chandler's question. The rest of the lecture was useless to the room full of students. A mini memoir by a man who was apparently far more self-centered than I had realized.

There was a student or two who stayed to ask Chandler questions. Henry had given me a little wave before he left the room, and I assumed I'd give his jacket back the next time I saw him at class. My gaze turned back to Chandler, still interacting with the students. I hated the way he was acting, like the idea of their presence was literally the most dreadful thing he could be doing with his time. Between his arrogant posture, the exasperated tone he took, and the annoyed look on his face, it was difficult not to march right up to him and give him a piece of my mind.

I was appalled by the way he was treating these students. They were still bright-eyed and bushy-tailed, eager to learn because of their desire to stay behind and talk to him. The wonderful memory I had, the interaction between us on Soleil's stage at my audition, was evaporating with each second I watched him. I was getting so annoyed, I forced myself to focus on gathering my belongings and erasing the white board.

When the last student left, Chandler went back to his collection of things, opposite of where I'd placed my own. I watched him for a moment before I approached him. He must have heard me coming by the squeak of my still-damp canvas flats across the hardwood floors. Chandler's head jerked over his shoulder to look at me.

"You're still here, Ms. Blackstone? Is there something I can do for you?"

I did my best to offer a forced, small smile before I spoke. "I was just wondering if there was anything you needed from me before I left." I sat the marker down beside his bag on the table he'd been standing next to.

Chandler turned to face me, scratching at his well-manicured beard. Which I normally would have found attractive, with its flecks of gray interspersed with the thick dark browns matching his hair. It showed his age, and I'd thought it made him look attractive and refined. At least I had thought so at my audition.

Now he just looked like a pompous ass.

"Let's see," Chandler started. I hated that, despite how unbelievably irritated I was by his very being, his gaze had a dangerous hold on me. It gave me chills having nothing to do with still being a little damp from the rain. "Perhaps first and foremost, you could arrive on time from now on. That would be a sufficient starting point."

I sucked in a deep breath. "You already *publicly* chastised me," I reminded him, feeling my face twist despite every effort in trying to hide my annoyance. "I was meaning more—"

"You might also consider showing up to my classroom not looking like a drowned rat." Every single fiber of my being was seething. He was annoying the living hell out of me, and I didn't think I could tolerate it much longer. "There are such things as umbrellas."

"I had a fucking umbrella—" I started, realizing I'd just cursed at him. It immediately jerked me back to reality, and I grew rigid, reeling myself back in. "You know what." My voice went as calm as I could make it. "I don't want to argue with you about this. Yes, I know I should come to class more presentable. I'll make every effort to do so. Trust me, this is not the way I intended my day to go." It was so true, on a variety of different levels.

"Did you plan to spend it daydreaming, then?" The man was relentless. Chandler nodded behind me, and when I looked over my shoulder, I realized he was referring to the whiteboard I'd cleaned off a minute earlier. "You spent most of the class staring idly into space."

I'm surprised you noticed, you self-absorbed shit. He'd crossed the line again, but I decided to keep myself in check this time. Couldn't believe I was having these thoughts about a man I had idolized for so many years. He was making me feel so conflicted.

"I didn't think it was necessary for the students to take endless notes about your whole life history, Professor Moreau. *Perhaps,*" I emphasized the word, using the same condescending tone he'd used a minute earlier. "You might consider actually lecturing about Circus Maximus next time instead of rambling on for an hour about the myriad of reasons you chose to study aerial silks." Most of those reasons I'd known by heart, but I couldn't have possibly cared less.

I wondered why I felt emboldened to speak my mind so freely with him. It certainly hadn't been one of my brightest decisions.

Chandler's mouth hung slightly open, staring at me for a few moments. I'd definitely caught him off guard and as much satisfaction as it had brought me, I also knew there would be repercussions. It had been reckless to go toe-to-toe with him in this little sparring session our conversation had turned into. I needed this job desperately, and to lose it on the first day of classes... I absolutely couldn't.

Surprisingly, when Chandler recovered, he resumed picking up his things, throwing his bag over his shoulder before he returned his focus on me. His facial expression had become calm like he'd been completely unfazed by my belligerent behavior. It had been ignored.

"Don't be late for your private lessons," he said flatly. Turning away from me, he walked up the aisle.

I wondered, bleakly, if I'd have to deal with more of this nonsense with him. In the span of a one hour class period, I felt deflated—he'd ruined every shred of excitement I'd had at the thought of getting to work with him...

Realizing what he'd said confirmed he did know who I was after all, I spun around and watched as he walked away. "I'm not usually late," I called after him, attempting to defend myself.

"Whatever you say, Ms. Blackstone," Chandler replied, without looking back, just before he'd slipped out the door.

CHAPTER 3

CASSANDRA

A strange mood followed me around the remainder of my first day at the Dreamers Academy, even with the excitement of the new classes, the new city, and all the experiences I would be immersed in over the next two years. Chandler Moreau was nearly all I could think about, and I hated every second of it. He'd been so drastically different at my audition. There had been a kindness to him, a gentleness in the way he'd approached me, a sincerity about his concern for my well being. He wanted me to succeed.

Today, however, it had felt as though he was an entirely different person. He'd been mocking me, testing me in every possible way. And it frustrated me terribly as to why he'd been so different; it consumed my thoughts.

Late that evening, after I'd taken a short cab ride a few blocks outside of downtown Acrefort, I finally felt distracted. When I arrived, it was dark and unfortunately, still drizzling. The rain had severely worsened my mood.

The place I'd been told to arrive at seemed bizarre. When I stepped out of the cab, I thought I must have been mistaken but I triple checked the address, and the driver assured me I was at the right place.

In front of me, a large, old, abandoned church sat. The architecture was reminiscent of the Dreamers Academy buildings, so much so I wouldn't have been surprised if it, too, was French Gothic inspired.

However, unlike the academy, this building clearly hadn't seen use in a long time. It was covered in thick patches of ivy. Some of the stone exterior was worn down a great deal. A few of the windows were missing. The place looked like the last place on earth I should be meeting my best friend, Alex. But here I was.

"What the hell?" I muttered to myself, holding my sling bag over my head to shield from the drizzle, minimalizing the destruction of the work I'd done to make myself presentable. Alex had promised me a night on the town to celebrate my first full day in Acrefort.

I'd worn my wavy, honey brown hair down around my shoulders, pinning the side pieces up away from my face. Put on a bit of makeup, which was far from usual for me. Broke out the one "dressy" dress I had in my collection. One I'd worn to my senior prom in high school. I'd found it on one of my many trips to thrift stores by a stroke of luck. Perfect and classy and simple, just the way I liked it. A "little black dress" my best friend had approved of when I'd sent her a picture of it a few hours earlier.

When I thought about Alex, I heard someone call my name from behind me. I turned in time to spot a familiar face trotting down the sidewalk toward me. Alex Ledger was a short, curvy girl with raven hair styled in a trendy pixie cut. When I'd seen her the day of my audition, it had been longer. The new look suited her.

Alex wore her usual fare, which was entirely black. She'd matched the same look I'd gone for that evening, dark eyeliner and dark lips. The way she often looked might have caused some people to be intimidated, but what always captured everyone who knew her was her charming smile. It was spread across her face when she collided with me.

Even if it had only been a short few months since I had seen her, I had forgotten how much I missed her until we'd hugged again. It was such a comfort to be in her arms.

Who is the one person you trust most in the world? Chandler Moreau had asked me at my audition. Alexandra had been that person. We'd become attached at the hip in middle school. After everything that had happened, she would forever be that person for me.

"God, it's good to see you," I said once we'd broken apart. Alex fixed a few strands of my hair that had come loose in the humid rainfall, smiling at me. "But I've got to say I don't know what the hell you were thinking when you chose to meet up here... Is there some weird voodoo shit going on in the church I should know about?"

Alex grinned at me, nodding toward the church. The only singular building around. "Oh, there's some stuff going on there alright. Far from voodoo. And you're going to like it. Wait and see."

My friend linked her arm with mine, and the two of us started down the sidewalk again. I felt as confused as I had when I'd been dropped off. Worried Alex might have joined a cult in the last year she'd been in Acrefort. I wouldn't have put it past her. Not because she had an evil streak or anything. More because Alex would literally try anything once. It was the kind of person she was.

When we reached the far side of the church, we headed in toward the building, making a detour around the side. The minute we turned the corner, there was a line of people in front of us. The opposite side of the building was bustling. Cars were parked on the side of the road. People were headed toward us from across the street. A stark contrast to my arrival.

Alex and I took a spot under an overhang, shielding ourselves from the drizzle. I was grateful for the little bit of shelter. But I was still horrendously confused.

"Did you have to bring that ratty-ass thing with you? You look hot as hell, yet here you are dragging around that bag..." Alex smirked at me, nodding to my sling bag on my shoulder.

I knew she knew better, and she was only teasing, but I said it anyway. Those thoughts had been on my mind off and on the last few days, interspersed with all my annoyance with Chandler today. "You know why I brought this bag. I always bring this bag."

Alex nodded as we shuffled forward in line. I realized, when I paid attention to the people waiting, we were headed down a flight of stairs leading beneath the church. It took us a good fifteen minutes; all the while, Alex and I chatted about school and made small talk, catching up with each other.

When we reached the door, the bouncer waiting at a small podium asked for our ID's. Alex and I both handed him our drivers licenses. Unlike me, who did not look like a person who associated with Alex with her black skinny jeans and band shirts and combat boots, the guy at the door looked like he could be her twin brother. He was studying our ID's, his blue eyes accentuated by his eyeliner.

Eventually, he handed us our ID's back, and he smiled at me. "You're from Las Vegas? Do you live near the strip?" It was the infamous question everyone asked.

I nodded, though oftentimes I liked to pretend I had never lived in Nevada a moment of my life. It had all been a distant memory I wanted to forget, especially because of the last decade. I decided to humor him anyway.

"A little outside of it, but not far." I took my license, put it back in my wallet, then returned it to my bag. Meanwhile, the bouncer put a wristband around our arms.

"I love it out there. I'm a big fan of magic shows. Have you ever been?" He was still smiling. "I've wanted to do magic ever since I was a little kid."

"Cassie's parents were magicians," Alex piped up, and I knew while it had been well-intentioned, she'd also momentarily forgotten what a sensitive topic it was for me. I assumed, perhaps, it was because she had known them when we were younger, and they had adored her as much as she adored them. It was in her nature to talk fondly of them.

"That's super cool," he replied, looking at me. "What show were they in? Would I know of them?"

At that point, I knew my entire demeanor had to have shifted because Alex wrapped her arm around me again and smiled politely at the bouncer. "We're going to go in and get out of this rain. Have a good night." He nodded, and Alex tugged me along inside, apologizing once we'd gotten through the door. "I got carried away."

"It's okay," I assured her, but I was too distracted to elaborate. The minute we stepped inside, someone handed Alex and me a small black object. It was a little dark, my eyes adjusting, but I made it out quickly. It was a simple black mask, one which fit over the eyes and nose. Like something you'd wear at a masquerade ball. "What's this?"

Alex grinned at me, and I watched her fasten the mask to her face. I followed suit, still quizzical. "It's a thing here. Go with it." I nodded. Strangely enough, the mask instantly gave me a little air of confidence I hadn't felt before. Like I could have been anyone I wanted to be, and no one would have known the difference. Well, except for Alex.

We rounded another corner, and suddenly, the room opened up. I knew we must have been underneath the old church then. Above us, wooden beams ran across the rafters, similar to how old churches looked. While there were no windows, the ceiling had been beautifully painted to look like it was entirely stained glass. Whoever had done it had spent a great deal of time designing it.

One side of the room, the side I was following Alex toward, was a long bar. It had a different feeling than other parts of the room. It was sleek and modern with a smooth, metallic-looking counter. The chairs, however, resembled little wooden church pews, but they were painted black.

While someone might have thought the two different designs, the older, classical look, merged with the contemporary flair and various pieces of the building, was off-putting, it actually worked. I loved the aesthetic. So much so I was lost in it until Alex and I found a seat at the bar.

Alex leaned into me, placing her mouth against my ear so I could hear her speaking. "Welcome to The Crucible, Cass."

The place was pretty packed considering it was a Monday night in such a small town like Acrefort. I imagined a lot of these people had to have come from elsewhere; there were too many of them to have all been from the city itself. Possibly there were people from the Dreamers Academy. It would have been impossible to know, given everyone was wearing masks. The more I noticed, the more I liked it.

"So, it's a club," I said, after Alex had ordered us both bourbon and cokes. The bartender took off to make them, and I watched my friend turn in the unique pew seat.

"It's *the* club," Alex corrected me, looking out into the diverse crowd. While it struck me as sort of a gothic-style club, more up Alex's alley, there were really all sorts of people there. Men in both suits and casual jeans and shirts. Some women in fashionable, high-end dresses, some in simple dresses. It was far more varied than I'd expected it to be.

"This place is kind of a hidden gem," Alex explained. "But if you know about it, and you're into it... it's the place to go. I hear some people drive hundreds of miles to come to Acrefort for a few days to visit. It's the happening spot, as far as Acrefort is concerned."

"I can see," I agreed. Our drinks arrived in front of us, and Alex handed a credit card to the bartender, asking him to open us a tab. She must have known I was about to argue with her because she held up a hand to silence me. "Fine. Thank you."

"Cheers to a new city and a new adventure," Alex said, offering me a smile.

"Cheers to getting the fucking hell away from Nevada for good," I replied, clinking our glasses together. Both of us took a drink, and I surprisingly downed most of mine in one go. Alex had already warned the bartender I'd need another one and was laughing at me by the time I'd sat the glass down.

"Jesus, woman, pace yourself," Alex said, grinning at me and shaking her head. She took another sip of her drink and then sat it down on the bar.

"It's been a hell of a day," I replied, hating I had somehow reminded myself of the morning I had endured with my cocky as fuck professor.

"It's been a hell of a last decade, Cass," Alex said, eyeing me. "With everything you had to go through with Peter, the fact you managed to survive all the bullshit. The fact you're going to go all Justice League on him soon and keep the son of a bitch where he belongs, in jail. As soon as that shady fuck Andre Morales gets enough dirt on him..."

I waved my hand, trying to get her to lower her voice. Even far away from Nevada, far away from my Uncle, Peter Blackstone, I still didn't feel safe. Not even if I hadn't dealt with the man since I left for college. Sitting here with my best friend in a crowded club in a small town in upstate New York, I still didn't feel entirely secure. Better than I had in a long time, given he had been behind bars for a few years in Nevada—but I wouldn't feel satisfied until I knew there was no way he was getting out again. Or dead. I mostly hoped for the latter.

"Sorry," Alex said, lowering her voice and drawing close to me. "What I'm saying is this is a celebration. It's a new chapter. College was one thing. But this... Cassie, this has been your dream forever. Our dream. And it's here. You made it, kid."

Despite how shaken I felt at the mention of my uncle, her pride in me made me smile. I picked up my glass, raising it to her. "Cheers to that. We both made it."

"Hell yeah," Alex said, as we brought our glasses together, both finishing our drinks as two more arrived.

Between people watching and more conversation about school, we must have spent a good thirty minutes or so drinking and enjoying ourselves. Before I knew it, I'd downed my second drink and was definitely starting to feel it.

Alex was about to order me a third, but luckily, the lights in the room dimmed before she had the opportunity. Across from us, a large stage was set up. Something I hadn't noticed until a bright spotlight illuminated it.

A woman's voice came over the speakers, drowning out the noisy crowd around us.

"Good evening." The electronic dance music blaring across the room, where a collection of people had been dancing, softened. "As you're aware, it's another beautiful Monday in Acrefort, New York." The crowd cheered, and it puzzled me a little. Who the hell got excited on a Monday? "Mondays are an exciting day here at The Crucible. A crowd favorite, you might say."

More cheering. I looked at Alex. "What the hell is everyone so excited about?" My friend didn't answer me, raised a brow and grinned playfully, nodding back toward the stage.

"Please, give a warm welcome to the most erotic act in all of Acrefort. Here to entertain you tonight, as always, the one, the only... Maître!"

If I thought the crowd had gone crazy before, they went nuts then. It felt like I was at a ridiculous boy band concert with a bunch of teenagers, and people were about to start throwing themselves at the stage.

Oddly enough, the room went quiet. It took a moment for my eyes to adjust to see what caused the silence—a man towering over the crowd. He must have been over six feet, and he was built like a fucking renaissance sculpture, with lines of abs and muscles everywhere. Which was easy to see, given the only thing he was wearing was a pair of loose black cotton pants and the signature black mask of the club.

In the darkness, he had an air of mystery about him. I couldn't make him out entirely. Which maybe wasn't the worst thing because anonymity was part of the whole allure here. The only thing I could gather was he clearly had the attention of every single person in the entire room.

Including mine.

I felt something nudge me and realized when I'd taken a small break from gawking at the man on the stage, Alex was grinning at me. "Ha. I knew you'd get a kick out of him. I'm not into men, and I'd still jump his bones. I mean, damn."

The heat radiating through me was intense. My best friend had done an excellent job. This was the kind of distraction I needed. The man was gorgeous, in all his mysterious glory.

When I turned my attention back to him completely, I realized there was something in his hands. He'd been tossing it back and forth, twiddling it around as he moved about the stage. It was a beautiful, deep red color. Rope, I realized, in a bundle.

I watched him scan across the audience, my eyes all over him, watching his face, admiring his towering frame, and then back to his hands and the rope. Wondering what on earth he was about to do that had the entire crowd wound up.

"Bonsoir." His thick, gorgeous French accent rolled out of his mouth, deep and gravely. I shivered.

A few women in the audience squealed in delight, but the man was unfazed. He took a few steps forward from the shadows into the light. It was still hard to get a full picture of him. And honestly, I kind of loved it. There was an air of mystery about him. It made him all the more sexy.

"*Shibari* is a Japanese word that means tight bonding."His beautiful accent made the words sound like a caress. It was as if he'd stepped off a jet plane straight from France. I watched him toss the rope around as he spoke, completely lost in everything about him. "It's a style of bondage, BDSM, involving tying a person up with visually intricate patterns of rope."

Maître turned, taking another few steps forward, and looked out into the audience. He scanned the room a bit and for whatever reason, I felt like his attention had stopped directly on me. Though I must have been losing my mind, I couldn't honestly tell because it was so hard to make out his eyes from a distance.

"While the practice of Shibari is often for sexual pleasure, it is also very much a beautiful style of contemporary art. Which I will be demonstrating this evening, on a lucky individual."

The crowd lost it again, and I understood why. Maître was looking in my direction, and I couldn't help but feel like he was still staring straight at me. A shiver went down my spine, and I was grateful he finally turned again. I was able to breathe.

"I'd like to invite someone to the stage, now, if there are any willing volunteers—"

"She'll do it!" An enthusiastic voice resounded into the room. Heads turned, including my own, in the direction of the shout. I began sinking into my seat, when I realized it had been Alex's voice garnering everyone's attention. The woman had been pointing with bounds of enthusiasm straight at me.

"No, no, no, no," I whispered, slouching in my seat. Maître had lasered in on me again, and this time I knew he was looking dead at me. I couldn't look back at him, burning like I was on fire. "I am *not* volunteering, Alex," I hissed at her.

"Let her do it!" Alex shouted at the man, completely ignoring my plea. Somehow, I gathered the courage to look back up at Maître, who was studying me intently, hands still fiddling with the rope.

"I prefer to take willing volunteers," he replied, matter-of-factly. "Shibari requires a level of trust. A level of calmness. Level-headedness. There's no room for fear. You can't be afraid—"

"I'm not afraid."

My voice rang out with an air of authority. I meant it.

Before I knew what I was doing, I'd stood up from my pew seat at the bar, pushing myself forward into the room. After the fucking nonsense I'd endured earlier with Chandler Moreau, challenging me with every step, I had about had it with men telling me I couldn't do something. It wasn't about to happen again. Not today.

"Clearly you have some reservations," the man replied, still watching me. I had already started moving through the crowd, weaving my way toward the giant stage he was standing on. Moving my body without permission. I didn't know what the hell I was doing, outside of acting on instinct and being a little pissed off.

"I'll do it," I called out to him. "I'm not afraid."

The silence in the room ended when people started to clap for me. Maître's stance had softened a little, and he watched me closely as I made my way through the crowd over to the steps leading up to him. The applause encouraged me, despite everything.

I could hear Alex whistling at the bar. While I literally hated her in those moments, I was grateful for her, too. Maybe this was the exact thing I needed.

Of course, I'd blatantly lied. I was fucking scared shitless. But the last thing on earth I was going to do was admit it to this man. At least one time today, I was going to prove a point. Even if it was to this stranger who I was impulsively about to hand myself over to.

The gorgeous man on the stage hadn't once taken his eyes off of me, and it had been nearly the same for me. I locked in on him, and he came more and more into focus the closer I got.

By the time I'd reached the top of the stage, I could make him out clearer. There was less of an air of mystery about him. I could see the thick, dark hair on his head and could take in those vivid eyes he apparently had. They were a beautiful shade of green.

They instantly reminded me of Chandler Moreau. I felt myself frown, pausing at the top of the stairs. Forcing myself to forget anything and everything about that stubborn, self-centered professor. I was allowing myself the courtesy. To give into something, to let myself fall into fear, and perhaps, be surprised by it.

"Often, Shibari is practiced in the naked form,"Maître spoke again after I'd paused. I was in the darkness, not having stepped into the spotlight yet. While he'd looked briefly at the audience, his attention immediately returned to me. It was as if he was speaking only to me.

"But since we're on *this* side of the club..." Laughter trickled throughout the room, and I wondered what he'd meant. I would have to ask Alex about it later. "I will kindly ask our lovely volunteer to be in her undergarments for this demonstration. It will allow for a better experience."

Truthfully, I would have probably stripped naked for the man if he had asked me to, with his accent. I'd heard plenty of French people speak before. I'd always found the language lovely. The combination of those beautiful inflections with the deep, coarseness of his tone... I probably would have done anything he asked of me.

Which included removing the little black dress I'd been wearing. I did it swiftly, allowing myself as little time to dwell on it as possible. My heart was still thudding in my chest, wildly, as the fabric fell to the floor. All at once, I was standing in a room of close to a hundred people with nothing but my cotton blue undergarments and a pair of well-loved black flats. I kicked my shoes off, too, for good measure.

"Come here, little *papillon*." My focus snapped to Maître, in the center of the stage. Losing all sight of the crowd around us. He was honed in on me again, his hand outstretched toward me. *Papillon*. I'd heard the word before. French, I knew it. It meant butterfly, if I remembered correctly.

And I loved the way he said it, drawing it out softly to me. It had been both sexy and, in a strange way, also comforting. Like he'd used it as a pet name for me and only me. My body moved as soon as he'd called me toward him. As I walked into the light, I focused solely on the man in front of me.

Maître's eyes never left me. I thought for certain there was no other man on earth who could have had as captivating of a gaze as my childhood idol, Chandler Moreau. Undoubtedly, this man could compete with him. He'd hooked me like I'd been the easiest fish in the pond to catch. I was helpless the minute he had.

I took slow, deep breaths, continuing to walk until I met him in the center of the stage. Every second, taking him in. Admiring the way he stood so tall and confident; his presence dominated the entire room.

I'm sure to someone who saw him outside these walls, he probably would appear intimidating, insinuating he'd be anything but trustworthy. But there was something about him, something said he wouldn't harm me. Behind that firm exterior was a gentleness which would see me to safety.

When I reached him, my hand fell into his. Again, despite his exterior, his touch was as firm as it was delicate, the perfect blend of the two. Maître spoke straight to me, though he was also explaining to the crowd.

"We'll be doing one of my favorite ties tonight. The butterfly harness." I watched him draw closer to me, closing the already small gap between us. Looming over me with his giant frame. "I will warn you, you will be firmly bound in this demonstration, unable to move the upper half of your body. It involves trust. You must give into the fear of being at someone else's mercy. Are you prepared, little papillon? Will you trust a stranger?"

My breath rolled in and out again, slowly. I did my best to relax my hand on his own, keeping my gaze steady on him. Had he been literally any other person, I probably would have fled the stage. But a sense of calm came over me, as I stared at him. Feeling the warmth of his hand holding my own. I nodded.

"I will," I replied, keeping my voice as steady and confident as I could. Though I realized, I had been slightly trembling.

There was a strange look in the man's eyes for a moment, studying me. He paused for a second like he'd lost his train of thought. Those eyes scanned over me as if he was trying to place something. Then he continued, squeezing my hand gently.

He leaned forward, closer to me, whispering into my ear. So close I could feel the heat of his breath against my skin. "Remember, little papillon. Your concern is the performance. The experience. Not the audience. Not me. Forget your audience. Forget me. It's only you and this rope."

It was like time had frozen. The room stopped moving, stopped existing. The sexy French accent which had been dripping out of Maître's mouth on stage had dissipated, replaced by an all too familiar voice, with a hint of his French lineage coming through.

Every single word he'd spoken to me felt like déjà vu. As real, as vibrant, as the first time he'd coached me six months ago on stage in Soleil Theater. Those moments after I'd frozen at my audition for the Dreamers Academy.

Chandler Moreau had come to me, to bring me back. To calm me and reassure me.

The mysterious man behind the mask was no longer mysterious to me. Those green eyes, drilling into me fiercely as ever, made me feel like a fool at that moment. There had been no other human in my life with eyes like his. No person in the entire world who looked at me the way Chandler did. At least at my audition.

I stared at him for a few long seconds. Tried to gauge if he had any idea who I was, any idea of who he'd spoken to. Surely he had to have recognized my voice. Surely he knew who I was after what he'd said to me. Then again, after the morning we'd had, maybe he'd been too oblivious to care. I honestly didn't know.

It appeared as though he didn't. I was some nervous volunteer from his audience.

I couldn't say a word. As I stared at him, my mind raced. It was telling me to run from the stage. To get the hell out of this club, pretend this had never happened. I had no earthly idea someone like Chandler Moreau would have a side to him like this. It was unlike anything I had ever expected, and I thought I knew the man well enough by now.

Yet something told me to stay, whether it was the look in his eyes or the gentle way he was still holding my hand. Those comforting words he had said. Perhaps they'd all played a part in keeping me there. The whole morning, I'd been longing for the man at my audition to return to me. The one in Soleil Theater, who had been so kind. Who had seen my potential. Who had believed in me.

And it felt, somehow, like he was there again, staring at me on the stage. Pulling me back into that intoxicating grasp of his. I found myself willing to do anything he wanted.

But when my eyes drifted down to the rope in his hands, I realized it was more now. On the stage, my view of Chandler Moreau shifted. He wasn't the man I'd spent years of my life watching, one with the silks. There was more to him when he stood there, the red rope in his hands, watching me almost possessively.

I knew, despite everything, I wasn't going anywhere. He'd caught me like a little butterfly trapped in a net. His merciless papillon.

"Are you ready?" He finally asked me. He hadn't shifted back to the accent he performed with bravado to the crowd. Still sounded exactly like himself, which was taking me to some strange place I didn't think I'd be able to return from. Somehow, I found myself nodding in reply.

There was a faint smile on Maître—on Chandler's lips. A smile I had missed. The one I'd been mesmerized by all those months ago at my audition. At that moment, I knew it was over. There was no turning back. The smile lasted only half a second, but it was the only thing he had needed to do to seal our fate.

"Then let's begin."

CHAPTER 4

CHANDLER

Smells of dried chiles, cardamom, cinnamon, and cumin wafted throughout the giant room. Above us, the massive draped white ceilings of Cirque du Lys towered. There were string lights glistening from the support beams holding the permanent tent structure in place, twinkling like stars. The lights had been Abigail's idea many years ago, and they added a certain dream-like aesthetic to the place. I hadn't been too keen on them at first, but they'd grown on me since. Years would do that to a person, I supposed.

I had been lying on my back on the stage, staring up at the ceiling, lost in thought. Listening to the crowd around me as they enjoyed our weekly communal dinner amongst the troupe. This week had been my choice, and like every other time, I'd picked the local Indian place. Although I enjoyed the food, part of me craved it for the scent rather than the taste. The aroma always seemed to take hold of me.

Someone passed a styrofoam container over me, and by the smell of it, I assumed it was the large order of garlic naan, an Indian flatbread. Everyone else at the circus adored it; we always ordered multiple boxes. I was the only one who blatantly refused to eat it, preferring to avoid bread, and I always got made fun of for it.

Which, of course, happened shortly after I'd seen the box go by. My friend Thomas loomed over me, dangling a droopy piece above my face. He grinned through a mess of facial hair, and his brown eyes glinted with the playful spark they had when he was trying to get under my skin. "You know, maybe all the negative energy of yours is due to your lack of carbohydrates, Chandler."

I swatted away the bread, which was drawing annoyingly close. Thomas laughed and stuffed part of it into his mouth while I sat back up. Abigail and Thomas were seated on one side of me. Sebastian sat across from us, immersed in conversation with one of our silk aerialists, Penelope, who went by Penny. Recently, Penny had been training to switch to acrobatics. Why anyone would give up the silks, I had no idea.

My attention turned to my friends. Then, to the box of saag paneer, a spinach and cheese dish, which sat in front of Abigail. It was my favorite Indian dish, though I liked all of them—sans the naan. I must have been staring at it a while, still lost in my own head, because Abigail called out to me.

"You sure you don't want to eat something?" When I focused on Abigail, I noticed she looked concerned. "It's your week to choose the food and you aren't touching a thing."

"That's strange, especially for you," Thomas said, chewing his last bite of naan. When he swallowed it, he wiped the corners of his mouth, studying me. "Is it your knee bothering you?" I nodded, despite my desire not to talk about it further.

Admittedly, it had been a part of the issue. I looked down at my leg stretched out in front of me. I'd been forced to put the brace back on. During practice with Penny, it had flared up again, still an unwelcome occurrence from time to time, even though it had been six months since my accident. I fought through it, but it left me hesitant to do anything drastic.

By the time we finished rehearsals, my friends had caught on. Thomas knew me well enough by now to know I never did anything half-hearted if I didn't have to. The moment we'd stopped for the evening, Abigail had appeared with the damn brace. And as annoyed as I'd been to see it, I was grateful, too.

It was throbbing uncomfortably. I tried not to focus on it and decided to give in to my friends' nagging. I waved for Abigail to pass the saag paneer dish to me, and she looked pleased when I did. I grabbed a fork from the pile of plastic silverware beside Sebastian, and instead of getting a plate, I decided to eat straight from the container. There wasn't much left between the two dozen greedy, ravenous performers. We could eat the hell out of a buffet.

For a few minutes, I sat in silence, trying to enjoy the food I was eating. I listened in, vaguely, to the conversation Abigail and Thomas had been having about some new shade of blue they wanted to paint their bedroom the following weekend. Overheard Sebastian inquiring with Penny about her acrobatic training progress.

Nothing suppressed the thoughts in my mind. Which, for the last twenty-four hours, had been nothing but thoughts of Cassandra Blackstone. And it hadn't been because of the horrendous History of the Circus class I'd been forced to cover...

"I heard you took over Jeanne's classes this semester." Thomas seemed as though he'd been reading my mind. I knew it was an attempt to draw me out of my shell. I must have been acting far more reclusive than normal. It was for good reason.

I nodded, finished the last bite of the spinach dish, and put the empty container beside me. "Unfortunately, yes." My friends must have seen how clearly I despised that fact. Though, I was curious how they'd come to know the information. I had only found out a few days before I'd been forced to show up for the Monday morning class. I'd barely had time to come up with a lecture at all.

"How did you know?" I asked after a few beats, looking at Thomas.

My friend studied me, exchanging a look with Abigail, who ended up answering my question. "Cassandra told us."

"Fantastic," I muttered, adjusting myself. The sudden movement jolted my knee, and I winced. But I didn't dwell on the pain for long, too curious what else the woman had told my friends about the terrible first class we'd had together.

"I heard you were quite the ass," Thomas said, grinning at me. "Which, as unsurprised as I should have been given—well, you're you..." I frowned at him, and Thomas laughed. "It seemed you were more cantankerous than usual. She was pretty upset."

"—I think a little *more* than you're implying," Abigail corrected. She stared straight at me, a stern look on her face. As sweet as she almost always sounded, she was very serious. "You need to apologize to her, Chandler. It was her first day, for goodness sakes. I know you have a tendency to be direct and brash, but Cassandra's a sweet girl. You really rattled her."

Admittedly, on more than one occasion since the class, I felt guilty for the way I'd behaved. She hadn't done anything wrong, but I had taken it out on her, of all people. Outside of being late, which had gotten a little under my skin. Tardiness was one thing I absolutely did not tolerate. But it was something I could have brushed off, given it was the first day.

"—I may have been a little distracted by my father," I admitted to my friends. "The class was forced on me out of nowhere. I thought I'd fulfilled my little obligation to him with those auditions, but clearly, he wasn't through." My brow wrinkled, remembering how he'd barged into my office minutes before I'd planned to leave for the day, only to derail my life by informing me my forever-burdensome ex-wife had abruptly left, and I would have to take over for her.

Jeanne Tremblay had already fucked with my life far more than she should have been allowed to. The idea she'd gotten another jab at me and left me stuck with her bullshit coursework had been the final straw.

Perhaps the only good thing that had come from her abrupt exit, I had squandered within a few minutes. The one good thing about Jeanne's sudden absence was Cassandra Blackstone becoming my student. The exceptional talent I'd seen at those auditions months ago would be rightfully training under the wing she should have been learning under—mine. I should have been happier than I was. Instead, I'd decided to take my frustrations out on her.

"What happened to Jeanne, anyway?" I asked, wondering what ridiculous excuse she'd made to drop from the program moments before school had started. When I asked the question, I noticed a strange shift in my friends' expressions. Abigail and Thomas shared a look. "What?" I asked, feeling annoyed by their silent exchange.

"She hasn't talked to you yet?" Abigail asked me, and I shook my head. "Oh, I thought she would have by now. Given the circumstances..." She tapered off for a second. I was about to demand an answer from her, but she continued before I could say anything. "I'm sure she'll talk to you soon. It's not my place to say anything."

"That's all I get? Really?" My tone had gotten snippy. Between the throbbing pain in my knee, the botched rehearsal because of it, and one singular female student who would not leave my mind, no matter how hard I tried to force it, it was bound to happen.

"I'll tell her to come talk to you," Abigail said, raising her hands in the air. Some days, I hated the fact that, while Jeanne and I had gone our separate ways, we were still tethered in many ways, including many of my friends, who were also hers. She had thankfully left Cirque du Lys shortly after our divorce, but she still remained part of the board. Hell, her parents and grandparents had ties with my family. It was like she was some incessant, annoying fly I couldn't bat away.

"Fine," I replied grumpily. I wished I had more saag paneer to eat to distract myself. Instead, I settled for a few measly bites of the butter chicken. Sebastian had finished with it and the dish was sitting close by. I snatched up the container, stuffing a bite of the food into my mouth.

When I turned my attention back on Thomas and Abigail, I noticed my friend was laughing at me again, shaking his head. "Jesus, Chandler. For a forty-one year-old-man, you sure can pout like a little kid."

"I'm not pouting," I scowled at him, both at the reference to my age and the jab. "It's been a long few days. That's all." Long had been an understatement, and it didn't help in between all these frustrating thoughts I kept having about a *student,* my father's hold on me was ever-lingering. I hated it.

It was something my friends would never completely understand. To them, they saw a strained father-son relationship. It ran far deeper. Deeper than either of them would ever get to know about. I made sure of it.

"Okay, call it what you will—restrained seething..."

"Oh go to hell, Thomas," I said, although I couldn't help but feel slightly more lighthearted when I saw the amused look on his face. He cared about me and was trying to lighten the mood. I should have been taking solace.

So, I tried to as best I could. "I'll apologize to Cassandra."

"Good," Abigail said. "She idolizes you and has been waiting to get to work with you for ages. It wasn't that long ago when we all met. You were her age and were in her shoes."

"Wasn't that long ago?" Thomas piped in, and before he could crack another joke about my age, I glared at him. He laughed, shaking his head, but he refrained.

"Anyway," Abigail continued, smiling softly at me. "Apologizing is a good first step. And maybe you'll also consider going back to the doctor about your knee—"

When she reminded me about my injury, the pain came back into focus. It wasn't quite as bad as it had been, and I supposed the brace had been helping a little, along with staying off of it. Every time I'd had a flare-up the last few months, my friends had nagged me to go back to the doctor. I probably should have, but I hadn't yet.

Either way, I tried to humor her. "I'll think about it."

As much as I was trying desperately to forget about Cassandra, for a few minutes, something flickered into my mind. Something I'd wondered months ago when she'd auditioned and resurfaced during our conversation now, much to my surprise. Something I had wondered about from time to time but kept forgetting to ask.

"Cassandra wouldn't happen to be related to Oliver and Katherine Blackstone, would she?" I figured out of anyone, Thomas and Abigail would surely know, given they'd apparently been friends with her since she was young.

Thomas raised a curious brow at me. "Oliver and Katherine were her parents."

It shouldn't have caught me by surprise because it made sense. But the idea Cassandra's parents had been two people I had admired and grown up enjoying had been a surprise regardless.

"Really?" I tried my best to restrain my enthusiasm, figuring I was already coming off too strongly as it was. "The Blackstone Magicians? What a small world."

"They were talented people," Abigail agreed with me. "Kind people, too, like Cassandra. You would have liked them, I think. Driven you less mad than this one—" Abigail nudged her husband gently, and Thomas grinned.

"Oh come on, he likes it."

I shook my head but continued my train of thought. "I grew up going to their shows, believe it or not. My grandmother Lily used to take us whenever they were in New York. I had thought about them when she'd introduced herself at the auditions, but I didn't think they would be that closely related." For a moment, I sat silently, remembering little pieces of the Blackstone shows I'd been to. Another thought occurred to me. "You said 'were.' Are they not performing anymore?"

Thomas and Abigail exchanged another one of their private couple looks. Thomas spoke. "They died years ago, Chandler. You didn't hear about that?"

In all honesty, I'd completely forgotten about the incident until that precise moment. "The freak circus fire accident?" Thomas nodded after I asked. His words suddenly jerked me from all of the self-pitying, ridiculous thoughts I'd been having the last two days.

"I don't know what to say," I replied because those were genuinely the only words I could think of. "I remember how sad I felt hearing that. I can't imagine what that must have been like for Cassandra—" While I certainly had anything but a perfect relationship with my father, I was close with my mother. And still, I couldn't fathom the idea of experiencing their deaths in a fire, let alone as a child.

"It's very sad," Abigail agreed, both her and her husband looking somber. "And we lost touch with her for a while... We didn't hear from her until college. Thomas and I assumed she just needed distance from all of it. I'm not really sure."

It made sense; I couldn't imagine who wouldn't have wanted space if they had been in her shoes. "I guess that explains why she didn't pursue magic." It had been the other question lingering on my mind.

Suddenly, Abigail's face lit up again, smiling softly at me. "Oh, Chandler, she knew way before her parents passed away she was going to be an aerialist. Broke Oliver's heart more than once about it. Both of them knew they couldn't stop her. Not after she saw you."

When Abigail said the words, my mind drifted back to those moments in the theater at Cassandra's auditions. After my ex-wife had asked her why she wanted to be an aerialist, she'd looked me square in the eyes and told me her dream had everything to do with me.

While I knew I was an inspiration to many, and I took pride in the fact, something about the way she said it struck me in a strange way. Especially after I'd seen her talent.

"So don't go breaking the damn woman's heart, Chandler," Thomas teased.

And I found myself far more serious than he had been when I replied. "I'll do my best."

Early the following morning, before the sun had begun to rise, I decided to take a brisk walk around the Dreamers Academy campus. Normally, I took my walks downtown, where my condo was, but today I had the itch for different scenery. While I was not entirely thrilled about my residence on campus that semester, I still couldn't argue the view was beautiful. As much as I hated my grandfather with every fiber of my being, he had an impeccable eye for design and had spared no expense to do what he wanted.

As I finished my lap around the perimeter, about a mile and a half or so, I headed straight toward the campus' centerpiece, Tremblay Hall. I made my approach, admiring the outside of the building. The sun was starting to peek into the sky, and the brilliant orange and red glow danced off the stained glass windows, the light reflecting onto the gargoyle statues watching from above.

I slowed to brace myself against the heavy exterior doors. When I'd made it inside, I let myself catch my breath for a minute. Even though I didn't trust my knee enough to run, I'd really pushed myself, as evidenced by the perspiration on my face and my audible panting. My intention had been to head to the other side of the building, to my office. Since I hadn't gotten in contact with my ex-wife yet, despite making several attempts, I was charged with planning the coursework for her classes on my own. While this whole ordeal was already an incredible thorn in my side, this made it much more frustrating.

Instead of making the turn to circle around the Soleil Theater in the center, which had curved hallways wrapped around it, I paused at its wooden doorways. Even the doors were carved with intricate designs complimenting the interior of the building. That wasn't what caught my attention. It was the light pouring through the stained glass windows on either door.

Classes for the undergraduate students wouldn't start for another two hours. The graduate students, who mainly attended focused training for their specialties, often arrived later. So, I was surprised to see someone had already been in the building. Most of the lights in the hallways hadn't been turned on yet.

Something compelled me to step inside, whether to admire the theater again or my curiosity to see who it was; I wasn't sure. I slipped inside the door, carefully, and tried to make as little noise as possible when I shut it. Luckily, the audience of the theater was dark, and I was hidden in the shadows.

When I turned around, my eyes caught movement, immediately focusing on something flying through the air, high above the stage. Not something, *someone*. I took a few steps further inside for a closer look. Surprised to find Cassandra Blackstone practicing alone in the silks onstage, moving from a cross back straddle into an airplane drop.

Her movements were flawless, at least what I caught in those first few seconds. I watched her cascade in another series of turns and flips until she'd made her way from at least sixty feet in the air all the way to the stage.

There were a few moments as she stood there, catching her breath, I thought to walk down to her. Felt the overwhelming urge to apologize to her for my behavior the other day after the conversation with my friends the previous evening. But I halted when she began circling around the vibrant fabrics again, lost in her own little world. As much as I wanted to apologize, it would have to wait. Right now, she was focused—in her element.

And as someone who knew how incredibly important it was to concentrate, I decided to not move. To admire her from afar as she worked. I hadn't gotten to see her like this since her audition, which felt like eons ago instead of six months. While I hadn't forgotten how talented she was, it was still a welcome sight to see her work again.

Cassandra headed back up into the silks, not quite as high as she had been before. I watched her dangling, tied up in the fabric.

When Cassandra let go this time, I was already a few steps ahead of her. While my mind was still drifting momentarily, I'd predicted what she intended to do and was surprised I had been right. As I expected, it had been the wrong drop to start her descent with. Cassandra would lose all the momentum she needed to propel her into the rest of the sequence.

Sure enough, a few seconds into her second twist, I watched her flail. She panicked, clinging onto the fabrics, clearly trying to regain her composure after her slip-up. It took everything in my power not to walk down the aisle, as I had done months ago, to help her.

I made a step in her direction and opened my mouth to call to her, watching as she twisted around, returning to the stage. But I felt a hand on my wrist, which caused me to spin around so fast, I almost toppled over.

In the darkness of the audience, staring up at me, was another face I hadn't seen in months. Not since the auditions. And I had been grateful because she was one of the last people on earth I wanted to deal with after everything she had put me through.

Jeanne Tremblay's blue eyes were lasered in on me. I couldn't read the expression on her face. It was jumbled, and it seemed as though she could have been thinking and feeling any number of things. I watched her open her mouth to speak, but before she did, I twisted my hand around, reversing her hold on me, so it was I who had the grip on her.

We found our way back through the theater doors, and I did my best to close them as quietly as possible again. Hoped Cassandra hadn't noticed my presence in the theater. I had closed the door, turning back around to face Jeanne. When I did, I nearly stumbled in surprise.

My ex-wife looked like she always did. Jeanne had always been an attractive woman, despite the fact I'd never much cared for blondes. Her family, like my own, had a long lineage of exceptional genetics. And like mine, they also had their fair share of fatal flaws. Still, she looked more different than she ever had.

Jeanne was clearly pregnant. Made obvious not only by the bump protruding from her stomach but because she had the 'glow' reserved for pregnant people, or so they said. I wouldn't have known, never having been around a pregnant woman before, but apparently, it was true. Despite her evident glow, however, her facial expression itself was anything but.

"You're—"

"Pregnant, yes." Jeanne confirmed. Her face was stoic but firm, eyes locked on mine. "About seven months now." I wished she hadn't added the last part, because I immediately did the math in my head. It must have happened during our divorce proceedings. While I knew she had been sleeping with my ex-best friend for years, it still stung.

A thought occurred to me as I stood there wallowing in self-pity. My eyes flitted up to hers again after having drifted away, lost in my own head. "Is that why you two got married the second we signed the papers?" Jeanne and her new husband Patrick had eloped mere hours after we'd walked out of the lawyer's office.

Strangely enough, I felt my knee throbbing when I said it. And the pain gave me a small surge of anger. Despite it being my fault for letting emotions get the best of me, the injury had happened due to feeling distracted by her marriage announcement at rehearsal. Like, after all the torment she had caused me, she wanted to rub it in my face more.

Jeanne had blamed me for the accident. I'd dropped her during the sequence we were practicing. Certainly, it had been my fault, but I'd spent those horrifying next few seconds doing everything I could to stop her from tumbling to the ground. Tried my best to protect her, despite everything she'd done. And it had ended up costing me instead of her.

At least she'd left the circus after the incident. Thank God.

Instead of answering my question, Jeanne rebutted with one of her own."Do you make it a habit of *stalking* your students like that?" She raised a brow at me, and the look on her face made my stomach churn, despite the annoyance I felt toward her. I hated that look. Especially when I had no earthly idea what the fuck it meant.

"I wasn't *stalking* her," I replied. "She's a student of mine. I was waiting for her to finish practicing so I could use the stage." There was only a sliver of that which was true, and I should have known after two decades, Jeanne knew me well enough to guess. I watched her face flicker for a moment, but I didn't bother dwelling on it. I had my own questions, too. "How did you know where I was? What the hell are you doing here? I thought you were taking a leave of absence. Which, thank you by the way, for dropping your job in my lap at the last minute."

Jeanne's nostrils flared, eyes narrowing at me. "I saw you walking in," she replied. I realized she must have been standing there watching me the entire time I'd been in the theater watching Cassandra. It shouldn't have bothered me, but I could feel my stomach churning regardless.

"I don't think you have any room to judge me for stalking," I replied, and quickly added, "Which I wasn't, to be clear."

"Chandler," Jeanne replied, still looking annoyed with me. The feeling was mutual. "I think your infatuation with a student fifteen years your junior is far more inappropriate than me following you inside a fucking building."

I ignored her reference to Cassandra and focused on my bigger concern. "Again, I'll ask you. What the hell are you doing here, Jeanne? You disappeared for absolutely no reason and suddenly decided to show up again. Why? To rub more salt in my wounds?"

"It wasn't for no reason," Jeanne said, and I watched her facial expression shift. For a few seconds, she looked worried in a way I hadn't seen in a long time. Worse than worried. I didn't have time to dwell on it because she quickly continued, "And you were the one who contacted me, not the other way around. I was tired of your incessant emails. There's such a thing as a phone, Chandler."

I realized what she was referring to. All the lecture notes and information for her classes. She'd been teaching these undergraduate courses for far more years than I had. My teaching experience consisted of lecturing from time to time and offering lessons to some of the more exceptional students when I was needed. Otherwise, I tried very hard to avoid this entire school for a myriad of reasons. Nevertheless, I only needed a few emails returned, not a surprise visit.

"Jeanne," I replied, eyes narrowing again. "The only reason I will ever call you again is if you happen to be dying... Even then, I'm not sure I'd count on it."

My ex-wife did not look amused. "Do you want the lecture notes or not?"I nodded, but I would have preferred she combust into flames than exchange lecture notes. It would have been far more satisfying. Instead, I motioned her to follow me around the curved hallway toward where I should have gone in the first place. My office.

Even with my ex-wife beside me and how awful she had made me feel in only a few minutes, my mind wandered back to thoughts of Cassandra. High above in those silks, lost in her own little world. Wishing I was back in the theater, watching her still.

CHAPTER 5

CASSANDRA

My mind was lost in thought while I stood in front of a large framed poster hanging outside Soleil Theater. It was black and white; its subjects were my friends, Thomas and Abigail Little.

They were performing their fire act at Cirque du Lys, as evidenced by the flames caught mid-dance in the still photo. It was funny because I imagined most people would never guess they performed such a dangerous circus act upon meeting them. Yet, there was hard proof of it.

The photo was a nice distraction until I heard one of the theater's main doors swing open. An undergraduate student fled from inside. He was clearly distraught and crying. I watched him until he'd turned down the hallway into what I assumed were the restrooms.

Seeing the kid in a panicked mess brought my mind to Chandler Moreau. It had been two days since I'd last seen him, and I was dreading the idea he was waiting for me behind those doors. It was fairly obvious; I didn't know any other faculty members at the Dreamers Academy who had the ability to send a poor kid crying down a hallway. He'd nearly done it to me at class on Monday.

That fact paralyzed me in front of the beautiful doors leading inside the theater for a few minutes. I knew I would be late again, but I didn't care. Somehow, I eventually forced myself to head inside despite my overwhelming sense of dread.

Soleil Theater itself was dark outside of the stage. I made sure the door closed softly behind me before I turned back toward the aisle and started walking down. Chandler Moreau was wrapped up in a set of silks on the stage, completely focused on what he was doing.

It was hard to stop myself from watching him, even though I was late. I knew it wasn't doing me any favors continuing to let time pass by, but he'd captured my attention, and I didn't want to interrupt.

Chandler wasn't too high off the ground and was mostly performing rudimentary maneuvers. Things I had learned back in college, even in high school. Pretty basic maneuvers for a man I'd watched do a Kamikaze drop on many occasions, which was the hardest aerial silk move to pull off.

He performed so effortlessly—it was hard not to watch. The way his face looked, those brilliant green eyes of his, so lost in his desire to execute everything perfectly. I continued walking through the darkness of the audience without making myself known.

When he'd twisted himself in the silks, all the fabric wrapped around his arms, legs and torso, my mind drifted back to The Crucible two nights ago. Those moments when he'd wrapped rope around me with the same focus he had now. I was helpless when it came to him, even if part of me was still furious. Even if I was dreading these lessons for other reasons.

The moment he'd bound me in the jute on the stage, when he had called me by that beautiful pet name, I was lost. There was no way in hell I was ever coming back.

Suddenly, my mind was jerked back to reality. I saw Chandler, who had been so precise and elegant, tumble back to the stage.

I heard him shout into the theater a string of curses, then he bellied over a bit. I panicked, wondering if I should run to him, concerned and confused by what happened.

Then, I noticed the brace on his knee. The one he'd been wearing at my audition when he'd admitted to the injury he'd suffered. The injury he was trying to prevent me from having when I'd frozen up. I'd been forever grateful for him in those moments.

I decided to let him recover. Eventually, he straightened, looking as though he was forcing himself to breathe through whatever pain he was in. After, he stepped away from the silks and out onto the stage.

Unfortunately, before I had an opportunity to announce my presence, he saw me hiding in the shadows. I wished I hadn't watched him for so long, hadn't seen his stumble, because I knew—without a shadow of a doubt—he was aware I had.

"You're late, Ms. Blackstone," Chandler said, staring straight at me. The thoughtful look he'd had, the one I found so attractive and got lost in when he'd been working in the silks, had completely vanished. It was replaced by the look I very much disliked. The one he kept giving me in class on Monday. Like I was the biggest nuisance to him.

I stepped further into the room then, walking up to the stage after setting down my sling bag and jacket, leaving me in nothing but my typical exercise attire—a fitted t-shirt and leggings. Trying not to dilly-dally more than I already had, I headed straight up the steps. "I know, I'm sorry about that—"

"Let's not keep making this a habit. I don't particularly like tardiness and certainly won't tolerate it in a graduate-level student. You'll be on time from now on, otherwise we won't have a lesson at all. Understood?" Chandler wasn't focused on me by the time he'd finished, his attention back on the silks. He ran a hand through them.

For whatever reason, his fingers dancing in the fabric sent my mind spiraling back to Monday night. Remembering his fingers grazing against me as he laid the red rope around me on stage. I swallowed deeply, shaking my head.

"Of course. I'll be on time from now on. I promise." I stepped closer toward the silks. There were several sets of them hanging in various vibrant colors.

Chandler finally moved away from the fabrics. I watched him walk a few paces, clearly limping a little. Part of me wanted to ask him if he was okay, but I refrained. Instead, I waited until he turned back to face me and spoke again. "I'm not sure what you were taught in undergraduate studies, and the mediocre gym you worked at, given it was at a subpar state school. Most of your peers came from far better programs."

My face twisted in annoyance. He was already digging into me like he did at class Monday morning. "Most of my peers could *afford* those programs," I muttered, shaking my head.

Chandler continued with his thought, disregarding I'd said anything at all. "We'll start with the basics. I realize you have a fancy for the more challenging maneuvers..." When he said it, I realized he'd been referring to my audition. Despite my irritation, I was a little flattered he'd remembered. "However, I want to ensure you have the fundamentals down because you tend to get distracted and lose your focus."

When he said that part, I wondered what he'd meant. If he had been referring to my audition, it would have been strange considering it had been more about my nerves performing in front of him rather than my tendency to get flustered. Then I remembered earlier in the morning, when I'd been practicing. I'd been a nervous wreck about these damn lessons.

I could have sworn someone had been in the theater with me. It freaked me out so bad I had immediately left and went home. Standing on stage with him, I wondered if it had been Chandler watching me, and I wasn't sure what to think about it.

"Ms. Blackstone, did I lose you?" Chandler's voice brought me back to the room. He'd drawn back to the silks again, wrapping his hands around a pair adjacent to mine. Leaning inward, his green eyes locked on me.

I shook my head.

"There we go," he said, looking satisfied. There was a bit more warmth in his tone. Chandler released himself from the silks, taking a few hobbling steps backward. "Let's see what you've got. Nothing fancy, remember. Start simple. I'll instruct you once you get started."

I made brief eye contact with Chandler, watching as he steadied himself, a careful eye on me. He'd given me plenty of space to work. Then, my attention turned back toward the silks. A pair of deep maroon fabrics. I tried not to focus too much on the color because it reminded me of the jute rope from the other night... Making it nearly impossible to concentrate.

Somehow, I shoved it from my mind. When I wrapped the silks around my hands, I managed to settle. I moved in a circle, running through a sequence in my head for a few seconds. I entered the mindset I needed to be in—it was just me and the fabric; the rest of the room disappeared.

A few deep breaths later, I pulled myself into the air, drawing up about twenty feet or so, wrapping my legs around the silks below me. I'd decided on a sailor pose first, then I would move into a bungee. I imagined Chandler might expect my choreography, but perhaps I'd take him by surprise with the bungee.

Regardless, I let my body swing in a few swift motions, executing the first move. Then, before Chandler could instruct me to do otherwise, proceeded into the bungee.

I expected him to butt into my performance. Instead he stood there, watching me. I glanced at him from time to time, maddeningly curious about what was going through his mind, but I continued to work on my focus.

I decided to make my way up further for a second set of movements, already playing them out in my head. This time, however, I had been too distracted thinking about Chandler. Enjoying how intensely he watched me as I worked.

I started into the second movement, about ten feet higher than I'd been before, attempting something slightly more complicated than I should have been doing. Probably in an effort to impress him, which I so badly wanted to do. I immediately tumbled. Before I faceplanted onto the stage, I managed to catch myself.

My head was spinning and my heart pounded so hard, I could have sworn it was audible. As I got my bearings, I was surprised to see Chandler had rushed to me. Had I not been able to stop myself, he would have attempted to catch me to break my fall. Instead, he skidded to a stop in front of me, wobbling as he did.

"Fuck," he growled, and I watched him brace his leg. It had clearly hurt him to move so swiftly. Immediately, guilt washed over me. I started to apologize to him, but he beat me.

"I thought I made myself *very* clear at your audition." He was still growling at me, and while I might have found it incredibly sexy in another context, instead, he sounded menacing. "You have to fucking pay attention. That cannot happen. Not ever. You've been doing this long enough to know better. You're going to hurt yourself, or worse—" He faded off, but I could tell by his facial expression he was pissed. His hand had wrapped around the silks beside him. He took a few deep breaths, looking away from me and off into the theater.

"I'm sorry—"

Chandler's head snapped back around, meeting my gaze with those intense green eyes of his. "Don't apologize to me," he said curtly. "Focus on what you're doing. If I catch you doing it again, I'll make sure there's consequences."

While I'm sure he meant something entirely different, the intensity of his gaze and the way he'd said "consequences" sent a shiver down my spine. To steady myself, I took a series of breaths. Fighting back tears, no longer able to meet his gaze.

Even though he'd frustrated me on multiple occasions the last few days, the very idea that someone I had idolized for so long looked so disappointed in me was horrible. I felt it breaking me a little, as much as I didn't want it to.

He seemed to notice I was starting to unravel. The glare on his face, the towering, menacing stance he'd taken over me, was immediately withdrawn. His entire demeanor changed in a matter of seconds. I watched him release the silks, and he winced.

I caught his gaze, his face having completely softened. All at once, he'd seemed to look so much more like he had six months ago on this very stage. He'd grown calmer, more composed. "I'm sorry. I was being brash."

I blinked at his words, surprised he was apologizing.

He continued, "I'm trying to look out for you here. You are clearly exceptionally talented. Far more so than the students from those prestigious schools; you run circles around them." I felt myself smile a fraction. "I can't have you squander all that potential and end up like me because you can't get out of your own head."

We stood there, staring at each other. Me, uncertain how to reply. Chandler, looking satisfied, albeit still a little concerned. I decided to assure him I'd do my best to do as he asked from now on, but he spoke again before I could. "And, before we do anything else, I need to say something. Because this certainly isn't going to go well unless I do, and it's been bothering me for days now."

Those words made my head spin. He could have meant any number of things, but all I could think about was the night at The Crucible. Oddly enough, I wanted him to say something about it. For whatever reason, I hoped he'd known it was me. Hoped he'd felt the same energy that had been weaving around us Monday night and even now on this stage.

"I was an ass the other day." I realized he was talking about class on Monday. "It had nothing to do with you; I was in a mood for other reasons. No matter what, I shouldn't have made you a punching bag. I want to apologize."

I felt my mouth drop slightly when he said it, surprised. Out of all the things I had expected him to say, it had not been another apology. It caught me completely off guard, and I was unable to formulate a reply at first. Eventually, I nodded. "Well, thank you."

Chandler suddenly smiled. It was small, but he met my gaze when he did. "However, I have to say very few people have gone toe-to-toe with me. You have spirit, Ms. Blackstone, I'll give you that."

My own smile widened. I'd been furious with him at the time, but we definitely had some strange way of keeping up with each other. "I'd advise you not to do it again, of course. Especially to someone who may not be as lenient as I'm being right now. But, I appreciate your ability to keep me on my toes. You should use that energy when you practice."

We grinned at each other. It only lasted for a few more seconds, and then he nodded to the silks I still had wrapped around my hands. He'd turned his focus back on the lesson, which I was grateful for because he'd stirred up a mess of feelings in me.

"Let's practice on the floor for now," he decided, drawing closer to me. I watched him approach, a little wobbly, but there was something alluring about it, too. Chandler was still watching me intently, and his movements distracted me.

All of a sudden, my mind was back with him at The Crucible again. He was the sexy Frenchman in his mask, pursuing me. Wanting to bind me with red jute rope.

"Am I going to have to lecture you again about your focus, Ms. Blackstone?" Chandler's slightly irritated tone brought me back to the room. He was nearly on top of me now. "If I have to ask again, we'll stop for the evening."

Those words brought me to full attention. I nodded, and he looked pleased.

"You did a sailor pose before," he said, and I watched as he looped behind me until I couldn't see him anymore, only hear him. I shuddered, still trying to reel myself in from the memory of Monday night. I didn't know how much longer I could keep up this charade, to not admit to him what I knew. Perhaps I needed to do it, for both our sakes. Rip off the bandaid. Get it out in the open.

"I'd like you to do it again. I want to show you some of the things you're doing wrong. It will be easier if you're within reach this time and not hanging precariously above me, about to plummet to your death."

I wasn't sure if he was trying to be funny or not, but I indulged him. One foot at a time, I wrapped myself up in the maroon silks. This move required only the fabric around my wrists; the rest of it was up to my upper body strength, holding me into position.

When I had readied myself, I pulled my body into the air above me, splitting my legs parallel to the floor like I was doing the splits. I had been doing sailor poses for so long, holding myself up never was a problem, and I could do it for however long he needed.

Behind me, I heard footsteps as Chandler approached me.

"I'm going to adjust you a bit. I need you not to panic and drop yourself, please." Chandler was right behind me, and I was high enough in the air it felt as though his mouth was dangerously close to my ear. My emotions ran wild remembering how he'd spoken to me on his stage. Calm, collected, gentle.

I felt his hands wrap around my upper thigh. He did it swiftly, likely to startle me less, but the moment he'd touched me, his grasp softened. I felt him draw my leg outward a bit, making tiny adjustments. When he was satisfied, he moved down, rotating the way my foot had been positioned around the silks. When I turned my head, I could see him.

Chandler was focused on what he was doing, lasered in on my body like he was fine-tuning an instrument. Essentially, that was what he was doing. Fine-tuning me. I was his instrument.

My breath caught in my throat.

A second later, I felt his hands release me, and he moved in front of me. I noticed he wasn't hobbling so much anymore and hoped the pain in his knee had subsided.

His green eyes raked over me, from one foot, up my leg, across the length of my body, and then down the other leg. While I was starting to feel it in my arms, I didn't move a muscle. I didn't care; I wasn't budging.

Chandler didn't speak as he brought his hands up, covering mine, which were still entangled in the silks. I felt captive to his touch, remembering how nice it had felt when he held my hand. It was different this time, but still.

"You want to invert this," he noted as he adjusted me. He was completely zeroed in on what he was doing. I glanced up, watching him as he repositioned my wrists. "I'm assuming you've been practicing in front of a mirror, so you've been doing this the opposite way. From now on, you need to remember to do it this way. It might take a few times, but you won't get so wrapped up in the silks you fumble over your movements like you did this morning."

He'd said it by accident, likely because he'd been so focused on perfecting my form. But Chandler admitted he had been watching me earlier when I'd been practicing. He'd seen the mistake I'd carelessly made. Undoubtedly, he'd cared I'd made it by choosing to work on this pose. I wasn't sure if it was because he was my mentor trying to teach me or if it was something else.

I didn't ask. He quickly realized his mistake, but I let it slide. He made no further mention of it, nor did I. Instead, I let him finish. When he had, I was still watching him. Chandler glanced down at me, meeting my eyes. "And, done."

Before I could stop myself, I said the singular word I shouldn't have. The final word he had spoken once he'd finished tying me with the rope. "*Fini.*"

Both of us froze, eyes locked on one another.

My mind raced as I tried to think of anything to say to him, to divert from the fact I had said the one stupid word which would be my undoing.

I moved my legs out of the perfectly-positioned sailor pose Chandler had spent several minutes putting me in. Had I not been so horrified, I would have felt worse about it. I needed to be on the floor. Immediately. Before either of us spoke again.

By pure luck, I'd managed to unravel myself and get steadied on the stage before Chandler finally came to his senses. He still had his eyes locked on me, the expression on his face hard to read. "Why did you say that word?"

Every second I spent flailing, trying to come up with an excuse, was making the situation much worse. Chandler took a step toward me, staring me down. "Cassandra." It ripped a quiver down my spine when he said my name to me, something he hadn't done since my audition. "Why did you say that word?"

I swallowed deeply, trying to hold my gaze on him. It felt like, at any second, I was going to combust. I forced myself to take a deep breath—I couldn't come up with a lie. "Because you said it when you finished."

Chandler, who had been hard to read for those first few horrendously long seconds, suddenly appeared panicked. He stood there, looking like he was about to spiral out of control, frozen, mind racing a thousand miles an hour. I couldn't blame him; mine had been, too.

I watched him finally shake his head. "I fucking knew better," he snarled, talking to himself instead of me. "The moment you got on the stage, I knew I recognized you. I knew by the damn orange smell. The little head tilt of yours you did at your audition..." He trailed off, lost in his own head. Mine spun, trying to decipher what the hell he was talking about. "Jesus fucking Christ."

"Chandler, I'm sorry. I didn't mean to upset you," the words tumbled out of my mouth, trying to get him to come back to me instead of being all wound up on his own. "I should have admitted it earlier. After the show. I don't know what I was thinking. To be fair, I didn't know it was you until I was already on the stage..." I trailed off, not knowing what else to say.

I watched him stand there, head bowed, staring at the ground. Muttering things under his breath. He had wrapped a fist around the silks, and I could see how white his knuckles were. I had no idea what to do or say in those moments, so I waited. Hoped eventually he'd come around and settle down so we could talk about it.

When he looked up at me again, his face had gone stoic. He looked straight at me. "We're done for the night," he said flatly. "I need you to leave, Ms. Blackstone."

"Chandler—" I started, feeling another wave of guilt wash over me because I'd gotten him so upset. Not completely understanding why, but still sorry for it, nonetheless.

"Professor Moreau," Chandler corrected me, almost barreling right over top of me when I said it. "I'm not asking you again. Get your things and go. Right now."

We stared at each other for a few more seconds. I fought every urge to fight him yet again. To get through this stubborn air he now had about him. But I decided, after a few seconds of staring at the expression on his face, I couldn't do it.

Chandler was trying desperately to hide it, but I could tell what must have been going on in his head. This callous exterior was a façade; it wasn't what really was going on. I'd embarrassed him, and though I couldn't fully understand, there was absolutely no way I was getting through to him.

So, I nodded. Took steps away from him before turning back out into the theater. At the foot of the steps of the stage, I collected my jacket and sling bag. Threw the bag over my shoulder and began walking down the aisle out of the theater. I made it halfway down before I suddenly had a change of heart. Even if it would be my second stupid decision.

I glanced back over my shoulder at him, still standing on the stage, clinging to those silks for dear life. "Good night, Professor Moreau," I called out to him.

Chandler didn't budge. He hovered in place on the stage. I stared at him for a few seconds, unsure if I should've gone back to him and forced the conversation. But again, I decided against it. I turned back toward the door, leaving him there. Just as I'd started walking again, I heard it. Faintly, but I knew he'd spoken.

"Good night, Ms. Blackstone."

CHAPTER 6

CHANDLER

Stella Flores placed the bourbon on the rocks in front of me, and I swallowed half of it in a matter of seconds. Proceeded to slam the glass back down on the counter far more aggressively than I should have. Stella raised a brow, placing a gentle hand on my wrist to bring me back to the room. I looked into her hazel eyes, but instead of focusing on her, all I could think of was Cassandra Blackstone. As much as I didn't want to.

An entire week had gone by since I last interacted with her. I canceled the second private lesson of hers, claiming I'd been under the weather. At the two history classes we'd had together, I did my best to speak as minimally to her as humanly possible. She seemed to get the point and hadn't pressed me about it.

Still, she was all I could fucking think about. Even at my rehearsals with Cirque du Lys. At my condo, lying restless in my bed. I couldn't get peace.

If it had been only about her talent, objectively as her mentor, it would have been one thing entirely. Instead, every time I drifted to thoughts about her wrapped up in those silks, it was seconds before my mind went elsewhere. She was bound in rope again on the stage behind me. Completely at my mercy. And it was driving me mad.

She's your student.

"Fuck," I muttered under my breath, grabbing the glass and downing the rest of the drink. I tried desperately to think about anything else. The crowd was thick again for a Monday at The Crucible. The last thing on earth I wanted was to be there after everything. Which was unusual, given how much I loved this act. But it wasn't doing me any favors, not right now.

"You couldn't have known," Stella said, looking at me curiously. She had already poured me another round, but less than she had the first two times. I'd been venting to her over the last half hour, the singular person I had decided to tell about my unfortunate circumstances. Someone who I knew wouldn't judge me for it.

"I knew," I scowled, staring down at the drink. I wanted to throw it back again; I wouldn't have minded if I was a little inebriated this time around to help get me through the performance I was about to do. But I managed to stop myself, looking back up at Stella. "I think I tried to delude myself, pretending it was impossible. But it was right in front of me."

I couldn't help it. I gulped down the third drink Stella had poured me. She studied me, taking away the glass.

"I'd offer you another, but you have to go in a few minutes," she reminded me, letting the glass fall into the dirty bin behind the bar. "And I don't think you should be drowning your problems in bourbon, regardless."

My friend was right. I needed to settle down. Stop self-destructing to the point I'd do something stupid. I took a deep breath and nodded to her before I spun in my seat, checking out the sea of people. "Jesus, it's more crowded tonight than last week."

"You'd think as the owner of this place, you'd be happier. More people, more money, yes?" Stella smiled at me when I looked back at her. It was certainly true. Not only that, but the more profitable this place appeared to be, the better, for many reasons. Reasons Stella didn't know about, and I would likely never tell her.

"And more tips for you," I decided to say in reply.

"Speaking of which, I should probably tend the rest of the bar," Stella nodded to other patrons. The bar was packed with people. Even though there were two bartenders working, Stella usually was on fire about keeping up with orders. I hadn't meant to distract her for so long.

"Get to it," I said, nodding, and she disappeared.

I remained at the bar for a few minutes, twirling a paper coaster in my hand with The Crucible logo engraved on it. Lost in a variety of thoughts, unable to stop myself from thinking about Cassandra once again. I would have given absolutely anything to not do the Shibari routine tonight. Nearly called it off and claimed I was sick again like I had done for Cassandra's lessons.

But calling off here was bad for business. No matter how much I was being governed by my emotions, it was something I couldn't do. It was laughable how easily I could hear my father lecturing me when I thought about it. Moreaus weren't governed by emotions. There was no room for it. *Mieux vaut plier que rompre.* Adapt and survive.

Fuck that saying. Fuck my grandfather. Fuck my father.

I got up from the bar. It was probably close to the time when I'd need to get ready anyway, and it was better than sitting there drowning in self-pity. I had just started to move into the crowd when I stopped abruptly.

It had been lucky I was facing the direction I was when I stood up, or I wouldn't have seen her. It was packed—not a single seat available, save the one I'd just vacated.

The first thing I'd noticed had been the distinctive honey brown hair of hers. She'd worn it down the previous week, which had been one of the reasons I hadn't figured her out sooner. This time, it was up in a messy bun on top of her head—reminiscent of how she'd worn it the first day of class. I wondered if she'd worn it up purposefully. Perhaps she'd thought if she looked different, she wouldn't have been recognizable.

Cassandra hadn't noticed me. She was chatting with a girl beside her, the same one she'd been with last week. They were laughing about something, and as absolutely stunned as I was to see her sitting there in my club, yet again, I was momentarily distracted by her smile. Trapped by it, helplessly.

I watched her turn around from looking out at the people to take a drink. I stood completely motionless, a million different emotions bubbling up inside me, whether I liked it or not. *Emotions solved nothing. They were just a distraction.*

I forced myself to breathe while I watched her turn back out to look at the room again. Her hazel eyes flitted around beneath the mask she blindly assumed would disguise her. She probably thought I might glaze over her and not realize she was there.

I had been a mere few seconds from storming straight over to drag her out of this place as fast as humanly possible when I was caught off guard. Cassandra's head turned, looking over her shoulder. For whatever reason, her eyes landed immediately on mine.

Both of us froze. I knew the moment she saw me, she'd known it was me. Just like I had known it was her. Why she had thought she would fool me again, I had absolutely no idea. It didn't matter. As soon as I got to my senses, I finally moved, blazing across the length of the bar, weaving through the horde of people.

Cassandra's eyes grew wide as I drew up on her. She'd already started to get up from her seat. Before I could speak to her, I was rudely interrupted. The lights began to dim and the spotlight on the stage illuminated. Stella's voice went over the intercom, announcing the Shibari show.

"Fuck me," I muttered. It had been the absolute worst timing.

My attention went back to Cassandra, who had gotten up from her seat and clutched the back of it, steadying herself. She and her friend stared wide-eyed at me.

When Stella finished her intro, the crowd went wild. Initially, I intended to ignore Cassandra. To focus on the performance and deal with her later. But I was livid. While the crowd waited, expecting me to appear on the stage, I wrapped my hand around Cassandra's wrist and tugged her along.

Her friend called after us, and I heard Cassandra yell back something to the effect that it was fine. It wasn't, not by a long shot, but I appreciated I wasn't going to have to explain myself to a second person. Cassandra let me weave her through the crowd to the other side of the room, beyond the stage, and to a set of doors. Doors that led to the other side of the club. Another place in which under no circumstances did I want her going, but I didn't know where else to go.

There was murmuring. Stella announced something, but I hadn't been paying attention. Instead, I snatched the keys from my pocket, unlocked the door, and nodded for Cassandra to go inside. She went obediently. Though I had been trying my best to control my temper, I slammed the door behind me and locked it.

It was dark in the room until I flipped on the lights. This room acted as a transitional area between the bar side of the club and the more exotic area. The patrons beyond the second set of doors across from us were forced to leave their belongings in storage here. Everything that happened in those spaces was private. Discrete.

At least at the moment it wasn't open yet. This room hadn't been occupied, which I was grateful for.

"Where are we?" Cassandra asked me, and I watched her remove the mask she'd been wearing. The less she pretended to put on this act of trying to disguise herself, the better. I followed suit.

Instead of answering, I took a step toward her. Cassandra watched me, unmoving, letting me get close enough so I was towering over her again. "What the hell are you doing here?"

Cassandra stood, looking up at me, lost in thought. Eventually, she decided to answer. "My friend really wanted to have a drink again. She really likes this club. I didn't feel like explaining to her that—"

"Bullshit," I replied, my eyes narrowing at her. "You're here on a Monday. Again. Don't tell me this isn't on purpose, Cassandra." I hated that I'd let myself use her name because of the way it always twisted around me. It was beautiful. I loved every opportunity to say it, despite the fact I was livid with her.

I watched her let out a laugh, shaking her head. "You don't think I needed a drink after having to deal with your massive attitude problem at class again this morning? You are disappointing me far more than I ever thought you would." It was snide and rude, but she wasn't wrong. I had been giving her the cold shoulder since her first private lessons the previous week. Likely that had been a disappointment. But it had been for both our sakes.

"Why do you have a key to get back here?" Cassandra asked me, looking down at my hand still holding onto it. I slipped it back into my pocket when she asked.

I hadn't wanted to humor her, but I did anyway.

"I own this place," I replied, curtly. "I work here. And last I checked, I'm not at the Dreamers Academy right now. What I do in my spare time is none of your damn business."

Cassandra eyed me for a moment before she spoke. "I could say the same. It's a free country last I checked, Chandler."

I felt a shiver rip up the length of me. A thing she had done to me on a number of occasions when she spoke my name. I was a fish caught on a hook. It took every ounce of self-control not to react.

"*Professor Moreau,*" I managed to correct her. "I can throw you out of here, Ms. Blackstone. Don't think I haven't done it with other patrons before. I can do it again."

Cassandra circled around me again like she was heading back to the door we'd come from. When she'd gotten to it, she turned back around to face me.

"*Cassandra,*" she replied to me, accentuating the syllables of her gorgeous name slowly and deliberately. "We're not at Dreamers, remember? You said it yourself." My eyes narrowed at her, more than they already had. "And I don't think you'll throw me out. I don't think you *want* to throw me out."

Before I could stop myself, I moved closer to her again. Closed the gap between us until I was looming over her. She was driving me mad. I wasn't sure if it was anger or what the hell it was, but my entire body was on fire.

"Are you *threatening* me now?" While I had been impressed by how well she'd sparred with me the other day in the classroom, I was not so impressed now.

"No," Cassandra replied, and her hazel eyes met mine. I watched her tongue draw across her lips, which were presently a dark shade of red. She took a deep breath in and slowly let it out. "I'm just waiting for you to admit it. To stop acting so bothered and pissed off. I know it's all bullshit."

"What the hell are you talking about?" I stared at her, utterly confused and more annoyed than I already was. I felt like I needed to jump in the nearby Peace River just to fucking cool off.

"I thought about it," Cassandra started, still looking me square in the eyes. "After you figured it out the other day at my lessons. I thought about it a lot. I get why you were mad. You said something when you were all fired up, and the minute you did, I knew."

The woman was driving me crazy. "God damn it, Cassandra, stop throwing around fucking riddles. I'm tired of it. This is ridiculous."

"You knew it was me, didn't you? You said you recognized my smell. Some head tilt I did or *something*." This entire time, while I'd been towering over her, trying my best to come across as deathly serious as possible, Cassandra hadn't budged. She held her ground, just as she had in the classroom.

I realized I might have been coming on too strong. It suddenly occurred to me I was doing the exact thing I hated so much about my father and grandfather. The dominance they always asserted. I was doing the same thing to her. The funny thing was Cassandra was seeing straight through it.

"I didn't know until you admitted it last week," I argued back at her. Although I desperately wanted it to be true, some deeper part of me knew I'd been lying to myself. I knew better, and I'd blatantly ignored it anyway. Gave into temptation.

Cassandra was staring at me hard, unmoving. Her hazel eyes trapped me in place, nowhere to go. I hated it. I was pissed as hell, yet at the same time I was seconds from shoving her into the wall and giving in to the surge of emotions I was feeling.

For a moment, I thought maybe that had been enough of a response. Perhaps she'd drop it. Give up this ridiculous act of defiance and go home. Stay out of my business.

Of course I'd been an idiot with the assumption. Cassandra drew closer. Literally right on top of me, still staring up at me.

"You say that," she started, studying me intently. "But I'm guessing you're having about as much trouble getting that night out of your head as me." Cassandra had gotten so close to me, I could smell her now. The distinctive, alluring smell of citrus. Oranges.

Fuck. I couldn't take it anymore.

All at once, I acted. Plowing straight into her small frame, pushing her back until she'd thudded against the door we came from in one fluid motion. Cassandra let out a surprised "oof" just as my arms landed on either side of her, effectively pinning her there.

"You may *think* you're in control here, Ms. Blackstone, but believe me, you *aren't.*"

While I hated the very idea of losing control, my words were a blatant lie. I was barely hanging on. "I don't take kindly to this behavior of yours. Don't appreciate you barging into my place of work, my private business, and trying to get a rise out of me. Or whatever the hell it is you're trying to do."

Cassandra looked as if she was about to speak, but the minute I let out a growl at her, she snapped her mouth shut. "There's about a dozen bars in this city. I suggest you pick another one to enjoy with your friend. If I see you in here again, there will be trouble."

Cassandra's breath had hitched in her throat a moment; I assumed both because of the tone I'd taken and also because I'd all but trapped her. Surprisingly, she stood tall against me. Trying to make a point she wasn't going to back down.

I couldn't have given a shit less.

Finally, she nodded, not speaking another word to me. I broke away from her, realizing the entire time I hadn't been breathing. All at once the cool air ripped into my lungs again.

My entire body had turned away from her, unable to look at her. In fear that if I did, the minimal amount of self-control I was so desperately trying to cling to would dissipate. I was afraid I would give into the maddening temptation she was drawing out of me. Instead, I looked at the doors opposite the one Cassandra had been backed against. Which, unfortunately, did not help matters.

There was a noise behind me, and I realized Cassandra had opened the door. I heard her utter one simple reply. One reply to send me recklessly tumbling, knowing full well I wasn't going to recover. A reply which signified whatever act I was trying to put on with her, however I was trying to hide myself, it wasn't working. Cassandra saw right through it.

"Whatever you say, *Professor Moreau.*" And she left me.

CHAPTER 7

CASSANDRA

A few minutes after my confrontation with Chandler, Alex and I left The Crucible. We stood outside on the street corner together, my sling bag over my shoulder. My best friend had been quizzing me about my dramatic disappearance, and as much as I wanted someone to vent to, I also didn't want her to know about Chandler. Not yet, anyway. I would allow him that courtesy, at least.

When I had done my best to convince her I was okay, which I knew she could clearly see I wasn't, Alex left me, heading a few blocks down to her girlfriend Dana's apartment. Meanwhile, I had called for a car with the rideshare app on my phone to come pick me up. It was getting kind of late, and the cab system in Acrefort was slow. I assumed I'd be waiting a few minutes.

I sat down on the edge of the curb, looking back at the old abandoned church, still feeling fired up about my confrontation with Chandler. Truthfully, I hadn't known how it would go down. I had been honest with him; Alex had wanted to go back to the club.

What I'd failed to tell him is that I'd also wanted to go again. I had fought the temptation to volunteer myself again for his show to see what he would have done. I knew better. I knew he was lying about knowing it was me when he'd rambled on in front of me on the theater stage.

What I didn't understand was why he was trying to fight me about it. Why he wouldn't admit it, for both our sakes, so I wouldn't feel so crazy anymore. I needed to know he'd been lost in this place with me, too. We didn't have to feel alone in it.

Unfortunately, I was alone in those moments, whether I liked it or not.

While I was waiting, I fiddled on my phone. I realized I'd forgotten to answer Henry, who had texted me before we'd gone into the club earlier. We had been chatting back and forth since he'd given me his number the week prior. My mind had been elsewhere, and I'd planned to answer him once I'd gotten home.

Though it was late and he was likely asleep, I texted him back anyway. I had nothing better to do. I let him know we could get lunch together tomorrow if he wanted.

When I finished the message, I noticed a car driving down the street. It was the rideshare, so I got to my feet. As I did, my phone buzzed in my hand.

It was Henry calling me. At nearly midnight.

"Hello?" I answered, putting the phone up to my ear.

There was a laugh on the other end of the line. "So you're a night owl like me, I see." His enthusiasm made me smile a bit, despite my somber mood.

"Actually, I'm more of a morning person. I happen to be best friends with a night owl, unfortunately." The cab had stopped in front of me, and I opened the door, preparing to hop inside. Once I had, I shut the door behind me. "I wanted to answer you back. Sorry it took me a while, I was forced to go out tonight."

"Dang," Henry said. "I'm guessing you're probably worn out."

Surprisingly, I felt the opposite. Wound up with weird energy and agitation more than anything. The last thing on my mind was going to sleep. There was probably a small chance it would happen anytime soon with how much my mind was racing.

"Actually, I'm pretty awake," I replied, wondering why he'd mentioned it.

"Oh, well in that case—" Henry paused. I heard him take a breath, and continued, "This is going to be a little awkward I guess, but here goes. Listen, Cassandra. I know it's highly unlikely a beautiful twenty-five—"

"Twenty-six," I corrected him, unable to help myself from smiling from his compliment, regardless. "Continue."

"Right. Twenty-six-year-old woman. I know you probably don't go for twenty-year-old nerdy sophomores, and I'm sure you're super busy with all the graduate school work. But, a guy has to shoot his shot, right?" He was rambling, but it was admittedly a little charming, so I didn't stop him. "Anywho—uh, I was wondering. Since you're awake and all... Would you like to go for a cup of coffee? Get to know each other better?"

"Coffee? Henry, it's almost midnight," I laughed, looking out the window of the moving cab, shaking my head. "What are you doing drinking coffee at midnight, you weirdo?"

"Well, it goes great with pie," Henry explained to me, matter-of-factly. "You'll have to trust me. Do you want to? I'm losing my nerve over here..."

I smiled, although I could empathize a lot about the anxiety. It was very easy to relate, as it sometimes left me paralyzed at times. It was flattering he'd been brave enough to ask me.

I wasn't sure if I would have had the nerve to ask an older, attractive man out on a date in the middle of the night. Then again, I'd recently confronted my forty-year-old mentor about his BDSM hobbies...

I needed a distraction. Maybe it was a good thing to stop thinking about Chandler Moreau in ways other than as my mentor. I was at the Dreamers Academy to learn from him, even if it was among many other things that brought me there. The ability to work with him had been a huge part of it.

Maybe going back to the way things were before was for the best. Better for both of us. I was there to focus. To become the best I could be. That's what I needed to do.

The pie, however, sounded like a great idea. My stomach growled in agreement.

"Okay, sure. Where are we meeting?"

The rideshare driver didn't have to divert our drive; we were close to campus and not far from my apartment. He stopped in front of an aged brick building on Old Main Hill, which was one of the busier roads in town that sat in front of the academy. A rickety neon sign hung above a doorway glowing with the word DINER in bold letters.

I paid the driver, which soured my mood a little because I was running lower on funds than I wanted to be. My paycheck from the teaching assistant job wouldn't come until the end of the week, and somehow I'd have to make what little I had left stretch for four more days.

Which meant I probably shouldn't have taken Henry up on this outing after all.

I saw him in the window, sitting at a booth, looking down at his phone. I'd make it work somehow. It would be good for me to have a distraction right now. I headed inside. When I saw the clock by the door, I realized I was late yet again.

A waitress by the door looked up to help me, and I motioned toward where I'd seen Henry sitting as I headed down the aisle. I paused when I'd gotten close enough to see him again, admiring as he looked out the window, watching a group of people walking down the street. Likely students, I imagined.

Henry's ash brown hair was a bit of a mess on his head, an organized chaos but chaos nonetheless. A striking contrast to how put together Chandler always seemed to look. His dark brown eyes staring off like he was lost in thought.

I slid into the cushioned booth across from him. It was large and plush and red, and it looked like it had recently been installed, despite the place itself being older. I relaxed, reclining against the high wood seat back and sighing.

Henry turned his attention toward me, smiling brightly, happy to see me. "I was wondering if this always-running-behind pattern was a school thing, or if it was a general habit..."

"It typically isn't," I rebutted, but I was starting to see I was lying to myself. Between classes with Chandler and our private lessons... I was a few minutes late even now. Maybe it was a problem, after all. I looked back at him, shaking my head. "Okay, maybe I might have a problem. Or maybe it's been lately, for some reason. I don't know what's wrong with me. I should break the habit. In my defense, tonight I was at the will of the driver who got me here."

"Hey, I'm not one to judge," Henry said, shrugging. "I'm the world's worst when it comes to being on time." I watched him flag down the single waitress who had spoken to me when I entered. When she came over to the table, she appeared unenthused and exhausted. Henry looked at me briefly. "I hope it's okay I haven't ordered yet. I wanted to wait for you."

"Let me guess," the waitress said, eyeing Henry. "Coffee and blueberry pie." Henry nodded to her.

"Come here often?" I grinned at Henry, and he smiled right back at me. When the waitress looked at me, I paused. I hadn't had a chance to look at the menu, but what Henry ordered sounded great.

I remembered the ride share fee. Sat for a minute, trying to calculate in my head how much I potentially needed to get me through the next four days. Decided, after a quick bit of thinking, I probably should forgo the pie, as much as I didn't want to.

But I didn't want to draw attention to my predicament, so I looked to Henry. "I'll have a coffee. I'm not too hungry though. Mind if I have a few bites of your pie?"

"This is on me," Henry said and looked at the waitress. "Bring her a whole piece, Anne. She can take the rest home with her. You know she's going to regret it if she doesn't have a whole piece."

"That good, huh?" I asked him. I was gracious he'd offered to pay, though I wanted to argue with him and still thought I might.

"The best," Henry and the waitress agreed simultaneously, and I couldn't help but laugh. The waitress disappeared down the aisle, leaving Henry and me by ourselves again. There were only three other people in the place with us, another couple and a single guy, on the other side of the restaurant.

"Thank you for offering to get me food. You didn't need to." I offered him a smile.

"Of course," Henry nodded like it was no big deal whatsoever, but he had no idea how much it actually was. "It was the least I could do if you are going to let me keep you up all night." He winked at me. A second later, I watched his facial expression shift, his face growing a little redder. "I didn't mean it that way."

I laughed again, unable to help myself. Already this outing was doing me good, keeping my mind off Chandler at least. "The coffee, you meant, right? Lucky for you, I drink a lot of it. I don't think it'll affect me much. I wasn't tired anyway."

"Same," Henry said, as the waitress dropped off two coffees and a bowl of half-and-half cups for us to share. "How do you drink your coffee?" I noticed him pick up a few of the little cups to use, and I followed suit.

"If it's a diner coffee like this, I generally have to have a lot of creamer," I admitted. "But I can drink a lighter roast black if it's good."

"No sugar?" Henry asked, and I shook my head. Henry smiled again. "Me, too. Look at that. We're a lot alike, Cassie. Meant to be."

I rolled my eyes, still smiling, and poured more half-and-half into the dark coffee. "Our coffee preferences won't indicate if we're soulmates, Henry. It's just coffee."

"Just coffee," Henry scoffed. *"How dare you."* I knew he wasn't serious. Both of us sat there, amused with each other. "Okay, you need more proof? Let's see. More questions." I looked up after pouring a final cup of half-and-half. Henry looked pleased he had my undivided attention.

"Cats or dogs?" Henry asked me.

"Dogs," I replied, simply. "But I've never had either before. I imagine I'd like dogs more. They're friendlier. Less aloof."

Henry took a drink of his coffee, and I followed suit. When he finished, he sat the mug down, letting out a sigh. "Never had a pet, huh? Interesting. I actually have to say cats, unfortunately. They're less needy and more independent."

"See, there goes your theory out the window..." I took another sip of coffee.

"Fa-Hey now, not so fast," Henry said, staring me down. "Coffee is a much better indicator than pets are. At least you like animals though; that's a good sign. I'm a big animal lover. Grew up on a farm, actually, with my sister. I'm studying to be a veterinarian for circus animals."

I raised a brow curiously at him. "Really? That's pretty cool. I didn't know Dreamer's had a veterinarian program. Or that there was a need for circus veterinarians..."

"It's kind of a niche, actually," Henry explained, still looking at me. "I'm studying the pre-veterinary part online and mostly doing general studies at Dreamers. I'm planning to go to graduate school somewhere after this, but I wanted the whole circus experience, you know? Since that's where I want to end up and everything. Plus, my dad lives right outside Acrefort, so it was convenient. I live with my sister about ten minutes or so from here."

I nodded thoughtfully. "Does your sister go to Dreamers?"

"She's a nurse," Henry started, "at the hospital downtown. I'm the crazy one of the family wanting to go into the circus industry. My mom actually was the reason, if I'm being honest. We used to go to Cirque du Lys shows all the time when I was younger. S—She loved them."

The idea Henry had been a big fan of the circus I had grown up adoring was an endearing surprise. "Do you still go to shows with your mom?"

"Ah, my mom passed away a few years ago, actually," Henry replied. "Ovarian cancer."

The waitress returned with our huge slices of pie. They looked hot and smelled divine. After I'd unrolled my silverware from the napkin they'd been wrapped in, I looked to Henry again. I was about to tell him my parents, too, had passed away, but he was ready for more questions.

"Okay, here's a good question. A real 'get to know you' one." Henry looked serious when we met eyes, and I raised a brow, not sure what to expect. "Do you like pineapple on your pizza?"

I nodded. "But it also has to have jalapeños or else it's disgusting." Henry made a horrified facial expression, and I laughed. "It's good."

"To be fair, I've never tried Hawaiian pizza before, but—ugh. Pineapple on a pizza... What monster thought that was a good idea?" I was still laughing, stabbing my fork into the pie, but not having taken a bite yet.

"Don't knock it until you try it. I'll have to get you some one time."

"It's a date," Henry said, smiling at me as he took a bite of pie.

I followed suit, unsure whether to argue with him about the whole date thing. It did kind of sound like a nice idea. A good distraction. He was kind and funny and related a bit to me being a student. Sure, he was a little younger than me, but Chandler had quite a few years on me, and I hadn't cared. Why on earth I was thinking about Chandler as if there were any remote way I could ever date him was beyond me.

Much to my displeasure, my mind continued to drift back to Chandler. Remembered those moments at The Crucible the previous week when I'd been twisted in red jute rope. I felt the wood booth against my backside, and I couldn't help but remember the way he'd pressed firmly against me. I'd felt what I was doing to him, having me trapped in those ropes.

And he knew it had been me. With almost absolute certainty. Yet for whatever reason, he was choosing to fight me on it. The least he could have done was admit it. Instead, he made me feel as though I was losing my mind.

It's only you and this rope, little papillon...

"Cassie," Henry's voice brought me back to the table. When my attention focused back on him, I immediately felt my face flushing hard, though I tried desperately to stop it. It was completely out of my control. "What's with the blushing? Were you over there thinking dirty thoughts?"

Oh my God, I thought miserably, diverting my attention to my pie. The first bite had been delicious, but I'd quickly been distracted. I took another and hastily tried to change the subject. "This is so good." I hadn't been lying, it *was* delicious.

Henry still looked amused by my reaction, but he didn't pester me further about it. I was hoping he hadn't been assuming it had been anything about him. Almost thought of saying something to reassure him, but I stopped myself. The less everyone knew about this entire ordeal between Chandler and me, the better.

The two of us chatted a while about school, about me studying aerial arts. I did my best to weave Chandler out of the conversation, and I was mostly successful. Aside from a few moments when Henry complained about his teaching style, which I didn't necessarily disagree with.

After Henry paid for our food, which I thanked him repetitively for, we grabbed our leftovers, and the two of us headed out. I felt a little buzzy, happy I'd recovered from the experience earlier. I'd managed to be distracted. It was nice. Henry was nice.

We walked down the street a bit, side by side. Henry was about to call a rideshare with the app on his phone when he looked at me. "Do you need a ride home?"

I shook my head. "I live a few blocks down the road. Pretty close to campus."

"Want me to walk you back?" Henry asked me, smiling softly. "It's a nice night out."

He wasn't wrong. It was beautiful.

Admittedly, I hadn't met many people quite as chivalrous as Henry had been to me this entire evening, and it was refreshing. Still, there was no way in hell I was bringing anyone back to my shady as hell apartment, not if I could help it. If it had been under different circumstances, with how much fun we'd had, I might have let him do it.

"Ah, that's okay. It's not far. I appreciate it, though."

Henry nodded, having finished ordering his ride. "Okay, if you're sure. Text me when you get home, though? So I know you made it safe and sound."

Again, a simple gesture which sometimes people took for granted. It was something my parents would have done. I appreciated it very much. "You, too?" He nodded.

I was about to tell him goodnight and hug him goodbye when I noticed he was staring at me oddly. Henry hesitated for a second before he spoke.

"Hey, Cassie," he said, his voice soft. I could tell by his stance he'd gotten nervous. I had a guess as to why. "It's probably a long shot, but..."

It was obvious what was coming. Before he could say more, I reached out, putting a finger to his lips. I took a small step backward, breaking the space we'd been standing in, which probably hadn't been helping. We'd been standing close together.

As much as I hated myself, I said it anyway. "Henry, I can't."

I dropped my hand back to my side, trying my best to keep eye contact with him. He looked a little bummed out. I was a bit frustrated with myself since he was such a nice guy. We had a great evening. I should have let him take me out, maybe even let him kiss me right then. A little part of me felt like I'd have been okay with it if he had.

But the rest of me knew it would be a disservice to him. Because standing there with him, as nice as he was, as much fun as I'd had with him, I couldn't give him what he wanted. Not really. Not when I couldn't stop thinking about Chandler Moreau.

"Oh," Henry finally said. He ran his hand through his mess of hair. He was adorable. I knew I must have made him all the more anxious, and I hated myself for it. I didn't know how to comfort him without feeling like I was giving him the wrong idea.

So, I stood there awkwardly, while he continued, "T—That's okay. I had to ask. I had a nice time tonight, and you look pretty under the streetlight."

I looked up at the light above us, unable to stop myself from smiling. Eventually, I looked back down at him. "You're sweet. Thank you. I had a nice time, too, Henry." I wondered if I should give him more of an explanation. "I can't right now. I have a lot of things going on. My life is a complicated mess. If it were under any other circumstances, believe me, I would. You're charming as hell."

Henry grinned when I said it, bowing his head a little. "I try." I was glad it seemed to make him feel a little better. "Well, if you ever change your mind, you know where to find me." Almost the second he'd said it, the cab pulled up from around the corner. It came quicker than I thought it would.

"Well, that's me," Henry said, walking around to open the back door. I walked over to him, wrapped my arms around his neck, and pulled him in for a hug. He hugged me back gently until I pulled away. "Remember to text me."

"You too," I said, watching as he'd started into the car. "Goodnight, Henry."

"Night, Cass," Henry said, smiling at me as he disappeared inside, shutting the door behind him.

I watched the car drive away down the street, staring at it until it turned the corner. While I'd thought the nice outing with Henry had been a great distraction, and it had been mostly, watching as he left had me starting to feel hollow again. Feeling guilty I'd rejected him.

God, I was such an idiot.

I stood on the street corner for a long time, looking across the street at the Dreamers Academy. Thinking about the hell I'd been through the last decade of my life to get there. The entire time, there had been only a few thoughts getting me through, pushing me to the point I was at now.

One of those things was Chandler Moreau. Getting to work with him. Getting to be around him. Learn everything I possibly could from the best there was. I wanted to be like him; I wanted everything he had done.

I still did, truly. I wasn't about to give it up. But I had made a mess of things because I'd let my emotions cloud my thinking. Gotten distracted from why I was truly here. The reason I'd fought tooth and nail.

It didn't matter anymore whether Chandler knew. Didn't matter if he felt anything or not. What mattered was what was standing right in front of me. That school. This town. The circus I wanted to perform in. That was why I was here.

As desperate as I was to think about it as little as possible, I was also going to take my horrible excuse of an uncle down. By whatever means necessary. And I knew one piece of it was doing this. Being here. Because it meant he hadn't won.

My mind went back to earlier at The Crucible. I'd made up my mind.

Chandler Moreau was my mentor. The man I wanted to work beside some day.

And, I decided, once and for all, it was all he was ever going to be.

CHAPTER 8

CHANDLER

Above me, I watched Penelope Girard drop gracefully, her torso swinging downward as she bent into a gazelle pose within the confines of a set of purple silks. The move, which looked like an inverted leaping gazelle, was challenging to complete. She looked outward into the empty theater of Cirque du Lys until she'd gotten in place.

Eventually, her brown eyes dropped to mine. I was twisted not far beneath her, in a T, my body sideways on the silks, parallel to the floor. We watched each other, both mentally preparing for the next few movements. Total focus was required; the two of us were dangling precariously, at least fifty feet in the air.

I was steady, taking long, deep breaths. In preparation, I rehearsed the next steps in my mind. Penny and I had done this routine many times before. I'd done similar versions in other shows for decades. Even still, there was always some nerves. It was inevitable.

I gave her a nod. The composition we had chosen as part of the soundtrack to this season of the show grew louder, the piano picked up again, making its way through the theater. My mind focused on the sound for a half second before I swung outward, twisting myself back upright as Penny dropped from the gazelle pose straight downward. I watched her, but my mind left the room.

The next move was supposed to join us together. We would have linked hands in a series of falls and spins further down the silks, toward the stage.

I was still in this theater, still wrapped in the silks. But suddenly, it was Jeanne above me. Tumbling in a mess of fabric, straight toward me. Eyes wide, looking panicked as I'd ever seen her. Zipping by too fast for me to be able to catch her in time.

All at once, I plummeted. I tried to untangle myself from the way I'd been wrapped in the silks. Desperate to be fast enough to catch her before she slammed into the wooden stage floor.

The moment I was free enough, I shot downward, gripping the silks Jeanne had been attached to. To slow her descent. It worked, thankfully, as I fell toward her. When I was within reach, I gripped hold of her tiny frame, swinging her back upward above me. Simultaneously, I tried to anchor myself enough to my own set of silks to slow my momentum. My attempt, while somewhat successful, was not nearly enough. The floor rushed at me, my life flashing before my eyes. Then I slammed into it, Jeanne on top of me. Feeling the air thrust out of me, my entire body went limp.

It had taken a long couple of seconds for me to realize how much pain I'd been in. The wind had been knocked out of me, my head throbbed even though my lower body had taken the majority of the impact. When I finally felt the jarring awareness I hadn't made it out unscathed, when the pain finally set in, I rang out into the theater. Jeanne rolled off me, also yelling, competing with the music that hadn't yet been stopped. I hadn't heard her, pulling myself halfway up. Noticing my leg bent in an odd direction.

My entire focus was on my knee. I knew the fall had done its damage. And even worse than the excruciating pain I'd experienced in those moments was the fear it meant my entire career was over.

Penny's scream jerked me back to reality. The moment I refocused, I watched her tumbling beside me. This time, however, I'd been more prepared. Although I'd frozen for a few seconds, my mind worked on instinct. My reflexes took over, swinging downward just in time to latch onto her back legs before she'd gotten away from me.

After a few seconds of breathing to try to recover, Penny swung around to help herself down. While I'd managed to stop us both, I hadn't come out of it unharmed.

Once again, my entire leg pulsed with pain. It was everything I could do to get myself to the floor. The moment I had, I collapsed to the ground, letting myself fall, my back flat against the cool hardwood of the stage. Panting audibly. My mind was spinning.

Penny appeared above me, staring down. "Are you alright?" She asked, breathing as heavily as I was. It took me a moment, and I was thoroughly lying, but I nodded.

I watched her face twist, from concern to annoyance. "That was the third time this month, Chandler! You need to do something about this! You're going to get someone killed."

Even through the horrid pain I was feeling, I, too, felt guilt. I tried to steady my breathing enough to get an apology out, but she stormed off before I was able.

"Penny! Where are you going?" I heard Abigail's voice nearby, shouting after the young aerialist. Perhaps it was a good thing she was switching to acrobatics after all. Hell, it might have been entirely my fault she was doing so just to get away from *this*. I couldn't imagine how anyone would want to work with me. This was happening too often, and I was becoming far too unreliable as a partner.

I heard Abigail trotting down the stage steps, running after a very distraught Penny. Even still, I wasn't able to get myself off the ground quite yet. Just stared up into the lights on the ceiling, feeling very dazed—like I was slowly losing my mind.

A hand came into view, followed by Thomas staring down at me. He also looked greatly concerned. This time, I had recovered enough to be able to take hold of his hand, allowing him to get me to a sitting position. There was no way in hell I was getting up yet, not with my leg in as much pain as it was.

Thomas sat down beside me, and I felt him wrap a hand around my shoulder. "It was my fault," I replied to his touch, shaking my head. Wishing I had the ability to go after Penny and apologize, but there was no way in hell I could. If I moved in those moments, who knew how much more damage I would do to myself. The fall had been too much as it was.

"Another flashback?" Thomas asked me, and when I looked over at him, he was studying me intently. I nodded, frowning. "Have you even called a therapist yet like Abby suggested? Or gone to the doctor?"

"Neither," I replied, grateful I was able to speak again. My breathing had finally steadied enough. Thomas looked at me, a mixture of concern but also disappointment. "Stop looking at me like that, please."

"No," he replied, releasing his hand from my shoulder. "As your friend, I think I'm obligated to point out to you when you're being a stubborn shit." I scowled at him, somewhat annoyed, even though he wasn't wrong. I didn't care. "You're being a stubborn shit, in case it wasn't clear."

Just as he'd said it, I heard footsteps again and watched as Abigail returned, climbing back up the stairs to meet us. She sat down in front of us, her eyes locked on me. She looked similar to her husband. I was annoyed to see she had brought the damn brace to me again.

I watched her fasten it back to my leg without asking me permission. She was gentle and kind about it, taking her time to ensure it was on properly. Once she'd finished, she looked back up at me. "You haven't called the doctor yet, have you?"

God, they were relentless. "No, I haven't called the doctor."

"Chandler..." Abigail said, her eyes narrowing at me. While I loved her charming voice, it was already getting on my nerves.

"I don't need another lecture from you both," I replied somewhat snippily. Still in a great deal of pain but trying to fight through it. "I realize you're concerned, but—"

"I'm beyond concerned," Thomas replied, and I looked over at him. His face had shifted again, this time he looked more frustrated. "You can get away with being this way sometimes; we've put up with you for years now. But I swear to God, if you don't listen, Abigail and I will drag you there. I mean it. Especially since you're putting another person's life in danger again."

The moment the word came out, I saw regret on his face. But the damage had been done. I, too, realized it had been an accident. He didn't mean it. However, even when I'd been bellied over in pain after the accident with Jeanne, all I could think about was that I had been riddled with guilt.

What made it worse was I'd spent the last two weeks relentlessly after Cassandra for the same behavior. Her lack of focus. Yet here I was doing the same thing when my friends were right, and there were things I could do to prevent it.

For a moment, I thought I'd argue with them. I was annoyed, for certain. Hated the way they kept nagging me. But, I realized, too, they cared. And truthfully, I only had so many people in my life who truly did, so I needed to be gracious.

I looked to Thomas, then to Abigail, before I said a thing. "I'll call the doctor first thing tomorrow. I promise." Both of them looked satisfied, relieved even, I'd said it.

Thomas got up first, followed shortly by Abigail. The two of them reached down, one on either side of me, to help me up. My knee felt horrible, but the two wrapped me around them and helped me carefully down to the seats of the theater. I settled down, and then they came to sit beside me. Abigail took my hand the minute they had, giving me a little squeeze.

"I'm sorry this keeps happening to you," she said.

When I looked at her, I offered a small, saddened smile in reply. "Me too."

The three of us turned our focus back to the stage. Rehearsals had not ended for the evening, and all the attention that had gathered on me had finally dissipated. People had gone back to what they were doing. It had been a while since I'd just sat and watched them all practicing their own acts. We were a month or so into practice for the winter show. Yet most of them looked as though it was already a dress rehearsal.

I supposed it was to be expected considering most of the people in this room had been with this show for years. When you knew something so well and had done it so much, it became second nature. Even with new routines and ideas, entirely different shows every time, they still knew what they were doing.

I was grateful I was there to witness it; I was proud of every single one of them. Except myself, who I had been beating up in my mind. It didn't even have to do with just what had happened minutes earlier. I'd been beating myself up ever since the night at The Crucible last week.

We were silent for a long while, watching. But eventually, I became so annoyed with my thoughts, deterring me from what was going on, I sighed loudly.

Thomas looked at me; I could see him in my peripheral vision. I turned my attention toward him. "If you have been sitting there the last twenty minutes berating yourself, which knowing you was likely the case, you need to stop it. It was an accident. It's over now. You're going to do something about it, which was the point we were trying to make."

"I'm not just beating myself up for that," I found myself admitting. Suddenly, I wondered if I was about to do what I thought I was going to do. Sure enough, I continued before I lost my nerve to do it, feeling as though I needed to talk about it more. Stella wasn't here, and I had probably driven her crazy enough about it. "There's other things on my mind, too."

"Like what?" Abigail asked me. "Did you talk to Jeanne yet?"

I looked back at her, repeating what she'd asked in my head first. "What? Why do you keep asking? I saw her last week, actually, but besides the fact she's pregnant, I didn't get anything else out of her."

Abigail looked relieved. "That was what I meant," she replied, studying me. "I was worried you were going to be upset, given everything. I figured you'd see her eventually. Thomas told me she should have warned you beforehand, but I didn't think it was any of our business." She hadn't been wrong. I was bothered by it a little, as much as I hated it. Bothered by all of it, but I tried not to be.

"It is what it is," I replied, shaking my head. Trying to get rid of those thoughts Abigail had brought up, not having realized it had nothing to do with what I'd been really bothered about. "That's not what's concerning me, however. Though, in hindsight, I wish it was."

When both of them honed in on me, I suddenly regretted bringing the topic up at all. Hated myself a little for it, but I'd already started, so I decided to finish it. "I'm distracted by Cassandra," I admitted.

It was true, obviously. But for more than just the reasons I assumed my friends would think. They had no idea about my side business, and as innocent souls as they were, I doubted I'd ever tell them. I could only imagine Abigail's face if I announced to her I'd done erotic rope bondage on a sweet, innocent girl she'd known since childhood.

After the previous week's events, I knew Cassandra better. Probably more than Abigail at this point. Because while she may have appeared that way to most, I definitely knew better. She wasn't as sweet and innocent as Abigail believed she was. Not by a long shot. There was a fire in the woman which had gotten loose, and while I was doing everything to tame it, it wasn't working well.

"What do you mean?" Thomas asked me, though I could tell he had an idea by the way he was looking at me. "You are her mentor, after all. We all saw how excited you were about her at the auditions. It's understandable you'd be a little wound up about it. You have a tendency when it comes to your work. I don't personally understand it because the thought of dangling fifty feet in the air by a piece of fabric that could rip on you at any second..." He trailed off.

I couldn't help but laugh in a very genuine way. Which, despite my knee pain and the myriad of thoughts plaguing me, was a very welcomed thing. "You're one to talk. At least I won't go up in flames."

Abigail laughed, nodding in agreement. "He has a point."

There was silence between us as we smiled over the last bit of conversation. Seconds passed in which I'd convinced myself I was about to admit to them the feelings I'd been having for my student. It might have given me some semblance of peace by talking about it.

I stopped myself at the last minute. Frustrated, I sighed.

"I need to go home and rest," I said, deciding to get up from my seat. I regretted the instant I did because the pain shot up my leg again. But I didn't want to sit there any longer. I turned back to them, trying my best to stay steady. "Thank you both for your concern about my leg. I'll call the doctor tomorrow, I promise you."

Thomas and Abigail looked like they wanted to say something more to me, but neither of them did. So, I took it as my cue to leave, gathering my belongings and heading out of the theater without another word.

Before I left, I made a beeline to the restrooms by the front of the building. I felt like I needed to splash some cool water on my face before my entire body burned to the ground. I got to the sink and stood there for a long while, letting water run over my hands and onto my face. When I finished, I looked back at the mirror, staring at myself, water dripping down my cheeks and neck.

I looked tired. Angry. In a massive amount of pain, despite trying to hide it. Not at all how I wanted to feel. Looking at myself, seeing what all of this was doing to me, made me suddenly feel angry. Not at anyone in particular or anything. I just felt angry with myself. The thoughts I was having. The decisions I was making.

An explosion of glass brought me back to reality. I heard it clatter to the ground, making a mess. I hadn't really cared. No longer was I staring at myself, only a few broken remains on the wall. The rest at my feet. Relieved there was no longer a face in front of me of a man spinning out of control. Now it was just a wall and my bloodied knuckle.

Even still, I felt like shit.

CHAPTER 9

CHANDLER

The following morning, bright and early, I was waiting in Tremblay Hall. Whether I liked it or not, I was trapped in the classroom for the semester. I sipped on coffee from a thermos I'd brought with me, watching as half-asleep freshmen and sophomores dragged themselves inside, looking as unenthusiastic to be there as I felt. Trying my best to shove all the irritated chatter in my mind away.

I was still in quite a bit of pain from the previous evening. The knee injury had been burdensome enough. Why I had thought it necessary to inflict more misery upon myself by taking my frustrations out on a mirror, I had no idea. It wasn't my finest moment. I'd had to stop at a drugstore on my way home to get something to help stop the bleeding. The impact had done more damage than I would have liked. It was certainly something which would be a further nuisance at rehearsals. Regardless, it was done now.

While I was distracted for a moment by the incessant bits of pain I was in, which was *not* doing favors for my mood, it didn't last very long. My attention lingered at the doorway of the classroom. Cassandra had her hair down, falling around her shoulders, a bright smile on her face. I'd noticed the minute she'd rounded the corner and entered the room, along with the fact that the door had been held open by someone. Another guy, who had come in behind her.

At first, I thought it was just a polite thing. Almost looked away from it, trying my best not to give her more focus than necessary. Instead, I continued to watch as they paused at the back of the classroom, lost in conversation.

Cassandra had been laughing at something the guy had said. Both of them were smiling at one another. She placed a hand on his shoulder, and I felt a weird flicker of annoyance the instant she did. Desperately fought myself to look down at the lecture notes for the class. Tried to do anything besides stare at her. At them.

Despite the arguments in my head, I was determined to be a masochist. I continued to watch the two converse for a few minutes as the last of the students trickled in. Wrapped up in each other and whatever it was they'd been talking about. The kid was looking at her, clearly as infatuated by Cassandra's damn smile as I always seemed to be. I didn't like it. Couldn't take it.

"Let's get started," my voice rang out into the room. When I looked at the clock, I realized there was technically a minute or two before class was actually able to begin, but I didn't care. "Today's topic will be Circus Flaminius."

Cassandra whipped around, trotting down the aisle, while the guy she'd been with took a seat. Finally, I was able to breathe again. The minute she arrived beside me, I turned, tossing the whiteboard marker in her direction, more aggressively than I'd intended.

I watched her snatch it from the air like we'd been doing this routine for a while. She was ready for it, looking completely unfazed by me, even if the little action I'd done had been done partially out of my annoyance with her.

For the love of God, I was *jealous.*

I immediately forced my attention back to the room. "Circus Flaminius was another large circus in ancient Rome," I began, watching Cassandra out of the corner of my eye as she scribbled across the board. "It was placed at the southern end of Campus Martius, near the Tiber River. Gaius Flaminius Nepos, the Roman censor, built it in 221 B.C. Can anyone tell me what the primary function of this circus was?"

At first, I thought the entire class would stare blankly at me, which was irritating enough. But what made it exponentially worse, was when the shaggy-haired kid Cassandra had been talking to a minute earlier shot his hand into the air. I pretended not to notice.

"No one did the reading?" The idea that the rest of them weren't prepared frustrated me further. As petty as I was being, I wasn't going to call on the kid. I realized he'd been the one who had been answering the majority of my questions the last few days of class. It was getting ridiculous at this point. The others were going to have to try, eventually.

"Taurian Games. Horseback racing around turning posts." A voice piped up behind me, and when I turned, I realized Cassandra was looking at me, her eyes steady. I couldn't read the expression on her face, although it seemed she might have been a little pissed, if anything. I wondered if she'd noticed I'd completely ignored her friend.

"Ah, that's correct," I said, scratching at the side of my beard. Before I turned my focus back to the students, I added. "Though I wish I'd been answered by one of my first years and not a graduate student." I shot Cassandra a look when I'd said it, trying to make it clear I disapproved of her answering on behalf of the rest of the class. But, again, she appeared unfazed. "You're required to do the readings. If I don't start hearing from some of you, I'm going to start calling you out."

They didn't want me to, but I would if I was forced. "These 'Taurian Games,' as they were called, were used to appease Gods of the underworld. Because of that, they were also symbolically grounded—always performed at this circus, never changing place."

I decided not to ask further questions during the lecture. Cassandra continued to write behind me, keeping up. When I finally glanced back at the clock, it was just in time to hear the bell going off, signaling the end of the hour. I finished up my thoughts as students clamored to their feet and scattered quickly.

One woman stayed behind to ask a question, which had been fairly straightforward. I was grateful because I wasn't remotely in the mood. Distracted by the several different places on my body that seemed to be relentlessly reminding me I was not in perfect form anymore. Even if the spry twenty year old version of me still housed in my mind constantly argued otherwise. I'd been on my feet too long, for certain.

As I was gathering my things, I drifted to Cassandra, who was clearing off the whiteboard. Unfortunately, she was also talking to the guy from earlier. Again, I watched them together, unable to look away. She hugged him, and it lasted far longer than I would have liked. Then he took off down the aisle, leaving the classroom. And as frustrated at myself as I was for the way I was behaving, it made me breathe a very gracious sigh of relief when he had.

After I'd put most of my things in my bag, I realized Cassandra had sat down at the desk by the whiteboard, nose buried, very intently, in a large stack of papers. I watched her for a moment and then couldn't help myself. "Are you grading last weekend's homework assignment?"

She nodded but didn't look up at me. I waited for a few seconds more, hoping she would, but when she didn't, I decided to sit down at the desk across from hers, where my belongings were. Instead of leaving for my office, which I had initially planned to do, I pulled out the lecture notes for the following week and the textbook for the class.

Another *thrilling* day, this time trying to force students to feign an interest in Philip Astley. I stared at the hideous-looking painting of him in the textbook Jeanne had given me. He was as dreadfully boring to look at as he was to read about, and I was certainly not enthusiastic about having to lecture about him either.

For a few minutes, I attempted and failed to distract myself by preparing for the following week. Eventually, I looked up at Cassandra again. Still busy working, giving me no attention whatsoever. And before I could stop myself, I regrettably began asking questions I shouldn't have been asking. Partially because it was inappropriate. Mostly, however, because I didn't actually want to know the answer. "Who was that you were talking to?"

"None of your business," Cassandra shot back at me, still looking at the papers she had been so furiously working on. I was slightly startled by how short she'd been with me, not expecting it. I should have been a little more on top of correcting her for her behavior, but instead, I found myself more curious than anything.

"Ah, well... Would you like any help grading?" I tried to change the subject nonchalantly, despite wanting to pry more about her friend. It was a very pathetic attempt to try and get her to give me any focus at all.

"I'm almost done," she replied, still refusing to look at me. "Thank you, though."

"Of course," I nodded, leaning back in my chair, trying, once again, to ignore my knee and hand, both at constant war with me now. My eyes still locked on her, waiting and hoping she'd give me a solitary ounce of acknowledgement. I hated I wanted it so badly. And even as mortified as I was for doing it, for behaving like I was some lovesick teenager, I still sat there for several very long minutes. Doing nothing at all. Just staring.

Eventually I couldn't help myself and spoke again. "Ms. Blackstone, about the other night—"

"We don't need to talk about it," Cassandra said, and finally, after what had felt like eons, she looked up at me. Which, after how ridiculously long I'd been sitting there begging for her to do so, caught me by surprise so much, it sent a shiver down my spine.

I swallowed deeply, trying not to get lost in those eyes of hers. She was looking at me fiercely at first but after a moment or two, she seemed to soften. "You made your point very clear. I overstepped. I shouldn't have pushed you about it."

I leaned forward, letting my arms rest on the desk in front of me. "Cassan—" I stopped myself abruptly. "Ms. Blackstone, it startled me. That's all. I wasn't expecting to see you there again after what happened at your lessons. I thought you'd have realized how much it bothered me."

My eyes darted around the room, suddenly getting the unsettling sensation I was being watched. I knew we likely weren't. But with a man like my father in charge of things, I was never certain what he was capable of. And that feeling I got was far more regular of an occurrence than I would have liked. The last thing I wanted to do was get her wrapped up in anything to do with Gabriel.

"Not many people know about that side of me," I explained, trying to stay steady. "Not even my closest friends. And to find out you, of all people, knew... I'd done what I'd done to you—"

"I'm sorry," Cassandra said, and I watched her bite the edge of her lip. It was hardly noticeable, but with how intently I'd been watching her, I caught it. It sent me unexpectedly spinning, fighting to bring myself back quickly, since she'd continued. "I won't go back there again. I promise. Like I told you, it was my friend Alex's idea. I was curious, that's all. I guess I had different feelings about it than you clearly did. I was projecting or something..."

If she had any idea at all. I knew she knew better, knew she was trying to do a kind thing for me in those moments, and I appreciated it. Still, I was riddled with guilt because I wasn't exactly being truthful with her.

"It can't happen again," I replied, trying to keep my face as neutral as possible. "Perhaps if you looked elsewhere, but nothing between you and I. You understand?"

She nodded, but I could see the hint of disappointment on her face. And truthfully, the idea of anyone else doing the things I had done to her—touching her in the intimate ways I had, binding her in those ropes, having that control I had over her—I had to force myself from thinking about it. Hated how strongly it was making me feel. Even the idea of doing another Shibari routine with someone else was beginning to torment me so much, I wasn't quite sure if I would be able to do it. And with how much I had enjoyed those Monday night shows for years, one of my few serious interests outside of my career, it was a devastating blow. She was woven in now, whether I liked it or not, and this had been the consequences.

In an effort not to crumble in front of her, as ridiculous as I felt I was being, I decided to change the subject. Another thing I was dreading having to say, but something I felt necessary, regardless.

"I also think it might be best if we switched you to a different class," I spoke softly, trying to tread as light as I could. Unsure of how she would react. "Work for another professor as an assistant."

Cassandra jerked her head back up. It had begun to drift back to the work she'd been doing. Her disappointed look vanished. "Excuse me?"

"It's for the best," I said, calmly. "Considering there is something—" I hesitated, unable to say it. I couldn't say it. "Considering the circumstances. You can still work as a teaching assistant, obviously. It would just be with someone else." My thought had been, if we could have at least gotten *some* distance between us, it would help matters. There was no world in which I saw myself giving up mentoring her for her private lessons, since she clearly was meant to be studying under my wing. I wouldn't have allowed it. Somehow, I'd have to figure that part out. But this job was less detrimental. An easy fix. A way to give me some semblance of room to breathe.

"I don't want to work with someone else," she argued, staring dead at me. "Why are you asking me this? Because of what happened at The Crucible?"

"Please don't talk about it here," I asked her, keeping my voice low. She snapped her mouth shut. "Ms. Blackstone, I have my reasons. I think it would be more appropriate if you were working with someone other than me, that's all."

"If it's because of the silly crush I have," she started, getting up from her seat, steering herself around the desk and walking straight toward me. Her approach had my entire focus, unable to break away. "I'll get it under control, I swear. It's a stupid crush. I'm sorry I came back the other day. Sorry I was fighting you so much on it. I was being stupid."

"You weren't," I replied, wishing I hadn't, but I couldn't help myself.

Cassandra blinked at me. Then continued, "I can't lose this job, Professor Moreau. I don't have an option."

I was still trying to recover from the fact she'd openly admitted having some inkling of feelings for me. Fought every urge to tell her the same, feeling some small shred of relief about it, despite everything. Instead, I was distracted when she added the second part. "Why don't you have an option?"

She bit at her lip again, and I felt my body sinking into the chair, begging her in my head to stop before I lost all control of myself. Every second of this was torture. Dragging emotions out of me I hadn't ever recalled experiencing before and it was becoming overwhelming.

"I'm barely scraping by," Cassandra admitted. "I'm broke. I live in a shitty hole-in-the-wall apartment, in what is probably the worst possible area of this city. Which is ridiculous because Acrefort is nice. You may think I've been a mess over our situation all week, but I've also been panicking, wondering if I'd even make it until Friday with enough money to eat."

My head was spinning again. Now worried if she had been eating, completely distracted by the topic at hand. "Do you need me to buy you lunch?" I offered without thinking about it. It wasn't remotely a concern. Something I would have done in a heartbeat, had I known it was necessary.

I watched her narrow her eyes at me. "I'm not trying to get pity." She paused for a second, trying to gather herself. "I need you to not switch me. Because if you switch me, it will stir up trouble I don't want because I don't need to worry about losing my job. And also because I want to learn from you. Not someone else. That's one of the biggest reasons I came here in the first place."

My mind was buzzing with a million different thoughts, all rushing around in various directions. I tried to steady them and formulate what I wanted to say. Made my usual attempt to problem solve. "My father," I said quickly, developing a plan as I spoke. "He owns this property. My family has run this place for several generations now."

"I know this already," she said, and I raised a brow, curious as to why, but didn't inquire. "Please don't let the next few words out of your mouth be—"

"Let me ask him to get you a better job. Something that pays more. Or a raise."

"Of course, you do *exactly* what I knew you'd do," she frowned, walking steps closer to the desk I was at. "I hate I've barely been around you for a few weeks, but I can read you like a book. Clearly, I have a problem. You've been the centerpiece of my life for far too long."

I was unsure what she had meant by that. "Let me help you," I insisted.

"I'm not some charity case for you," Cassandra said, flatly. "I know your entire family is loaded. You can throw around money and not bat an eye. But it's not why I fucking said what I said." She snapped her mouth shut after, likely realizing she'd let curses fly again.

"I'm trying to make your life a little easier," I argued.

"You literally got through telling me we can't do this—whatever it is we're doing. And that's fine, whatever. But if you think trying to use your father's authority, your family's money, to give me some sort of advantage isn't a little over the line... You're an idiot."

For a brief second, I felt a tinge of annoyance at the fact she'd said the last bit. If I had been any other teacher at this school, she wouldn't have gotten away with it. With me, she shouldn't have gotten away with it, but I let it go. Too caught up with other thoughts.

Despite the bit of trouble my knee had given me today, I still got up from my seat. Chose to ignore it as I wound around the table, walking straight up to her. The closest we'd been since our altercation at The Crucible. I wanted her undivided attention.

"Ms. Blackstone," I said, and it had taken every ounce of effort not to call her by her name. "You're my student. My concern for you is purely for the sake of you and your studies." How I planned on convincing her I'd meant those words when they sounded like an outright lie to me, I had no idea. But I continued. "If you're coming to your lessons worrying about feeding yourself, I would assume most people would be a little concerned. You're an athlete. And it's not even that. You're a human being. You need to eat."

"I'm not starving or anything," Cassandra rebutted. "I was trying to make a point."

"I didn't say you were," I said, trying to catch her eyes with my own. "But I'd still like to help you. Please let me help." She threw her hand up when I tried to continue, stopping me abruptly.

"Professor Moreau," she said, keeping her voice calm and collected. "I'm asking nicely. Don't move me to another professor. Don't start stirring things up because I have feelings for you. I wanted something I couldn't have. It was inappropriate, and I'm sorry. I promise it won't happen again. I won't step foot back inside of The Crucible."

I was seconds from telling her the truth. Opened my mouth, unable to take it any longer. Then I watched her turn away from me, walking over to snatch her things off the desk and stuff the remainder of the papers she'd been grading back in the atrocious sling bag she always toted around. Realized at that moment she probably couldn't afford another.

"Where are you going?" I asked her, dumbly. I watched as she finished packing, throwing the bag over her shoulder. She didn't look back at me.

"I'm supposed to be meeting Henry for lunch," Cassandra replied. She finally looked at me again, briefly. "Do you need me for anything else, or are we done here?"

"Henry," I said, pondering for a second. Feeling like an ass for continuing to ask about it, after everything. "Is he–is he the one you were talking to earlier?"

"Oh my God," she said, shaking her head. "It's none of your business." We stared at one another for a few seconds before she added. "Please don't move me from the class, Professor Moreau. That's all I'm asking."

I watched her take off across the room without another word, the door slamming behind her. Stood there, unable to comprehend what had just happened. Tried to calm my jumbled mind. I hated that everything she did kept making it worse, no matter how desperate I was to stop it. It was becoming almost impossible, no matter how hard I tried.

If she asked me not to move her, I wouldn't. I would likely do whatever she asked at this point, feeling absolutely powerless. Knowing full well, if I didn't stop this, didn't stop her, didn't stop myself... There would be consequences as a result. Dangerous consequences that I knew better than to get her involved in. But I was barely hanging on, almost beyond the point of caring.

And regardless, whether she liked it or not, I was still getting her the damn raise.

CHAPTER 10

CASSANDRA

A swirl of colors draped around me. Silks in purple, maroon, green, and gold. Somehow I'd always been drawn to the same ones since my audition all those months ago. My hand was wrapped around the dark red fabric, tangling it in a fist. Feeling it in my hand, pulled firmly against me, but at the same time soft.

My eyes looked out into the empty theater. Everything was dark and eerily quiet. Pretty much as I expected it to be, given it was a Thursday evening, and most students had fled the campus for the night. Abigail had been kind enough to let me have a key to get into Soleil Theater on my own. She knew exactly why I'd wanted it.

If anything could keep my thoughts at bay about this day, it would be the silks. Losing myself in all the intricacies of the movements, the way I dropped and ascended and spun. If anything would protect me from the memories all those years ago that always haunted me, it was this cocoon of fabric.

Music was playing in the background on my phone, which was barely hanging on. It was as loud as possible and paled in comparison to the sound system in the theater. But I didn't have access to it, and I knew the silence wouldn't help me.

The song I had picked had been one I first heard in high school. A variation of a Shaker hymn by Aaron Copland. It was a sweet, upbeat classical song. Surprisingly, despite my somber mood, when I'd seen it on a playlist as I'd been trying to pick, it felt like just the thing.

At the start of when the winds come in, right before an upbeat section of strings, I went to pull myself into the air. Ready to do another sequence. I surprised myself and stopped instead of darting upward. I stayed low to the ground and practiced a very basic movement. The one Chandler had helped me with the other night at lessons: the sailor pose.

Where I would have usually let my body move on its own, having trained it for so long some of the motions were almost robotic, I instead took my time. Carefully wrapped my feet into the silks first, taking care to be precise, like I'd been instructed.

Before I pulled myself back up off the ground, I made sure to wrap my hands opposite of what I'd done for years. Noticing when I had, my grip felt stronger. After I lifted off the ground, I split my legs apart again, adjusting myself the way I needed to.

It felt like I'd succeeded. I paused there in place for a while, lost in thought. Tried my best not to let my mind wander to Chandler.

I had been so happy about the idea of being immersed in his life and getting to be around him for years, it felt like a torment to force myself to stop thinking about him. That the thing I loved the most, the thing which took me far away from every shitty moment of the last decade, had somehow become tainted.

Yet I couldn't stop. Didn't want to stop.

Hell, I was grateful in those moments he'd drifted into my mind again, like he had a million other moments prior, because at least it gave me a moment to breathe. A moment to be whisked away from this horrible day, as far as I possibly could.

When I finally dropped back down to the floor, I heard clapping from down the aisle across from me. My head turned, feeling a wave of panic. As much as I had wanted to be alone, it also was terrifying. Not because I couldn't stand it, but because I feared something terrible would happen if I were alone for too long.

I was grateful to find Alex had stepped out of the shadows and into the light of the stage. She was smiling, clearly having been watching me for a bit. The minute she'd reached the top of the stairs, I'd already made it over to her. The two of us wrapped together in a hug, which I needed desperately.

"That wasn't anything special," I told her once we'd split apart. "What are you doing here anyway?"

"I went to your apartment looking for you, but you weren't there. I figured the next best place to look was here. I sent you a couple text messages because I didn't think I was going to get inside. But luckily there was a nice janitor who let me in. I guess he trusted I wasn't a serial killer or about to rob the place."

"I mean, you're the spitting image of a serial killer," I noted, which made her laugh.

"You shouldn't be practicing on your birthday," Alex said, nudging me. While I knew she was well-intentioned, Alex also knew why the hell I was here. I looked up at her, giving her a look. "I know why but I'm just saying. You're only going to be twenty-six once, you know. Let me take you out to celebrate. Dana wants to go to the pizza place again."

"I don't like celebrating my birthday," I replied, brushing hair out of my face and behind my ear. "Besides, I'm trying to get these moves down, so I don't have to hear about it later."

"Professor Moreau still giving you a hard time?" Alex raised a brow at me.

A hard time was an understatement. If only she knew everything. I hated not telling her. Wished I could because maybe she would be able to give me advice. But I felt obligated to keep what I knew about him a secret. "We're trying to work on fundamental stuff. He said I have trouble with the basic movements. Get carried away wanting to do all the fancier stuff."

Alex grinned at me. "Sounds about right. You've always been an overachiever."

"Shut it," I said, unable to help myself, smiling back at her. "And also, I'm hoping if I practice these enough and he sees it, he might actually teach me again."

"Did he bail on you today?" Alex asked me, looking surprised. I nodded. "What the hell? I'd say something if I were you. That's his job. Did he say he was sick again?"

"He switched it to tomorrow," I replied, spinning the maroon silk around my hand. "Which I'm grateful for, so I'm more prepared this time." It hadn't been the only reason I'd been grateful. The last thing on earth I wanted to do was deal with the overwhelming amount of emotions the man brought out of me on the worst day of the year for me. I might have literally snapped.

"Okay, well, all the more reason you should let me take you out," Alex said, offering me another smile. "I know you don't like celebrating. I know this is a hard day for you. But consider this a distraction. It'll keep your mind off everything, and I think it'll do you good." *Keep your mind off other things.*

I again made a terrible attempt to shove Chandler from my mind. Alex, meanwhile, was still rambling on. "Dana was going to drag her brother along with us. She thinks you'd like him a lot. He's a nice guy. A sophomore, I think. His name is Henry."

"Henry—" I blinked, looking at Alex. "There's a Henry in the class I'm assisting Chan—Professor Moreau with. He and I had lunch together. He's the one who took me out for pie the other night. He's studying to be a circus vet—"

"Circus veterinarian!" Alex finished my sentence and laughed. "Oh my God, that's hilarious. I didn't realize he was who you were out with. I'm guessing you're the one he won't shut up about. Dana said he's been going on and on about a girl from school since the first day of classes."

I shook my head, having tried to shove the fact Henry had a crush on me out of my mind. It had been for his own good. As stupid as I was for not indulging him and chasing the ridiculous feelings I had for my *professor.*

"Small world," I decided to reply, trying not to think about it. "Okay. If they're coming, and you're so adamant about it, we can go. You can't mention anything about today, okay? It's my birthday. That's all." Alex nodded in agreement, and I let the silks in my hand go.

The first time I came to the hole-in-the-wall pizza parlor on the outskirts of downtown Acrefort, it had been in celebration after my auditions six months ago. It had been the first time I'd met Dana Thorpe, the girl Alex had been dating. They met when she'd ended up with a bad flare up of her prior meniscus injury, after her first lessons at the Dreamers Academy. Dana had taken care of her at the hospital, and the rest had been history.

Visiting it again brought back fond memories from when I'd first arrived in town. I had been filled with so much excitement and adrenaline from how well my audition had gone. I was on a high I'd never experienced before in my life, having gotten to meet my childhood idol face-to-face. That he'd been so impressed with me.

When I walked into the restaurant with Alex, I was overwhelmed by the smells of wood-fired pizzas being made close to the entrance. On the opposite side was a small arcade, where Alex and I had played a million rounds of some dancing game together, and she had beat me every time.

The place was packed for eight-thirty on a Thursday. By the look of it, it seemed like a lot of students were there, given it was a younger crowd. Even the bar was filled up. A contemporary jazz band was playing in the back. Oddly enough, they were playing a song from an old Cirque du Lys show. I recognized it after a few measures, and it made me smile.

Alex had taken my hand, weaving us through the aisleway, avoiding a few servers and people shuffling out of the restaurant. We found Dana sitting near the back, close to the small stage in front of the musicians playing. And I knew from the back of his head, seeing the crazy mess of hair, it was definitely Henry sitting across from her.

The minute I'd slid into the booth beside him, I watched his head spin toward mine, grinning broadly. "I couldn't believe it when Dana told me who you were! That's hilarious."

"I hope it's okay if I sit next to you," I replied, figuring Dana and Alex would want to sit together.

Henry shrugged at me, waggling his eyebrows. I laughed. "I guess I'll survive."

The waitress came as we'd settled in. Henry and Dana had already ordered and gotten their drinks, and since Alex and I got the same thing at every pizza place, we decided to order, too.

"Medium Hawaiian pizza with extra jalapenos, please." Alex flashed a smile at the waitress, handing her back both of our menus. "And two hard seltzers, if you have them. This old lady needs a drink for her birthday."

Henry, who had been making a face about the Hawaiian pizza, turned his attention to me. "Wait. Is it your birthday?" I nodded in reply as the waitress wandered off from us to put in our order. "Happy Birthday! I wish I had known. I would have gotten you something."

"You don't need to do that," I assured him, smiling even though I wasn't exactly thrilled everyone now knew it was my birthday. I tried to deter the conversation. "You're going to have to try the pizza tonight, remember."

"Ugh, I forgot all about our deal," Henry replied, making a face again. "Why can't you be normal like us and eat a vegetarian pizza?"

"That's right," Alex piped in, and I glanced at her. "These freakshows don't put meat on their pizza. They think we're the weird ones..." She made me laugh again, which I appreciated. She turned her attention back to Henry. "Don't knock it till you try it. Cassandra here made me a convert. I used to make those same faces, too."

Dana fake gagged next to Alex, and Alex nudged her playfully in reply. "Sweet food does not belong on a pizza. Ew. No thank you."

The jazz band started playing another song, which distracted me from the conversation for a moment. I looked out, watching the piano player and the saxophone player. Several people had gotten up to dance. I couldn't remember the last time I'd danced. Senior prom, probably, and even then it had been minimal.

"Do you know how to dance?" Henry's voice brought me back from my daydreaming, watching the people out on the little stage. I turned my attention to him, noticing he intently focused on me.

I shook my head, offering him a small smile. "I know how to sway to music. That's about the extent of my dancing knowledge. I have absolutely zero rhythm."

"Bullshit," Alex said from across the table. "You have plenty of rhythm. You should see this girl on the silks. She can move to music like nobody's business." Dana nodded in agreement, and I felt my face getting hot at the attention.

"I can't wait to see her," Henry said, smiling at me. He looked out at the people dancing. The song which had been playing ended, and a new one started. Unlike the one before, it was a little on the slower side. "Want me to show you how to do a few moves? This is a pretty good song to dance to for a beginner with no rhythm."

"When did you learn how to dance to jazz music?"

"Our grandma used to get us dance lessons when we were kids." It was Dana who had answered instead of Henry. "She was a ballet dancer when she was younger, so she was adamant everyone in the family should know how to dance."

"They're excellent dancers," Alex agreed. "Come on. I need to prove how much you're bullshitting anyway. No rhythm. Psh." She nodded toward the dance floor, and I got up with her, Dana and Henry following suit. Once we'd all gotten to our feet, Henry offered me a hand, and I took it, letting him lead me out.

When we'd settled, Henry swiftly put his hand on my hip and took my other in his own. "It's not too hard, I promise. Follow my lead. I've got you covered." For whatever reason, I appreciated the little bit of encouragement. Henry waited a second before the two of us took off across the floor. He explained little things as we went, but sure enough, he made it easy to follow along. It hadn't been hard at all.

I tried to lose myself in the music and the simple series of steps he explained to me. Made it like I was wrapped up in the silks doing a series of movements. That's all it was. Except it was on the floor this time.

No sooner had I thought about the silks again, my attention turned back to the room we were in. Peering over Henry's shoulder at the crowded restaurant as people chatted away at tables and at the bar. I'd barely started to look around when I came to a staggering halt.

He was hard to miss, sitting at the booth a half dozen seats behind where we'd been. I assumed he must have come in after us because I would have noticed him otherwise. And I might have admired him a little more if it hadn't been for the fact those ridiculous eyes were locked straight on me.

Why Chandler Moreau was at a little hole-in-the-wall restaurant, I had no earthly idea. I noticed the person sitting across from him. She looked familiar, her profile angled in such a way I could make out the side of her face. Eventually, I realized she was one of the bartenders at The Crucible. I remembered because Alex had gushed on and on about how gorgeous she was.

I hadn't disagreed at the time, but it hadn't fazed me until that precise moment. Looking at her sitting with him, I noticed just how beautiful she really was. Her dark brown hair fell around her shoulders, and interesting tattoos lined her arms, accentuating them. She was wearing a dress cut in such a way I could see most of the way up her shapely legs.

My stomach was churning. I realized I'd been agonizingly attentive, and when my attention turned back to Chandler, he'd stopped looking at me. Turned his focus back on the woman across from him, and she on him.

I wondered, briefly, if he was on a date. While I had been a little surprised Chandler would have shown an interest in a woman as eccentric as she seemed to be, her stunningly attractive looks screamed otherwise.

My attention snapped back to Henry, who had been speaking to me. "You're a natural," he said matter-of-factly. "Get ready. I'm going to twirl you now."

"You're going to wha—" I hadn't been able to finish, and I was spun outward and then, just as quickly, returned back to Henry's arms. "Oh my God." Once I'd recovered, I started laughing. "I wasn't expecting you to do *that*."

"I'm full of surprises," Henry grinned at me.

"You sure are," I agreed, smiling at him and shaking my head. While we danced to the rest of the song, I glanced over at Dana and Alex, who were lost in a world of their own. I loved watching Alex with her girlfriend. It was obvious how over the moon they were about each other, and it made me happy. Alex had a terrible time coming out with her parents, so Dana had certainly made it all worth it in the end.

As much as I hated myself for it, thinking of Alex and Dana and how happy they were somehow made me think of Chandler again. My attention drifted back over to his table, and I wished it hadn't. The woman had her hand wrapped around Chandler's wrist. She was laughing about something Chandler had said, and he was smiling back at her, shaking his head.

I adored his smile. Felt trapped in it, like it was impossible to look away from. He hadn't done it too often, so it was always a welcome surprise. It warmed his face so much. And while I should have been happy about him smiling, somehow it made me sad. I wished it could have been me he was smiling about instead.

"You okay?" Henry asked me. I realized the song had ended. I shook my head, bringing my focus back to him. I nodded, and Henry smiled. "Good. Wanted to make sure you were having a good time, seeing it was your birthday and all."

Dana and Alex had walked past us, my best friend pointing toward our table. When I looked, I noticed our food and drinks had been delivered. Henry and I split apart, heading back in the general direction. Before we'd made it, I looked back one more time down the aisle, unable to help myself. Met Chandler's intense gaze, staring right at me again.

I swallowed deeply, choosing to look away, sliding down into the booth next to Henry. I had to stop it. This was getting ridiculous. Instead of dwelling for too long, I immediately reached for the metal spatula on the Hawaiian pizza to get myself a slice. Before I put one on my plate, I dropped one on Henry's.

"Oh *God,*" Henry scrunched his face in response. "I was hoping you'd forget."

Much to my satisfaction, it turned out Henry didn't hate the Hawaiian pizza after all, but it was decided he would still stick to his and Dana's vegetarian style. I was still happy he'd humored me. The four of us got lost in conversation together, inhaling pizza and drinks until I felt so full I could barely breathe.

"They're bringing you a dessert," Alex said, glancing at me as I leaned back into my seat, holding my stomach. Regretting I'd eaten the last slice.

"Oh God, I don't think I can do it," I grumbled. Then I'd fully realized what she'd said. Remembered my friend and her tendencies. "Please don't tell me you did what I think you did."

Alex grinned at me, and I heard singing from down the aisle. Mortified, I put my face in my hands. She'd done this to me for the millionth time. Every single year of undergraduate. I didn't hate it, because I always enjoyed the free food. The public humiliation, I supposed, was my price to pay.

The group singing arrived at the table a few seconds later, and I managed to draw my face from my hands. They finished a "Happy Birthday" song, in a cute mix of English and Italian. Once they were through, they sat down what they'd brought for me.

It was a little piece of tiramisu. I hadn't had the dessert in a very long time, but I remembered liking it the last time I had. They'd put a few candles on top and written 'Happy Birthday' in chocolate around the edge of the plate.

The next minute went by in what felt like slow motion. I barely had time to process what had happened. Alex leaned forward, trying to read the words on the plate, tumbling her glass, liquid spilling all over the table. As soon as she had, Dana and Henry came to the rescue, offering their napkins to help clean up the mess.

As Henry passed off the napkin, I watched the edge of it as it wisped over the candles. He'd held it over them a second too long, and it ignited rapidly, right in front of me. The minute it did, my heart leapt out of my chest.

Instantly, it was thirteen years ago. I was standing outside the circus tent my parents had spent the last few months traveling across the country with. Back in Nevada, which had been a welcome sight after being away for months. Watching big, black, terrifying columns of smoke billowing into the sky, flames engulfing the white tent. Some of the other colleagues of my parents had been forcing me away, but all I could remember was watching the entire thing tumbling to the ground, screaming. Knowing my parents were still inside. They weren't coming back.

A terrified gasp flew from me.

I immediately returned to my senses. Henry had already managed to put the flaming napkin out by dunking it in Dana's water glass across from him. Everyone's attention had now turned on me, and I realized I must have made a sound after all. It wasn't just my imagination, all wrapped up in that horrific memory.

"Cassie, are you okay?" Alex was studying me, watching me as I clutched my chest, trying to force myself to breathe. I hadn't felt this way in a long time, but suddenly I knew I was going to burst into tears at any moment. My entire body raced in panic.

I shook my head, jumping up from the booth. Alex had started to get up to follow me, but I managed to tell her I needed a minute and turned away, fleeing down the aisle, into the hallway. I tried to force myself to not completely break down until I'd gotten away from the crowded room. Until I was someplace I could be alone.

In my frantic attempt to get away, I saw Chandler for half a second as I darted by the table he'd been sitting at. His green eyes lasered in on me as I raced past him. I didn't have time to read the expression flickering across his face. Didn't care in those moments. The only thing on my mind was to get as far away as I could, as fast as humanly possible.

When I'd gotten to the restroom and realized I was alone, I breathed a sigh of relief, going to a stall and locking myself inside.

And the minute I had, I let myself lose control. Falling to the ground, sobbing.

CHAPTER 11

CHANDLER

After a terrible morning dealing with my father at a faculty meeting with the Dreamers Academy, I didn't think I would make it the rest of the day. By the time the afternoon rolled around, I had decided to, once again, cancel my lesson with Cassandra. Only because I feared my foul mood would trickle through, and the last thing I wanted to do was upset her further than I already had.

Especially since I'd gone against her wishes and asked my father to see about a pay raise for her anyway. Much to my surprise, I had been successful with that endeavor, which was rare with him. What I hadn't expected was his inquiry about her afterward. The incessant amount of questions he'd asked left me rattled.

With no private lessons and an empty evening, Stella had taken advantage. It was her day off on Thursdays. When she'd called me to go out to dinner, I didn't have an excuse not to. So, I met her. Thought I could probably use the distraction.

We had settled in a booth amongst the very lively crowd at a hole-in-the-wall pizza place my friend had chosen. Stella knew I was not a huge fan of pizza, never enjoying all the bread involved, but I humored her anyway. While I wasn't thrilled about the location, at least the music was decent. I enjoyed jazz. Unfortunately, it was painfully hard to hear with all of the people around us.

"It's loud in here," I frowned, feeling irritated that I nearly couldn't hear myself think, nor enjoy the music playing. We'd put an order in for pizza. At least Stella had let me order a thinner crust with enough toppings to justify the bread intake.

"It's loud in most restaurants, Chandler," Stella replied, raising her voice so I could attempt to hear her. She took a sip of the wine she'd ordered. Some sort of fruity red wine, which I would never drink because of how sweet it was. I'd decided on a seltzer water, not so much in the mood for alcohol, despite the excessive noise giving me a headache.

"This is precisely why I order in," I replied, glancing across at her. Every time I looked at Stella lately, when I noticed her eyes, I made comparisons between hers and Cassandra's. Stella's were more of a bluish tint, while Cassandra's favored a more green color.

"It would do you some good to get out of the house every once in a while and socialize. Be in a crowd for a while. Lord knows you could work on your table manners." Stella grinned at me. I narrowed my eyes at her, which only proceeded to make her laugh. "Point, exactly."

The two of us sat quietly, watching people in the crowded restaurant, sipping our drinks. Waiting for the carbohydrates Thomas said I supposedly needed to fix my moodiness. I tried to listen to the music as best I could. The band was playing a lot of songs I recognized. Some of them we'd used in Cirque du Lys shows before, which was maybe the reason I liked them as much as I did. It was helping keep my thoughts at bay. Cassandra had drifted from my mind for a little while, and I was somehow able to focus on Stella. A much-needed distraction.

Unfortunately, it didn't last for as long as I would have liked. The waiter had brought our pizza to us, and the moment he'd left, I happened to glance up toward where the musicians were. They'd started into another song. I wished I hadn't looked at all because the moment my eyes had started toward the stage, they went a little too far to the left and landed on the one person I'd been trying desperately to keep far from my mind, for both of our sakes. Cassandra had been sitting with a group of people a few booths down.

There were four of them. I recognized the woman across from her, Alex, if I remembered right. Another brunette sat beside her, and next to Cassandra, there was someone else. The moment I saw that hair, I knew who he was. I frowned. Henry Thorpe. I'd looked him up after she had told me his name. A sophomore student.

I felt a gentle nudge against my leg, and realized it had been Stella under the table. When I focused back on her, she'd dropped a piece of pizza on my plate. I scooped it up, stuffing it into my mouth. Trying my best to focus my attention back to her and not think about the group a few booths down.

"You're daydreaming again," Stella noted after she'd swallowed a bite of her own food. Admittedly, it was pretty good even with the crust. It wasn't the worst thing I'd ever eaten.

"I have a lot on my mind lately."

Stella nodded to me, taking another bite. Luckily, she didn't press me on it further. We sat enjoying our food for a minute or two. As another song started to play, I glanced up and noticed Cassandra and her friends had gotten up, heading to the dance floor together. Of course, much to my dissatisfaction, Henry had chosen to dance with her.

I hated how much it was irritating me. Thought perhaps I'd quit having these ridiculous jealous thoughts after our class together the other day. But it was a constant struggle to stop watching them. All I could think about was wishing I was dancing with her. Any excuse to get her away from the twiggy, dorky kid.

"Chandler," Stella brought me back to the table again. She looked over her shoulder, noticing where I'd been staring intently. "Oh, they're all dancing! That's cute. I love it when they dance." There was a smile on her face, and I watched her for a moment, admiring them all. "Was all your intense staring you were doing some hint you wanted to dance? I'll dance if you want to."

"No," I said flatly, looking straight at her. Stella laughed at my seriousness and took another sip of wine. "I haven't danced in years. Jeanne and I used to go occasionally, and she had to drag me. I'm not a dancer by any means."

"At least not a dancer meant for the ground, anyway," Stella noted, giving me a wink. Perhaps that was true. Practicing aerial silks was a lot like dancing in a variety of ways. I never thought about it like that before.

My attention went back to the group. Watched as Henry spun Cassandra out and pulled her back to him. Wrapped his hand around her waist. The simple little movement had my mind drifting, thinking about the night at The Crucible and how it had felt wrapping the jute rope around her. What I would have given to have the opportunity to do it again, as absolutely impossible as it was.

At this rate, I didn't think I was ever going to stop thinking about it. Maybe I didn't want to and I needed to give in. Stop this ridiculous charade of mine. It clearly wasn't working. If anything, it was making me slowly lose my mind. And driving her further away. While I tried to justify it had been the correct decision, it wasn't at all what I had wanted, if I was being honest. Far from it.

I let out an annoyed sigh, briefly irritated with myself, yet again. Then quickly returned my focus to Stella. "That's Cassandra," I found myself saying, nodding out toward the stage.

Stella glanced over her shoulder again, following my gaze. I focused on her for a moment as she looked. "Well, I certainly see what you see in her. She's very pretty. And a brunette, too. You seem to have a thing for brunettes."

"That's something Jeanne used to always say," I said, and instead of feeling annoyed about it, I actually smiled in response. "I suppose it might be true." I glanced at Cassandra again, watching her laughing at something Henry had said after they'd finished dancing. They were returning back to their table. My attention went back to my friend. "But I'm here with you tonight, and lucky for me, you're also a brunette."

Stella laughed, shaking her head at me.

The two of us lost ourselves in conversation. I mostly let Stella do the talking, enjoying listening to her and eating far more breaded food than I normally ever ate. Knowing I'd probably regret it later, but trying to enjoy it regardless. We'd nearly finished our pizza, Stella finishing up some story about her latest dating fiasco, when something caught my eye.

Cassandra had moved in a flash by me, but I'd seen her long enough. Noticed the look on her face, which was enough to draw my entire focus. She looked like she was doing everything she could to hold back tears. I supposed the reason I recognized it so quickly was because she'd had a similar expression at her lessons the previous week when I'd gone off on her about her lack of focus.

My gaze followed her as she fled down the aisle, turning my body and watching her until she'd disappeared behind a door in the hallway. I'd assumed she'd gone into the restrooms.

For the next few moments, my body was entirely out of my control. I got to my feet, grateful tonight my leg was more cooperative than it had been a lot lately. Stella said something to me, and I replied I'd be back in a minute. Before I knew it, I was walking swiftly in the direction Cassandra had taken off in.

When I reached the women's restrooms, I stood paused outside. Finally coming to my senses and realizing what I was planning on doing was ridiculous. There could have been others in there. Even if it had just been her, I also could have startled her, which likely wouldn't help matters.

Despite all the arguments in my mind, I couldn't help myself. I leaned into the door, listening. All I could make out was the muffled sounds of sobbing. It was the only thing I needed to hear to send me shoving myself inside.

I barely took a step in, struggling to take in the sounds of her crying. It wasn't often I had heard people cry. Jeanne had never cried, in the history of our relationship. Abby had once or twice maybe, maybe Stella. But it was a rare occurrence and hard to hear.

It occurred to me I didn't know what I'd say to her. How would I be able to explain why I was there? We'd made it very clear to one another nothing was happening between us. And I'd been adamant about that fact. I couldn't do this.

Instead of heading further into the room, like I initially had planned to do, I stepped back outside. It had been one of the hardest things I'd had to do in a very long time. Hated that I'd left her in there like I had. Eventually, I steadied myself at the door, deciding I'd help in another way. I took up the majority of the doorway, blocking anyone from entering.

Sure enough, a minute passed, and two women came wandering down the hall. They stared at me as they approached. Before they could ask, I spoke. "Occupied." They both stared at me for a few moments but eventually walked back the way they'd came.

Shortly after, another person rounded the corner. This time, I recognized her. Alex, Cassandra's friend who had been with her both nights at The Crucible. I had seen her in the halls from time to time at Dreamers. If memory had served me right, I was quite certain she was training to be an acrobat and a year ahead of Cassandra.

I watched her eye me once she'd realized I was standing there. At first, she stared blankly, then quickly realized who I was. She walked straight up to me. Had it been any other circumstance, I would have been more amused by the fact I nearly swallowed her whole standing in front of her. She was significantly shorter than Cassandra was.

"Professor Moreau?" Alex asked me. "What are you doing here? Is Cassandra in there?" She looked terribly confused.

I cleared my throat, trying to formulate what I would say to justify my behavior. If there was anything I *could* say. I was certain she was gathering her own opinions about the situation, regardless.

"Yes," I replied. "I saw her go inside. She looked—ah—a little distressed." A little distressed was an understatement, but I figured if I came across any more concerned than I was trying to be, it would become abundantly clear I was far more involved than I should be. "I was trying to prevent someone from barging in on her. It looked like she wanted a minute alone."

"Well, uh... thank you," Alex was still studying me with a strange gaze. "Can I get past you and go check on her? If that's okay with you?"

I immediately stepped away from the door, off to one side. The woman made her way over. Before she went in, I surprised myself, putting my hand on her shoulder to stop her. It wasn't a habit of mine to abruptly physically interact with people without warning, especially not a student. I always took great care in announcing it at lessons. But I panicked a little and needed to stop her before she'd gotten away.

Alex stopped abruptly, not seeming to have cared that I'd touched her. She looked up.

"I was never here," I said, keeping my face neutral. Before she could say anything else to me, or I could condemn myself any more than I likely already had, I took off.

The following evening, after most of the students had left for the day, I was waiting in Soleil Theater for Cassandra to arrive. Instead of practicing, like I normally did in between lessons, I had situated myself on the stage. In a fashion not unlike our communal dinners at Cirque du Lys, I had laid out several containers of Indian fare across the floor in front of me.

While I had no earthly idea if Cassandra liked Indian food, I went with the hope she might. It had been the best way to disguise my intentions with the whole ordeal. If she presumed I'd done it for my own benefit, perhaps she wouldn't have realized I meant otherwise by the gestures. Wouldn't gather how much her admission earlier that week had been bothering me. I continued to justify it in my head that it was purely out of concern for her as her mentor. I wanted her at her best. In reality, I knew I was deluding myself.

I'd been busy helping myself to my favorite dish, the spinach and cheese saag paneer, when I heard the door of the theater close. When my attention drew up, I saw Cassandra walking down the aisle, dressed in her usual set of skin-tight athletic pants and a t-shirt. I smiled for a second that her shirt of choice happened to be a Cirque du Lys tour shirt from a few years ago. Clearly well-loved by the look of it. I'd almost forgotten about the specific design. It didn't hold my attention for too long, however. I focused back on her hazel eyes, watching me intently. I took another bite of food, trying to appear as innocent as humanly possible.

And for a little while, I thought it had worked in my favor.

She had set her things by the stairway leading up to the stage before she came to join me. I could tell she was trying to place the smells, her head tilting a little in an attempt to sniff the air. It was rather cute to watch, even if it only lasted a few seconds. I knew I had to be smiling a little in amusement, watching her.

"What is that?" Cassandra asked as she approached. She sat down across from me, staring at all the food spread out in front of us. "And did you get enough of it? I assumed you had an appetite, given you're about as neurotic about training as I am and likely need five thousand calories a day to sustain yourself. But not quite this much of one."

I couldn't help but continue to smile at the comment but didn't answer, my mouth still full of food. Eventually, when I swallowed, I met eyes with her. "Indian food," I replied. "There's a place downtown I like. You should ask Abigail and Thomas next time you see them how often I order it. I'm sure they'd make fun of me. Thomas would, anyway."

It was Cassandra's turn to smile. She looked down at the food, having become more curious about it. "It smells spicy."

"It is," I replied, adjusting myself so I was looking more at her. It was a relief to see she'd been less standoffish toward me compared to our last interaction in the classroom. Which, hopefully, would continue if I didn't reveal exactly why I'd ordered enough food for a half dozen people. "Not spicy as in hot, necessarily. Just flavorful, I suppose. Which is a lot of the reason why I like it so much. I could sit and enjoy the smells for hours."

"It's definitely smelly," she said, thoughtfully. I wasn't sure if she had meant it in a good way or a bad way but didn't have long enough to think about it. "What are all the dishes? I've never had Indian food."

I raised a brow, both because she'd never had it, and that she was curious. It gave me hope that my plan had potentially worked. For the next few minutes, I explained to her about all of it in probably much more detail than I needed to, but I'd been excited.

"I never would have expected you to have so much enthusiasm about food," Cassandra laughed as I finished up my speech. "Or have so much knowledge about it. You clearly do like it a lot."

"You should try some," I suggested, hoping it had been casual enough of an idea it wouldn't faze her.

As luck would have it, she let her curiosity get the best of her. "Okay, sure. I haven't eaten dinner yet. Let's see what has Chandler Moreau so off-the-charts excited, and it doesn't have to do with the silks for once." She looked up at me, still grinning. It was a relief to see again, and between that and her usage of my name, which I didn't correct her about, I, too, couldn't help but smile.

I watched Cassandra as she proceeded to inhale half of the food on the floor in front of me. She ate so fast she barely spoke, but

I hadn't minded, wrapped up in the content look on her face as she did. Clearly enjoying it, as I had hoped she would.

When she finally slowed her pace, she looked up at me again. "You haven't eaten anything," she noted, studying me curiously.

"I ate before you got here," I said, which had pretty much been the truth, though my intention had been to save as much as I could for her. "I was enjoying the fact you ended up liking it. Sometimes I think I'm the crazy one with the addiction. At least Thomas and Abigail like to tease me relentlessly."

Cassandra ate a piece of naan, which I had gotten explicitly for her to enjoy, otherwise I wouldn't have bothered. She sat and enjoyed herself for a minute lost in thought. Again I found myself wrapped up in the soft, content look on her face. Once she'd swallowed, she held out the container to me. "Do you want a piece?"

"I don't typically eat bread," I replied swiftly. It wasn't until her facial expression shifted a little that I realized I'd slipped. I tried my best to recover, helping myself to my feet.

"We should probably get started," I said, looking back down at her. Meanwhile, she had closed all the styrofoam containers, stacking them. Once she finished, I offered her a hand up, and she took it graciously.

As the two of us made our way over to the silks, I heard her speak beside me. "If that hadn't been one of the best meals I've eaten in a long time, I'd be more pissed off at you right now." I'd been completely wrong in my assumption my plan hadn't been foiled. She continued. "Thank you, regardless. Even if you're so easy to read, it's ridiculous."

"It was the naan," I assumed, turning around to face her once we'd reached all the dangling fabric in the middle of the room. My hands wrapped around the purple set, eyes falling down to meet hers. "I thought I'd done a pretty good job up until that point."

"Professor Moreau," Cassandra said, giving me a look that had the hairs on the back of my neck standing on end. "I knew the moment

I saw you surrounded by a thousand boxes of food. Give me a little more credit."

I couldn't help but grin at her. She had smiled at me a little, too, which had been a relief, considering I'd assumed if she'd figured it out, she'd be furious. "I'm glad you enjoyed it, at least."

"I'm taking the rest home with me, too," she noted.

"Good," I replied, feeling satisfied with the way it had all turned out. I turned back around, looking up at the silks, trying to get focused on what we should have been doing. I was certain half our time was already up, but I'd get as much accomplished as I could, regardless.

"I decided to humor you tonight," I told her, and when I looked to my left, where Cassandra had come up beside me, I saw she was looking at me curiously. "I know that itch you've been having to do more complicated moves. I'm sure my desire for you to practice fundamentals has driven you a little mad."

"Maybe a little," she confirmed, smirking.

I nodded, turning my attention back to the fabrics. "I'm the same way, so I understand. Once you've gotten into a routine, it's hard to fall back. You're always looking for the next challenge. Which is why I decided to compromise. Our aerialist at Cirque du Lys gave me inspiration, actually."

Cassandra watched me as I turned back to face her again. "We'll do a little sequence. Let's start off with the gazelle and go from there." I watched her mouth curl a little more in satisfaction, happy I'd given in to her desire for a challenge. The gazelle move, which Penny had been doing moments before our fall the other evening, was a good middle ground.

After I stepped away from the silks, she went to pick the ones she wanted. Which, like every single time I'd seen her on this stage working, were the maroon silks. I wasn't sure if she had done it on purpose at this point, given everything that had transpired between us, but I forced myself not to think about it. We had work to do.

Once I'd given her a nod to begin, I watched her get into position with a single foot lock, which was the prerequisite maneuver before she could complete the gazelle. I admired how she'd become completely relaxed and focused. It was her and the fabric again. I had disappeared from her mind, which was a good thing. I needed to be the last thing she was thinking about, especially since this movement required her to hold herself upside down.

She completed it, her body falling gracefully forward until she was dangling upside down. Both her legs and her waist were securely fastened within the fabric that suspended her. Once she'd steadied herself, I approached her again.

"I shouldn't be surprised you pulled this off better than the sailor pose," I said, walking around her in a circle to get the full idea of what she had done. Sure enough, she'd shown more finesse with this move. I wasn't quite sure if it was due to her focusing more, if the complexity had her more enthusiastic, or if it was a combination of the two.

Once I made a complete circle, I drew up to her from behind. I announced myself as I had done at our previous lesson and with every student I'd ever assisted. "I'm going to adjust you now." This time, it was more imperative she stood still while I did because if she dropped, she could easily snap her neck. I tried my best to refrain from thinking those thoughts.

Cassandra nodded, and I swiftly placed my hands onto her thigh. While I could have been more focused on the fact my hands were on her in an intimate way, my mind had done what it was supposed to. Calculating every little adjustment required of me. Between her upper thigh, where her foot had been entangled with the fabric, and over to the other leg, which was bent at an angle, to secure the other piece of silk around it.

When I was satisfied with what I'd done, I took a half step back to check on her. She seemed relaxed and focused, staring straight ahead, breathing steadily. My hands returned, landing on the fabric that had been around her waist. She had put herself at an awkward angle, despite her nearly flawless leg positioning.

"I have no earthly idea why you're situated this way, but it's wrong," I said, my hands having fallen onto her hips in an attempt to turn her correctly. The moment they had, I'd suddenly lost my train of thought. When I had wrapped my hands around her and I felt the muscles of her stomach underneath the fitted t-shirt she'd been wearing, I froze.

Instantly, I was back at The Crucible. Cassandra had been standing on the stage, having appeared in the spotlight directly in front of me. I had been holding onto her hand, doing my best to reassure her. All the while, my eyes had been raking down her half-naked body. Admiring those same muscles I'd been feeling now. Transfixed with how well she'd been built. A true athlete.

She'd moved a fraction, and her scent had caught the air. The subtle hint of oranges. My mind had shifted back to when I had been near her in Soleil Theater months earlier. I had stopped myself when I'd gotten too close for comfort, realizing how attracted I was. Somehow, I'd garnered my self-control.

I wouldn't have forgotten that smell. Even if it had been months prior. It had been so distinct like everything else about her. Every time I thought about her, I remembered that scent.

I had known right then and there, exactly who she was. Without a shadow of a doubt. I had tried to read her, wondering if she had recognized me. After I had so dumbly assumed she hadn't, I had decided to give into temptation. I'd let desire win.

It had been a terrible mistake, and it was costing me.

I heard Cassandra speak. "Professor Moreau, I think I need to change positions. I'm getting lightheaded." The moment her voice broke me from my thoughts, I released my grip on her.

"Alright," I agreed, taking a step back. "Come back up and we'll try something else. You have a good hold on the gazelle for the most part. We'll just have to figure out the weird positioning you had with your torso later."

Cassandra, in a beautiful swing of her body, got herself back upright. She unfolded herself from the silks in just a few simple motions and landed back on the stage. I stared at her, mesmerized. She was truly in her element.

I noticed she had steadied herself with her arms dangling above her head. Hands and wrists wrapped around the silks. The way she was suspended was both terrifying, and beautifully distracting. Not at all aiding my mind that had been precariously trying to hold on to the room and not drift back memories that would not let go.

It was like she had trapped herself there purposefully. The fabric that was so close to the color of those jute ropes, wrapped around her. Capturing her in front of me. The look on her face, in her hazel eyes, which were lasered in on me, seemed to say things. But I was starting to believe it had to have been my mind playing tricks on me for certain.

"What do you want me to do next?" Cassandra asked, as her voice brought me back yet again. I shook my head, forcing myself to focus. To stop behaving the way I was. My student was waiting for me, eager to learn tonight.

I approached her, trying to think what I'd wanted her to do, but I couldn't come up with anything to save my life. My mind was still too scrambled.

"I could do an iron cross," Cassandra suggested. It was a good idea considering the position she was in. It would require a simple roll or two of her body to pull her up off the ground.

"That works," I replied, nodding. I was happy she had made the suggestion to avoid flailing any more than I already was. "Stay down here. I know it's not as much fun as dangling fifty feet in the air. And I would let you do it, since you are clearly focused this evening. But I'd like you close by. Just in case I need to adjust you at all."

Cassandra gave me a simple nod, and I watched her gather her thoughts again. She secured a good hold on the fabrics, pulling herself off the ground and into a roll, which she completed twice. It was enough to get her maybe six inches off the ground or so.

After she'd completed the move, which left her body dangling like a cross, I approached her. She had executed it in perfect form, not unlike the gazelle. I was proud of her this evening, certainly happier with her than I was with myself and my wandering mind.

"Excellent job," I praised, and I watched Cassandra's face break into a radiant smile. She dangled in the air as I made way behind her to look. There hadn't been a need. It was fairly obvious she'd done it perfectly, but I wanted to anyway.

My hands fell through the remainder of the maroon silks that hung as I walked by, and I found myself dragging them along for some reason.

I circled completely around her, still holding onto the fabric. Not having grasped my own intent. It latched on and when I finally stopped, I realized I'd ended up wrapping it completely around her.

Cassandra's breath hitched, as surprised by my actions as I had been. My mind had definitely been elsewhere. Instead of stopping myself, instead of dropping the silks immediately, I held on. I was out of her view when I felt the desire to admit what I had done yesterday. Having her somewhat trapped, dangling as she was, gave me the courage I needed.

I tried to keep my voice calm, hoping if I said it gently enough, perhaps she wouldn't have the urge to punch me or something similar as a result. It would be difficult, especially considering her hands were bound at the moment, but I took the precaution anyway.

"I got you a raise," I said softly, a few inches away from the backside of her neck. Getting a good whiff of the scent that very nearly drove me mad. I tried not to linger on it after the admittance of what I had done. I was tired of my dishonesty with her. If I had been able to admit my feelings to Stella, I could tell Cassandra the truth. I needed to tell her.

She was quiet for a few moments, processing what I had said. "You got me a rai—" She paused for a second and then proceeded to frantically flail in place, clearly livid from what I'd just said to her. "*Oh my God,* Chandler. After I *explicitly* told you *not* to. What the absolute HELL is wrong—"

In an attempt to calm her, I drew closer. Found my hands wrapping around her hips yet again, this time with an entirely different intent. My lips drew next to her ear, my entire body lured toward her. I hadn't been this close since we'd been at The Crucible.

"I knew it was you," I said simply. The words came out effortlessly this time. Like it had been an utter relief to say them. Cassandra stopped flailing, much to my satisfaction. I kept my hold on her regardless, paused in place. I didn't need to say another word. She had known exactly what I'd meant.

An indeterminable length of time passed, which had felt like an eternity, but it was likely shorter than I'd imagined. Eventually, I felt her stir again and realized she was attempting to get back down. I stepped away from her and watched as she brought herself back around, looping her body opposite the way it had initially come until she'd arrived back to the floor.

When her hands unraveled from the fabric, she released one of them but held onto the other. I watched her spin in place until she turned to face me.

"I didn't think you'd realized," I admitted, somehow managing to make eye contact with her. She had a strange look on her face, one I couldn't read. Regardless, I was going to tell her. "I wanted to do it anyway. Let myself do it regardless. And honestly, as much as I have struggled with it since, I still don't regret having done it. However horrible of a human that makes me."

"You are not horrible," Cassandra said to me, and while my gaze drifted for a second, it returned. Her face had softened a great deal.

"I told you Alex dragged me back on Monday, but truthfully, all I wanted was for you to do it again. I was there for selfish reasons."

"It shouldn't have happened," I said, feeling guilty I had woven her in so deeply. It was something I didn't talk to anyone about outside of Stella, and then Jeanne, years ago. No one else had ever known. It had been my secret.

Part of the reason I'd opened The Crucible in the first place was to have somewhere to be able to practice Shibari with another person. I'd enjoyed it immensely, always getting lost in the art and the intricacies of it. Jeanne had always seen it as perverse and bizarre. She hated me for it, but she'd missed the point entirely. It was a meditative thing for me in a way. A small means of escape from the chaos of my life. Getting lost in all those twists and turns and nuances of something as simple as a piece of rope. Not everyone really understood it.

Truthfully, it was very similar to how the silks were for me, too.

And as much as it had bothered me at first that Cassandra had figured me out, now it was almost a relief. She wasn't looking at me in those moments like Jeanne had all those years, drawing all sorts of unnecessary, inaccurate conclusions. Wasn't standing there completely convinced I was some deviant human she'd been mistaken about. Even though she'd blatantly admitted her curiosity, I could tell, too, by the way she was looking at me, Cassandra understood where I was coming from. Far more than I had imagined she would.

"Probably," Cassandra agreed. "But it did. And I'm glad you told me. I was starting to lose my mind thinking I was alone in it, honestly."

She hadn't been alone in it. Not any in the least.

Despite having already told myself not to, I took a step toward her, closing the small gap between us. I felt overcome with an intense need to give in now that we both knew. To let this insane obsession I had with her have its way. Even if it was wrong.

What stopped me wasn't the fact that I was her mentor and we'd be breaking rules. Wasn't that I was older than her. None of the superficial, obvious reasons mattered. It was all the other lingering things within my life. Things no one knew. Secrets I carried on my own, for good reason.

My desire to protect her from that was what had stopped me in my tracks.

It hadn't been enough, though. Not after Cassandra broke me from my thoughts with a singular question that would change everything. "Why did you get into Shibari, anyway?"

I looked up to her again. In an instant, I was lost in her gaze. Trapped there in all those captivating flecks of color. The greens and browns and grays. Truthfully, I could have just answered. Probably said absolutely anything at all, and it likely would have satisfied her.

But it wouldn't have been enough. Not now. My desires had taken control again.

"Can I show you?"

CHAPTER 12

CASSANDRA

The entire time we'd made our way to downtown Acrefort, I was a nervous wreck. I shouldn't have been surprised when a town car picked us up, nor the fact that it drove us to the tallest building in the entire city, but all the while I was in awe.

Chandler and I barely spoke to each other as we rode. I wondered if he was as anxious as I was. Then again, I wasn't quite sure what was about to happen. He hadn't given much context outside of the fact that we were heading to his home. I'd been surprised when we didn't go back to The Crucible, but he'd insisted it was purely for discretion. And I'd blindly followed him regardless, which was something I rarely did with anyone, especially over the course of the last few years of my life.

But he had been a man I almost felt like I'd known for half my life now, though we'd only met face-to-face a few months ago. I knew so much about him, small details I doubted some of his friends knew, from years of research and interest. After today, I knew intimate details that no one else knew, or very few anyway.

When we'd gotten into the elevator of the building, and I watched Chandler insert a keycard into a slot by the panel of buttons and press the top one, I finally managed to speak some of the first words

I had since we'd left the school. "You live in the *penthouse*?" I shook my head, reminding myself who he was and what I knew about his family. "*Of course* you live in the penthouse."

"What is that supposed to mean?" Chandler eyed me as we made our way upward. He was staring at me strangely, and I felt a little lurch in my stomach.

I hesitated before I replied. Feeling as if I shouldn't elaborate exactly how much I knew about his family for a number of reasons. "I meant that to be in my head. You own a popular nightclub. I should have assumed you had money."

"Money comes with a price," Chandler replied, looking back at the elevator doors. While I could have inquired about what exactly he'd meant, I had a fair share of ideas. So instead, I silenced myself.

We rode up the rest of the thirty-eight floors without speaking. I realized, halfway up, how close I'd been standing to him when I felt his hand graze against mine. It lingered there, and I swore he kept making little attempts to touch me, however briefly. Then again, my mind very well could have been playing tricks. It must have been an accident. Still, I focused on it, the entire rest of the ride up. Enjoying the subtle bit of affection, regardless of what it meant.

The elevator opened into a small entryway. There were two end tables on either side of a set of intricate wood doors which reminded me of the ones at Soleil Theater.

"Do all the Moreaus like these classic designs or something?" I wondered aloud as I followed Chandler forward. Instead of a lock, there was a keypad with a slot for the same card he'd used on the elevator. Chandler swiped it, and I heard the door click open.

"I actually prefer a more modern look," he replied. "But those doors came with the property." I nodded, following him inside after he'd gone. Chandler fiddled with a set of switches by the door until the lights illuminated the huge room.

It was an open space, stretching across what I imagined was the entire span of the building. On the far side, across from a lengthy leather couch, was a row of large glass windows which stretched from floor to ceiling. They ended near the kitchen area, on the opposite side. Across from the kitchen, there was a fireplace with a large television above it. Something told me, knowing everything I did about Chandler, it didn't get touched much.

"I'd like it if you removed your shoes, please," Chandler interrupted my thoughts, and I noticed he was eyeing my feet. I nodded, sitting down on a sleek bench by the door.

As I unlaced them, I realized, upon looking back up at the room, Chandler hadn't been lying about his particular tastes. His entire home was modern, almost the same sort of style as part of The Crucible. I wondered if he'd designed the club in the style on purpose, trying to merge the old and the new.

"It keeps things cleaner," Chandler said, offering me a hand once I'd placed my shoes near the others by the door on a neat little rack. I enjoyed the way his hand felt around my own. It had been the second time he'd done it tonight.

"You definitely keep it clean in here," I noted. The place was absolutely spotless. The windows looking outside looked as if there was nothing there at all. I admired the view.

"It's something I can control," Chandler admitted. "I'm a bit neurotic about it."

I noticed a flicker of lights from the windows and veered closer. "Do you mind if I take a look?" My attention went to Chandler briefly, and he nodded.

I walked forward across the room, hearing him following behind me. After I reached the glass, I paused, staring out at much of a twinkling and lit up downtown Acrefort. I could make out the Peace River faintly, which wove around on the outskirts.

"I don't know how you don't sit on your couch and look at this view all day," I replied, somewhat in awe of it. It would have been what I'd done, for certain.

Chandler stood beside me, and I saw him shrug in my peripheral vision. "Sometimes I do. I've lived here a long time, though. You get used to it after a while." I noticed he was looking at me, and I turned toward him. "You're giving me a new appreciation of it again, however."

I smiled. "It's a nice view."

Chandler seemed to have lost focus of anything else, staring intently at me. "It is."

For whatever reason, I got a little chill from his words, mixed with that consuming gaze of his. I watched him reach up, running a hand through his hair. He looked a little nervous. It surprised me, but I found it a bit endearing nonetheless. Chandler never struck me as the anxious type. I certainly was, so it was nice I wasn't entirely alone in it.

He turned away from me, looking at a little bar situated beside the kitchen area. "Would you like a drink? I can give you a little tour after, before I—show you some things."

"Sure," I replied, following behind him as he'd already started walking. When he'd reached the bar, he immediately reached for an unmarked bottle and two glasses.

"What would you like?" Chandler asked me, but his focus had been on pouring himself something first. I glanced at the few shelves full of a few different liquors, feeling a bit overwhelmed by the selection. I didn't drink often, so I didn't know much about it.

"What are you having?"

"Bourbon, neat," he said, glancing at me again once he'd finished pouring his glass. He'd given himself quite a hefty amount, surprisingly. "It's my drink of choice after a long day."

"Sounds good to me," I replied, though I usually had my bourbon with a soft drink or something else to help dilute the taste. I definitely wasn't a huge fan of the taste by itself. Something told me there was no soda in Chandler's home, given I'd read an article about him a few years ago about his strong dislike of sweets. "It's been a long day?"

Chandler, who had poured me a glass less than his but still an ample amount, turned and handed it to me. He offered me a small smile. "It has nothing to do with you," he reassured me. "You've been the highlight, actually. It's little things. Little things I don't prefer to talk about right now." After he said it, I watched him take a pretty substantial drink. Half of it, at least.

I nodded, taking a drink myself before I followed Chandler, who had already left without me again. He waved around the room, toward the kitchen and his living room.

"Obviously this is the kitchen and the living room. I don't really use them often. Not really much of a cook, and I don't watch a lot of television."

"You weren't wrong; you must like modern architecture a lot. It's so white and sleek here." I saw Chandler smiling a little as he weaved his way around a corner behind the wall with the fireplace and television and into a hallway.

He nodded to the first, slightly ajar door. "My bedroom."

While my curiosity was maddening, and I tried to look inside, it was relatively dark. I couldn't see much of anything. Chandler didn't move to turn on the light or show me anything further, which probably had been the appropriate thing to do. After all the thoughts racing through my mind, seeing his bed of all things wouldn't have helped at all.

Chandler started walking again, nodding to the next door. "Restroom, if you need it." He didn't stop, heading to the final room in the hallway. I assumed it had been a second bedroom. Which it well may have been, but I quickly learned Chandler had utilized it for something else entirely. "And this is the room I practice Shibari in when I'm at home."

My gaze went directly toward the door and then quickly back to him. Chandler hesitated, and I watched him finish off the glass he'd been drinking. I did too, feeling a wave of nerves hit me, wondering what he was thinking so hard about. He took the glasses and asked me to wait. I watched him walk back around the corner, likely taking them straight to the kitchen. That little thing about him that I hadn't ever really known about, had me smiling yet again. A minute later, he returned, coming to stand near the door again.

"I'd like to show you another tie. Something a little more complex than the butterfly harness from before." He'd drifted off, looking away from me, and I wondered if he was embarrassed or something.

"I'd love that," I replied, trying to keep my voice as collected as I could, though I was incredibly excited at the idea. It had not been what I'd expected him to do, despite the fact he'd taken me back to his condo. I wasn't sure what I had expected, truthfully.

Chandler stepped in front of the door and turned toward me. We were separated by maybe a couple feet of space, and still, I moved a step closer to him. "There are a few rules before I let you in here." I raised a brow, but didn't reply, letting him continue. "Number one: under no circumstances will you speak about this with anyone. I'm showing you this because I trust you. Understood?"

While it had been implied at other points, I was flattered he said he trusted me. I nodded in reply again but decided not to say anything further.

"Good," Chandler replied. "Number two. As you might remember from my little speech at The Crucible, I know Shibari tends to be—ah—sexual, in nature." The way the words came out of his mouth sent a little shiver through me. I tried my best to restrain my thoughts, focusing on him. "This is purely artistic. I need to make myself clear. I wanted to show you what I mean. I wanted to share this with you because you clearly have as much of an interest as I do. But that's all this is, Cassandra. Nothing can happen outside that. This isn't some prelude to something else. Only a demonstration. Understood?"

I knew better than to assume it would turn into anything else. Secretly, something inside me hoped it might potentially lead somewhere. He'd have me in his grasp again and realize this thing between us was inevitable. That we shouldn't be fighting it. But I gathered he was doing his best to keep his composure. So, instead of challenging him, I nodded again.

"Number three." Chandler's green eyes honed in on me. It brought me to full attention. "From the moment this door opens until we exit, you'll do exactly as I tell you to. You can ask questions, and I can give you explanations if you need it, but I'm in charge from here on out. I won't have any of this constant need to challenge me."

I gave him a look, but he seemed unfazed. "If you do have an issue, however, if you start feeling anxious or like you can't handle it, all I want you to say is the word 'feather,' and I'll stop immediately. We can leave, and you can go back to your apartment. Understood?"

"Of course," I replied and regretfully added, "Whatever you say, Professor Moreau." I had meant it as a simple joke. Trying to be a bit playful, perhaps lighten his intense mood. It hadn't been a good idea, however, because I watched Chandler's eyes narrow.

"I mean it, Cassandra," he replied, still focused on me. "No games. You'll listen and do as I tell you, or this will end. Do you want to get started?" I gave him another small nod, but he didn't look satisfied. "I need to hear you say it."

"I want to get started, Chandler," I replied calmly, my attention focused straight back at him. Neither of us wavered. He seemed satisfied with my answer but paused for a second before turning and opening the door without another word.

Letting the two of us inside. Feeling as though I was entering a doorway to a new reality I wouldn't be able to ever come back from.

CHAPTER 13

CHANDLER

Some of the longest moments of my life were when I had turned away from Cassandra, opened the door, and let her into the room. As we stepped through the threshold into this other reality, I realized there was no turning back. The two of us had gone to a different place. While I was absolutely set on nothing happening between us, it still had my heart racing.

As I strolled inside, flipping on the lights, I allowed Cassandra to take in everything before I said another word. Watched her beautiful hazel eyes, wide and eager, scanning around, trying to get her bearings.

On one wall directly across from us, there was nothing but mirrors stretched from floor to ceiling. Additionally, some mirrors were directly above us, positioned to allow the other hanging devices to have room. Most of the carabiners and ropes dangling from the ceiling were utilized for suspension purposes. Something I wouldn't be doing with her tonight.

While this space had never been used with another human, I'd designed it with the hope it would be used at some point. Went to great lengths to finish it after Jeanne and I had started our divorce proceedings. Mostly, my practice at home had been on mannequins sitting in the corner of the room and sometimes on myself.

Cassandra had wandered in another direction entirely, toward a wall housing several dozen different types of ropes. She walked down the length of it, studying them all curiously. Running her hands over them like she was trying to take them in.

Once she'd made it from one side to the other, I walked up to join her. She turned to face me just as I'd started to speak. "This is my rope collection. Not all of it. I have some in storage. It took a few years to collect some of them. They come from everywhere. Some are even from overseas. All different materials, weights, lengths, and colors..."

I pulled one bundle off its hook on the wall beside where she was standing and offered it to her. It was a deep shade of red, bound neatly together and tied.

"This," I said, as she took it from me carefully, "is what I use at The Crucible most of the time. What I used on you."

"Jute rope, right?" Cassandra asked me, and I couldn't help but smile and nod. "I looked it up when I got home. I was curious."

"That's jute, yes," I replied. "It's very commonly used for Shibari because of the way it looks on the body and how it feels on the skin. Some people don't like it as much because it's a little coarser, but I think that's part of the point. You're supposed to really feel it."

"I liked the way it felt," Cassandra agreed, her eyes focused on mine.

I had to look away from her, trying to regain my composure after she'd said the words.

All I could think about was the way she'd looked the previous week. In a matter of minutes, I'd get to look at her in the same way all over again. This time, with a more complex design. Something I hadn't done in a very long time in practice. And never on another person.

The way my entire body stirred at the idea had me staring in another direction until I had a handle on myself. If she was still looking at me like she had been, I feared I might drive her into the empty section of the wall behind her and throw caution to the wind.

"It's supposed to," I said, finally managing to come back to her. "But anyway—" I glanced at the wall again, eyes scanning over the ropes for the specific kind I wanted for the evening. I plucked several from their hooks. They were a deep shade of purple. "Each of these ropes gives a unique experience because they all feel differently." I handed her the collection I'd gathered while I placed the jute back.

"You aren't using the jute today?" Cassandra asked me, curiously.

"I actually wanted to use this tonight," I explained. "Bamboo. It's a bit softer. If I'm going to be working for a little while, and you're new at this, I want you to at least be comfortable." Cassandra smiled when I said it, and I continued, trying to just plow through the next part before I lost my nerve.

"I'll leave it up to you, but you can leave your clothes on this time or undress like you did the other day. The latter would probably give you a better experience, but you choose what makes you comfortable."

Cassandra looked up at me, studying my face. "And here I thought you were going to ask me to get naked. I was trying to prepare myself for it."

I wasn't sure if she was joking or serious. It didn't matter. I narrowed my eyes, trying to maintain a steady expression. However, the imagery of what she could have possibly looked like with those ropes around her, nothing on her body inhibiting them, had my breath trapped in my throat.

When I managed to exhale, I spoke again. "No, Cassandra. I need you to at least wear your undergarments, please. For both our sakes."

Cassandra looked as though she wanted to say something more but stopped herself. I watched as she drew her shirt up over her head in one fell swoop, followed by looping her fingers on her skin-tight pants, tugging them to the floor. In seconds, she was standing in front of me in nothing but her undergarments again.

As many times as I repeated to myself I wasn't going to react when she'd finished removing her clothes, I knew I had failed miserably. I couldn't help but draw my eyes down the length of her, admiring the way she looked. While I'd seen her somewhat clearly on the stage, it was much more apparent in this room with the lights overhead instead of a bright spotlight shining on us...

"Earth to Chandler," Cassandra brought me back to the room, my head snapping up.

"Sorry," I apologized, clearing my throat and trying to not make a big deal about how obvious I had been staring at her. "I usually think it's best to stretch beforehand, but since I won't be taking as long with this, I think you'll be okay."

"You can take as long as you want," Cassandra said, her eyes steady on me.

I sucked in a breath of air. "What's the safe word?" I asked her again.

"Feather," Cassandra replied almost immediately.

"Good," I replied, nodding. "Use it if you start feeling overwhelmed, okay?" Cassandra nodded, and I decided to begin, stepping in front of her. "I'm going to start. I usually work in silence, but if you have a question, feel free to ask."

I circled around her after a moment. Unlike how I usually was at Dreamers when we were working, warning her before I would approach, this time I planned to just act. Part of the experience was the anticipation of everything. If I warned her ahead of time, she'd be ahead of me, and I wanted her to get everything out of this.

Even though I hadn't acted yet, I could hear Cassandra's breathing picking up.

"Take deep breaths," I gently reminded her. "In through your nose, out through your mouth. Try to stay steady. I'm going to get started."

She nodded, and I picked up a piece of rope, unraveling it. I came around to the front of her. Noticed her eyes locked onto me as I wrapped the rope around her neck, laying it neatly on her skin. Taking great care to make sure it was exactly the way I wanted.

I started on a series of half hitches. Each hitch's location depended on the body type of whomever you were binding, but the first knot was usually placed at the center of the chest. I let the rope fall down her body. Studied it for a moment before I made the hitch. I carefully lined it where I wanted, feeling the backs of my hands brushing against the fabric of the navy blue bra she'd worn.

Cassandra swallowed deeply, and I glanced at her, making sure she was okay. She was staring straight ahead, breathing the way I'd instructed her to. Satisfied, I continued downward. One hitch at a time, over her stomach and belly button. The little grazes of my fingers against her skin made trails of goosebumps, and my entire body buzzed with the visual, wound up with excitement.

With Cassandra being significantly shorter than me, it started to become difficult to work from the distance I was at. I carefully dropped down, one knee at a time, until I'd made it to the floor, sitting on my legs. At an appropriate level to be working.

When I'd settled and looked back at what I was doing, I instantly regretted having moved to the floor at all. Immediately distracted by the damp fabric between her legs. Had to force myself away from continuing to stare and contemplate if it was actually happening. That it wasn't my imagination running wild.

My mind raced, trying to draw myself back to what I was doing. I heard her breaths becoming labored above me and looked up. She'd been staring down at me, eyes wide. I noticed she'd abruptly halted her breathing again. Before I could stop myself, my hands reached up, landing on her hips, trying to brace her.

"Cassandra," I said calmly, latching onto her gaze as best I could. "You need to keep breathing, or else I'm worried you're going to collapse on me. And I would prefer you not to do that this evening, for the sake of my sanity."

While she'd looked momentarily distracted, my attempt to bring her back worked. She smiled at me, appearing as if she'd returned to the room, and she took a deep breath. I felt satisfied I'd gotten through to her and went back to what I'd been doing.

I tried desperately to ignore that she was clearly aroused by what was happening to her. Specifically, what *I* was doing to her. I myself was having a similar response, and was fighting myself at every turn to come down from it. It didn't help that I was close enough that I was consumed by the smell of oranges.

It was making it nearly impossible to think.

I rattled off the steps I needed to do next in my head. Gently, I tried to nudge her legs a bit further apart without having to explain it to her. Quite certain hearing myself say it wouldn't help matters for either of us. She did exactly as I had wanted. Once she'd settled, I let my hand slip around her thigh, pulling the rope around, so it fell in the crevice of her leg. Wrapping it around and tying it off on the half hitch. Doing the same thing to her other side.

I'd been busy repeating the pattern in an attempt to design a somewhat improvised harness, focused on the overall aesthetic, when I suddenly felt something running gently across the top of my head. It startled me for a second or two, but then I realized what was happening. Cassandra's fingers had laced into my hair, drawing over my scalp, holding herself steady by way of my head.

When I looked up at her, I noticed she had closed her eyes. Wondered if she was trying to give in to the sensation of the rope being wrapped around her. The idea of how consumed she was throttled me a little, to the point when I returned my focus to what I was doing, I made every effort to make the process slower and more drawn-out than I already had.

Once I'd finished with the ties around her hips and thighs, I resumed working on the half hitches. Out of habit, focused on the usual layout of the design, I completed the final hitch and slid it right between her legs. Tugged it upward from behind until it settled against her and I'd tied it off along her lower back.

It wasn't the tightened grip on my head that sent me spiraling again, but the small gasp she emitted once I'd situated the hitch against her.

I knew better than to use the tie. It most certainly wasn't appropriate in this situation. Would only worsen what this was already clearly doing to her because of its position against her. Every move she made after, she'd feel the rope there. The last place I needed her to feel it because of the consequences it could have as a result.

My original intention was to deter from using it at all, but when I felt her hands in my hair and saw how she looked lost in the motions of everything, I was compelled to draw her into the experience more. Lost sight of myself and did it without thinking.

Cassandra writhed a little. When I looked up, her eyes were still closed, but I noticed her mouth had opened a fraction, and her breathing had picked up.

I felt her fingers still drawing over my head, softly and rhythmically. Had to stop myself abruptly from verbalizing, with some sort of pleased sound, my enjoyment of the sensation. I didn't recall ever having felt someone do such a thing to me before. It was hypnotizing and relaxing, to say the least, and I almost hadn't wanted her to stop.

However, I *absolutely* needed her to cease the rocking of her hips, both because it made things more difficult to do, but also because it was doing dangerous things to me. And I needed to be focused. Needed to stay collected in those moments.

Luckily, I also needed to get up from the floor. While I immediately missed the feeling of Cassandra's fingers roaming over the top of my head, it at least allowed me to breathe steadily again.

For the next few minutes, I focused on weaving a new piece of rope over the front of her and around her back. Created several rhombus shapes down the length of her torso, weaving the rope around her chest and in between all the hitches in the center of her body.

While I was focused on what I was doing with the design, I couldn't help myself, letting my fingers brush against her skin every now and then, enjoying the way it felt and the way she reacted when I did.

The little twitches she made gave me occasional shivers. The goosebump trails across her skin paused my breathing when I noticed them. I tried to take every second of it in, savoring it as best I could because as quickly as it had started, I was already nearly done.

After I'd finished crisscrossing the rope around her back down near the underside of her belly button, tying it off at the hitch again, I looked back up at Cassandra, and she still had her eyes closed. Her head was tilted back a fraction. Still breathing just as I'd asked her to.

For the entire few seconds I was looking at her, with how close I was and how captive she held me, I thought about taking her by surprise. Plant my lips over her own. My curiosity was maddening.

Instead, I realized I'd finished.

"And *fini*," I whispered, mostly to myself. Meanwhile, Cassandra was still oblivious, eyes closed. Likely thinking I was still working and waiting patiently for me to continue.

Although I had managed to stop myself from kissing her, I still reacted in a way I probably shouldn't have. Felt compelled to give her some small bit of affection, regardless.

I found myself reaching up, brushing a few pieces of her hair, which had mostly been up in a ponytail, away from her face. Tucked it behind her ear.

The simple little act had drawn Cassandra's eyes open. She brought her head forward, making eye contact with me. "I'm finished," I said quietly to her, smiling. Carefully, I reached for her shoulders and rotated her around in a circle until she was facing toward the mirrors on the wall.

Both of us stood together, while Cassandra tried to take in what I had done. She looked absolutely mesmerized. "Wow," she said, almost inaudibly. "It's beautiful. What's it called?"

"It's a tortoise shell tie," I explained to her, still watching as she stared at herself in awe. "When people think of Shibari, this is something similar to what they imagine. It's a popular tie. I thought it was a good one to demonstrate since it covers the whole length of the torso."

Cassandra's hand drew up, and I watched her fingers trace one of the rhombus shapes along her stomach, running over the half hitch in the middle."I can feel the ropes everywhere. It's like a hug, almost."

I smiled at the comparison. Before I could help myself, my hands fell off her shoulders, drawing along her backside. My fingers ran along the lengths of rope I'd tied back and forth along the length of her spine. Pushing gently into her skin, allowing her to feel the pressure of it against her.

Cassandra's eyes closed again, lost in the feeling of it. The fact she'd done so had me continuing without thinking much of it. Tracing all the lines of the rope on her back until they drew around in front of her. I stepped forward, my body almost pressed into her, fingers carefully zig-zagging across all the shapes on her stomach. Finding I was using different pressure at different points, so it would give a different sensation every time.

I'd been so caught up in what I had convinced myself had been an innocent act, admiring my work, I hadn't heard the way Cassandra's breathing had picked up again. It had taken me a few moments to realize she had started gently rocking herself back against me.

The moment I realized she was without a doubt feeling what this was doing to me, something I *did not* want her to know, I backed away from her. Just in time to watch her eyes flutter open. She spun around to face me. Before I had a moment to think, she'd drawn her hands up to my face, wrapping them around behind my head, gently tugging me forward.

My breathing stopped. I felt trapped in her gaze, unable to move myself at first. Watched her bore into me with those beautiful eyes. I wasn't going to make it.

I suddenly managed to come to my senses, gasping and ripping backward from her. Cold air rushed into my lungs as I took a long breath. My eyes narrowed at her, feeling a wave of annoyance. "Jesus Christ, Cassandra. I told you outside, that *wasn't* going to happen."

"Why not?" Cassandra surprised me with the question. "What is so wrong with it you are panicking at every turn? Clearly you want it, too." I watched her eyes divert downward, briefly, and the attention she gave me paused my breathing yet again. Ramped my heart a little in my chest. "I don't understand you."

"It could get us both in trouble at Dreamers," I argued, though it hadn't been remotely the reason. "It could jeopardize your future career. Not to mention I'm, as much as I hate to admit this fact, quite a few years older than you." I rattled off the obvious things, yet none of the actual reasons. Just superficial ones. If that had really been all it was, I would have allowed myself that opportunity the moment I'd realized she felt the same.

The real reasons stopping me, I would never tell her about.

Cassandra was as fired up as I had been. But I did my best to hold my ground. Stared her down until I watched her shoulders sink.

Instead of acknowledging the fact I was in agreement with her, wanting nothing more than to quit denying myself—denying both of us what we wanted, I simply changed the subject. Ended something I hadn't wanted to end.

If it could have gone on indefinitely, I would have let it. But the reality was it couldn't. I should not have let it get this far. The temptation had been far too much to handle. And there was too much of a cost.

"Let me get you untied."

CHAPTER 14

CHANDLER

When Cassandra had been relieved of the ropes, she offered to assist me with my neurotic need to clean up after myself, helping me bundle the ones I'd used with her and put them back on the wall.

After we exited, I flipped the light switch off and prepared to close the door behind us. She caught me off guard, still gazing back into the room. She'd been looking at something, but I hadn't been quite sure what it was. Like she was longing to be back there. Truthfully, I was too. It felt strange being over.

I noticed, though Cassandra had put her shirt and pants back on before we'd left, there were remnants of the ropes which had made lines in her skin. The imagery of it held my attention for a moment, so much so I found myself reaching out to run my fingers across where I saw it, around her neckline.

She shivered when I touched her, her eyes flitting up to meet my own. I felt her lean into my fingers as I traced around it. Almost liked that I'd marked her, in a way.

When I realized how long I must have been standing there touching her, I pulled away abruptly. Cleared my throat. "Those rope marks will go away after a while. Sometimes it happens. It doesn't hurt, does it?"

"No," Cassandra said, her gaze still locked on mine. "I think I can feel it in places, but it's like a nice reminder more than anything." It certainly had been a nice reminder. I thought I'd be more composed since it was over, but I still felt like I could unravel at any moment. All the pent up, overwhelming feelings I'd been having were still running rampant inside me.

"I can draw you a bath if you'd like," I said, realizing seconds after I'd said it how odd it must have sounded. It had been something I was accustomed to doing when I practiced on myself. Something second nature for me to suggest.

"It helps relax your body, and make those places where you're feeling the ropes right now less noticeable. They call it after-care I suppose, though I've never really been a fan of all that BDSM terminology–" I paused for a second, realizing I'd been rambling. Wondered if I'd been embarrassed momentarily but I shook it off and continued. "I know you weren't bound for long, but it's good to get in the habit."

Good to get in the habit. I hadn't a clue why I'd said those words. By the shift in her facial expression, Cassandra had noticed what I'd spoken but both of us chose to ignore it. Instead, she decided to amuse herself with the other thing I'd said.

"Chandler Moreau, drawing a bath, never would I have ever—"

We had stopped in the hallway together, almost directly in front of the doorway to my bedroom. I turned to face her, noticing she was smiling at me, and I couldn't help but smile at her in return. "I don't particularly go around advertising that information, but I suppose it couldn't be any worse than you knowing other hobbies of mine." I nodded back toward the room we'd just exited.

"I think it's cute, personally," Cassandra said, that adorable smile of hers still lingering on her face. "I'll take you up on it. I can't remember the last time I took a bath."

"Well, all the more reason to indulge yourself," I decided. I nodded down the hallway. "Go get yourself a glass of water from the kitchen first. It's good to do after a Shibari session. The glasses are in the cabinet left of the stove. Drink the entire glass."

"So bossy," Cassandra said, raising a brow at me. I chose to ignore it.

"I'll be in my bathroom when you're done. Just come through here," I propped open my bedroom door. "There's no tub in the other bathroom. I'll go get you set up."

Once I'd watched Cassandra disappear around the corner, I cut through my room to the bathroom. By the time she had returned, I'd gotten the water to a satisfactory temperature and was adding Epsom salts and some eucalyptus essential oils I'd gotten from underneath the cabinets. Enjoying the smell of it, lost in my head.

When I came back to the room, I looked over my shoulder, noticing Cassandra leaning against the doorframe, sipping on a glass of water. When she'd stopped, she smiled.

"I figured I should drink more than one glass."

I nodded in agreement, returning to what I was doing, not yet satisfied. As I added a bit more of the salts, listening to the rush of the water, I felt Cassandra come to sit beside me at the edge of the tub. "You have a beautiful bedroom, and bathroom. A beautiful house in general. And I definitely haven't taken a bath with a view like this one."

When I looked at her again, I noticed she was admiring the scenery from the slightly tinted window behind the tub, overlooking the city. "Now you see why I enjoy them," I retorted, my lip curling a bit. I finished with what I was doing, turning off the faucet and standing up to return what I'd been using back to its proper place under the sink.

Cassandra had been running her hand through the water when I turned back. "I made the water hotter than you may be used to, but try to relax into it."

I paused for a moment, drumming my fingers on the countertop beside my sink, looking at her. She seemed a little overwhelmed by the bathroom, still taking it all in. "There's a towel for you on the counter. Hang it up when you're through, if you don't mind. I'll get it tomorrow. If you need anything else, let me know. Otherwise, I'll leave you to it."

We looked at each other, and I admired her perched on the side of my tub, with the frosted window overlooking the city behind her. I felt as if I wanted to say something else to her, it was on the tip of my tongue, but I couldn't figure out exactly what it was.

Eventually, I remembered. "I thought I'd offer you to stay the night since it's getting late. Treat you to breakfast in the morning, if you want."

Cassandra raised a brow at me. "Chandler, you need to stop worrying about my food situation," She was staring at me hard. "I've managed just fine the last five years of my life. I promise you, I'm a grown woman. I'm capable of handling it."

I'd been a handful of feet away, still at my sink counter, watching. For whatever reason, I took the steps back, moving right in front of her. Looming over her as she sat beside the tub.

"I'm sorry to inform you," I said, unable to help a smile from breaching my face. "I've been worried about you since I first saw you in Soleil Theater all those months ago. And it's not because I don't think you're capable. I'm quite certain you are very capable of a lot of things. I've seen proof. I have no doubt."

Cassandra stared up at me, eyes wide, allowing me to catch all the flecks of colors in them. Trapping me there. My smile grew a little more, and I found myself running my fingers across her cheek once again. Tucked those few loose strands of honey brown hair back around her ear. "I just decided from the moment I saw you auditioning, you were worth worrying about."

I watched her eyes close for a few seconds, my fingers lingering on the side of her face. It was warm. "You should stay for tonight.

It would make me feel better, knowing you were safe. I admit, ever since you told me about your living situation, I've worried a bit."

Though I'd offered and it had been with good intentions, it still felt dangerous to say. There was only so much left I had in me, keeping me from giving in to her completely. What I had wanted, despite my every argument against it. I was playing a dangerous game with her, and I knew it. Knew I should have kept my distance.

But against my better judgment, I chose to ignore it. I convinced myself, like when I'd let her experience the Shibari again, this was innocent. I was just looking out for her.

My hand dropped. The moment it had, Cassandra's eyes fluttered back open. She gave me a small smile, shaking her head. "Fine. I'll stay." I felt a little bit of relief when she'd said it, my shoulders dropping. I stepped a few steps away.

"I'll see you when you're done. Take your time." I snatched her glass from the counter before I turned.

By the time I'd made it to the door, I heard Cassandra call out. Turned my head over my shoulder to find her still watching me. Saying a few simple words, which were further proof of how quickly I was still undoing. "You're worth worrying about, too." Regardless of my concerns, I smiled at her before I disappeared.

I shut the door behind me once I'd left. Shortly after, I heard the water splashing and assumed she'd gotten into the tub. Tried not to think about the image for long, instead focusing on the alarm clock on my nightstand. It was already a few minutes shy of eleven. How it had gotten so late so fast, I had no idea.

After returning the glass to the kitchen, I changed the sheets on the bed, deciding to offer it to Cassandra and take the couch for the night. Lost in thought while I did. A noise across my bedroom suddenly brought me back. It was coming from my bathroom. I panicked, worried there was something wrong, so I went quickly over to check on her. My hand had been near the door to knock when another noise caused me to stop. It wasn't the noise of someone in distress—far from it.

Cassandra had been moaning, and not at all softly. It was echoing across the tile of the bathroom, loud enough I was certain I might have heard tiny bits of it, even if I had been in the other room. And when I expected myself to immediately back away, convinced I had enough willpower still in me to do so, instead I leaned into the door, wanting to listen. The moment I had, it opened a fraction. I must not have closed it properly.

My entire body froze, waiting for some indication she'd noticed. By the sound of it, she certainly hadn't because all the noises continued on loudly. I took a step forward, ignoring the tiny whispers in my head fighting me. They'd started to fade, my temptation becoming too strong to resist. The sound had lured me in.

Through the tiny crack, I could only make out the mirror and the sink, across the room. But it had been enough. In the reflection, I saw the bathtub, with the frosted window behind it. Saw the upper torso of Cassandra's body, laying in the tub, making out everything above her shoulders, which had my imagination running wild at what the rest of her could have looked like. But my attention drew quickly to her face, and I locked on.

Her head had been rolled back, leaning against the back of the tub, mouth hanging slightly open. Eyes closed, much to my relief, giving me another layer of protection from being spotted. She was still moaning, letting out little gasps, her body writhing.

I noticed she must have taken the retractable end of the tub faucet off. Ignorant as to why. Seconds later, it occurred to me, and my breath hitched in my throat.

Another moan escaped her. A string of curses.

If I thought I'd been losing my mind, it went to a completely different dimension the moment she'd started verbalizing actual words. "Oh God, oh God..."

Her body tensed, and I watched her head roll again, body rocking upward. She shook involuntarily, and I realized what was happening. Was completely transfixed by the sight of her as she brought herself to climax in my tub.

"Chandler—"

I nearly fell into the door. Felt my body responding to the sight and sound of her so fast I barely had time to think. For a matter of a few seconds, I panicked. But it was fleeting. She likely had no way of knowing I was standing there, clearly far too distracted.

And she was saying my name. No—*moaning* my name, over and over, ringing relentlessly in my mind. I'd never thought it could sound more indefectible. Wanted it to continue indefinitely, convinced I would never get sick of hearing it said in the ways she had been, mixed with all those gasps and moans in between...

Temptation had finally gotten the best of me. My hand had snaked its way down and before I realized what I had done, I had fallen right alongside her. Unable to help myself. Completely transfixed by the sight in front of me and the sounds she was making.

"Chandler—"

"Fuck." I gasped, hoping I was quiet enough. But I quickly realized Cassandra had looked in my direction. I should have moved, should have stopped and walked away. When she turned back, still lost in those last moments she'd been experiencing, I stayed put.

Cassandra moaned again, and I watched her free hand grasp the side of the tub. I found myself growling at her in a whisper. Calling back her name, voicelessly. She had slowed, but her body still bucked and writhed from time to time. I watched her attention look back in the direction of the door again.

When I saw her eyes, they were quite possibly right on top of mine. Quite possibly having realized I was just beyond the door. I didn't care, already falling off the precarious cliff I'd been dangling from, unable to stop it. My free hand braced against the wall, legs shaking a little. Watching every second of the scene in front of me.

By the time I'd come to my senses, I realized I was audibly panting. My hand was clutching against the door frame so tightly my knuckles had grown white. I let myself stumble away from it, feeling a very intense wave of relief flood through me. I quickly searched for something to clean up the evidence I'd left behind as a result.

I managed to, as quietly as I possibly could, take care of the mess. Once I had, I slipped out of the bedroom. Cassandra had yet to leave the tub.

When I collapsed onto the couch, I felt my knee throbbing a little. It wasn't horrible, but I was tired of the constant reminders I was still injured. Reminders it may never go away.

My eyes drew up to the ceiling. Watched the large fan in the center of the room spinning around rapidly. Lost in the movement, trying to come down from the whirlwind of emotions and feelings I was having.

I'd finally started to settle, thinking I'd just relax and it would be fine, when I felt my insides twisting. I thought I'd be elated after everything, but instead I was filled with a nagging panic rapidly worsening with every second. Realized everything I was doing was complicating the situation. Every decision I'd been making was reckless. Governed by emotions.

The Moreaus weren't emotional creatures. They couldn't be, not leading the lives they did. Not without risking everything. I might have thought I could have been a person who could protect her. Keep her safe from all the things worrying her. Things that were worrying me. The person who could let her in, and everything would still be okay.

But I knew better. I'd been a fool.

Really, it should have been me I was protecting her from.

I heard footsteps rounding the corner. Brought myself to a sitting position, feeling further out of control with my emotions when my knee throbbed again.

Cassandra leaned against the side of the wall, watching me intently. She'd dressed again. By the expression on her face, it was evident she knew there was something wrong. Which was only confirmed when she asked. "Are you okay?"

"I think I need you to go, Cassandra," I said, trying to keep my voice neutral and steady. Trying not to let any sort of emotion run rampant on my face. Despite the bit of pain I was in, I got to my feet. "I'll have my driver take you back to your apartment."

"Chandler—" Cassandra started, taking a few steps toward me.

"I need you to not argue with me," I told her. "Please." I moved swiftly back toward the condo's entryway. Grabbed the ratty sling bag of hers next to where she'd placed her shoes. Cassandra had followed after me, and when I turned, I handed the bag to her. "He'll be outside by the time you reach the lobby."

I hated the way she was looking at me. Confused. A little hurt, trying to make sense of what I was doing. I wondered if she'd try to argue, but she didn't. Instead, she went to sit on the bench beside the doors. Stuffed her feet into her tennis shoes. Stood up, took her bag from me and threw it over her shoulder.

Before I could feud with myself otherwise, I moved the couple of steps over to the doors. Opening one for her and stepping aside. Cassandra followed me, moving through the doorway. She turned to look back at me, still looking distraught. "Chandler, please don't—"

And, as much as I absolutely loathed myself for it, I knew I couldn't handle hearing the rest of the sentence. "Goodnight, Cassandra." I shut the door. Left her standing on the other side without any further explanation. I heard her footsteps receding and breathed a sigh of relief, even if I still felt like shit.

After I'd downed a full glass of bourbon, in a poor attempt to mask my thoughts and distract me from my knee, I went to my bedroom. Decided all I wanted, after everything, was to sleep. To get some peace for a few hours.

I settled down on the side of my bed, the side closest to the door, facing it. It was the side I had slept on nearly my entire life. When I didn't, I couldn't sleep. Spent the night tossing and turning, panicked. Needed reassurance that I was as close to escape as I could be, if necessary.

On my nightstand was an old picture of mine in a black frame. It caught my eye for a moment, and it both made me feel better and worse at the same time. A picture of my cousins and I playing in Lily's apple orchard in France, which she and my grandfather Elliott had owned. The four of us, happy. Naive. The world had been different. We hadn't known any better.

When four suddenly became three, it had grown darker. Reality had set in. The truth had been a bitter kick to all of our faces. I missed them. It had been a long time since we'd spoken. Not since we'd lost Frederick.

The picture was all the reminder I needed. I'd made the right decision with Cassandra. Though it had hurt us both, I had protected her. And, more than anything, it had been all I wanted.

I'd just been about to lie down, lacking any desire to change out of the clothes I'd been wearing. Too desperate to escape my thoughts. I would have done it. Had already reached out to turn the lights beside my bed off in preparation.

Then I noticed. Which had been surprising, given the fact I'd been so distracted and lost in my own head. But as soon as my attention came back into focus, it was clear as day.

There was something missing. A small black journal I kept sitting on my nightstand beside the picture. One which hadn't changed in location for probably at least a decade, if not more. And I knew, with how neurotic I was, how I needed to be in control of literally every aspect of my life, there was no way in hell I had put it elsewhere.

No one had stepped into this condo in a long time. I couldn't recall the last person who had. Maybe Thomas and Abigail, for a brief bit of time, on occasion. It might have been so long ago now, it had been Jeanne. It had been a while.

Only one singular person had been in my home. One person I had left alone in the confines of my bathroom, the confines of this room, without my eyes on her.

It occurred to me how little I actually knew about Cassandra. How utterly ignorant I'd been. She was nearly a stranger. One I'd become completely infatuated with. I had lost all sight of reality because of her.

My father's voice was whispering in my ear. I'd been a fool. There were far too many consequences for my ignorance. I knew better. After all the years I'd lived now, lived in this hell I'd been trapped in for so long, I knew better.

Cassandra had taken the journal. And I needed to know why.

CHAPTER 15

CASSANDRA

The towering ceilings of Tremblay Hall echoed with the sound of students wandering up and down its hallways. I'd looked up, admiring the intricate designs, tiled and arched, supported by columns in the middle of the hallways. It was no wonder the sound was so loud; there were few soft surfaces for it to be absorbed. It was hard not to appreciate how fantastical it looked inside this building. Like you were walking into a magical castle.

Except it felt anything but magical in those moments. The last place I had wanted to be Monday morning following the Friday evening I'd spent with Chandler Moreau. He'd abruptly sent me home without any sort of explanation. I absolutely hated the fact I was supposed to be in the History of Circus class with him. I looked at the clock against the wall I had passed and noted I was late at this point.

I didn't care. Pondered the idea of leaving altogether and going back to my apartment. Not sure if I could face him after everything.

The nagging reminder I didn't have an option came crawling back to me. I was stuck. I wished I'd taken him up on his offer about switching professors. Though it had been the last thing I'd actually wanted. Truthfully, I hadn't wanted to have to look him in the face. At least not today.

What brought me to turn back, walking toward the classroom, was when I told myself under no circumstances was I going back to Nevada. It was far too dangerous. I'd come across the country with the intention of making Acrefort my home. My real dream had been to perform at Cirque du Lys. To spend as much of my career working alongside my idol as I possibly could. It was all I had wanted since the moment I first saw him.

Now it felt nearly impossible. My dream was fading away with every second.

When I reached the obnoxious wood door leading into the classroom, I hesitated. I found myself remembering to breathe, and as much as I hated it, it was Chandler's voice who had reminded me. *In through your nose, out through your mouth.*

I finally got my wits about me, pulling open the door. As usual, the audience was dark, only lit by the sprinkling of colorful light from outside reflecting from the stained glass windows on the far wall.

It had been eerily quiet when I entered, and after I'd shut the door behind me, I realized why. Henry, who had been directly across from me, had his head down, staring intently at a piece of paper in front of him. They had a quiz today, and I had completely forgotten. At least it might have excused me a little from my tardiness. There hadn't been a huge need for me if that's all they were doing for the first part of class.

As I slowly descended down the aisle toward the front of the room, my attention turned to Chandler. He was sitting at his usual place behind the desk adjacent to the one I typically used. Looking down at what I assumed was the History textbook he'd been lecturing from. By the way his eyes looked glazed over and distant, I assumed he was lost in thought versus actually reading anything.

I took the opportunity to try to sneak past him and get myself situated. Hoped if I didn't draw too close, and he happened to casually notice I'd arrived, he might not say anything about it. I imagined he likely didn't want to make a scene in front of the entire class. At least, I was going to assume he wouldn't.

Once I'd gotten settled, having been surprisingly quiet, I decided to busy myself. I pulled out homework needing to be graded from last week. I'd almost finished, but there was a bit more to do. For a few minutes, I lost myself in what I was doing. At least attempted to, though my mind wandered a lot. Not once looking up at Chandler, in fear if I did, he'd be staring at me. And I didn't want to stare into those green eyes.

At the tail end of finishing grading a terribly done homework assignment, I begrudgingly put a bright red D on top of it and glanced up at Chandler. His green eyes were piercing into me. Glaring so fiercely it was like he was driving a knife through me. He looked pissed as hell.

"*Stop it,*" I mouthed at him, somewhat annoyed and distracted. I looked back down for a few seconds. The room had been almost dead quiet, so I was blatantly aware when he'd let out a low growl.

Jesus Christ. I wasn't going to get anything done.

I got immediately to my feet and swerved around my desk, storming straight over to him. Planted my hands on his desk and leaned forward, so I could get across the tone I wanted to have, but hopefully still not draw a lot of attention. Because if I could have helped it, I likely would have flat out yelled at him. Smacked him. I was so annoyed.

"Are you fucking *five years old* or something?" I glared at him, my nostrils flaring. It didn't matter what I'd said, too livid he'd acted the way he had.

Chandler glared back at me, holding steady. "You're late again, Ms. Blackstone. Don't think I didn't notice."

"And that warranted you sitting there giving me that murderous glare?" I shook my head at him in disbelief. "You can be upset with me, but there's such a thing as talking about it. Not trying to distract me from getting work finished."

"I'm about done with having to lecture you on your tardiness at every turn,"he said. I hated the look on his face. It always reminded me of the first day of class. The one which would make me forget the other side of him, the kind side, the affectionate side. He twisted into some sort of evil version of himself. I loathed it.

"Well, if it's any consolation, the reason I'm fucking late is because I was struggling to come into this classroom at all after you had the audacity to kick me out of your condo for no good—"

Chandler's hand wrapped around my wrist. He stood up from his seat, weaving around it, dragging me gently along. As much as I had wanted to protest and thought I would, I followed him obediently. Hoped if I did what he wanted, maybe, perhaps, he'd explain his behavior.

There was a door on the wall with the stained glass windows. A fire escape which led outside. I watched him push into it, leading us out into the alleyway. It shut behind us, leaving a room full of students taking their tests. Like he hadn't given a care in the world about it.

Once the door shut, Chandler drew up on me, much like he had the night at The Crucible when I'd come back to see him. Backed me up against the door, trying his best to act like he had control over the situation. Looking as livid as he had before.

"First of all," he said, glaring at me, his tone menacing as ever. "I don't want to ever hear you mention what happened last week inside these walls. Under no circumstances."

I blinked at him. While I wasn't one hundred percent sure why he'd said it, I had an inkling of an idea. Still, I felt like putting up a fight with him regardless, incredibly annoyed with his behavior.

"Why? You're suddenly embarrassed about it?"

"I'm not obligated to explain to you why," Chandler replied, shortly. "And I'm not asking you. It's not a suggestion. I am telling you, don't mention it. Not a hint. Are we clear?"

"You're being a fucking ass right now," I said, my eyes narrowing at him. "I don't understand why. Everything was fine. We were having a nice time. It was a good evening. Then you decided to lose it on me without any explanation." I took a deep breath, trying to steady myself. "You know, you may be tired of me running late all the time. And I'm sorry, truly. But at least I'm not treating you like shit for no reason at all."

I must have looked visibly distressed because at least for a few moments, Chandler looked like I'd gotten through to him. He seemed like he might have calmed down a little bit. I watched him take a few deep breaths, his green eyes boring into me.

"I don't know you at all," he finally said, his voice dropping quite a bit. "I let some deluded infatuation distract me from that fact. Got caught up in some fantasy version of you. Maybe you were doing it on purpose, I have absolutely no idea..."

I was boiling over. "Do you remember the other night at the club when you were bitching at me about talking in riddles? I could say the same right now, Chandler."

Chandler, who had briefly looked off in a different direction, snapped his attention straight back at me. As swiftly as he'd done the previous time, I watched his arms come crashing down on either side of me. Pinning me against the door.

"You are such a *control freak*, I swear to God. You think I'm going to run away—"

"Are you going to admit to it or not? Tell me why you did it?" Chandler asked, his gaze unwavering. It was intense. I was actually a little bit afraid. "I know you're not stupid, Cassandra. Clearly, it seems, since you had the ability to somehow get past me. And, trust me, that's not an easy feat for most people."

"What are you *talking* about?" I raised my voice at him, starting to feel more freaked out, my heart racing in my chest. Struggling to get breaths out. Though I'd been asking the question, I had a suspicion I knew exactly what he'd been referring to. Suspected it was the whole reason for his attitude. Still, I wasn't about to divulge the information. Not with him acting this way. "I need you to back the hell up right now. Please."

Surprisingly, Chandler didn't move an inch. I let out a gasp, feeling like I was going to pass out from the amount of adrenaline rushing through me. I couldn't take the surge of anxiety I was suddenly experiencing.

"Chandler, please. I am not joking. I am begging you. This is triggering me right now." Chandler hesitated for a second more, still looking furious with me. But it was only for a second, and then he moved away.

I felt like I could breathe again. I stood, trying to regain my composure. But it clearly had been too long because while I'd been staring at the ground, unable to look at him, I heard the door open and shut again. When I looked up, he was gone.

I let myself recover for a couple of minutes, making sure I was steady. I followed him back into the classroom. Completely mortified, I'd left my bag unattended at the front of the room. Chandler had distracted me so badly, but I didn't dwell on it. I stuffed everything I'd sat on the desk back into the bag, snapping it shut again, and throwing it over my shoulder.

The second I had, I started to storm out of the room. I'd almost made it to the aisle when I felt a gentle grip on my wrist again. It sent me spinning around, straight into Chandler's gaze. Still as frustrated as he looked outside. "Where are you going, Ms. Blackstone?"

"I quit," I snapped back at him, knowing I'd raised my voice. "I'll find another professor to work for. I'll get a different mentor." It was hard to keep my gaze on him. I had lost it, so upset this was happening. "Congratulations. You may have driven me out of this school, out of this town, and ruined a dream I have had since I was in middle school. I don't care anymore because I clearly thought you were someone you weren't. Thanks for being a huge fucking disappointment, *Professor Moreau*."

There had been a flicker on Chandler's face as he watched me. His expression shifted, looking as if he was seconds from offering me some sort of explanation, maybe attempting to stop me. I didn't care. It didn't matter what he said. I was done.

I turned around again, this time leaving, not stopping. Two dozen students' eyes watched me. I tried desperately to ignore it, so angry that it was difficult to do. As I'd reached the door, Henry had gotten up from his seat. Probably having seen and possibly heard my altercation with Chandler.

"I'll text you later," I assured him swiftly. I couldn't stay in the classroom another second longer than I had to. "I have to go take care of something first."

I left. Not caring about letting the obnoxious wooden door of my classroom slam on my way out.

Fortunately, the next place I intended on going was in a building adjacent to Tremblay Hall. One I didn't recall the name of. I only knew about it because it was where Chandler's office also was, and I'd been there once after a History class to get paperwork to grade.

This time I wasn't headed to Chandler's office. I was headed further down the hall.

The door to the dean's office was closed at the moment. There had been no secretary at the desk to ask if he was there in the first place. I had been so infuriated, so completely and utterly done, I acted on instinct.

I knocked on the ornate-looking door, similar to the one leading into the classroom in Tremblay Hall. The theater, too. In fact, this building, while not quite as majestic as Tremblay Hall, still had the old French charm within it. It was beautiful, even if it was a bit more simple in its construction. I might have been more interested in taking a better look around if I hadn't been so determined about what I needed to do.

When I still hadn't gotten an answer after what felt like a decent amount of time had passed, I turned to leave. The doorknob clicked, and I heard the door itself swing open. "Can I help you?" A man called out to me.

The moment I spun back around, I was face to face with someone I could have sworn had been Chandler. Had to blink and really stare for a lengthy amount of time, completely surprised by it. He had the same booming height, the same broad frame and sharp facial features. The same thick hair and beard, only much more gray.

What had been the real giveaway, however, had been his eyes. Piercing and green and absolutely unmistakable. It certainly hadn't been Chandler standing there, but I was one hundred percent sure they were related. The man was a Moreau. And I almost knew for certain who he was but hadn't expected him to be the one to meet me.

"I'm looking for the dean," I said, trying to keep my voice steady, despite my body raging with adrenaline. "I need to lodge a formal complaint."

Chandler's older doppelganger studied me in silence. He motioned me into his office, and I followed. He shut the door behind us, and I weaved my way around his desk, taking a seat at the chair opposite of it. While I had wanted to talk to the dean, I was not expecting who I thought this man happened to be. Suddenly I wished I hadn't come here at all.

I watched him rest his arms on the desk in front of him. Still studying me for a minute before he spoke. "What seems to be the problem, Ms—"

"Blackstone," I said, somewhat curtly, though I hadn't meant it. The way he inquired about my name triggered me a little. Sounded exactly like Chandler. His voice, the inflections he used were so similar, it had me utterly convinced I was right. He had to have been related somehow.

It started to make me worry this conversation might not go in my favor. "Cassandra Blackstone. I'm a graduate student in the aerial silks program. I study under Chandler Moreau. And I need to be switched to someone else to work for. Someone else to be my mentor."

Again, the man stared, his eyes almost boring into me. Exactly the way Chandler often did, except he sent a chill down my spine, which was more uncomfortable than anything. I didn't like the way he was looking at me, truth be told. And I didn't like the words coming out of his mouth. "I'm aware of who you are."

"You are?" This conversation had already taken a turn I didn't like. I was about to inquire further, but he had decided to answer the question I was going to ask.

"Ah, yes," he offered me a small smile. Again, it made me more uncomfortable than anything else. There was something off-putting about it I couldn't place. "The daughter of the famous Blackstone Magicians. I had heard about you auditioning earlier this year. Did a little research on you because of it. Your parents were a favorite of my son's when he was younger."

My eyes narrowed a little bit. "I'm guessing your son must be Chandler Moreau," I replied, my stomach sinking. My assumption had been right after all, but again, I hadn't expected he was faculty at the school. Only had known he'd acquired it from his father, Elliott, when he'd passed away.

"Gabriel Moreau," he replied matter-of-factly. "Chandler is my son, yes. But I assure you, if you're here with concerns about him, it's my duty to assist you if I can. I don't prioritize my son's personal feelings over my duties of running this school. You paid good money to be here, and if the rumors serve you correctly, you certainly deserve to be here. If you have an issue involving him, I'll do my best to assist you."

So, he had been the dean after all. I realized Chandler had mentioned it in passing before. I had forgotten for one reason or another. Felt stupid I had. He'd been the one who had given me the raise, I was certain, because he'd mentioned it after class one day. It would have slipped my mind entirely otherwise. "Well, I appreciate it. I need to work with another faculty member. If I can't, I'm going to leave the program."

Gabriel looked surprised by what I'd said. He pressed me further about it almost immediately. "What exactly prompted this? If you don't mind my asking?"

For whatever reason, as furious as I was at Chandler, if he'd been another person, I might have indulged him. Thrown every minuscule concern I had left about Chandler's privacy out the window and told him everything.

But looking at him, I decided otherwise. I hadn't liked the strange way he was acting. The way he'd known about me, about my parents. Even if he was the dean, it still was off, and I couldn't figure out why.

"The reasons are irrelevant—" I started to say, trying to glaze over that fact.

"I assure you they aren't," Gabriel replied, studying me intently. "If he's gotten you to the point you need to remove yourself from him entirely, that you're considering leaving the program after all the work you put into getting here..."

Again, he rubbed me the wrong way. What he'd said could have been purely innocent. He could have meant it in any number of ways. I was certain it could be in regard to any student auditioning to get into this school. It was the premiere school in the entire country, probably one of the best in the entire world. You had to have worked hard to get here. But something told me he'd meant another thing entirely.

Which is why I didn't elaborate. "I know you need an explanation, but I can't give you one. I don't think we work well together. And if I'm going to succeed in this program, and I'm going to be able to stay here, I need to be learning from someone else. That's all."

I had already gotten up from my seat, deciding I felt too uncomfortable and on edge to stay any longer. I didn't want to offer any words to a man who was making my stomach churn looking at him.

Gabriel still seemed curious about me. I wasn't sure if it was because I'd skirted around the issue, if it had something to do with me and what he apparently knew, or if it had possibly been a combination of the two. I didn't care. I wanted to leave.

"I'll see what I can do, Ms. Blackstone," he replied, clearly having realized I was ending the conversation. "Thank you for bringing it to my attention." I nodded at him, weaving my way around the chair I'd been sitting at, and immediately heading out of his office.

I fetched my phone the second I'd closed the door and started back down the hallway. Typed a text message to Alex, more unsettled than I was angry. *I need to talk to you. It's important. Call me the minute you can.*

My phone had nearly been back in my pocket when I heard it ring. Looked to see who it was and was relieved to see it was my best friend. I put the phone to my ear, bringing my voice low. I was a good distance away from Gabriel's office, but I was still anxious. I understood why Chandler had been so paranoid about me remotely mentioning what had transpired between us the previous week at this school.

Something told me it didn't so much have to do with being embarrassed about it. I wondered if he'd meant it out of fear someone was listening. Because suddenly, after those few minutes in his father's office, I had a strange feeling too.

"I need to talk to you about something, but I need to meet you off campus. I need your advice on whether I should call the guy again. Andre Morales. The one who's been helping me with Peter."

There was silence on the line for a minute. "Did you find something?" Alex finally asked, and I could hear how her voice sounded both worried and curious simultaneously.

"No," I replied. "But I'm going to."

CHAPTER 16

CHANDLER

As I paced the steps outside a series of three-story townhomes southwest of downtown Acrefort, I found myself wishing I was anywhere but there. I stared up at the aged brick, feeling sick to my stomach. It had been enough that I'd had to deal with the altercation with Cassandra earlier. She'd decided to quit working with me, perhaps decided to leave the program, too.

I had tried to convince myself I didn't give a shit about it, but truth be told, it had bothered me the entire day. Almost made me more infuriated than I'd been about her taking the journal. I had nearly avoided this entire event and looked up the information at Dreamers Academy about where she was living. Even if it was highly inappropriate, and I would likely be breaking several rules.

There was no way in hell I would let her quit. No matter how pissed I was or she was at me. The woman had far too much talent to squander it because of her emotions. I wouldn't let her, even if it meant she worked with someone else. She wouldn't give up something she worked so hard for, not because of me. Not because of anyone else.

So, I'd decided, because it was almost impossible to get out of this unbelievably inconvenient monthly dinner with my parents, I would attend to it immediately after. It deserved my prompt attention, but I had to get this obnoxious obligation out of the way first.

Still, it was taking everything in my power not to flee anyway. It happened every single time I stood out here. The same sense of dread. I wanted to be anywhere else, but I couldn't be. This was a required arrangement.

At least I could take a minute to try and compose myself.

When I finally felt like I had my wits about me, I managed to walk up the stairs and immediately ring the doorbell before I lost my nerve again. Seconds later, the door swung open, my mother Madelyn standing in the foyer behind it. I couldn't help but smile when I saw her. She was the singular reason I forced myself to get through these evenings.

"You're late," she said. If it had been me saying those words, I would have been annoyed. My mother, however, was still smiling. "It's good to see you."

"Dad happens to be the only person who cares if I'm on time," I noted, stepping into the foyer with her. I realized it had been something we both shared. The same irritation over tardiness. And I suddenly was annoyed at myself for it.

The house was beautifully decorated. I took it in as my mother retrieved the light jacket I'd been wearing and hung it on the rack beside the door. It wasn't anything I'd ever do in my own home, a little more old-fashioned than I preferred, but the decorations had been my father's choosing. The same tastes as my grandfather, Elliott. French inspiration everywhere. Perhaps I still liked it because it reminded me of my childhood when I stepped inside.

My mother had lived her entire adult life trapped under the will of my father. For nearly the same reasons as I had. Why she hadn't left him, I never could understand. Somehow she had always stayed, as loyal as ever. I supposed neither of us had a choice, but her fierce dedication to him still baffled me.

It was likely why we took solace in one another so often.

After she'd hung my jacket and turned back toward me, I hugged her. She was pretty much the only person in my life I hugged, outside of Abigail and Stella on occasion. My mother was a bit shorter than me, around Cassandra's height. For a brief moment, despite everything, my mind drifted back to the previous week with her. When she'd run her fingers through my hair. It had felt so foreign, but I missed that small bit of affection, truthfully. It was a rare occurrence.

We kept our hold on one another for a while. I felt like I needed it more than I normally did. "I wish we'd see you more often. I miss getting to hug you."

A little part of me felt guilty when she'd said it. I avoided her as much as I did only because of my father. If it had been just her, it would have been one thing, but she was nearly always attached to my father's hip. And I wanted to be around him as minimally as humanly possible. It was already enough that I had to deal with him at the school.

"It's nice to see you too, Mom," I replied, as we'd broken apart. I smelled something coming from the kitchen. If I had to take a guess, it was my mother's famous French-inspired chicken and potatoes. She'd made it every time my cousins and my Aunt and Uncle had come to visit from France. I rarely ate potatoes anymore, but she'd humored me in recent years and made a bowl of greens for me, too. Her chicken, however, was something I lived for.

"Coq au vin?" I asked, and when my mother nodded, I smiled. "You're too good to me."

"Well your father likes it too, from time to time. I figured I'd try to please you both, as rare of a thing it is to do." She wasn't wrong. My father and I agreed on a few things, but it was hard not to agree when it came to my mother's cooking.

All at once, I heard a throat clearing from the hallway beside the foyer. When I turned to look, I realized my father had been watching us. "You're late," he noted, which I had already been expecting.

"The food your mother worked so hard on is getting cold, Chandler. I'd expect for you to have better manners."

Before I could get in some snide reply, my mother nudged me gently, nodding down the hall in an effort to distract me. It was probably the right decision for me not to get into it with him first thing after I'd arrived.

"Let's go eat," I decided to say, weaving us in the direction Gabriel was looming in. We followed behind him as he turned, heading back the way he'd come.

The array of food was already laid out on the dining room table. I let myself enjoy the wonderful smell of the French dish I adored as I sat down at the table. Tried not to focus on my proximity to my father, who yet again reeked of cigar smoke.

The three of us sat in silence for a few minutes, helping ourselves to all the food my mother had lovingly made. After a few bites, I looked up at her. She had apparently been watching me eat, which wasn't unusual.

"It's wonderful, as always," I assured her. My mother beamed at me, clearly waiting to make sure I enjoyed it. When she returned her focus to her own food, I took a bite of salad greens.

"I take it things have been going smoothly with taking over for Jeanne?" To the left of me, I heard my father ask the question. After I'd swallowed my food, I proceeded to take a long drink of the water my mother had provided before I acknowledged him.

Truthfully, it had been a thorn in my side momentarily, but I'd started to adjust—until this morning. "It's been fine," I replied, not at all in the mood to discuss things with him at great length. "Not really any issues I can recall."

My father raised a brow at me. I didn't like the look of it and almost inquired why. He spoke before I had the opportunity, "That's surprising to hear."

"Why?" I replied, still confused by his reaction.

"If I had a student barge into my office today, threatening to leave the program because of you, of all people, I would have assumed there might have been an issue. That doesn't happen often, even when *you* happen to be teaching."

I would have been more irritated by the last bit he'd said if I hadn't been so utterly distracted by the first part. Undoubtedly, Cassandra had been the one to visit him. The idea of her speaking to my father sent a wild variety of feelings rushing through me. I didn't let it be known I knew what he was talking about, or rather, *who* he was talking about.

"Someone had an issue with me?" I asked, trying to sound as neutral about the situation as I possibly could.

My father was looking at me intently. I could tell by the expression on his face, having seen it so many times over the four decades of my life, he knew I was bullshitting him. I continued to play dumb regardless. "You don't recollect having upset the Blackstone woman? I would have thought your abundant enthusiasm with her being in the program would have made you aware if something like that were to occur. I'm quite sure, in fact."

"I might have wondered if something was wrong," I tried to steer the conversation a bit, hoping I could give a satisfactory answer without condemning myself. "It hadn't occurred to me it was *so* bad she was considering quitting, however. I'll have to speak with her about it. I appreciate you bringing it to my attention."

I prayed he would drop it. There'd be no further inquiries for Cassandra's and my own sake. But it had been a foolish hope.

My father took a bite of his food, still eyeing me. I felt compelled to do the same, so I could look away from him for a moment. Every second, I feared I was giving myself away somehow. He'd break me with his gaze like he often did.

"Would you care to enlighten me about what you could have possibly done to make a student you so clearly have a vested interest in, threatening to give up her education? Her career? Surely you must have some sort of idea. This whole presentation you're putting on isn't fooling anyone. You should know better."

"Why does it matter?" I found myself asking since he'd clearly seen through me. He was right; I should have known better. Wished I could have been capable of being more steps ahead of him. Every attempt I ever made had been futile. He always had the upper hand, no matter how hard I tried. "The two of us don't get along. If she wanted to switch professors, then that's her decision. It's her education. I'm not going to stand in the way."

Every single word was bullshit. I intended to deal with it the moment I left this house. If my father didn't destroy me first.

"I didn't get an answer from her, either," my father said to me, his facial expression growing hard to read. "With how irate she was with you, she was still trying to protect you. And it seems you have the same intent. All I want to know is why. Because, if she does change who she's working with, if it resolves the problem, it isn't the only thing going on here."

"What exactly do you think is going on?" I asked him, though I had some inkling of an idea. If it was what I thought, I didn't want him to answer the question at all. But my curiosity was far too overwhelming not to inquire.

"I'll have you know fraternizing with students is against school policy." My father said the words I'd been dreading he'd say. And though he'd been entirely right, I knew it was also some manipulative tactic to disguise whatever he was really after. A way to get to me if I was refusing to give him what he wanted. "If either of the two of you were involved in any way, I would have an obligation to remove her from the program. You know as well as I do."

Again, it was exactly what I knew he'd say. I felt sick to my stomach at the idea and wished I hadn't pressed the issue with the journal at all. Whatever fears I had about her and the journal were starting to feel more and more irrational by the minute.

This conversation, however, was terrifying to me. I wouldn't allow myself to be the reason Cassandra's entire belief of her purpose since she was a child was taken away from her. I refused, no matter what I had to do to stop it.

I'd go so far as to bend to my father's will, as much as I hated myself for it.

"What do you want from me?" I asked him, and I found I was almost pleading.

"I'm not sure if there's anything you can do, Chandler. Not at this point. It's evident by how you're reacting right now, you knew what was happening. And you know the consequences. You aren't stupid." My father's eyes were burning into me, and I wished I could say a million things to him in those moments, but I fought myself. Forced myself to shove every ill thought away.

"I'll do whatever you want," I said, staring back at him, not breaking my gaze. "Including staying away from her. I swear it. Don't make her leave the program, not because of me."

Gabriel leaned back in his chair, studying me. Meanwhile, my mother sat in silence, still eating her food, but she looked worried. I abhorred my father more for constantly putting her through this bullshit. Myself a little, too.

"I suppose I can find something for you to attend to. Hopefully, something to keep you distracted." I knew whatever it was he was implying wasn't anything I wanted to be distracted by. I didn't care. I had been serious—I'd do anything.

"I'll switch her to a different teacher," my father decided, much to my relief. "And you'll keep your nose out of her business from here on out. Otherwise, I'll see it's dealt with. You know I'm a man of my word. So, I suggest you keep yourself in check this time."

I knew *very* well he was a man of his word. If it had been any other person, it may have been an admirable trait. But his intention had made it a threat. It hadn't been pure, not any in the least. If I was out of line, he'd ensure I'd face the consequences.

"I'll stay away from her," I promised. As horrible as it felt, I knew it was probably what I should have done in the first place. Especially after all of this. I was miserable at the idea I wouldn't be able to teach her. The woman who had stunned me on the stage at her audition all those months ago. I'd squandered the dream she'd had. My father had squandered the dream she had. And I couldn't think of a time I detested myself more.

For the next two months, both Cassandra and my father got exactly what they wanted. I tried to stay as far away as humanly possible. She'd been placed with a faculty member I despised, who I knew with absolute certainty wouldn't remotely give her the training I would have. But it was the best I could do for the moment. The only way I could protect her.

Someone was better than no one instructing her. At least I tried to convince myself, as much as I couldn't stand it.

I did everything in my power to keep myself distracted, including helping my father with things I would have never done otherwise. But I did, to protect an innocent person I'd gotten wrapped up in this bullshit.

The week following midterms, I arrived at the conference room adjacent to my father's office for the meeting which occurred every semester at this time. It was meant for faculty to plan out the remaining months of the semester and ensure everyone was on the same page.

It was also a way for my father to keep himself in all of our business, though I was certain most of the others involved didn't see it that way. After all the time I'd known him, I knew better.

At the meeting, Abigail, Thomas, Sebastian and I sat together at the far end of the table. All of my colleagues knew my disdain for my father and were supportive of protecting me from it as best they could. It was something I'd always been grateful for.

The meeting, which I didn't attend every semester since I didn't always teach, droned on for a long time. Two hours, at least. The group of us had gotten so bored with all the drabble, we started quietly discussing Cirque du Lys to keep from losing our minds. Conversing about Penelope Girard, who had just made her transition to performing with the acrobats, and our dilemma of acquiring a new aerialist for the winter shows that were in a month.

When the meeting adjourned, and most everyone had left, my father caught me before I had gotten out the door. Outside the dinners I'd been forced to attend and these little errands I'd been running for him as a consequence of what had happened with Cassandra, I did everything in my power to avoid him. So, when he'd managed to catch me before I could make my escape with my friends, I'd been disappointed, to say the least.

"I need a word with you," he said to me, nodding toward the door to his office.

It was the only thing he said before he walked over, disappearing behind it. It left me unsettled. Still, I followed him back to his office. I'd forgotten how awful it usually smelled until I stepped inside. Reeked of cigar smoke. I remembered why I hadn't been in there in over a year.

"Close the door," he told me, and I did what he asked. Afterward, I stepped over toward his desk but decided not to sit down. I hoped whatever he wanted would take as minimal an amount of time as humanly possible.

"I need you to take care of something," my father said, and I loathed every single word of the sentence. I knew whatever followed was something I did *not* want to do. Not remotely. But I listened anyway because I didn't have a choice. "While I'm impressed at your ability to maintain some sliver of self-control with the Blackstone girl, I am going to ask you to break my rule. For one circumstance."

"Why?" I asked, already not liking where this was going.

"It's not your concern," he replied swiftly. "There's something I need to know. And I figured you were the best person to do it, given your interest in her."

"I'm not interested anymore," I argued, which had been a blatant lie. While I'd somewhat done what my father had asked the last few months, and had been careful at every step, there had been many times I'd still been reckless. Gave into temptation.

Several times a week at least, I would sneak into Soleil Theater, to watch her practice. Made sure, even if I couldn't teach her myself, she was still learning. And much to my satisfaction, she improved every day. Occasionally, I'd follow her after seeing her in a hallway, to have some little shred of knowledge she was alright, despite everything. I'd done my best to be careful. But I was lying. I still cared, far more than I should have.

And as usual, my father was steps ahead of me. "If what you were saying were true, I don't care one way or another at this point." The fact my father glazed over his suspicions of me made me all the more concerned. "I'm not asking much of you. You'll attend her next lesson. Say you're sitting in to observe or whatever suits you. I need you to check on her. See if she says anything at all to you. Specifically in regards to you or the Moreaus in general."

"What are you talking about?" I asked, though I assumed it would be a futile question.

"Let me know what you find out," my father replied, simply. Then he honed in on me again. "And know, if I find out any differently, what I said to you before still holds true. Don't think I won't remove her and send her home. You've both already broken the rules as it is. I'm being lenient at this point. This isn't anything dire—I'm checking in."

It was bullshit, of course. I knew better. But I humored him anyway. "Fine."

Between the horrible anxiety he had given me and the headache I was getting from having to sit in the cloud of rancid cigar fumes, I started to flee from the room as fast as I possibly could.

Something stopped me moments before I reached the door. I almost didn't catch it. But it had stopped me dead in my tracks the moment I saw it. Took the air right from my lungs.

Sitting on my father's bookshelf was the journal from my nightstand. The one which had been missing the last few months. The one I had sworn Cassandra had taken from me. I knew it was what I'd been looking for since the emblem on the outside was the original logo for Cirque du Lys. And there was a tiny bend on the far right corner of the leather cover.

The journal was one of a few small things I had gotten from my grandmother, Lily, before she'd passed away. The only thing which had actually been entirely mine and not dangled over me by my father, like her circus had been. Something I treasured more than most things.

It was the reason I'd become so rattled when I'd thought Cassandra had taken it. My concern as to why she'd done it had been another thing, but it had been so small in comparison, it hadn't mattered.

Staring at it now, sitting on the bookshelf, I spun with a whirlwind of emotions. Fought off the urge to turn around and confront my father head-on. If he had it in his office, if it had been with him the entire time, then somehow, he must have been in my home without my knowledge of it. That fact alone left me so rattled I could hardly stand it. However, I wouldn't say a word to him. Not then. Not until I'd had time to think.

I wasn't sure what to do, if there was anything I could do. Whatever my father was looking for, while it might have been small, maybe less significant than I was worried it was, it was something regardless. Something which left me greatly unsettled and knowing my attempts to keep Cassandra safe hadn't been working.

As I left his office and headed for Tremblay Hall, my first thought was to find Cassandra. Without a shadow of a doubt, I knew exactly where she was this time of day. It was where I had sometimes gone to spend a few moments with her without her knowing. Any excuse to watch her talent from afar.

It might not have been the best idea, might have been a terrible idea, but I needed to see her. This couldn't wait. I had to do something. If my father had only wanted something small from her, something small from me, the fact he wanted anything at all was enough to leave me concerned. I had to act. I couldn't do nothing.

So, I did the first thing I could think of. I went to her, intending to tell her as much as I could afford to. To explain the singular reason I had pushed her away. The only reason I had been so concerned about her months ago. Otherwise, nothing would have stopped me. If it had been as simple as keeping it a secret to keep me from getting fired, I likely wouldn't have cared. I would have taken the risk.

The fact it was so much more complicated, and now it seemed as if she was somehow woven in, made it all the more imperative I couldn't keep it from her. Not anymore. I hoped if I told her enough, she'd be able to help me. Because honestly, I didn't know what to do. Had absolutely no idea what he possibly could have wanted from her, and maybe she did.

Minutes later, having jogged nearly the entire way from the building adjacent to Tremblay Hall all the way to the doors of Soleil Theater, I immediately went inside. I didn't want to waste any more time. When I stepped through the doors, I saw Cassandra working on the stage in the center of the room. But what had me stopping the door behind me, and trying to remain quiet, had been the fact she wasn't alone.

The small group she'd been with that evening at the pizza place, including Alex and, much to my annoyance, Henry, and whoever the other girl had been, were all sitting around her on the stage. Talking together while Cassandra was focused on something with the silks. Little tricks I would have been more interested in if I hadn't been so panicked.

It was certainly not what I wanted to interrupt. My sudden arrival might prompt more questions I didn't need. More attention would make things worse. I needed Cassandra alone, so I had to be patient. There was no other option. I had already gotten her weaved into all of this mess, and I couldn't afford adding anyone else. Especially not people she cared about. Including Henry, despite how much it annoyed me.

I had been about to leave the room, to wait somewhere outside until they left. Find the first opportunity to get to her, to get us to a place where I could speak to her alone. Off campus. My first thought had been to take her to The Crucible if she'd let me. It felt like the only place I knew, with nearly full confidence, would be safe.

Cassandra spoke, stopping me in my tracks. I'd made it far enough into the room to hear them talking, though it had been hard to make it out entirely. But I had caught what she had said, and I had almost ran into the room despite her friends bei ng there.

"I'm going to go back to Nevada," Cassandra had announced to her friends. I watched her walk across the stage, leaving the silks she'd been at. "I can't take it anymore. Professor Larson is a joke. I honestly can run circles around her. I miss Chandler."

For a few seconds, I stood there reflecting on those last few words she'd spoken. I had missed her too, nearly every single day regretting I'd made the decisions I had. Then my mind came back. The professor Cassandra had been referring to, was the individual she'd been placed with to avoid me. And she'd been absolutely right. Being barely into her career, she far exceeded Elizabeth Larson's abilities. I had known from the minute I'd found out about it. There were many nights it kept me up out of frustration.

"Cassie," Alex argued with her. "You absolutely cannot go back there. What the hell are you thinking? It's not safe there. Even if he is in prison. You got here after everything. This is your dream. You can't give up now."

I hadn't known what Alex meant regarding her safety. Truthfully, it barely fazed me. I was too distracted by the fact she was planning on leaving. Not only because I couldn't imagine her ever doing so, but also because, if she did, it would be much more difficult to protect her. From whatever I'd so carelessly gotten her into with my father.

My mind was racing. I was literally seconds from acting, running into the theater to argue with her otherwise. But I knew the consequences. There was no way in hell I could do it, no matter how panicked I was. There had to be another way. Something I could do right then, potentially deferring this plan of hers.

Then, thank God, it occurred to me. Just an hour ago, the answer had been right in front of me. All at once, my thoughts settled. I felt my body calm a minuscule amount.

I knew exactly what I needed to do. While it may not have been a permanent solution, it could be enough for now. Enough for me to be able to figure out a way to stay steps ahead of my father before anything else happened. Enough to ensure I could keep Cassandra safe. It had been almost the perfect timing.

And I needed Sebastian Taylor to do it.

CHAPTER 17

CASSANDRA

The two months that had passed since I'd last stepped in the classroom with Chandler Moreau, since the last words I'd spoken to him, were some of the worst of my entire life. While I'd never had a serious intimate relationship that had left me in heartbreak before, I imagined what I'd felt every moment after the last altercation with Chandler must have been exactly what it was like.

Except it was as if I was experiencing it over and over again. Not only the loss of someone I'd genuinely started to care about, who I had thought cared about me, but also the loss of a person who had been the centerpiece of my life for as long as I could remember. The loss of a dream I'd had since I was a kid. The loss of the career I'd wanted past my life at Dreamers Academy—the one I had wanted with Cirque du Lys.

The loss of my mentor.

It was unbearable. Crushing me further every single day.

And while I had been angry with Chandler that day in his classroom, while I'd wanted to be done with him, to never look back—I wouldn't have done it. Couldn't have done it, no matter how hard I tried. If he had shown a solitary second of remorse for his behavior, if he had come to me after, I wouldn't have hesitated. There wasn't a human on the planet I had been more devoted to in my entire life, and Chandler hadn't realized. Wouldn't have ever known. It didn't matter. If he'd come back to me, I would have let him.

The absolute worst part of it was, the part which felt devastating beyond belief, was he never did. He stayed away from me. Disappeared, like he'd completely forgotten I'd existed at all. Gabriel had found me another mentor to study under, who had only made it worse with how blatantly I ran circles around her. I wished I would have never gone to him at all, wished I would have attempted to sort things out with Chandler on my own.

Truthfully, I had tried. Many times I went to look for him. I thought I might have gone as far as to beg him to not leave. It couldn't be the way it all ended, not after everything. But everywhere I looked, every attempt I made, it was like he was purposefully absent. He wanted nothing more to do with me.

Sometimes my imagination seemed to play tricks on me, with how much I longed for him to be there. I would sometimes feel like he was with me in Soleil Theater when I was practicing, watching me in the darkness of the audience. Got a little chill when I'd do a certain sequence, hearing the ways I thought he'd critique me about it in my mind.

Occasionally, I'd wander down a hall and assume I saw him out of the corner of my eye. Desperately looked, but no one was there. Only me, alone. Having lost so much in my life now, it was breaking me into a million pieces I would never recover from.

Nearly every day since I would spend my time outside school locked away in my apartment. Lost in a million thoughts. Today was much the same after I'd left my friends at Soleil Theater. Except today, I'd finally reached my breaking point. I didn't think I could stay in Acrefort any longer. It was too agonizing, pining after a man who had clearly vanished, taking my hopes and dreams along with him. There wasn't a reason for me to be there anymore.

I was sprawled out across the old and somewhat uncomfortable twin mattress I'd been sleeping on for months, staring up at the wobbly ceiling fan, when I heard my phone ring. It was an Acrefort area code, but I didn't know the number.

Eventually, they left a voicemail message. I decided to check it, though I'd been feeling more and more unsettled lately and felt a surge of anxiety when I did. Especially after the confrontation with Chandler's father months prior. I'd been working with Andre Morales, the shifty guy who had also been helping me with my uncle. While I hadn't been able to pay him much, and he hadn't divulged too much information, the little bits I was learning about Gabriel worried me.

Before I'd gotten to the Dreamer's Academy, I'd known some about the Moreaus. Purposefully, of course, because I felt like I needed every shred of information about Chandler I could consume. Inevitably, with it came information about his family.

Everything I'd learned about Gabriel before led me to believe he wasn't the greatest person. Assumed he was probably a bit of a shady type. Andre, however, made me realize it was substantially more. Chandler's father was likely involved with dangerous people doing dangerous things. What, exactly, I wasn't sure. But I knew he wasn't safe. Which had me all the more worried for Chandler at every turn.

When the voicemail started, it brought my focus back to the room. I was surprised to find it was my new aerial instructor for the last few months.

"Cassandra, this is Elizabeth Larson. Abigail Little gave me your number. I was calling to let you know someone will be subbing for me for your next lesson. It's been moved to this evening. They know what we've been going over, but either way... Keep working on those techniques we went over last time. I'll see you next week."

The last thing I had wanted was to go to lessons. Especially tonight. I had every intention of calling in sick, still highly debating if I was going to get the hell out of Acrefort. But when Professor

Larson had left me the message, I couldn't help but wonder who was subbing for her. For whatever reason, I found myself hoping if it had been anyone, perhaps it was Chandler.

Which was the only reason I was pacing nervously outside the intricate doors leading into Soleil Theater in the evening. Flip-flopping back and forth if I was making a stupid decision by coming. If I should have stayed away. This was all a mistake.

Eventually, I found the courage to pull open the doors and step inside the theater. Tonight, I was surprised the seats in the audience were lit up, which usually wasn't the case. It showcased the entire room, which I didn't think I'd seen in its entirety since my audition. It had been a long time. I stood looking at all the beautiful architecture for a few minutes, caught off guard.

When my attention came back to the audience, I noticed someone was sitting on the edge of the stage. He'd had his nose buried in papers in his hands, giving no attention to the rest of the room. For whatever reason, I felt like I recognized him. His brownish blonde hair and those green readers sitting on his nose were vaguely familiar.

Despite my reservations, I decided to make my way down to him. Didn't say anything until I'd gotten relatively close by. "Excuse me," I said, and the man looked up the moment I had. "Are you the person substituting for Elizabeth Larson?"

The stranger smiled at me, his eyes glistening behind the glasses. His smile looked familiar, and I didn't understand why. "Ah, if it isn't the infamous Cassandra Blackstone. The gifted aerialist I've been hearing so much about these last few months." I stepped closer to him until I was able to shake the hand he'd outstretched to me. "I'm sitting in for Elizabeth tonight, yes. I wouldn't say I'm substituting so much as—ah—observing, if you will. Sebastian Taylor. Nice to see you again."

"You look so familiar... I'm sorry. I can't place where I know you from."

"I was on your audition committee," he replied to me, still smiling. "Back in the spring. I'm sure that's what you must be thinking of. I doubt you'd recognize me as a ringmaster."

Immediately, I realized I recognized him from both. "The ringmaster from Cirque du Lys! Yes, I know exactly who you are. And I remember you from my audition, too. I didn't recognize you. I was pretty nervous."

"I remember," Sebastian nodded. "We were glad Chandler got roped into those auditions. He certainly saw your potential right off the bat. But yes, I work for Cirque du Lys. I've been with them for years now."

"I know," I replied. "Almost twenty, right? If I remember correctly? You knew Lily?" It had been a while since I'd read about him, but I was pretty sure I was right.

By the look on his face, it was clear I had been. "Chandler wasn't kidding about your dedication, that's for certain." He got up from where he'd been sitting, turning his attention to the silks on the stage. "Now, I'm no master of the silks, but I've been a fan for many years. Thought I'd offer to help tonight and get to see Chandler's protégé in action." He winked at me, and while the flattery was nice, I was a little saddened at the mention of the fact I'd been Chandler's protégé. I hadn't been for months now.

Sebastian clapped his hands together, distracting me. "Let's not dilly-dally, Cassandra. We have an hour together. Let's see what you're made of!" *What I was made of.* Suddenly, I felt confused as to why he was there at all. I decided not to question it. Not yet, anyway.

Instead, I spent the next hour showing off my skills to a person I barely knew. But surprisingly, I'd enjoyed it far more than I had the last two months with Professor Larson. While he didn't know much about the silks, he knew enough little things to keep me focused. Asked enough of me and tried to challenge me. It had been the first time since I'd last worked with Chandler, in which I was actually excited to be working with someone.

When we were wrapping up, I did a final set of movements for Sebastian like he'd asked me to. Feeling a bit on cloud nine. Hopefully, maybe, by some miracle, I could ask him if he'd teach me. Regardless if he hadn't known too much about what he was doing, at least I might not lose my sanity. At least maybe I could still be somewhat excited to be here.

I'd been coming down from the last set of drops, landing softly back on the floor, when I saw him walking down the aisle. For the first time in two months, he was there again. Right in front of me. Seeing him took my breath away.

Chandler Moreau had made himself evident. I watched him, dressed in a Cirque du Lys t-shirt and a pair of black cotton pants, focus his green eyes straight on me. My stomach flipped. We might be speaking to each other in a matter of seconds for the first time in what had felt like a millennium.

"How long have you been there?" I couldn't help but ask him as he drew up next to Sebastian, who'd been standing off the stage watching me.

Sebastian turned, looking over to see Chandler as he approached. "Ah, Chandler! Perfect timing, my friend. We were wrapping up." Sebastian walked over to meet him. "I think she's *wonderful,* like you said. Better than Penelope, but let's not tell her that. I don't think we'll have a problem at all."

I moved away from the silks, heading toward them. Walked down the steps of the stage, feeling perplexed. Like I was an outsider to this whole ordeal between them, and I shouldn't have since they were clearly talking about me. "Is someone going to tell me what the hell is going on?"

Chandler looked at me, and I watched his face soften. It nearly made me crumble straight to the floor. He wore the affectionate gaze I'd been longing for from him for so long now. Something I'd missed so desperately, I hadn't realized how much until I saw it again. And it grew exponentially more surreal when his face broke into a smile.

"Get your things, Cassandra. The three of us are taking a little field trip."

Despite the fact I was mesmerized by him, completely distracted and unable to break away, I still found the ability to reply.

"And where are we going exactly?" I was distracted, but I was also terribly lost. And still had some lingering feelings, like I didn't know whether to trust him after everything. "I'd like to know before I pack up and follow you both. The last time I did something like that—" I stopped myself when I watched Chandler's facial expression shift a little. Paused for a second and rephrased. "I'd appreciate it if someone could clue me in on what's going on."

"An opportunity," Sebastian said, smiling at me broadly. He glanced at Chandler, who was looking back at him. "And much deserved, I'd think."

An opportunity. Evidently, they weren't going to explain anything. And despite my better judgment, I decided to play along. Even if I'd end up regretting it. After seeing Chandler smiling at me like he was, I'd lost sight of anything else.

"Okay then. Lead the way, boys."

While it should have been alarming for a young woman to be following two older men in the darkness of night down the streets across the Dreamer's Academy campus, I'd decided to anyway. We'd headed a few blocks north. It took almost the entire trip before it started to occur to me where the hell we could be going.

The reality hadn't sunk in until we turned the corner onto the strip of buildings, and I saw the top of the white circus tent looming in front of us. I'd passed it a few times since I'd been in town, but never had I been so close to it as I was now and seen it in all its glory.

By the time we'd made it to the front, I was forced to stop. My entire body was in shock. I'd planned to go see their show, of course.

Especially before everything had happened between Chandler and me. I wouldn't have dared miss an opportunity to see him live in the circus I'd wanted to be a part of since I'd first gotten into aerial silks. In Acrefort, the place it started.

And there it was, towering above me. Cirque du Lys. Chandler Moreau's pride and joy. The place I'd been hoping to be part of for so long. It felt like such a faraway dream until the moment I was standing there.

"Is this real?" I said, still unable to move from where I was standing.

"Yes, Cassandra," Chandler replied. Both he and Sebastian had stopped, letting me take it in. I watched him take a few steps forward, turning around to face me.

Those green eyes locked on to mine. His face was still softer than I'd seen it in a long time. And calm, too. "No student, not even some of our best graduate students, has gotten the opportunity to come inside of this building during our rehearsal time. This is very much a privilege."

It had been an understatement, to say the least. I tried to repeat what he said to me back to myself. Tried to process it. "We're going inside?"

Chandler nodded, and I blinked, my mind racing. Wondering why I was an exception to this rule. Why everything over the last hour and a half had occurred. I didn't dwell on it long, watching as the two of them started off again, and I followed along quickly.

Straight inside the building.

I had seen thousands of pictures and videos of the place. It paled in comparison to seeing it as I walked through the front doors. The lobby, which had been recently updated to a more modern design reminiscent of Chandler's condo, was mesmerizing, even empty. But, reality didn't truly hit me until we'd gone into the center of the building. The place where all the magic happened. The audience. The stage itself.

While it didn't have the architecture Soleil Theater had, the wild feeling of being under a gigantic circus tent, despite it having been made to be a permanent structure, was far more exciting to me than the theater had been. I admired the lights above, the ones Abby had installed. Took in the beautiful lush red seating throughout the room.

And I stood enthralled, looking at the stage. Most of the performers were hard at work at rehearsals. I knew nearly all of them, outside of maybe one or two newer ones I hadn't kept up with. I'd been so completely distracted, so incredibly mesmerized and unable to do anything but stare in every direction, I hadn't noticed Abigail approaching.

"Cassie!" She shouted as she reached me. I was pulled into a hug, which I graciously returned. Thomas had been following alongside her, playfully ruffling my hair a bit. "Oh, I'm glad you got over here safe and sound. I guess Sebastian liked you after all. All of us assumed he would. I thought it was the perfect idea. I can't believe neither of us thought of it sooner. Thank God for Chandler, I suppose."

"What are you talking about?" I asked her, blinking. Now, standing in this theater, I felt as confused as when I had left the school. Wondering what the hell was going on. Thought perhaps maybe they'd let me watch a rehearsal. For what reason, I had no idea. It was the only thing I could think of.

"They didn't tell you?" Abigail studied me, and I shook my head in reply. Her attention darted toward Chandler and Sebastian, who had been talking amongst themselves behind us. "You let her walk all the way over here without knowing what she was getting into? The poor thing! You both were giving her all sorts of unnecessary anxiety..."

"We want you to take the place of our old aerialist," Thomas explained to me, when I'd almost been at the point of demanding someone tell me. "Penelope started working with the acrobats, and we need someone to replace her. With the shows coming up in a month and all..."

"And Chandler made the wonderful suggestion a few hours ago—it should be you!" Abigail said, beaming at me. "It made perfect sense. Beats trying to scramble for a replacement when we had such obvious talent right in front of us."

I looked over my shoulder, back toward Chandler, who had been looking back at me. The look on his face was still gentle. He looked like he was smiling a little, though it had been subtle. I might have returned the look had I not still been in complete disbelief.

"You want me to replace Penny?" I knew who Abigail had been talking about. She'd been working with Chandler at the show since Jeanne had left.

"Only if you feel up to it, of course," Thomas said. "I realize it's a lot to ask, and you'd have to catch up quickly since we're coming up fast on the show. But I don't think I've ever seen Chandler so confident as he was pitching you. Maybe with the exception of when he was doing it after your audition." He smiled at me and glanced at Chandler.

Once again, I looked back at Chandler, feeling stunned. He'd been looking at Sebastian, but he was smiling, and I savored every second of it. Couldn't believe he'd been speaking so highly of me to all of his colleagues. It was flattering. But still, I felt strange accepting the offer. Considering hours ago, I wanted to flee Acrefort for good. To get out of this mess I'd gotten in.

"I don't know if I'm ready," I admitted, though it hadn't really been the reason. While I wasn't one hundred percent confident in myself, I wasn't lacking in confidence. I was sure I could make it work if I put enough effort in. But it was the only thing I could think of to say, which wasn't anything damning Chandler or myself.

"Cassandra, a word," I heard Chandler say, and my attention darted back to him. He was staring intently, motioning away from the group which had gathered around us. Despite everything, I followed after him.

He stopped once we'd moved far enough from the group, and it was just the two of us. "I didn't put in a good word for you to let you squander it." While I expected him to be annoyed, he looked the same as he had the entire time I'd seen him. Calm. Steady.

"Why exactly did you put a good word for me?" I rebutted. Chandler didn't look the least bit fazed. "You could have picked anyone. There are people who would have come from everywhere to get this kind of opportunity. Yet your first instinct was to pick me?"

"Because I know how talented you are," Chandler replied, his gentle facial expression unwavering. "I know how much you have to give. I wanted you to have the opportunity. And, as much as you may be thinking about pissing it in the wind, I'm not going to let you go back to Nevada."

"I am not—" I stopped when I realized he'd mentioned Nevada. "How the hell did you know about Nevada?" I blinked, completely confused. The only time I'd mentioned it had been a few hours earlier in the theater. Unless somehow he'd been in there with us when I'd said it, and I hadn't realized it. I wouldn't have put it past him.

"I'll explain later, I promise," Chandler assured me. After everything, I truly believed him. "But right now, we have work to do. I have to get you up to speed in a month, and while I know you're capable, I also know you have a lot to learn. Things I want to be able to teach you."

It hadn't mattered in those moments that I didn't understand how he knew about Nevada. Didn't matter about those two months I'd been so upset with him or how angry he made me in the classroom before it had all happened. When he'd made me leave the night at his condo. Absolutely nothing mattered except those simple words he'd spoken to me.

My entire world, everything I had wanted for so long, all my dreams and my hopes, all came rushing back to me. When the man I had admired more than anything stood there, with a fond look on his face, completely as wrapped up in me as I was with him. And he'd said those words to me.

You have a lot to learn. Things I want to be able to teach you.

"I can't tell you how much I've wanted to hear those words from you," I said, hardly able to say it, still barely able to process what was happening.

Chandler reached out, and I watched him, in one gentle motion of his fingers, sweep the hair away from my face, and tuck it behind my ear. Something he'd done a few times now, and I knew I would never get sick of it. He held his hand against my cheek, staring at me. "I'm sorry it took so long for me to say it."

All at once, there was commotion behind us, the group we'd left behind calling us back to them. Breaking Chandler and me from the small moment we'd had. It didn't matter. It was all I needed.

"What do you say, Cassandra?" Thomas called to me as Chandler and I made our way back to them. "Ready for the big leagues?" And all I could do was smile back at him, feeling as light and as happy and as absolutely whole as I'd been in a long time.

CHAPTER 18

CHANDLER

Watching Cassandra Blackstone weave amongst the performers rehearsing beneath the white canopy of my grandmother's circus as she made her way up to the sets of silks for the first time was like living some sort of familiar dream. Very distinctly, I remembered the first time I had come into this room as a performer.

It was one thing to have watched from the audience my entire childhood. Another thing entirely when I was finally invited to cross that threshold and step into the massive arena at the center. A new world. And, perhaps, I relished watching Cassandra even more than I had enjoyed my own experience.

I let her lead the way, allowing her to take time to savor it all. Truthfully, I'd been just as happy watching her hazel eyes, wide and eager to take every little nuance of it in. I could hardly imagine what it must have been like. Someone who probably knew more tiny little details about this building than even I knew, getting to experience it all for the first time.

There would be no way I would rush her, no matter how eager I happened to be.

Some of my colleagues introduced themselves as we passed. She didn't immediately go straight to the silks, instead wandering the perimeter. Soon, she'd get to see this entire show in action as one cohesive unit. The experience of a performance with Cirque du Lys was unlike anything else.

However, I imagined my absolute favorite thing was what was bound to happen any minute now. When she finally found her way to those beautiful sets of fabrics on the far side of the room. And while I intended to be as patient as she wanted, I admittedly was far more excited about the idea than I was outwardly expressing.

Or, maybe I'd been expressing it more than I'd thought.

Cassandra looked at me and proceeded to point out the ridiculous-looking smile I'd had on my face. I had nearly forgotten every single thing which had been worrying me, overcome with the sheer joy of giving someone so deserving of it exactly what she wanted.

"You look happier than I am," she said, breaking me from my thoughts. I'd been watching her, trailing behind, as she walked around. A casual observer, just enjoying the experience. When I focused on Cassandra, who had stopped to look back at me, she was also smiling. "I don't ever think I've seen you look this happy. And I've seen an embarrassing amount of photos and videos of you over the years."

I couldn't help but laugh and shrug, having stopped beside her. We were maybe two dozen feet away from the silks, and I watched as her head turned in their general direction. She looked up, high above us, to where they were suspended on the beams in the catwalks near the ceilings.

"You've never gone that high before," I said, drawing up behind her, and placing my hands on her shoulders. She still was looking up when I continued speaking. "The silks at Dreamers go seventy feet. This is another fifteen." I paused until she had turned her attention to look up at me. "Do you think you can handle it?"

The smile on her face widened. “I’m more worried about you, actually. Down here having a panic attack every time I do a Rainbow Marchenko.”

I realized it hadn’t occurred to her yet. She was still thinking of herself as a student, practicing on the stage in Soleil Theater. I had purely been her instructor. The man admiring her from the wings.

Now, it would be so much more.

I must have been smiling even more ridiculously than before because she looked back up at me, both confused and amused simultaneously. “What are you smiling about now?”

I nodded back to the silks, watching her head turn back to them. Leaned in to place my head beside hers, my mouth near her ear. “Cassandra… I’ll be up there with you.”

When I had thought I couldn’t have been enjoying her entire experience any more than I had, completely wrapped up in everything about it, it had peaked then. I watched her take a step away, letting my hands drop from her shoulders. She twisted around to face me. Those beautiful eyes of hers locked onto mine, her face so in awe. I felt like I was looking at an excited, mesmerized kid on Christmas morning.

“Really?” Cassandra sounded in complete disbelief. Like, despite how talented she truly was, somehow she couldn’t realize it. Even if it had been obvious. She didn’t understand how much she deserved this. I’d been a little biased in my decision with my feelings for her, I was certain. But every single one of my colleagues knew it, too.

“Come on,” I said, reaching out, and wrapping my hand in her own. Our hands had come together on a few occasions, and every time I’d been aware of it. But this time, it had felt like such a natural thing to do.

Finally, she let me lead her to those beautiful pieces of fabric hanging in the air. And we stood there again, enjoying their presence in the room. I appreciated there was someone in the world who loved them in all their simplicity as much as I did.

My patience had started waning. Only because she'd made it exactly where I'd wanted to be. And the only thing I needed in those moments was to do what I had wanted to do from the moment I first saw her at her audition in Tremblay Hall.

The one thing I knew she wanted more than anything, too.

"Let me show you what we've been working on," I said. Cassandra turned to look at me, holding onto those silks, as wide-eyed and eager as I'd ever seen her. Ready to do whatever I asked. I'd give her everything I could.

We started on the ground for a while. Talked through the routine together, everything Penelope and I had been doing. I played her the songs we'd chosen over my phone for a few minutes, letting her listen.

"'The Flower Duet,'" Cassandra said, barely a few measures into the opening. She met my eyes momentarily, her face splitting into a smile. "I love this song. It's beautiful. It's your favorite opera song, right? I remember reading it somewhere."

The minute she'd made the observation, I couldn't help but laugh again. I shouldn't have been the least bit surprised.

"I changed this today," I replied, smiling softly back at her. She raised a brow. "Do you remember your audition? The song you chose from *Serse*?" The curious look on her face still lingered. She nodded, and I continued. "I can't tell you the last time I watched a performance, heard the music with it, and it made me experience things like what I did watching you with that song."

My mind drifted back to Soleil Theater, watching Cassandra high in the silks as the aria wrapped around the room. I stayed there for a few seconds before I came back, focusing on her.

"I realized earlier I wanted that again. It was what's been missing for me for so much of my life with these performances. I've been so wrapped up in the technicalities, trying to perfect every little thing. When you chose that song that day, when I was watching you, it was so undeniably obvious what I had been missing for so long."

"What was that?" Cassandra asked me, watching as I wrapped my hand around the silk adjacent to hers, leaning into her a little. Neither of us paid an ounce of attention to anything else in the entire room.

"You made me *feel* something again," I said, simply. "Which I'm not quite sure would have happened had you not shown up. And after knowing you were going to be here, that we were going to get this opportunity together—I wanted you to have that, too."

I paused for a second, realizing how wrapped in the silks we were, buried in a sea of all the fabrics. We stayed there, both silent. The world was going on noisily around us, but it was like a distant memory.

"Okay. Let's go." I finally spoke. Breaking us from the little moment we were having, but realizing, too, I'd grown impatient. I couldn't wait any longer.

Cassandra transformed before my eyes in the next minute or so. Still my student, still willing and eager to listen to me. But at the same time, she'd become something else entirely. Something I didn't think I'd ever truly have the way I had imagined if my career didn't completely end after the accident had happened.

When you were high in the air in those fabrics, dangling precariously, the only person you needed there with you was someone you trusted. Someone who was right beside you, in perfect unison. The person who could predict how you'd react before you even did. Someone who knew you backwards and forwards.

Despite every doubt I'd had since I'd first started out in this theater, it had somehow finally happened. I'd found my partner.

Somehow we'd both made it happen years and years ago, when I'd still been a young and learning performer, and she'd been eagerly admiring me from afar. Watching me, her entire life had turned upside down because of me. And I was grateful because mine had been now, too.

"Let's try something. Improvise, maybe?" I asked her, feeling like I'd been stuck in my head far too long, trying to savor every second of this. Like at any point, I might wake up, and it had been a dream.

She nodded to me, smiling, hands still wrapped around the silks.

"We'll be up high," I gently reminded her. Making sure I had her undivided focus before I continued, which was a remarkably easy thing to do. She'd honed in on me like I had been the only thing in the room. Me and the silks.

I watched her settle in front of the fabrics she'd chosen, a pair of vibrant green ones. Her hand flowed through them, wrapping it in a fist. Eyes locking onto it, everything else disappearing in the room around her.

Behind me, I searched for Sebastian. He had been busy talking to another performer, but he met my eyes within a few seconds. I motioned up toward the speakers on the ceiling without calling out to him. He seemed to understand what I meant and walked off.

My attention turned to Cassandra, who was breathing steadily. Her eyes had still been focused on the silks, trying to prepare herself. When the strings began to play over the sound system within the theater, I watched her head shoot up toward the ceiling. Paused for just a second or two, surprised to have heard it all around us.

I hadn't needed to prompt her. She began, pulling herself upward, drawing those silks around her small frame as she went. Climbing high into the air as the two women began their duet. The French lyrics pulled me in every time. It was perhaps one of the reasons that while I simply tolerated most opera songs I'd heard, I adored this song.

Every time I heard it, every time I got lost in those little nuances of the language, it brought me back to summertime in Melun, France. Playing on the hills overlooking the city, lost in the grasses filled with wildflowers. Climbing into Meme's apple trees. Perhaps the time in my life when it had felt so simple. All there were, were the memories of when I'd been happy.

And if there was any place I wanted to be, as I watched Cassandra ascending above me, knowing in seconds I would be right beside her, it was in those memories again. Bringing her with me.

The first stanza finished, and my mind immediately centered. My hands had already been wrapped in the silks without having to think about it. She paused, and I saw her attention drift downward. We fell captive to one another, and it was all I needed to see. I knew it was my turn to go to her. She was waiting for me.

In the same fashion she had moments earlier, I began my way up the silks beside hers, which had been a deep royal purple color. The entire time I made my way high into the room, I immersed myself in the French lyrics, the strings complimenting every rise and fall of the two women's voices. Some moments, I'd lose myself in what I was doing, taking careful note of all the little adjustments my body was making. Other times, my attention drifted upward. Until finally, I was just beneath Cassandra.

When I paused again, I took a few deep breaths, steadying myself. Focused entirely on the beautiful woman above me, who was just as attentive to me. I nodded to her, signaling I was ready, prepared to follow her in whatever she had thought to do next.

At the precise moment when I had met her, she had already begun moving herself into a sailor pose above me, legs splitting, and much to my satisfaction, every single part of her in perfect position. All the small details I'd shown her the first lesson we'd had together were as pristine as when I'd helped her myself.

I would have taken more time to truly enjoy how proud of her I felt if she hadn't twisted downward, dropping her torso straight toward me in a graceful fall. Before she'd completed it, I knew what she'd done. A Rainbow Marchenko. A famous move of Jeanne's for many years. But watching her as she settled into it, I would have thought it was hers alone.

Cassandra's hands dropped, releasing the silks. Dangling inches away. The only thing holding her in the air was the precise folds of those green fabrics wrapped around her legs.

Looking into her eyes as she hung there, waiting for me to act, all I could do was smile. She'd been focused, lost in her own world, but she'd come back to me. We were together again in the very place I had wanted to be with her ever since I'd seen her flying through the silks at her audition. I had dreamt about it every time since, every lesson we had, every time I'd watched her from the shadows of the theater while she practiced.

I had taken her to those fields in Melun with me, high in the trees. Trapped us both in those treasured memories, made all the better knowing she was there.

"I've got you, Cassandra," I called out to her, gently. Steadying myself, my body locked in place. Breathing slow and rhythmic and calm. I watched her take the same breath as I had, waiting for the little drop in the lyrics before the next few lines began.

The moment their voices bellowed into the theater again, she let herself drop in a salto. In a gentle sweep of my body, I caught her gracefully into my arms. Twisted us together, letting the silks take hold of the two of us as we swung across the room, dozens of feet above the stage below us. Falling like two feathers locked together, dancing into the wind.

When the fabrics released us, I swung us outward. Our bodies drifted apart again as she spun around me, both of us still descending toward the floor. As beautiful as she looked, circling outward away from me, the moment she had, I wanted her back. I used my legs to give myself enough momentum to swing forward, latching on again once she'd appeared.

Cassandra had been so close I'd felt her breath against my face while we dangled above the stage. I got lost in the way it felt to be tangled up with her, a mess of bodies and fabric. Consumed by it. Convinced I might never let go of her again.

As we'd traversed the rest of the way back to the stage, I didn't. The two of us descended together as a singular unit, just her and I and the fabrics. Improvising the graceful fall we were doing, finding little tricks and motions to carry out, all the while never leaving her side.

We'd both reached the floor, perfectly in sync with one another. I heard a gentle thump as we landed. Followed by the sound of both of our light, audible breaths. Steadying ourselves back on the ground.

Even having left the air, the silks still wrapped around us. Neither of us had freed ourselves. Cassandra was still in my arms, something I realized, when I hadn't been so caught up in what we were doing all those feet above us, was happening for the very first time.

The sweet smell of oranges overwhelmed me. Her beautiful hazel eyes, those captivating flecks of grays and greens and browns, drowned out the world around us. I watched her breathing softly, holding her to me and those silks holding me to her.

And in those next few moments, every single solitary thing keeping me from her since the day we had met no longer existed in the little reality we were trapped in. Every fear I had, every reservation, disappeared. I tightened her to me, my hands capturing the sides of her face in a gentle sweep, as elegant as every other thing we'd done those last few minutes.

Our mouths fell together, and I lost myself in her. Trapped in those profound and so unbelievably relieving seconds in which the things that had stood in our way no longer mattered.

I hadn't thought anything could have surpassed the experience the two of us just shared. Undeniably, it had been the best minutes I had ever spent in those silks in my entire career. As simple as it had been. And we had barely started. This was only the beginning.

But this moment now was just as wonderful. As perfect as I could have hoped.

Cassandra sighed, her hands drawing up against my face. I lost track of time, wrapped up in every detail, every feeling until we eventually drew apart. I felt my heart still racing, both from our time in the silks and the perfect ending to it we'd shared.

Now that it was over, I remembered there was one more thing. One more thing I had to do before I could truly have some peace. We could finally have everything we'd wanted without anything stopping us anymore.

Both of us untangled ourselves from the silks. I noticed many of the performers had left for the evening. Only a handful left, including my friends, who had been across the room. Apparently they had not noticed what had transpired between Cassandra and me.

"I want you to go to the condo," I said, keeping myself steady despite feeling a whirlwind of emotions. I tried to bring myself down from the high I'd spent the last few minutes of my life in, though it had been the last thing I wanted. "You can get some things from your apartment if you need to. I'll have my driver come pick you up after. But you have to promise me you'll go as soon as you do."

Though she looked confused, Cassandra didn't argue. "I will."

My hand reached up, cupping the side of her face. I leaned in, planting my lips against hers one more time, wanting one more second, trying to hold on to it despite knowing what I had yet to do. She sighed just as we'd split apart again.

"I'll be there soon," I promised her. "We'll talk. I'll explain everything."

While my initial plan had been to take her to The Crucible, assuming it had been the safest option, I'd changed my mind last minute. Wherever we went, I wanted to be with her when we did. I assumed she'd be safe for a few hours until I could get home.

As I walked down the steps out into the audience, I could hear Cassandra following behind me. When I reached for my things lying on a chair, I dug through my bag, pulling out my keycard. Grateful she'd been right behind me, so I could hand it to her.

Surprisingly, she didn't ask questions. She seemed to trust that whatever I was about to do was important.

"Lock both the locks when you get there. Call me and let me know you made it safe." Cassandra's eyes had grown a little wider, and I knew she had to be wondering what the hell was going on. But still, she nodded.

Before I lost all nerve and succumbed to my reservations about what I was going to do, I walked away from her. Threw my bag over my shoulder as I did, heading straight out of the theater with only one thing on my mind.

CHAPTER 19

CHANDLER

With the desire to keep Cassandra under a watchful and familiar eye for the next few hours, I allowed my driver to get her back downtown to my condo. Which was why I had spent the last twenty minutes commuting from Cirque du Lys, in the back of a taxi cab, to the outskirts of Acrefort.

The driver had been one of those who reminded me how grateful I was that this was not a regular occurrence. He'd made every attempt to strike up conversation with me as we went. But I must have been highly disappointing, constantly shooting him down. Far too distracted about what was waiting for me at the other end of the car ride.

By the time we'd arrived, it had started raining outside, though nothing terrible. I stood in it as I paid for the drive and then watched the car disappear back down the road. It was the perfect setting for the mood I was in, ominous and brooding.

The moment the sedan disappeared around the corner, headed back into Acrefort proper, I turned my attention behind me. I'd been standing on a small suburban street lined with street lights and trees and a row of craftsman-style houses. All of which faced out toward the Peace River, which wove around the outskirts of town.

Down the same road, Thomas and Abigail had resided for at least a decade, if not longer. And I wished I was outside their door instead. There were few places I would have hated more to be than standing outside this green and white house with the red front door. Etched into my memories for all the wrong reasons because the last time I had seen it had been before the beginning of the undoing of decades of my life.

Like myself, Patrick Sullivan had grown up in this circus town between the hills of upstate New York. Spent his entire life here, to this day, despite how much Acrefort could be as much a curse as it appeared a blessing. We had been inseparable growing up. While Patrick hadn't come from the lineages of performers like myself or Jeanne had, it had perhaps been one of the things that made him so refreshing. He hadn't been tethered to all of it. Allowed me some semblance of escape from it when necessary.

I had been gracious after everything, even if he still was a ghost haunting me. At least he led his life as far away as possible. Barely in Acrefort now. Outside visits with Thomas and Abigail at their home, I never came out here. My life was deep inside the city.

Except for now, standing there in front of the damn house I had practically grown up in. Left to him by his late parents, both of whom I adored almost as much as the family I'd abandoned in France. Another glimmer of normalcy, which otherwise, I would have never gotten growing up.

This was the place Patrick and I had spent years of our lives together, Jeanne with us, too, assuming it would always be that way. This tiny town would be unable to separate us. Nothing in the world would be able to tear a bond like ours apart.

How very wrong I'd been.

I finally decided to move, not wanting to waste any more time than I already had. Both because it was of the essence, for Cassandra's sake, but also because I had already wasted far too much of it on both Jeanne and Patrick as it was.

Walking up those steps, preparing to knock on the door, they were already taking more time away from me. I despised it, but I had no choice. All this was showing was how, despite my every effort to maintain control of things in my life, the truth of the matter was I never really had it. No matter what I tried to do.

I rang the doorbell the moment I'd been within reach of it. Checked my watch, realizing it was after ten. Hoped my ex-best friend might still potentially have the same night owl tendencies he had in our youth. That either of them would open the door in the first place once they saw who was standing outside.

It had taken an agonizing long length of time, of which I spent fidgeting in place, distracted only by thoughts of wondering if Cassandra had gotten to her apartment safely. If she'd been commuting to my home at that point. The sheer amount of stress in my life over the last few months made me surprised I hadn't lost the remainder of my brown hair yet. That it wasn't all gray.

The red door swung open, and I looked straight into the eyes of a face I hadn't seen in two years. The last time I had, the last seconds I remembered, it had looked in far worse shape than it did now. I'd nearly beaten the shit out of him, blinded with rage. I'd arrived home for the evening, the events playing out like some fucking ridiculous scene from a movie, finding him in the throws, underneath my sheets, in my bed, with my then-wife.

Patrick had been lucky I hadn't killed him. It had been a wonder I hadn't.

While he had certainly aged those last two years since our altercation, gotten a few more gray hairs mixed in with his dark brownish blonde ones, just like I had, he looked much the same as he always did. He'd always been a kind of average-looking guy, next to two humans who had been gifted, though I would be far more inclined to say cursed, with the genetics both Jeanne and I had. He seemed like the type who would never have interacted with us in the first place. But at one point in our lives, we'd been inseparable. Even genetics hadn't divided us.

It wasn't clear how long either of us were just standing there, but at some point, I heard footsteps behind Patrick. A familiar voice calling out to him. Seconds later, Jeanne appeared beside him. Looking so pregnant, I knew she had to be weeks or days from labor. A fact which I didn't want to focus on. Not then, with both of them right in front of me.

As paralyzed as Patrick and I had both been, the expression on Jeanne's face had seemed to indicate she was in a stranger place than we were. While I certainly had no empathy for the woman, given everything she'd done, I could only imagine what could have possibly been going through her mind.

"Chandler?" Jeanne finally broke the silence between us, which had seemed to stretch on far longer than it should have. I should have acted sooner. There wasn't a lot of time for me to sit trapped in an emotional whirlwind. I had things to do. Things of urgency, which didn't need to be worsened by two people who had already made my life hell enough.

"I need to talk to you," I said, staring straight at her. Forcing myself to look at her head-on, because as much as I had convinced myself to hate her, how I'd spent the last few years convincing myself she was as despicable of a human being as members of my own family were, the truth of the matter was, some minuscule piece of me still cared about her. Still had her in a place in my mind where I found some solace in the two decades we'd spent together and that every second of it hadn't been in vain.

And I hoped if I still had held onto that, as tiny of a feeling as it had been, perhaps somewhere inside the infuriating, self-centered brain of hers, she had felt it too. I needed her, if it was possible.

Which is why I was also grateful, as much as I hadn't wanted to see him ever again, Patrick had been there too. Because, after knowing him as long as I had, if he'd been plagued by guilt about this entire situation, if he had any shred of remorse at all, if Jeanne was still not convinced, he might be able to sway her.

"Why? What was so dire you came all the way out here at night?" Jeanne was still locked on me, but I saw a little flicker on her face. She knew me well enough. If I was here like this, after everything we'd been through, whatever I needed to say was of the utmost urgency. I wouldn't have wasted my time otherwise.

"Can I come in for a minute?" I asked, maintaining my eye contact with my ex-wife for a moment before I looked at Patrick. Making every attempt to swallow all the feelings I had when I did, to focus on the matter at hand. Which was Cassandra, and I absolutely couldn't lose sight of that fact. "I won't be long. I just don't feel comfortable discussing it out here."

Jeanne and I gave each other another silent look. One we'd shared so many times over the years, both knowing what I'd meant when I said things like that. While I hated the air she breathed more often than not over the last few years, she was one of only a small handful of people who truly understood many nuances of my life. A life in many ways we both shared, even if it was on different battlefields. It still wove us together at points.

"Fine," Jeanne said, and I watched her wrap her hand around Patrick's arm. My friend had still not said a word to me, which hadn't really surprised me. I'm sure the last person on earth he ever expected to see again was me. The feeling was mutual.

I followed my very pregnant ex-wife as she basically waddled her way across the familiar house to their living room. And as petty as it probably had been, I allowed myself a second to amuse myself with the image, despite everything. Jeanne still had her usual air of authority about her, like the pregnancy was a part of the act. It was convincing.

When we reached the living room, I took a seat in an armchair, while I watched Jeanne and Patrick sit on the loveseat. Both of them were locked onto me, and both looked more concerned than they had when I'd first seen them at the door.

"It's not as dire as you're thinking," I tried to reassure them both, realizing my abrupt appearance, demanding to speak to them, might have led them to think otherwise. Felt a little bad I hadn't clarified sooner. Still, it was dire enough for me. Enough I'd subjected myself to these awful minutes of my life.

"Well, clearly it isn't nothing," Jeanne replied, leaning forward, studying me intently. "I can't imagine a place you'd hate being more right now, except perhaps maybe at your parents' stuffy dinners." If it had been any other circumstances, her empathy for those atrocious obligations my father forced on me might have made me laugh.

There hadn't been time.

"I need your help with an issue with my father," I said. "A simple vote with your seat on the circus board. A minor inconvenience. You and I both know I can't sway anything in my favor if you aren't on board with it. So, I need you to put your gross disdain for me aside and help me, just this once."

"What are you trying to do?" Jeanne asked me, her facial expression having remained stoic. She at least hadn't shot me down already, which I was grateful for. But I also didn't want to answer because, knowing her well enough, I was certain she'd have zero desire to help me.

"I hired a new aerialist for Cirque du Lys," I tried to explain, treading as carefully as I possibly could. "Someone to replace Penelope. She's finished her acrobatic training and wanted to transition. We needed a replacement, quickly, with the winter shows coming up."

"You couldn't have called me about this?" Jeanne stared at me, looking in disbelief now. Like she didn't understand me at all. "Is the entire show crumbling apart or something? What is it you found so urgent you had to come running to our doorstep? I'm sure there's more to it than you need a simple board vote, Chandler. And if you want me to help, you're going to have to tell me what's going on."

"Because without your vote, as much as I hate this, my father will have the final say in the decision." I paused a minute, watching Jeanne's blue eyes honed in on me. Patrick looked as if he was trying to figure me out, too. "And he absolutely cannot. I have every single other person willing to help me. All I need is you, as inconvenient as it is for both of us, I realize."

There was a long, drawn-out silence then, in which I had some minuscule hope my ex-wife wouldn't press me further. She would do as I asked, maybe with the desire to get away from me as soon as possible and end this horribly awkward encounter.

I should have known her better, as easily as she knew me. Jeanne locked eyes with me again.

"We all know what I think of your father after everything he and Elliott have done to my family," Jeanne started, and I swallowed deeply at the mention. While I had never been directly involved with any of it, I knew it was one of the many reasons our marriage had been destroyed. After everything, it seemed impossible for it to have continued.

"But this clearly has little to do with Gabriel. You're making your normal attempt at bullshitting me right now, and I know you know better than to think you're succeeding."

Jeanne leaned forward toward me more, and I absolutely hated the look on her face. She knew how right she was. She was about to get exactly what she wanted. Because I was desperate, and she wanted to dangle it over me like she normally did.

"I want to know what the hell is making you so desperate to be showing up at our doorstep in the middle of the night. I know you hate your father as much as I do, but that's not what this is about. I am not an idiot, Chandler. I'm familiar with all these little Moreau games."

"They're certainly not any worse than the Tremblay games," I retorted, finding myself glaring back at her, unable to take her tone and the way she'd spoken to me. "Don't act like you're so high and mighty, Jeanne. I'll stop with the bullshitting, fine, but you're as tainted with shitty genetics as I am, and you know it."

The two of us sat glaring, playing an internal game with each other we had a million times over the course of our divorce proceedings. Trying to determine who could outsmart who, though we both were hurting regardless. It was a completely pointless game which didn't solve anything at all. But I suppose when two people were in pain and coming at each other the way we had over the last few years, it sort of drug you in eventually until you'd lost sight of everything else.

As much as I hated it, I was thankful for Patrick's presence. Or else nothing might have ever gotten solved. Jeanne and I would have spent an indefinite amount of time sparring with each other, still trapped in all this emotional baggage of ours which had been lying around for years.

"Chandler, what do you need from us?" Patrick asked me. He hadn't said a word since my arrival, but the words he spoke then were a welcome reminder of the person he'd used to be for me.

The tone he used was calm and collected, far more than Jeanne and I had been. He had his usual air of calmness about him, which, perhaps, was what I assumed had attracted Jeanne to him. She and I had always been a whirlwind of emotions and chaos. It came with the territory, living the lives we had, with the family we had.

Patrick was a refreshing reminder of normalcy.

I shook my head, leaning back into the chair I'd been sitting in. Relaxing my shoulders, which I hadn't noticed had gotten so tense in the last few minutes, they were actually hurting. I shook my head, trying to steady myself. To admit to both of them the reason I was really there. Which I knew if I did, it was highly unlikely Jeanne would have any interest in helping me at all. But I'd try anyway, regardless.

"I'm trying to help someone," I admitted, first looking at Patrick and then, as much as I hadn't wanted to, to Jeanne. "Someone I care about, who seems to have my father's undivided and unwelcome attention at the moment. I was trying my best to protect her."

"You're stalling, Chandler—" Jeanne started, clearly annoyed with me.

"Cassandra Blackstone. My student. The one from the auditions in the spring." It felt like I'd nearly shouted at her to get it out. All the air had left me for a moment. "I need you to vote to let her work for Cirque du Lys. If you don't, my father will ensure it doesn't happen. And I'm not quite sure what else he'll do. As usual, I can never get ahead of him. All I know is I need this. I need you to have some ounce of empathy here and help me."

Jeanne pondered after I'd said what I said. I watched her facial expression shift over the course of a minute. It had been expressionless, but then suddenly she seemed to have come to the realization of who I'd been talking about. "The silk aerialist? The one you were so clearly infatuated with? That's her, right?"

Despite my every desire not to, I nodded. "Jeanne, you saw her exactly as I did. She's beyond talented. Deserves a career. She's wanted this since she was a child. Wanted to attend our school, be in our circus..." I tried my best to hold steady, as emotional as it was making me think at any moment, I could have stripped it from her. "My father is trying to take that from her, and she doesn't deserve it. I can't allow him to do it. And if you have any shred of decency in you, if you can remember how excited you were about her, like the rest of us, maybe you could listen to me and do this. I'm not asking a lot. A vote from you, that's all."

"Why is your father trying to get rid of her, then? What could she possibly be doing that is so threatening? Is she involved with your father's bullshit? Does it have to do with that?"

"No, no, nothing like that," I assured her. Cassandra was as far removed from the chaos Jeanne and I lived in as I could imagine. In fact, it had been my own guilt about wrapping her up in all of the shadows of my family and my life which had been more concerning. I completely trusted Cassandra.

Jeanne studied me again, trying to get a read on me. I prayed I wouldn't have to elaborate further because, after everything, if I did, I was sure she wouldn't humor me. But, as unsurprised as I should have been, she seemed to figure it out before I had the need to say anything at all.

"You have feelings for her," she decided, her gaze on me locked on again. "I know the look on your face right now. It's been a long time since I've seen it, but I know it. I know exactly what this is. You went and pissed him off because you were breaking rules by falling for a student, and now he's threatening to kick her from the program. You did this all to yourself, and now you're panicking that you ruined a gifted student's career because of it."

How I hated, with every fiber of my being, every single solitary word coming out of her mouth had been true. I had absolutely no words of which to argue with her. But I was desperate. And more so, I was still worried about my father. Even if he had been pissed at me and followed protocol.

Maybe that had been true. But I would never rest confident that every single move he made didn't have a thousand reasons behind it. Far more than the obvious ones.

"If that's all it is, if that's what is truly happening, then fine." I sucked in a deep breath of air, feeling mortified to have to admit she was right. "I fucked up, Jeanne. I made a mistake. A terrible one, of which I am regretting beyond measure."

Each word of admittance to her was like it was stabbing and twisting itself into me. "Please don't let my lapse in judgment be the end of the woman's career. If any shred of you has any decency at all, you won't let it happen. You're an aerialist. You've lived this life for decades, like me. And I know you saw her talent in the theater. I know you know a fate like that would be a disservice not only to her, but to everyone who wouldn't get to experience her talent. Please, I am begging you. Help me protect her and her career."

The three of us sat there for a long while, none of us speaking. I tried to distract myself, with the agonizing wait for her decision, by admiring the room we were in. Reflecting on all the good memories I had there growing up. Saddened how it all ended.

Much to my surprise, it wasn't Jeanne who spoke, but instead Patrick. "We'll put in the vote for her, Chandler."

Jeanne's head immediately snapped in his direction, eyes growing wide. "I didn't agree to this. Last I checked, Patrick, it was *my* seat on the board. Not yours."

Patrick turned to her then, and I watched him somehow soften her. After all the years we'd been married, it was something I had never been able to do. Perhaps it had to do with his nature. How it was the perfect compliment to personalities like my ex-wife and my own, in its way to lure us down from those precarious cliffs we often put ourselves on.

As much time as I had spent hating him over the last few years, all I could do was sit in awe as I watched him manage to speak reason to her. Despite everything. He was somehow able to tether us both together, to sort through all the chaos we'd built around ourselves and see the forest from the trees.

"Jeanne, what if it had been you?" Patrick asked her. I had nearly left the room, they were so lasered in on one another. "If it had been Gabriel Moreau threatening your career? I don't know this woman you two are talking about, outside recalling you mentioning her auditions. And I am pretty sure you were as excited about her as you were saying Chandler was. It had been a long time since I'd seen you that enthusiastic about a student. It was refreshing."

I was surprised to hear it, among the many things which were catching me off guard. If Jeanne had seen through my infatuation with Cassandra the day in Soleil Theater, I hadn't been alone in it. She, too, had been engulfed in her career for decades. Jeanne saw talent as clearly as I did. It was perhaps one of the few things she and I actually had so much in common. The only thing holding us together after so much time hating one another. Our love for our careers.

Jeanne, who had her attention focused on Patrick for a while, trying to absorb what he was saying, eventually turned to look back at me. Her face, which had been more intense before, had softened a great deal. "I'll let the board know in the morning."

When she had said those words, it had almost been enough for me to go to her and hug her. I had thought, for a fleeting second, I might have. But I left it the way it was. Got immediately to my feet. The only thing I had wanted was to get to Cassandra now that this was settled.

Patrick and Jeanne followed me back to the door. I had already pulled out my phone to call a cab to come and get me. Startled to see there were a dozen missed calls from Cassandra over the last half hour. The only reason I had put her in my phone had been for purposes related to her work at Dreamers. But I was grateful I had, so I knew it had been her calling me so furiously.

I'd been so distracted by my phone I'd missed Patrick and Jeanne both walking me out. It wasn't until I felt a grip on my wrist I truly came back to my senses. When I looked up, Jeanne was staring at me in the doorway. The intense look back on her face. Patrick, it seemed, had left us.

"I know you know this well enough by now, after everything," Jeanne said, and the way she was speaking immediately made me start to feel sick to my stomach. Compounded when she finished her thought. "Don't think my help doesn't come with strings attached. Patrick may have been your saving grace for now, but if you think you will get away with not owing me for doing this for you after everything Gabriel and Elliott have done, then you're an idiot."

"I wouldn't have expected anything otherwise," I found myself replying, staring straight back at her. "And if that's the cost, so be it. Thank you regardless."

Jeanne stared at me for a moment more, releasing my hand. And then she disappeared behind the door, leaving me alone out on her porch. It was still drizzling a little out, so I stayed where I was, immediately calling Cassandra back, still feeling as unsettled as when Jeanne had been threatening me moments earlier.

Surprisingly, it wasn't Cassandra who answered but another familiar voice. "Chandler?"

"Alex?" I asked, quite certain it was who I had been speaking to. Between our bit of silence, I could hear someone freaking out in the background, a mess of hysterical crying and shouting. It was completely inaudible, but I knew from the second I started hearing it, having heard her so clearly in my mind at every turn for months now, there was only one person it could be.

"You need to come to Cassandra's as soon as you can. It's urgent."

All of my worst fears were tumbling through my mind. Worried somehow all of this had been my father, when I'd been trying desperately to handle the situation. He was still steps ahead of me. "What happened? What's going on?"

"Someone mugged her," Alex explained to me, managing to stay far more calm than I heard Cassandra being in the background. I felt helpless listening to her losing it, hating I was nowhere near her.

"I guess she was coming home from practice, from what I was gathering. Somewhere around campus. Chandler, he took something of hers, and I swear to God if she loses it, she won't make it. I can't tell you more, she'll have to because I wouldn't do it to her. But she was pleading with me to get ahold of you. And I can't leave her, not like this."

"They took her bag," I guessed, and I could tell by the silence on the line I'd probably been correct in the assumption. Anyone who knew her well enough, who saw how religiously she clung to the atrocious-looking thing, could have guessed as much. And while I couldn't understand why, it hadn't mattered, all I wanted was to do anything to help. "Tell me as much as you know. I'm coming right now."

While I would have given nearly anything to have gone straight to Cassandra's apartment after I'd made the drive back over to the Dreamers Academy, in the heart of Acrefort, I didn't. Alex had been there, and I knew it was enough, at least for now. There had been other things on my mind, other ways I needed to help.

The rain had picked up again by the time I'd been dropped off on the outskirts of the campus. It was late then. The streetlights were the only thing really lighting up the streets and sidewalks around me. Most of the buildings at the school were dark.

Somehow, Alex and I had managed to get some semblance of information from Cassandra to be able to help me. I knew her path back to the apartment she lived in had taken her in the direction I had started to head. While I'd never actually visited her home, I knew roundabout where it was and was fairly certain of the ways she'd gone to get back.

I didn't really know what exactly I was going to do, how I would remotely be able to help in searching for what the person who had attacked her had taken from her. But I knew, both by the fear in Alex's voice when she'd said it, and how many times I'd noticed her fierce protection of the bag, I didn't have a choice but to search anyway.

It had been a relief, at least, this clearly didn't seem to have anything to do with my father. At least, I was highly doubtful. Seemed as if it was some shitty human being who had wanted to steal something of value for whatever reason or other. Why they thought it would be inside the ratty bag of hers, I had no idea. But the idea someone had attacked her like they had, had put her in danger, took me to another plane of existence.

If I found them, I wasn't sure what I would do.

My walk took me all the way from where I'd been dropped off, circling around a portion of the school campus and then the entire way back to Cassandra's apartment. I would have been more distracted by how unsettling this part of town was and how annoyed I was with myself I hadn't forced her out of this place sooner. Instead, as I drew up to her building, I was more concerned I had nothing for her.

If I walked into the apartment without anything, if she knew whatever it was she was clinging to so desperately was still missing, I feared what Alex said would be true. And I didn't think, despite everything about my family and the things which had happened over the years, there had been few times I'd felt more unsettled.

As I rounded the corner of the building, dreading those last few steps I had to take to get to her apartment, I noticed something. It had been subtle, and I might have missed it entirely had I not been looking in the right direction at the right moment. But as soon as I saw it, my entire body halted.

Sitting on the porch of one of the apartments a handful away from where Cassandra's had been was a scrawny-looking guy with wild, stringy gray hair, sitting in a wrought iron chair, a cigarette dangling from his mouth. Even over the wooden railing in front of the porch, the white paint badly chipping away, I could see what he was doing in the dim light illuminating him from above.

The bag was permanently seared into my brain, having seen it far too many times now not to recognize it immediately. Whatever contents had been inside of it were mostly spilled out on the ground beneath him. He'd been emptying it out, clearly looking for something. I could only assume any valuable Cassandra had.

It had been a very long time since I had felt such an overwhelming surge of emotion rip through me within a matter of a few seconds. My body took off involuntarily, charging through the grass leading up to the porch at lightning speed. The world rushing around me, every cell within me ablaze.

My entire focus was on the man in front of me. And while I should have been grateful, I'd found the bag of hers. I wasn't about to go back to Cassandra empty-handed. All I could feel was a rage unlike anything I had before.

The guy hadn't seen me coming, too distracted by what he was doing. By the time he realized, I was leaping over the wood barrier of his porch. When my feet hit the ground on the other side, a horrible shooting pain ripped through my injured knee. For maybe one solitary second, it distracted me.

I snatched him out of the chair, my hands bundling around the ratty old long-sleeve sweatshirt he'd been wearing, twisting it in my fist. Brought him straight up off the ground, like he was a rodent I'd caught by the tail. Truthfully, there wasn't much to him. He was not much bigger than Cassandra was.

His body flailed in my grasp after I'd gotten him so far into the air he was writhing. Watched him frantically scrambling in my grip, trying to break himself free. Gagging and gasping due to the fact I'd been choking him in the fabric.

Before he had the opportunity to do much, I spun him around, taking a few steps forward to slam him up against the wall surrounding his porch. Took some shred of enjoyment hearing the loud thud of the impact.

"What the fuck were you stealing the bag for, you piece of shit?" I growled at him, my eyes drilling into his. They were wide, looking straight back at me while he was gasping and choking, still desperately trying to fight me off. I loosened my grip a little in hopes instead of choking, he'd formulate some semblance of words.

"—I don't know what you're talking about," the guy wheezed at me. "It's my bag!"

The sheer amount of rage I was feeling unleashed itself from me. I slammed him into the wall again and brought my knee up in one swift moment to follow up with a brute impact to his groin. The man screamed out in pain, much to my satisfaction, but it was masked by the realization I had neglected to remember it was my bad knee.

When the pain shot through me, my grip loosened on him. I was too focused, trying not to lose consciousness with how absolutely intolerable it was. Somehow, I managed to find my way back to someplace where I could steady myself again. The guy was scrambling over the railing I'd come from, trying to escape.

I caught him by his foot at the last second. In one swift yank, sent him slightly backward, doubling over, the top part of his body slamming into the railing. When I released his foot, he crumbled downward onto the ground below him.

There was no way I'd be able to make it over the railing, I realized. Not without hurting myself again, which I couldn't do. Not if I wanted to remain conscious. And I absolutely had to, in fear if I didn't, the guy would steal her bag again. Which was the last thing I wanted.

Instead, I watched him lay stunned for a few seconds before he managed to roll himself off the ground again. Angered by the fact he was going to get away from me. But I had to prioritize. He was staring at me, wide-eyed, as he tried to come to his senses.

"I know where you live, you piece of shit," I said to him, my voice as low and menacing as I had ever heard myself speak. I sounded much like my grandfather, Elliott Moreau, as much as I'd tried to shove down those memories of him. I didn't really care after what had transpired. Wanted the guy to know how serious I was.

The man took off a second after I said it, scrambling across the grass away from me. I watched him until he'd disappeared around the row of apartment buildings. Still pissed as hell he'd gotten away.

Once I got my wits about me again and had recovered somewhat from the pain I'd been in, I managed to collect all the things off the ground. Surprised most of it had been a substantial amount of paper. Why it had mattered so much to Cassandra, I wasn't sure, but I was beyond relieved somehow I'd found it.

I triple checked I had gotten everything I could lying on the porch. Once I had, I did my best to get myself back over the railing again. It hurt like fucking hell, but I managed to fight through it. All I wanted was to get the bag back to Cassandra, in hopes it would give her much-needed relief.

When I arrived at the door, I was about to barge in because I'd been so lost in my head, but I stopped myself a second before I did. Realizing after everything, it would likely have scared the shit out of all of them.

I knocked, waiting for a few seconds. Heard a voice on the other side of the door and then a click of a lock. When it swung open, Alex was on the other side. A few feet behind her was Cassandra. She looked miserable, in every sense of the word. While she wasn't crying like I'd heard her on the phone a short while earlier, she certainly looked like she had been. Her face was distraught, completely empty, unlike I'd ever seen it.

When her eyes met mine, I could instantly see the relief. And when I held up the ratty sling bag to her a moment later, the color slowly came back to her face. She paused for a half-second like she was trying to process what she was seeing.

Then, in a blur, I watched her come flying into my arms, throwing herself around me. And through the pain, I latched back onto her, doing my best to ignore it. Grateful to have her in my arms yet again.

"Thank you," she managed to whisper to me.

CHAPTER 20

CASSANDRA

The entire drive from my apartment to downtown Acrefort, I was in a dreamy haze. Once Chandler had arrived, having found my bag I'd lost, the adrenaline running rampant throughout me dwindled away. By the time we were both in the town car, I could hardly keep my eyes open, resting my head against Chandler's shoulder.

Every once in a while, I would come to for a few seconds, feeling his head lying against my own. Our hands wrapped together. I wanted to know if he was still there and that this hadn't been a dream I was going to wake up from.

Eventually, the car pulled up alongside the building Chandler's penthouse sat on top of. When it stopped, I finally stirred, hearing a seat belt unbuckle. Seconds later, I realized mine had been unbuckled too. I looked up in a sleepy haze, seeing his green eyes on me. Felt his arms wrap into my body, pulling me to him. Realized I was being lifted up from the seat, and he was drawing me out of the car after his driver had opened the door.

"You don't need to—" I murmured, feeling a little embarrassed he'd deemed it necessary to do what he was doing when I was entirely capable.

"Cassandra," Chandler said once he'd gotten to his feet outside the car. He pulled me close, putting his head against my own. "Close your eyes, and let me help you. Please." While I had a tiny urge to argue, my exhausted body decided otherwise. I laid my head against his chest, feeling the warmth of it and the steady grip of his arms around me.

I couldn't help but notice it seemed Chandler was off-kilter a little when he walked. I was about to tell him to let me walk, but he'd already made up his mind.

The driver assisted Chandler in getting through the doors using the back entrance. I had already returned his keycard, which he used to get onto the elevator. As we rode up several dozen flights, my eyes opened and lingered on the side of his face. He'd been staring straight ahead, looking lost in thought.

My hand reached up, my fingers drawing against his cheek. I felt the skin right at the divide where his beard began. Traced the line of dark hair, speckled with gray, accentuating his face. Mesmerized by how sharp his features were, how he could exude such a strong, overwhelming presence yet still be so gentle in everything he did.

Chandler closed his eyes when I touched him, falling into it. I heard him let out the softest of sighs, and it made me smile a little. "Thank you," I whispered loudly enough for him to hear me. He nodded in reply, and I felt him squeeze me gently, and I sunk back into him, closing my eyes again.

Throughout the walk from the elevators to Chandler's apartment, I stayed in the sanctuary of his arms. Listened to the sounds of him opening and closing the door. He locked both of the locks like he'd instructed me to do earlier. I heard him kick off his shoes by the door, and I felt myself smiling a fraction at the image.

Afterward, he walked his way through the house, and I knew exactly where we were going even though my eyes were closed. It had been months since I'd been there, but I could remember it in my mind like it had been yesterday. Heard the sound of him opening the door to his bedroom.

From the door to his bed, my eyes opened again, trying to make sense of the darkness around us. Making out the shapes within the room and the silhouette of the man carrying me.

Chandler placed me softly onto his comforter, laying me in such a way my feet were still dangling off the side. I felt him carefully remove my shoes from my feet, and once again, I smiled as to why he did it. I heard him set them beside the bed shortly after while I slightly repositioned myself. Shortly after, he turned on a light on his nightstand, dimly illuminating the room.

"How are you feeling?" Chandler asked, his green eyes lingering as he adjusted himself beside me. I got lost in them for a while. They were twinkling a little in the glow of the lamp he'd switched on.

I found myself sighing once I'd realized what he had asked. Truthfully, I wasn't sure. It was all in a haze, with how rapidly I had come down from being so overwhelmed with emotions. Finally, I brought my attention to him, brushing my fingers against his cheek. Letting my palm rest against his face, holding onto him.

"Grateful for you," I replied, my face breaking into a soft smile. "You don't understand what you did for me. God, this entire day, everything you've done—"

I trailed off, absorbing the magnitude of it. If I had ever had doubts about this man, what he thought of me, or his intentions, every single bit of them had dissipated. There was no world in which someone would have gone through the lengths Chandler had for me for any other reason than caring about them deeply.

"I wish I'd done this months ago," Chandler admitted to me. He'd rested his arm opposite of my body, so he was leaning down over top of me, watching me intently. I could tell by the expression on his face he was riddled with guilt, with frustration. "If I'd realized what the hell my father was up to sooner, I wouldn't have wasted so much time."

"What do you mean?" I asked, confused. My fingers danced across his cheek, running along his beard line again. Chandler closed his eyes, falling into the motion, a subtle but very serene smile lingering on his face. I heard him sigh softly again.

After some time, he opened his eyes. "Do you have any idea why he might have developed a sudden interest in you? I know you're aware he's the one that runs the Dreamers Academy." The words had come abruptly out of his mouth.

A violent shiver ripped down my spine at the mention of Gabriel Moreau and his association with me. Abruptly, I was terrified that my recent nosiness had gotten the best of me somehow. He knew something, maybe even Chandler too, and I was about to be in a very bad situation. All the anxiety that had been dwindling from me started to ramp up again.

"What did he say exactly?" I asked, unsure of how else to try to get more information from Chandler. "The only time I ever spoke to him was a few months ago when I went to complain about you..." I bit my lip at the thought of that incident, still hating the fact that I'd done anything at all. I should have just let it go and resolved it with Chandler instead of wasting all the time I had.

"I knew you went to him," Chandler replied, nodding at me. "He was the reason I stayed away from you for as long as I did, despite my every desire not to. Somehow he'd figured out what had been happening between us, that things were getting personal, so he threatened to expel you. If that had happened, I would have never been able to forgive myself, so I did the best I could to convince him otherwise."

My thoughts about his father and my worries faded away a little with his words. I stared up at him in disbelief. "And here I thought the last few months you hated me and wanted nothing to do with me anymore. You just—vanished. Honestly, I did wonder if it had anything to do with your dad, but I wasn't sure. I thought I'd never see you again."

Chandler, who had been still smiling as I continued to let my fingers roam against his face, reached up to clasp his hand around my own, kissing it softly and then bringing it down to his lap. "If you only knew." He shook his head, looking off in a different direction for a moment, but then quickly returned back to me. "Last week... Wednesday, I think it was—Elizabeth had you practicing a hip key roll up, into a pencil drop..."

My head spun, remembering practicing the sequence he'd mentioned in Soleil Theater. I didn't have any time to think about it because Chandler continued. "You were flawless with that first bit, getting the fabrics laid right and your leg positioning." Chandler let out a dreamy sigh. He was sitting there like he was remembering the entire scene perfectly in his mind. "You missed that third little twist. Not your first time missing it either, but you made a good recovery. You were clearly focused." I could tell he was proud. "And you're getting better at it. Honestly, I think the whole issue is Elizabeth teaching you. You run circles around her, and it messes with your practice. Luckily, that won't be a problem anymore..."

"You were watching me?" My voice came out breathy and hardly audible. Still in utter disbelief of the words he'd spoken, even if he'd been singing me praises.

He nodded, his green eyes latched on mine. "Cassandra, I will never stop watching you."

My hand, which had still been wrapped in his own, reached up, finding the hem of the shirt he'd been wearing beneath a jacket. I bundled it in my fist, drawing him down in a gentle tug. His upper body fell gracefully down into mine.

All at once, those lips of his were consuming my own. They were as firm and authoritative as they were gentle. A little grittiness to them in the way they moved against me in a sexy way, somehow matching how his voice sounded sometimes. Though I'd been the one to ask for it, he was the one commanding the kiss, pressing himself against me.

My hands drew up around his head, fingers wrapping into his thick head of hair. It had been in disarray from him being out in the dreary weather outside, but it made him all the more charming. I remembered how it had felt when I'd last been able to touch it. We'd been in his Shibari room together, and he had been kneeling on the floor. I hadn't been able to help myself.

It felt as wonderful then, soft and textured. I gripped it as I decided to take over and deepen the kiss we'd been sharing. Chandler let out the smallest of sounds, something between a pant and a groan. The sound shook me, and I moaned softly in reply, bucking my lower half up against him, gripping his head tighter.

Our kiss continued, growing more and more frantic every second that went by. All of those agonizing moments we'd spent together, so close to this point but never quite making it there, crashing out of us with reckless abandon. We kissed until we were breaking into pants, realizing we had to stop to breathe.

My entire body was so ablaze it felt like a wildfire, raging wildly. When we stopped, I still writhed beneath him, my body moving almost involuntarily. I knew, by the look on Chandler's face, still catching his breath, he was as lost as me.

"I need you inside of me," I whispered, still panting, my hands clenched against his head as he loomed over me, hands on either side of my body.

Chandler let out a low growl, raising the hairs on my neck. I pulled him toward me, and despite how desperately we were trying to catch our breaths, we kissed again regardless. It was sloppy and wet and spiraling rapidly out of control. He moved in a swift motion, pulling himself from the place he'd been sitting and drawing over the top of me. Straddling himself over me, capturing me underneath his towering frame, encompassing me like a cocoon.

He steadied himself there, those delicious eyes of his boring into me. Face steady, still breathing audibly but allowing himself time to recover. I hadn't let him go, stroking my fingers against his scalp and bucking myself against him. Every time I did, I knew I was feeling how much he wanted me, too.

For a moment, I thought I would get what I wanted. Watched as he dipped into me, pressing us together. His face fell into the side of my own. I felt his lips sear my skin several times as he kissed up the side of my neck until his mouth landed against my face, near my ear. The heat of his breath was pounding against my skin.

"Cassandra," he said so quietly it was barely audible and had still been panting a little. My entire body erupted with goosebumps at the sound of my name whispering from his lips. "I promise you, I'll give you what you want. Believe me, for every time I've had to control myself in your presence, this is by far the hardest thing I've ever had to do." I could almost feel him smiling, though I couldn't see it. "I want to show you the other side of Shibari. I want you to feel what it's like to take it all the way..."

"Oh my God," I gasped, my hips thrusting into him. Desperately, I wished there hadn't been fabric between us. "Please do it. I can't wait anymore. I need you now."

Chandler's face came in front of me again. He drew back over my mouth, roughly. Kissing me with force. Authoritatively. Like he was demanding every ounce of my attention. I sighed, sinking into it for the moments it lasted until he pulled away again. This time, he paused a few inches away from my face. Staring straight down at me.

"Please," he said calmly, face steady, panting a little again after the intensity of the kiss he'd just given me. "For tonight, I want you to rest. You went through a traumatic experience. You need to relax. Let yourself recover, just for now. There's time for us to—" Chandler stopped himself, and I watched him visibly swallow the words. "—Time for that, later."

I silently studied him for a little while. Eventually, I nodded and watched as it caused Chandler to break into a small smile, looking relieved. "Will you lie here with me at least? I want your arms around me again. It makes me feel safe."

The smile on Chandler's face grew substantially with my words. I watched him get back up, situating me so he could wrap the blankets around my body. He disappeared out of my sight, over to the other side of the bed. I felt him crawl beneath the sheets until he'd reached me. Felt him mold himself against me, wrapping his arm tight and holding me close.

The two of us laid there, breathing steadily together. So much time had passed without either of us speaking, I thought perhaps he might have fallen asleep. Then I felt him draw in closer, burying his face into my hair for a short while. He sat up a little, and I felt him kiss against my shoulder, over the fabric of my shirt.

When he moved again, he twisted himself, drawing his mouth against my ear. Kissing me again so gently it almost felt like it hadn't happened.

"Don't think I wouldn't fuck you right now. I've been lying here consumed by the idea." Chandler said, in that low voice of his, which was so unbelievably sexy he could nearly weaponize it against me. I felt my entire body tremble. His lips drew over my ear again, and the following words he whispered to me, made my soul ascend from my body.

"Get some sleep, Cassandra. You'll need it. It's the last time you will until I've done everything I want to you."

CHAPTER 21

CHANDLER

Outside my window overlooking downtown Acrefort, I heard the rain picking up again, puttering against the glass. My focus had been on Cassandra, whose small frame was nestled into mine. I could hear her breathing steadily while she slept. She had the subtlest of snores, which I never thought I'd ever enjoy the sound of, but it made me smile. I watched her body rise and fall, twitch every once in a while, knowing she was asleep. At peace.

The last few hours, I had felt such a wild rollercoaster of emotions—more than I had ever recalled feeling in my life. Which had been saying something, with all the hell I had lived through the last four decades. Knowing Cassandra was here now, she was safe in my arms, gave me some comfort. I'd at least somewhat solved a problem, and the rest I would figure out with her beside me.

Even still, thoughts plagued me for hours. There was so much I still needed to say, so many questions I now had for her. Everything had felt deceptively calm for a short while, as much as I knew it wasn't. And though I was trying to savor these moments, grateful for every second of them, my worries didn't cease.

I glanced at the clock on my nightstand again, realizing it had been barely twenty minutes since the last time I'd checked. The same thing had been happening over and over for the last few hours. My mind was too wound up.

At that point, I'd given up on any semblance of relaxation. And as much as I'd wanted to lie there with her still, I started to feel so agitated I couldn't any longer.

Carefully, I wove myself away from Cassandra. Leaned forward to plant a kiss on the back of her head. As I tucked the covers back around her, I took one last look, admiring her lying so serenely, before I slipped from the bed. I seemed to have not disturbed her, her light snoring still audible as I crept across the room.

After I shut the door behind me, I made my way out into the living room. Walked across the far side along the windows, taking in the view. Cassandra had been right the first time she'd looked out into the skyline. You could lose yourself staring at it. I did for a minute before I walked over in the other direction, heading toward the small bar by the kitchen.

I made myself a glass of bourbon, probably more than I should have been drinking, but I had been so wound up and anxious I didn't care. Once I'd fixed the drink, I took a long sip, downing most of it before I headed over to my couch. Midway there, I'd already decided what I wanted to do. Something I hadn't done in what felt like forever.

When I sat down on the white leather sofa, I realized my knee was still aching a bit from earlier. It likely wasn't helping me sleep. It had kept me up many nights before, throbbing. I moved myself, propping it up onto the couch and stretching my legs out. After I had taken another drink, I sat the glass on the end table beside me.

It took a few minutes of searching on my phone, but I found what I had been looking for. Uploaded to a storage site filled with other photos and videos I hadn't looked through in ages. Mostly Cirque du Lys-related things, marketing campaigns, and footage from shows.

This, however, was something entirely different. I fumbled, trying to figure out the settings on my phone. Feeling my age a little when I found myself squinting at the screen, trying to find what I'd been looking for. When I did, the video pulled up on the large television across from me. Something which hadn't been touched in a long while.

The video was old now, at least fifteen or twenty years old. Shot on a camera before cellphones were a common thing. The camera I used was a luxury. The aged footage was still completely recognizable as a circus act beneath a red and white striped tent.

As the act started, I noticed a body leaning against the wall near the hallway in my peripheral vision. I paused the video momentarily, looking at Cassandra lingering in the dim light, watching me.

"You left," she said to me, walking closer. I couldn't help but smile at the sleepy way she'd said it and how her brown hair was in disarray. She was beautiful in the glow of the television as she approached. "Are you okay?"

"I was having trouble sleeping," I admitted, looking up at her as she stopped beside me. "Too many racing thoughts, I suppose." When I shifted my body a little, I winced, feeling a sharp pain shoot through my knee and into my leg.

Cassandra's eyes narrowed at me in concern. She looked down, staring at my legs stretched across the couch and met my eyes again. "Is your knee bothering you? I could feel you limping a little earlier. You shouldn't have carried me inside."

"I realize," I said, still looking at her. "I wanted to do it anyway."

"You're very stubborn," Her lip curled a little, shaking her head.

"As everyone likes to remind me," I agreed, smiling back at her and laughing a little. "I'm aware." I winced when I laughed. For whatever reason, it hurt again.

I watched her study me, and she moved herself down a few steps toward my legs. She grabbed a throw off the back of the couch, wrapping it around her before she slid down, sitting right after where my feet were. I was seconds from asking her why she'd done what she did, but my question was answered when she gently lifted my legs a little, sliding underneath them. They fell back onto her lap, my thighs resting against her. It had hurt a mild amount when she'd done it, but I was too curious to care.

"Do you mind if I try something?" Cassandra asked, glancing back up in my direction. I nodded to her and watched as she turned her attention down to my legs in her lap. She gently placed her hands down. "It's the left one, right?" She looked up at me again for a second, and I nodded again. Briefly, I started to worry about her doing something, concerned it might make things worse. But I quickly convinced myself to relax, deciding to indulge her.

She sat still for a moment before I watched her reach to tug the hem of my left pant leg up my leg. They were a pair of light cotton pants, ones I typically wore to rehearsals. She dragged it upward, and I lifted my leg a little for her until she pulled the fabric up to my mid-thigh, exposing the majority of it.

Once she had, she looked over at me briefly. "I'm going to put my hands on your thigh," she explained to me, so reminiscent of how I always announced my intentions before I worked with her on her silk movements. I nodded and felt her hands fall into my skin. Pressing down into my thigh, drawing down my skin with her palms toward my calves.

I felt a sharp bit of pain which made me hiss a little in response. She immediately stopped, startled. I moved my hand from beside me, reaching down to touch her arm, reassuring her. Gently nudging her to continue.

I tried to fall into her motions. The firm pressure of her hands as they slid down the sides of my legs. Let myself give into the pain a little bit, finding when I'd started to accept it, it subsided.

"What were you watching?" Cassandra broke the silence between us, and I found my focus turning back to the television. I reached for my phone to turn the video back on. The introduction to the show began again, the announcer speaking inaudibly to the crowd. Meanwhile, a pair of silk performers took to the center of the stage.

"It's Robinson and Ebbard," I said, my eyes trying to focus on what was playing on the screen, but my mind was lost in the rhythm of her hands against me. The pain I had been feeling started to feel like just a murmur in the background. "This is a show I went to back in the nineties in New York City. My best friend Patrick and Jeanne and I, during Christmas."

"They're the aerialists, right? The Esposito Circus?" Her pressure deepened. I let out a small sound at the sensation, starting to enjoy how it was affecting the tension in my leg. "Are you okay?"

I nodded, motioning for her to continue. All the while, I was smiling. "You are something else. A wealth of circus knowledge."

Cassandra laughed at me, shaking her head. "One may call that being a nerd."

"Or passionate," I replied to her, still smiling. Our eyes met briefly before I watched her turn her focus back. She had shifted what she was doing, her palms working more into my quadriceps now. "About many topics, I suppose." When she looked back at me curiously, I nodded to her hands.

"Alex tore her meniscus in early college," She explained to me, still working against my thigh, focused on what she was doing. "After it had mostly healed, she still went to physical therapy for a while, and whenever it would flare up, I'd help her. I assumed you probably never had anyone do this for you, so I thought I'd give it a try."

"Well, Thomas did offer once," I said, and she looked up at me, realizing I was joking. I laughed, sinking back down onto the couch and turning my attention back toward the television again. "This was one of the last shows they performed before they retired. I haven't watched this video in years."

The movements Cassandra had been making shifted yet again, focused now more with her fingers, gently massaging the tissue surrounding my kneecap. While I had relaxed into what she was doing, this had been entirely different. I found myself involuntarily rolling out a long, quiet gasp into the room.

She must have realized I hadn't been in pain, more just in shock about how what she was doing was impacting my knee. Whatever she was doing was like she was relieving a hundred-pound weight that had been sitting on it since the accident had happened. Those bursts of relief were far more intense than I'd been anticipating.

"Have you gone to a doctor about this?" She asked me after she'd been attending to my knee for a little while, and I'd gotten lost in the video on the television again.

If anyone else had nagged me with the question, I might have gotten more annoyed. Instead, I surprisingly felt calm about it. "I went with Thomas and Abigail a few months ago, actually," I replied, glancing back at her, but she was still focused on what she was doing. "They said it's probably developing into osteoarthritis. Supposedly, knee injuries can accelerate the process."

I hesitated for a moment, closing my eyes and letting myself enjoy the feeling of her being so thoughtful in her attempts to relieve some of the pressure on my knee.

Finally, I managed to say the rest. The part I hadn't wanted to think about. I hadn't talked to anyone else about it, not even my friends. "I was told it's just going to get worse over time. They made it clear it was going to impact my career eventually. I've just been doing my best not to think about it. As persistent as a reminder as it seems to be."

"You still have plenty of time," She reassured me, finally looking back over and smiling softly. "If you take care of yourself. People live with things like that. Look at you earlier. I would never have guessed you were any different than you were the first time I saw you."

It was a sweet sentiment, and for a short while, I smiled because of it. My eyes drifted up to the ceiling, looking at the large spinning fan above us. Eventually, I sighed. "I'm getting old, Cassandra.

I'm not the same spry athlete you first laid eyes on when you were younger."

She paused what she'd been doing. My knee felt so much better than it had. Like it was lighter and far more relaxed. Most of the pain had subsided. I felt her slide out from under my legs. Watched her as she moved to her feet. The moment she did, I pushed myself up to a sitting position. We met eyes as she drew over top of me, straddling my lap.

Whatever wallowing I had been doing in those moments immediately ceased. My full attention was on the woman in front of me, whose hands had gone into my hair. Studying me intently, looking everywhere except my eyes at first. After some time, she looked straight at me. "You're right," Cassandra replied.

I blinked, surprised. Curious as to what she'd meant by it. Before I had an opportunity to inquire, she'd already enlightened me. Drawing her body into mine, her voice having grown so low and sultry, I lost every thought I'd been dwelling on. "You're far better. Far better than I'd ever imagined you could be." I felt her fingers drag from my hair, over my beard, cupping my chin. "Gray hair and all."

In the middle of the age jab, I had already been in motion. I captured her face between my hands, drawing her the rest of the way to me. Responding to her with a kiss, which wasn't at all subtle. I wanted all of her. She sighed, pushing herself against me.

Soon after, I found myself gripping around her. I pulled myself up from the couch just as she wrapped her legs around my waist. With her in my arms, I headed around the perimeter of the room with the video still playing in the background.

"You really are stubborn," she laughed, wringing her arms around my neck. I walked down the hallway until I'd made it to the end near the final door. It had been shut for months now, not having been used since the last time she had been in my condo.

The minute I stopped, I felt her slowly slide off me. She'd done it slowly and deliberately, riding her body against me in a motion so graceful, I felt like we'd been high in the silks again, moving against each other.

I pushed her forward in a firm, swift motion. Watched as she fell back against the door she'd been standing in front of. Let out a surprised 'oof' when she did, eyes growing wider.

"What's the word I told you?" I asked, drawing up on top of her, my hand snaking around her body to put my hand against the doorknob. "Do you remember my rules?"

Cassandra's face broke into a delicious-looking smile. She paused for a second and nodded before she drew the word out, accentuating the two syllables.

"Feather."

I was drowning in those playfully seductive eyes of hers, feeling myself latching onto the word like it was the key to the door behind me. I drew back into her, kissing her again as I pushed into the room. Leaving another world behind us as we went.

CHAPTER 22

CASSANDRA

As I wandered back into the mysterious back room of Chandler's condo, I realized it felt similar to the awe I felt when I walked around the Dreamers Academy campus. Caught up in all the little pieces of the scenery. The lush landscapes. The nuances of the French Gothic architecture. How the sunlight reflected off the stained glass windows, and the gargoyles watched you from high above.

It kept me captive in another place and time. I took in every detail like it was the first time I had seen it. Because truthfully, this was the first real time. It wasn't held back by fear and restraint.

We could be whatever we wanted now, in this room, together.

I watched Chandler from the mirrors as he closed the door behind us. All the while, I'd laced my fingers underneath the hem of my white cotton shirt I'd been wearing, prepared to draw it over my head. I had hardly started when I heard him let out a low whistle which shot me to attention, spinning around to face him.

"What did I say, Cassandra?" He asked me, as he made a dramatic approach toward me like he was in pursuit. It was sexy as hell, and I found myself paralyzed watching him until he'd drawn up on me, twisted me around, and pushed himself against me. I watched him in the mirrors as he dipped down to my ear, speaking in that low tone of his. "You're *mine* in this room, little papillon. Do you understand?"

A violent shiver ripped through the entire length of my body. I watched his lip curl, looking clearly satisfied. "I missed that," I admitted. "Does it mean butterfly?"

He looked surprised, but when he smiled, I knew I'd guessed right. "It does. It's French. I always remember it from a book my grandmother used to read me when I was little. It was about a caterpillar turning into a butterfly. When you were brave that day, getting up on the stage, I thought it fit you. A little papillon, coming out of her cocoon."

He kissed my shoulder gently before looking back up at me, still smiling. "Surprisingly, it fits you more than I could have ever known."

My hand snaked up around us, reaching up to draw onto his cheek. We watched each other in the mirrors for a few seconds, and I saw him lace his fingers underneath the hem of my shirt. I moved with him, helping as he drew the fabric over my body in one fell swoop, letting it fall to the floor behind us.

He continued immediately after, tugging the exercise pants I'd been wearing down to the floor. I kicked them off once he had, realizing I was standing in front of him wearing those same undergarments I had on the first night he'd seen me at The Crucible. His gaze had latched onto me again, looking almost possessive, and he drew up, pressing himself into me. I watched him nod above us, and I followed where he'd been looking.

"Do you see the cabling and hooks above you?" I noticed what he'd been talking about. Things I'd seen the last time I'd been in this room but hadn't been quite sure what they were. His face pressed against mine. I could feel the heat from his mouth, radiating against my cheek, while I studied a thick red cable running along the ceiling, reinforced with a separate cable and carabiners like they used for mountain climbing. "Do you know what it's for?"

"For suspending someone in the air?" I asked, focusing on him.

A small smile trickled on his lips in such a tantalizing way I felt myself tremble when I saw it. Watched him as he brushed my hair off my neck before he leaned down to kiss me. Each time, it felt like it had the last time he'd done it, searing into my skin.

When he whispered his reply to me, I had to brace myself. "It's for suspending *you* in the air," he corrected me. I shivered again. Tried to keep breathing.

His hand fell against my backside. I felt him lace his fingers swiftly around the clasp of my bra, twisting it in one simple motion until it loosened and fell off me. He didn't look back at me yet, finishing what he'd started, tugging down the underwear I'd been wearing. Once again, I kicked it off to the side once he had.

When the gorgeous man's green eyes returned their focus on me, I was lost in the expression on his face. He looked ravenous, raking down the length of me. I had seen him do it before, both at The Crucible and the last time we'd been in this room. But this was on a new level entirely. The man was devouring my entire being with his gaze.

He dipped into me, mouth drawing down beside my ear. *"Je te trouve belle."* Every single one of those intoxicating French words were laced with the accent oozing out of him the night I'd seen him on the stage. My legs wobbled a little, and I felt him catch me by the waist, holding me against him.

"Dear sweet *God*," I breathed, feeling the goosebumps on my neck. He laughed behind me, still holding me for a moment. "I know you're French and all, but where did you learn to speak it so well? What did that mean?"

With his hands wrapped around my naked hips, he looked amused and smirked as he drew his mouth back onto my neck. And, when I had thought I was about to dematerialize the moment he'd spoken the sexy French to me, it compounded when he gently nipped my earlobe.

"Are you ready, Cassandra?" He asked me once he'd drawn back again, eyes meeting mine in the mirror. I nodded. He circled around me then, his hand grasping my chin, tilting my head upward so he could plant our lips together. I sighed, savoring those few seconds he lingered there.

When he drew away from me, I noticed the confident presence he'd exuded had wavered just a bit. His hand swept through his mess of hair, looking off across the room, lost in thought. I lifted my hand up to his cheek, trying to draw him back to me.

"I've thought of this a few different ways," he said, his voice sounding like he was a little anxious. Unsure of himself, even. He glanced up at the carabiner and ropes above us. I gently stroked his cheek until his attention returned to me.

"Don't think, Chandler," I smiled at him, lost in his eyes again. "We're high up in the silks now. There's no time. Just breathe. Focus."

It had been enough of an answer. His nervousness dissipated, and he broke into a soft smile. He kissed me once more and then whispered. "Wait here." I watched him go over to the wall across from us, his rope collection hanging across it. I had forgotten how many there actually were.

He was swift, clearly having known exactly what he was doing. He plucked several bundles of red and black ropes from the wall, carrying them in his arms back to me. I watched as he let most of them fall to the floor, save one red bundle lingering in his hand. He approached me again. "Do you remember this from the first night?"

"I won't forget it," I replied, watching him as he drew close to me, taking the rope and skimming it across the flesh of my cheek, across my face. I took in a large breath as it passed my nose, savoring the scent I'd almost forgotten. "It smells like honey."

My words got a curious brow raise from him, immediately moving to smell it for himself. It was clear by the expression on his face he agreed. "It does. Like some sort of pungent citrusy smell. Almost like you do, actually."

I watched him unravel the bundle of jute he'd been holding onto and let most of it fall to the floor. It made a beautiful, familiar sound I'd first heard at The Crucible. But it was more pronounced in those moments. My attention dropped down to what was in a pile on the floor.

"Face the mirrors, so you can watch."

I adjusted myself away from him, trying to stand tall and patient despite the adrenaline coursing through me. He circled around me, holding the end of the jute in his hand. I breathed steadily, and when we met eyes with one another, I nodded to him.

He carefully picked up my wrist after looping the end of the rope together. He slid it around, tugging it firm against me. "This is called a lark's head knot," he explained while I stared down at what he'd done. "The tighter you pull, the tighter it gets." He tugged a little harder, constricting my wrist more. Then he released, taking off again around me, dragging the rope with him as he went. It fell across my body in a slow, tantalizing fashion.

The first time, he circled my upper chest. It had been so relaxed, so fluid. When he'd done it a second time in a very rapid tug, raking the coarse rope against my naked skin further down. I gasped in surprise. His face flashed a wicked smile as he moved in front of me again.

"One of the things with Shibari," he continued, letting the rope dance against my skin. I could feel the rough texture as it dug into me a bit, and I found I rather enjoyed the sensation, writhing a little at the touch. "The rope can express anything. Any emotion you want, any experience you want to convey. It can all depend on how you tie someone. How the rope falls on the body."

"I wonder how you're going to tie me then," I said, thoughtfully. He swept his way around me again, looking up into the mirror and meeting my eyes. He dipped his mouth into my neck, pausing there like he was breathing me in.

Then he unraveled the red jute from me until most of it hit the floor again. I stood steady, breathing as rhythmically and calmly as I could. My body felt completely relaxed and ready for what was next. While I was trying to stay focused, lost a little in my head, I felt his fingers draw across my backside, making a line on the skin between my shoulder blades.

"This first tie is called a pentacle chest tie," he explained to me. "It's similar to the butterfly harness in a lot of ways but with different embellishments." I felt him kiss the side of my ear before he whispered again. "I'm going to start now."

Once I nodded in reply, he took the rope over my body, sliding it down the center of my chest, weaving it under my armpits, and then securing it with some sort of tie. When he brought the rope back around, I focused on the gentle touches of his fingers. Felt the tickling against my skin as he laid the rope in various ways across me. I was completely unfamiliar with what he was doing, but I enjoyed watching him.

Falling captive to his touch and the sensations of the rope, I closed my eyes again. Let myself enjoy the surprise of not knowing where he was going next. It relaxed me a great deal, sinking into the sensations. I focused on how it felt versus how it looked.

When I felt his lips draw on mine for a brief second, my eyes fluttered open. He moved around me, and my eyes immediately went to the mirrors behind him. Studying what he'd done as he finished on my backside. Admiring the pattern crisscrossed over my collarbone and how the ropes accentuated my entire torso. It really did look like a harness with a pentacle at the top, very similar to the first tie he'd completed.

"What do you think?" He asked me, appreciating his work in the mirror alongside me. He'd used both black and red ropes to create the design, and the way he'd woven them together was beautiful.

"It's really intricate," I replied, my eyes following along the ropes like I was tracing them. Eventually, I looked back up at him, watching as he spun me around, so I could see myself from behind. I looked over my shoulder, mesmerized by the pattern. "Wow..."

The next words out of his mouth sent my head spinning yet again. "Are you ready to be bound now?" It would be the first time it had happened since the night at The Crucible. I could still vividly remember how intense the feeling had been. So overwhelming but also so serene and peaceful. Completely giving up power to him.

And I wholeheartedly wanted every bit of the experience again.

When I smiled and nodded, he spoke. "I'll take that as a yes. This is called 'hands behind the head tie.'" I watched him pick up another piece of rope off the floor and move back around in front of me. "Hold out your arms." My arms came out in front of me seconds after. He wrapped the rope around my wrists snugly multiple times. After, he lifted my arms into the air and back behind my head.

I watched him in the mirror as he trailed back around me. He paused, looking at me again like he was checking on me. When I nodded to him, he seemed satisfied. He wove more rope in between my bound arms behind my head, and then I felt him fasten it to the design on my backside.

All at once, I was locked into position. My heart raced a little in my chest at the realization.

"Are you comfortable? You should feel restricted, but you shouldn't feel any discomfort."

"I'm comfortable," I assured him, watching as he wove around me and began working on another tie. It was familiar this time, the first he'd ever done, with the loops running down the center of my body. When he reached near my pubic bone, he went down onto his knees again, and just like the first time, the sight overwhelmed me.

When he looked back at my body, he studied me for a few seconds before saying anything. "Spread your legs." He'd said in such a way it ripped a quiver up my spine.

I did exactly as he'd asked, moving my legs apart. My hands were still dangling, tied behind my back, and I'd been looking away from what he was doing. "Are you going to do the same tie again? The one you did last time?" My attention fell back on him.

There was a wicked smirk on his face. I waited for a moment, curious about what he'd been thinking. "No, Cassandra," he replied, and I felt him draw his fingers lightly over the small patch of hair on my pubic bone. It caused me to gasp, jerking my body even more. He didn't stop, roaming straight between my legs, brushing over me in a gentle sweep. "I don't want anything in my way later."

I panted softly. He'd barely touched me, and my entire body was trembling. Heard him make a small noise of his own as he drew back over me a final time. Then he continued what he'd initially intended to do, wrapping the rope around each of my thighs, one at a time.

As he worked, I continued keeping a steady watch on him. When he finished, he got back to his feet again, fastening the rest of the rope to my backside. I realized he'd made another harness on my lower half, woven intricately down my legs and across my pubic bone. I was covered in ropes hugging me in all the right places.

He had drawn up behind me, looking at me through the mirror. His hands had fallen on my hips, and I felt his fingers against the ropes there. His mouth came down against my face, whispering yet again. "I'm going to suspend you now."

All of my thoughts were spinning wildly in my head. I was starting to get the delirious feeling again, knowing I had given myself completely to him. Somehow, I managed to nod, and he walked me a few paces to the side, adjusting me so I'd been lined up underneath some carabiners on the ceiling.

He reached up, pulling one of the ropes with the hooks attached at the end downward, attaching it behind me in one swift motion. I dangled there like a piece of meat on a hook waiting to be devoured by the sexy Frenchman. His eyes raked down the length of me through the mirror, seeming satisfied.

"Now to get you in the air."

For whatever reason, I hadn't fully realized he intended to take me off the ground. The idea was a little overwhelming, and it caused my heart to pick up pace in my chest again. I watched as he twisted around me, reaching for another rope dangling from the ceiling. This time, it was attached to several other stronger-looking ropes and a carabiner. It was fastened almost like a pulley, with a rope dangling off one side of it.

He snapped the carabiner to a portion of the harness he'd made on my lower half, locking it into place. Once he had, I watched him wrap his hand around the rope attached to the pulley. We met eyes, this time straight toward each other and not as a reflection. He flashed a playful look at me just as I felt myself being swept straight off the ground.

I drew in a sharp breath of air, my mind spinning as I dangled above the floor. While I'd spent so many hours flying high above the ground, wrapped in silk, this was something entirely different. When I'd been performing, I had complete control. Knew how to get back down to the floor and was able to manipulate myself however I wanted.

Now, I was completely at the mercy of the man who was perched in front of me, standing between my legs, still holding onto the rope he'd used to tug me off the ground.

"What are you going to do to me like this?" I couldn't help but ask. The question was almost overwhelming. I looked down again, watching as he secured the rope he'd been holding onto, then dropped it. Coming to the full realization I was completely off the ground. It felt surreal. Hard to wrap my mind around entirely.

"Oh, I plan to do all sorts of things to you like this, little papillon," his voice had gotten low again. My attention went to the ceiling, realizing there were mirrors above us too. I'd forgotten about them. I watched and felt as he raked his fingers down the inside of my thighs, somewhat roughly, before he moved away from me, circling around my helpless body, trapped in the air.

He came around in front of me, so I saw him looming over my head. I was so distracted by how absolutely mesmerizing he looked, towering over me, completely dominating every piece of me. I hadn't realized it when he'd drawn his fingers over the ropes, pushing them into my skin. I could feel the coarseness of the jute raking against me, and it was taking me to another place entirely.

"God, I can feel everything everywhere," I gasped, his touches continuing, tracing every single rope he'd drawn against me like he was thoroughly checking the work he'd done. "Every time I move, every time I breathe, I can feel all the ropes..."

"That's the point," he replied, softly. He dipped down a little, pausing. I felt his hands wrap around my head, pulling me upward so he could plant his mouth against me.

A soft sound escaped me into his mouth, letting him kiss me deeply for a short while. Then he broke free, reaching up above me to adjust the ropes on the ceiling until I felt myself being lifted, so it was like I was almost sitting in the air. Once he'd finished, I felt him gently push against my body, sending me spinning around in a circle.

When I stopped moving, he was right between my legs again. He'd positioned me so I could see us both in the mirror behind him, but his gaze remained on me. Once again, I felt him rake his fingers up my thighs in an agonizingly slow fashion. The look on his face was so intense it had me shivering.

The next words that came out of the man's mouth completely obliterated me.

"Do you want me on my knees, little papillon?"

I couldn't even utter a reply. The feelings I was succumbing to were so overwhelming I was struggling to breathe. All I could force myself to do was nod. He dropped a second after, and my eyes darted back and forth between watching him in front of me and then in the mirrors as he settled on the ground.

His head was right between my legs. So close I could feel the heat from his mouth beating into my skin. I was already writhing again, completely unprepared to feel his fingers delicately drawing against me. Everywhere except where I wanted them to be. Taking great pleasure in torturing the fuck out of me for what felt like forever.

I was a half-second away from begging him, and I wouldn't have been surprised if that had been his intention all along. Likely would have humored him, feeling so desperate at that point. But then I watched him draw forward. Felt him everywhere, all at once.

And in that moment, I realized I was his. Existing purely to be entertained by Chandler Moreau.

CHAPTER 23

CHANDLER

My heart had been pounding furiously in my chest nearly the entire time Cassandra and I had been together in the back room of my condo, adrenaline running wildly through me. Even still, I somehow managed to stay steady. Reminded myself to breathe enough to take in these moments the two of us were experiencing. We had returned to the place I didn't think we ever would, and I was grateful it had happened.

The last time we'd been in this room, I'd been so overwhelmed by her curiosity, her desire to understand and experience everything, I'd almost lost sight of myself. It hadn't really occurred to me what it meant to be able to share this with another person. Someone who enjoyed it as much as I did. Getting lost in a simple thing like rope. It felt a lot like the silks—not everyone understood the depth and nuance of two pieces of dangling fabric.

Cassandra certainly had. Far more than anyone I'd ever met.

I'd known it those first few moments she'd begun her performance for her audition. Seen it repeatedly every time I watched her practice, wholly consumed by everything she was doing, taking nothing for granted. Giving in to the entire experience of it without reservation.

It was precisely what she was doing now. Trapped beneath all those twists and turns, folds and knots of red and black jute enveloping her. There wasn't an ounce of fear inside her, no hints of doubt. She'd given in completely. It was nearly as mesmerizing to watch her like this as it was to watch her on stage—not quite the same experience, but overwhelming all the same.

As I knelt between her legs, listening to the noises she'd been making, watching the writhing and bucking of her frame trapped in all of those precise patterns of rope I'd delicately woven across her, I got lost in it. Lost in her, like I had so many times over the months since we'd first met one another.

"Chandler."

Cassandra's elongated moan of my name brought my wandering focus back. I'd been wrapped up in what I was doing. Savoring the opportunities I had to figure out little things I could do and what responses they would bring out of her. Something I could have continued on with for an indefinite amount of time had it not been for that sound she had just made.

I hadn't heard it since I'd seen her in my tub all those months ago. It was like listening to it for the first time again. The second it drew out of her mouth, my little game of tormenting her, my enjoyment of being able to dictate everything that was being done disappeared from my mind.

My fingers inside her had elicited that moan. The moment I'd curled them against her, she couldn't stop herself. I watched her entire body twisting and jerking, trapped in the position I'd placed her in, unable to do anything except take precisely what was being given. Her eyes had been closed, but the minute I'd made that slight motion, they'd shot open again, immediately looking into mine as she moaned my name. It twisted around me like it had every time before. I'd never heard that designation so magnificently said in my entire life.

There hadn't been a doubt in my mind about what I intended to do. Not after I heard her speak those two exquisite syllables to me. I'd been all wrapped up in a million different things happening all at once, but those last few seconds had tethered me back. My fingers twisted again, similar to before.

"Oh my God," Cassandra gasped in response, her body a constant mess of movement beneath all the ropes around her. Completely helpless to do anything at all. I enjoyed her reaction quite a bit. It captured me. Still, it hadn't been what I'd wanted, and I was bound and determined to do whatever it took to get her there again.

In the few seconds following that thought, I decided I didn't need to wait. Didn't need to waste time figuring out how to draw it out of her. There was no reality in which I remotely wanted to, and I knew I didn't have to. Cassandra was devoted to my every word, willing to do whatever I asked of her. She tried to please me with everything she did.

All I had to do was tell her what I wanted.

I paused the motions I'd been making. Drew so close to her that she must have been able to feel my breath between her legs. I stayed completely motionless until I watched her drifting gaze return to me. The moment those hazel eyes fell back on my own, I spoke—no—*demanded* the singular thing she had to do.

"Say my name."

We were both so fiercely enraptured by one another the room vanished. Cassandra's breath hitched for a solitary second until I curled my fingers again. She moaned into the room wordlessly, and I could only assume by the quivering of her body I was dragging her closer. It wouldn't be long.

I wasn't about to let her have it. Still waiting, motionless, until she did what I asked. I watched her tossing and turning helplessly, eyes on me. Making desperate attempts to get me to act, but she certainly knew better than to think she would succeed in that endeavor. The image of her there, merciless in front of me, wrecked with desire, so close to giving in and giving me exactly what I wanted, was so surreal...

I decided to indulge her. Let myself fall into a rhythm against her, enjoying how it rocked her in those colorful ropes suspending her above the ground. The breaths she'd been taking started to become audible. She was shaking, her body falling into my fingers' motions.

As I admired her, I realized I didn't want it to end. Not yet, anyway. And what was even more of a revelation was the idea that however long I took, even if she was desperate for relief in those moments, was entirely in my control. Whatever I wanted her to do would just take a little bit of effort to figure out how to drive her mad enough to get her there.

When I'd pulled away from her and got up from the floor, Cassandra's gaze lasered in on me, panting hard. "What are you doing?" She gasped, looking as lustful as ever but also a little bit confused. I took a step forward, planting myself right up against her naked frame, standing between her legs.

Drawing forward, I raked my fingers around part of the pentacle chest tie I'd woven around her a short while earlier. Looping around the rope and tugging her entire body toward me in a gentle sweep so I held her hostage in front of me, our faces a few inches away from one another. She was dangling off the ground, completely at my mercy, and I never thought I could be more consumed by a sight in my life.

Cassandra let out a surprised gasp, eyes growing wide. That look sent a wave of satisfaction through me, glad that she was focused on me and nothing else.

"Do I have your attention, my little papillon?" My eyes were latched onto hers, unmoving. Cassandra took several trembling breaths, nodding as she did. "—Ah, Cassandra. You know better..."

"You have my attention," Cassandra replied in a breathy whisper. My lip curled a bit, pleased she'd gotten the hint. I tugged her closer, just for a second, to plant my mouth on her own. Just long enough that she knew I'd done it, but that was all. Then, in a gentle motion, I carefully dropped her back to the position she'd been in previously.

"I know what you want," I said, my voice low, letting my fingers rake somewhat roughly against the inside of her thighs. "And I fully intend on giving it to you…" I drew inward, watching as she started to writhe and gasp a little again, feeling utterly satisfied I had continued this game just a little longer. "But you need to remember, little papillon…" I abruptly stopped my motions, so she honed in on me again. "You're trapped in my net right now. There's no escape. Nothing left for you to do but give in and submit to me. And you know *exactly* what I want from you right now."

Cassandra's breath hitched, and the moment it did, I growled at her, my fingers still paused on her thighs. "Tell me what you want me to do."

"Oh my fucking God," Cassandra gasped loudly, bucking desperately in place, her gaze still boring into me. "Chandler, move. Do anything at all. Please, I am begging you. I need—"

Her pleading never finished, interrupted by her loud moan as I resumed what I'd been doing, pushing back into her and falling into that rhythm I had before. "Thank you, Chandler," she managed to say in between those little gasps she was making from what I was doing to her. My entire being savored every single word she'd just said.

While I worked against her, I dropped back down to the floor again. Seeing that desperate look on her face, all those involuntary jerks and twitches she was doing, she was barely hanging on now.

My gaze was steady, keeping a careful watch on her, waiting for the precise moment…

"Beg me to make you come, Cassandra." That same demanding tone came flying out of me again, but I hadn't stopped what I was doing. "I want to hear you say it."

Her head rolled back again, gasping loudly, "Chandler, oh my God."

There it was. The sound that throttled me. Without even thinking about it, I'd fallen down between her legs, mouth working in tandem with my fingers. Willing to give her what she wanted, assuming she would do what I asked. My free hand reached up, raking over all the twisted jute around her. I watched her magnificent body trapped there, taking every single touch I gave, unable to do anything at all about it. All the while, I was drowning in the sounds she was making, all the gasps and moans.

It was apparent she was moments away, still writhing in the ropes, all those noises continuing relentlessly. I pulled myself back again, and I didn't have to wait because I immediately had her undivided attention. I repeated myself. "Beg me, little papillon."

My fingers drug against her, and I watched Cassandra lose her mind, her body making little involuntary twitches and jerks. Her arms trapped behind her back, still tossing and turning in those ropes, desperate for relief. She wasn't going to last.

And much to my satisfaction, she did exactly as I asked.

"Please let me come, Chandler... Please let me—"

Midway into her pleading, I'd already resumed what I'd been doing. Every sound that had just come from her mouth had utterly obliterated me. Left me feeling as if my entire being might explode into individual atoms and dissipate into space.

I was relentless against her, knowing with utmost certainty she would lose control any second now. Even still, I gave her every ounce of effort I had in me, wanting her to know what saying those simple, tantalizing words had done. They'd wholly devoured me.

In an instant, Cassandra let go.

Her entire body was a mesmerizing mess of movement, succumbing to what I'd done. I was captive to the imagery in front of me, all those resplendent sounds she never stopped making, trapped in that jute like a butterfly in a net. My merciless papillon...

All those beautiful rope designs were tight against her skin, likely taking her to an entirely new place with the experience. This was the whole point. It was meant to accentuate everything else. And every time I'd practiced on myself in years past, it often reminded me of those same sensations of the silks wrapped around me.

Something I assumed it surely must have felt like for Cassandra, too.

"Chandler." Even if my mind had only drifted for milliseconds, her voice, the satisfied groan she'd twisted in with my name, snapped me back to attention.

This time, Cassandra was digging into me with her gaze. I watched her breathing, heard it in the room's quietness, her entire body moving as she took in gasps of air beneath the ropes that trapped her.

The look she was giving me ripped a shiver down my spine. I held steady. She had mostly settled. Occasionally twitched and bucked a little still, whatever she'd been experiencing tapering off. I'd hardly been able to focus on anything other than those hazel eyes boring into mine. Didn't think I could feel more distracted by her doing so.

Clearly, I was mistaken. When that gorgeous woman in front of me knew she had my undivided attention, she spoke a few simple words. Words that *could* have been a simple request to give her what she wanted since it was blatantly evident by the state she was in that I was most certainly in charge of that.

But she hadn't been asking. Not remotely. Even trapped helplessly in those intricate jute patterns dangling in front of me.

Cassandra was demanding *me.* Not unlike what I'd done minutes earlier with her.

"I need you inside of me."

I hadn't needed her to repeat herself. I moved in a swift motion from the floor. Quick to remove my clothes, far less graceful than I'd been removing Cassandra from her own. But she was waiting after that all-consuming command she'd just given me. And I wasn't about to delay any longer than necessary.

The minute all the fabric left me, my attention returned to her. Noticed she'd been raking her eyes down my entire length. I hadn't recalled ever seeing her do it before, and I stood there admiring her as she did.

"Do you see something you like, my little papillon?" I asked her as I took the two steps forward, gripping the ropes that suspended her and spinning them around. Cassandra's eyes widened. I took a second to adjust how she'd been positioned to make her almost parallel to the floor. Exactly how I wanted her.

I spun her again, enjoying the sight of her dangling there in anticipation. Her hazel eyes locked on me every second they could as she circled. When I stopped her, I drew up between her legs. The place I had been a minute earlier.

Her breath hitched, and a million different emotions were rampant on her face. She didn't move, looking completely paralyzed by me standing there.

For whatever strange reason, the sight made me smile. My hands fell down on her hips enveloped in those ropes. Steadying her as best I could. Bringing her back to me.

"Breathe, Cassandra," I said, gently. And like any other time I'd spoken those words to her, she did as I asked. Resumed her calm and rhythmic breaths. I took the same ones she did, feeling like I had hours earlier in the silks at Cirque du Lys, both of us steadying ourselves. Waiting for the moment when we were in total sync with each other.

When I saw it, I drew forward into her in a swift and graceful motion, hands still wrapped around her hips. Watched Cassandra's back arch, gasping into the room, entirely as overwhelmed by the sensation as I was.

I knew there wasn't much left of me hanging on. I wouldn't last long. I was dangerously close already. Every second of that experience had unraveled me so quickly that I barely had anything left.

Even still, I watched her moan my name to me, mixed in with all the other little sounds she made. Every time she did, it dragged me closer. Heard myself gasping and groaning right alongside her, wrapped up in every second of it.

Her eyes had been closed, head tilted back, lost in the moment. I crashed into her, wanting her focus, and in an instant, she returned to me. Eyes open wide, capturing my attention. Those breathtaking colors trapped me.

"*Cassandra,*" I gasped, completely overwhelmed by the sight of her, those beautiful eyes right on top of mine.

I could see it on her face, knowing she was right there too. The second I'd said her name, she'd lost control. And I watched every second of it, letting go right alongside her, falling captive to the rush of the entire experience.

When I finally released her, Cassandra watched me as I spun her again. Stopping her so I could plant our lips together briefly. "Are you ready to be untied?" I asked her quietly, brushing my fingers against her cheek and tucking her hair behind her ear.

"Please keep touching me," she replied, nodding.

The rush of water filling my tub echoed off the walls of the bathroom as I sat on the edge, fixing things the way I liked them. Cassandra sat naked beside me, watching me as I worked like some sort of alchemist, trying to get it exactly right.

"You're quite the expert at this," Cassandra noted, and I looked over my shoulder at her. I reached my hand out, running my hand across her face and into her hair, pulling her toward me. We kissed for a moment, and I enjoyed the little sigh she made in response. Cassandra nudged me once I let her go. "That was a lot of fun. Thank you for sharing it with me."

I smiled, my attention turning back to the bath as I finished. "Believe me, I enjoyed it as much as you did. I've wanted to do that for a very long time. It's one thing doing all of those demonstrations at The Crucible. I enjoyed them, but they'd gotten to be routine. Nothing like what we just did." I turned off the faucet, looking at her again. "I'm glad you enjoyed it so much. Not everyone is quite as enthusiastic."

Cassandra raised a curious brow at me, watching as I put what I'd been using in the bath back under the sink. As I walked back to her, she spoke again. "You mean Jeanne?"

"Ah—yes," I replied, feeling slightly uncomfortable that I'd brought her up at a time like this, but I continued anyway. "She spent years and years hating me for it. It's part of the reason I started those demonstrations at The Crucible. Otherwise, I might have stopped altogether."

"I'm glad you didn't," Cassandra replied. I watched her get up from her seat along the tub, slowly stepping over the edge and sliding into the water. I joined behind her, sinking into the heat. Before Cassandra leaned back against me, I admired all the lines the ropes had etched on her skin. It made me smile a little in satisfaction.

We laid together for a while. I listened to the gentle laps of the water against the side of the tub, and the calm, rolling breaths Cassandra was taking. Enjoyed her lying up against me with my arms wrapped around her, so close to her hair I got whiffs of her scent.

"Thank you again for finding my bag for me," Cassandra whispered. She'd drawn my hand into her own from behind, lacing our fingers together and squeezing. "I don't know what I would have done if you hadn't."

I smiled, though she couldn't see it, and gently kissed the back of her head. "You've been toting that thing around ever since I first met you. Clearly, it's important." I paused for a moment, enjoying Cassandra playing with our hands, cherishing the sensation. Refocusing on the conversation, I continued my train of thought.

"Can I ask why it's so important? When I was trying to gather it all for you after I'd gotten it back, I noticed it was a bunch of papers."

For a few seconds, it was quiet again. I watched as Cassandra sat up from me, turning herself so we were facing one another. She looked me steadily in the eyes, taking a few long, deep breaths before she replied. "It's evidence," she said simply. "Almost five years worth."

It had been the very last thing I had ever expected her to say. I raised a brow at her, unable to help myself from asking, "Evidence about what?"

"Evidence that my uncle murdered my parents," Cassandra responded, her face very steady, eyes unwavering. "They died in a fire when I was in middle school. For a little while, I was convinced it was a freak accident. I lived with my uncle for years after they'd died. And I couldn't understand him the entire time. My dad, his brother, was the kindest person I knew. He wouldn't have hurt anyone. Peter, on the other hand..." She trailed off.

"He hurt you?" I stared at her in disbelief, unable to comprehend what I'd heard.

"Not physically," Cassandra replied. "More mentally. Like that constant fear that he *might*. I spent four years in high school in constant fear of him, of everything I started figuring out he was. I don't think I spent a single day not in constant anxiety. I started asking questions, started trying to understand him, wanting to figure out why he was so much different than my parents. It didn't make any sense."

My hands moved through the water to find her own again, wrapping us together. Cassandra gave me a soft smile when I did and continued. "I found all these documents one day in his office. Things about my parents' will and about me. I still don't fully understand it all, but I do know he'd taken my inheritance from me. Made accusations trying to condemn my parents for really horrible things. When I saw all of it, I knew he was responsible for the fire. I was lucky he got caught doing some shifty things and landed himself in jail a few years ago, but I'm not going to feel satisfied until I know he's permanently there. Or dead. That would be even better."

Cassandra stopped speaking for a little while, but I couldn't find the words to say either. I squeezed her hands again, and it seemed to break her from her thoughts.

"I've been working with some guy for the last few years, using all the evidence I had, trying to pin him down. It's someone Alex helped me find when I finally got away from Peter in college. He hasn't been great. Truthfully, he's been shady as hell. But he's all I can afford."

It was at that moment I realized why she'd been in a constant state of anxiety about money. She must have been spending nearly all she had in pursuit of this man. There was a trickle of anger ripping through me in those moments. And a little bit of helplessness, too, wanting to do anything for her but unsure of what. "Does he know what you're doing?"

When Cassandra nodded, I felt a lurch in my stomach. "That's why I was so freaked out about the guy taking my bag. I mean, I didn't want to lose the evidence either, especially since I'm too paranoid to put it on a computer for a variety of reasons. But I was afraid he was going to find someone to come after me. That he wasn't finished, even if he's locked away. I am never going to feel completely safe until I know he can't get out again. Or dead. And I sincerely hope it's the latter."

Though it had been wet, I released my hand from Cassandra's, drawing it up to cup the side of her face. "Nothing will happen to you, Cassandra. I promise you. I'll make sure of it." I felt her relax against me a little bit. A small smile crossed her lips. I could tell she wasn't entirely convinced.

Suddenly, it occurred to me that I had something to offer after all. Something which had seemed to drive Cassandra mad at every turn but perhaps, for once, would be useful. "What if I hired a private investigator? Someone more qualified than the clearly incompetent individual you've been working with. I'll take care of it. We can get the best we can find."

I sat for a moment, trying to anticipate Cassandra's response. Surprisingly, her eyes went wide, and her mouth dropped open a little. "You'd do that for me?"

It occurred to me I'd never told her about my own connection to her family.

"I used to go with my grandmother to your parents' shows when I was younger," I told her, smiling softly. "I wish she was still here to tell you how fond I was of the two of them. Thomas and Abigail reminded me shortly after you arrived at Dreamers about what had happened. About the fire. I never knew them personally, but it was still devastating to hear. I can't imagine what it must have been like for you."

Cassandra's gaze dropped a little. I could tell she was saddened by the memory. "It was the worst day of my life. I watched the tent burn to the ground, and it felt like my entire world was gone." She sat for a moment, her gaze off in a different direction. But it wasn't long until it was back on me again. Cassandra's eyes dug so deep into me, I was reminded of the way I had felt the first time she'd ever looked at me on the stage of Soleil Theater.

"My parents took me to see you the day before they died. It was a birthday present. I went with my friend Alex, actually." Cassandra's face broke into a soft smile at the mention of it. "It was the moment I realized I was going to do everything in my power to end up here. You autographed my playbill after the show, and I—"

She faded off again, still holding her gaze on me. I didn't move. "I think you've been the one thing I've been clinging to ever since that day. Like it was some sort of weird twist of fate I went to your show when I did. Every single moment of those darkest times of my life, I would cling to the memory of you. The dream of being able to be here, to work with you, to learn from you one day. I've been drowning for years, and you have always been my lifeline."

When she finished her thought, the two of us lingered there, both still lost in one another. I was still trying to process all the things she'd said, trying to understand the gravity of it all. There was so much I needed to tell her, so many questions I needed to answer for her in regard to everything that had transpired. Things I wanted her to know, things I needed to know to protect her. Protect us both. But I realized it didn't matter right this second. This was the only thing that did.

"Thank you for giving me yesterday," Cassandra said before I had a chance to speak to her. "Like I said before, I don't think you know what you did for me. It meant absolutely everything. You finally made me want to be alive again."

I felt myself smile when she said those words. "I know you probably wouldn't guess it, but it meant the same to me. You made fun of all my ridiculous smiles, but truthfully, Cassandra, I haven't felt that way in so long. I thought it would never happen again."

Cassandra drew her hands up out of the tub, dripping with water, planting them against my face. I let her pull me to her, our lips falling together softly. Stayed there with her, taking every second of it in until she broke away.

"Okay," she said, quietly. I raised a brow at her, wondering what she'd meant when she said it, but she'd finished her thought seconds later. "I want you to help me. I need to solve this once and for all. Finally have some peace."

"You will," I promised. Another time, I'd tell her the things I'd kept from her for far too long. Right now, I was too desperate to help her. To help the younger version of her, who had clung to the memory of me for so long.

I wasn't going to prove her wrong.

CHAPTER 24

CASSANDRA

High above, dangling from the catwalks near the roof of the giant white circus tent, lights shined down onto the theater stage. Throughout the entirety of the room, a guitar and piano were beginning a charming upbeat melody all around us. *Canarios*. It had been something Chandler and Sebastian had picked, a lighthearted classical piece I had been unfamiliar with before, but now every solitary note was ringing inside me.

Across from me, hands wrapped in a set of royal purple silks, Chandler Moreau's green eyes were watching. He was wearing a marvelous skin-tight black costume with streaks of green weaving throughout it, which nearly matched his eyes. It was similar to my own, except mine had been meant to compliment his silks with shades of purple instead of green.

As soon as the music began, I took off into the sky. Wrapping myself around those soft green fabrics as I did, my mind completely focused on what I was doing. The song had barely gotten a dozen measures in, and I had made it halfway up, dangling over fifty feet in the air, looking out into an empty theater when I paused.

It had been our first day of dress rehearsals, only two weeks out from the beginning of the winter showcase. Chandler had told me on multiple occasions how surreal it would be when it happened, and he hadn't been wrong. While there was no audience with eyes on me yet, I was performing like there was, lost on the stage and in all the acts before us.

I swung outward, gracefully twisting into a sequence I had only recently been able to perfect with the help of Chandler called the Split Arabesque. It was mostly done hanging in one position, twisting around the silks upward and dropping back down again. And while it may have looked deceptively simple to a casual observer, it was something I still felt a little nervous about after all the time I'd spent practicing.

As I pulled myself upward, I allowed myself to rotate in a circle, so I could look toward the ground. I saw Chandler below me. He'd moved halfway up his silks, drawing nearer every second. Watching him approach was the grounding I needed to remain focused on what I was doing. By the time he had settled about fifteen feet below me, I'd completed the entire move. When I glanced down, Chandler was beaming.

I listened as another few measures played, having been somewhat seated within the silks. The next movement was by far the hardest part of this performance. And though we'd continually practiced it, we had yet to get it right.

Tonight was another night, however. There was a different feeling in the air, and it came with a greater sense of confidence. At least for me, anyway. The guitar let out a bellowing strum, giving me the cue I needed. I had taken a calming breath beforehand, waiting.

I dropped backward, falling from my position high above the stage, shooting straight downward, silks twisting around me as I did. While it wasn't quite a Kamikaze, this drop was by far the most intense I had ever done. And as steady as I always felt, it was the opposite for Chandler lately, who had been tasked with the job of catching me as I passed him, swinging me outward into the air to circle the stage.

We were watching each other as I flew downward toward him in a rush. I saw it seconds before I'd reached him. His face had gone blank again, and he tumbled backwards from where he'd been positioned, falling straight down alongside me.

While I had been able to catch myself in time, wrapping enough of the silks around me to draw upward again and slow my momentum, Chandler had not been so lucky. I watched him in a sea of fabrics, flailing the entire way down helplessly. And I hated how far up I was still, unable to do anything but see him hit the floor. Hard.

In all the times we had attempted this, he'd struggled, never catching me like we'd wanted. But this was the worst of the experiences. Never had he taken himself all the way to the floor. I stared down at him, having gone completely limp, feeling a massive wave of panic.

Chandler abruptly shouted a string of angry curses into the theater. He managed to get himself sitting upright. By the time I'd gotten most of the way down, he'd turned his attention back to me. Watching me intently until I'd gotten back on the ground. I could hear him panting when I got to the floor next to him.

"Are you okay?" I asked, placing a hand on his shoulder. Meanwhile, the theater lights had all turned on again, signaling an abrupt halt to our rehearsal. "Are you hurting?"

"I'm frustrated," Chandler scowled, shaking his head. "My knee is fine. It was another panic attack." The more we'd worked together on these more complex moves, the more times he'd panicked or had flashbacks of the fall he'd had with Jeanne. "I was confident tonight, too. *God damnit.*"

"We'll get it," I assured him, crossing my legs, still resting my hand on his shoulder. Meanwhile, I saw Thomas and Abigail approaching us and, shortly thereafter, Sebastian. Some of the other performers had been watching from the wings.

"I saw when it happened," Thomas said, offering a hand to Chandler while Abigail helped me. "Maybe you two should consider taking out the drop. I know how much you love theatrics, Chandler, but it's better to be safe than sorry. Abigail was freaking out watching your fall."

Chandler looked annoyed but more in general than at any of us.

"I've decided to wrap up rehearsals early for the evening, anyway," Sebastian announced.

Abigail was looking at me, her worried face breaking into a soft smile. "Thomas was backstage in a bit of a mood. I think he's getting a little hungry."

"Well, I can't help it if I'm *excited,* Abby. I look forward to this day every year. The single day I can excuse myself for eating as much food as Chandler typically does in one sitting."

Even Chandler, who had been stewing beside his friend, smirked a little at the comment. "Food sounds good to me," he agreed.

The moment he'd said it, my attention drew out into the theater. A group of familiar faces was weaving their way through the aisles, containers in each of their hands. Alex and Dana led the way, along with Henry, and surprisingly, another woman beside him I didn't recognize. Trailing behind them was Chandler's friend from The Crucible, Stella. I'd met her a few times now, and she'd since become a lot less intimidating.

When Chandler, Thomas, Abigail and Sebastian headed back into the wings to fetch all the food everyone had brought and change clothes, I made my way down the steps of the stage, headed for my friends. All of them were taking in the theater, looking around in awe.

"This place is wild," Alex said, staring up at the ceiling. By the looks of it, her eyes were specifically on the silks. "And I thought it was insane how high up you went on the silks at Dreamers. Look at those things, holy shit. What is that, a hundred feet?"

"Eighty-five," I corrected, smiling. "Close enough."

I watched Henry weave his way around Alex and Dana, coming up to meet me. We hugged one another briefly before he turned his attention to the woman beside him. For whatever reason, she had the same sort of air as Henry did, with untamed, curly blonde hair and eyes as brown and enchanting as Henry's. She wore a pair of black glasses reminiscent of the ones Sebastian wore frequently.

"Cass, I wanted you to meet someone..." Henry said, glancing at the woman, beaming. "This is Elle Green. The girl I was telling you about."

Elle smiled at me, extending her hand, and we both shook briefly. "I've heard a lot about you. I couldn't imagine doing what you were doing up there in the silks. It looked terrifying, but it was so pretty."

I hadn't realized my friends must have been watching us rehearse. Silently, I hoped they wouldn't bring up Chandler's fumble to him to spare his embarrassment. No one said anything.

"You're Thomas' student, right? I can't imagine trying not to light myself on fire. It seems a hell of a lot more terrifying than a couple of pieces of fabric." I laughed a little.

Elle grinned at me in reply, shrugging. Henry spoke instead of her. "Elle's a little bit on the wild side. She loves all the dangerous stuff. Nearly gives me a heart attack every time she's practicing."

When Henry said it, all I could think about were all those times Chandler had been so anxious about me. He was fiercely protective in that regard. Though we'd been rehearsing together for a month now, he still worried. Which I appreciated because it meant he cared.

"Well, come on in," I finally said, ushering all of them toward the stage. "I think everyone was starting to get food together. Wait until you get to experience a Cirque du Lys communal dinner. It's crazy. I don't even know how Thanksgiving is going to go. I'm sure they went all out, knowing this group."

When I turned away from my friends, I headed back down the aisle. Sure enough, food was already starting to appear in the center of the stage. The entire troupe had all brought dishes for the event. Chandler had told me about it weeks ago, and I had been so excited at the idea of having a somewhat proper Thanksgiving. It was something I hadn't done since I was in middle school with my parents.

And it had made it all the better when Chandler had invited my friends. Including Henry, much to my surprise.

I spotted Chandler helping Thomas and Abigail with the world's largest trays of turkey. Definitely enough to feed the group, though I was certain it would still all be gone by the end of it.

As we approached the three, Chandler finally looked up at us. Despite what his mood had been a short while earlier, he had calmed down substantially. He even smiled when he saw all of us together. Stella weaved around us, offering him a hug.

When they broke apart, Alex approached him. I loved the way Chandler towered over her, swallowing her whole with his giant frame. Alex was barely five feet tall, making Chandler have nearly a whole foot and a half advantage over her.

My best friend looked up at him, grinning. "We meet again, sexy skyscraper."

I laughed so loudly and hard I cried for a solid minute. When I calmed down a little, the entire group was recovering from the comment, too.

"Well, I've never heard *that* one before," Thomas noted beside Chandler. "I guess I know what I'll be calling you from now on."

"Don't you dare," Chandler glared at him, but he had been laughing, too.

Despite every impending concern over the last month of my life, I had felt sheer joy at nearly every moment. I had been living with Chandler at his condo since the first night I came back. My weeks were filled with Cirque du Lys rehearsals. And though I no longer helped Chandler at the Dreamers Academy and was still working with Professor Larson for my lessons, we'd kept ourselves a secret from almost everyone else, and I didn't mind.

For the first time in a long time, I felt like so many things which had been missing were finally within reach again. I was living the dream I'd had since I was a kid. I'd found another person who completed me in nearly every single way and understood all the nuances of my passions for my career on a level most others couldn't.

As I sat amongst the crowded theater of Cirque du Lys, beneath the majestic tent covered in string lights, I felt joy like I hadn't felt since my parents had been alive. Like I was surrounded by family again and the warmth of being together and happy.

Chandler must have noticed my thoughtful expression because I saw he'd been watching me when I came back to my senses. I shook my head, grinning before I took another bite of the pumpkin pie I'd been eating. A dish courtesy of Elle. It was delicious. Chandler was smirking at me, shaking his head.

"What?" I said, swallowing down my food.

I watched him reach across to me, wiping off the side of my face with his fingers and shaking his head again. "No more making fun of my eating habits. Ms. Whipped Cream Face."

The comment made me laugh. I leaned over, tugging at his Cirque du Lys sweatshirt he'd put on, drawing him close enough to be able to whisper to him. "I happen to know you like it when I have whipped cream all over me."

When I heard Chandler clear his throat in response, I laughed again, releasing my hold on him. He smiled at me while I finished off the last bite of pie. After I did, I looked back up, realizing most of our friends had been staring straight at us.

"Get a room, hornballs," Alex grinned, a few people down from me.

I would have been more anxious at the comment she'd so obviously announced to the entire group if it hadn't been for the fact Abigail and Thomas had been smiling too. The entire group was, really.

"Wait, so does *everyone* know now?" Chandler asked, though he was mostly looking at Abigail and Thomas, who I had assumed he was most concerned about.

Thomas shook his head at him but was still smiling. "Chandler, my friend, you are by far the *least* subtle human being I have ever met. And I'm afraid you've rubbed off on *that* one. All you two do is smile. I haven't seen you this happy in years."

"I don't think ever," Stella added in agreement.

"You've certainly been our loveable, grumpy old man," Abigail said. Out of the corner of my eye, I watched Chandler scowl at her playfully. "But this side of you is nice. We're happy for you, truly."

Chandler and I glanced at one another, and I was certain it would still remain a secret elsewhere for now, but it felt like a tremendous relief not to have to keep it from our friends any longer. I leaned over, feeling completely comfortable, laying my head on Chandler's shoulder and lacing our hands together.

I felt him lean in, planting a kiss on the top of my head. He whispered quietly. "Happy Thanksgiving, Cassandra."

It had been a happy one, indeed.

We'd barely gotten lost in conversation again when I felt something vibrating. It must have been Chandler's phone in his pocket. The two of us broke apart from one another, and he dug for it. I noticed his eyes grow wide when he looked at the screen.

"It's David Finch," his attention turned to me, and I watched as he started to get to his feet. I blinked, the name not registering at first. Chandler had put the phone to his ear while offering me a hand off the ground. I took it, feeling him tug me upward.

By the time I'd gotten to my feet, Chandler had spoken. "Hello? David? Give me a second."

He started off across the theater stage, still holding onto my hand. He glanced back at me, noticing the confused look still on my face. I still didn't know who he was talking to.

"It's the private detective," Chandler explained, and the name instantly registered. We had spent the last few weeks hunting down the best person to help us with my uncle, Peter, and had finally decided on a private detective from Massachusetts with a pretty stellar background. Last week, we had sent him the evidence I had on my uncle.

Well, most of it, anyway. Chandler hadn't known about the fact I'd kept some of it to myself still, preferring not to entrust it with anyone until I was absolutely certain it was safe. Also, I did not want him to know that some of my more recent finds were about his father rather than Peter. Information I wanted him far away from until I had it sorted out.

We reached the wings of the stage, and Chandler, who had been limping a little, brought himself back down to the ground. I followed as he put his phone on speaker. "Okay, David, we're both here now."

"Great," David said with that thick Boston accent of his. "I wanted to touch base with you both since I've sorted through all this information Cassie sent. I'm pretty impressed you got a hold of some of this stuff. I'd imagine there are quite a few lawyers who would pay you a fortune to be as meticulous as you have been gathering evidence."

I smiled a bit despite my anxieties about this conversation. "I think I'm too curious for my own good sometimes," I admitted. "Hopefully, it comes in handy."

"Actually, I have a few leads," David replied, and I heard Chandler shift a little beside me. I glanced over at him, noticing he was wincing. Worried about how badly he was hurting after his fall, but I was too distracted, wanting to know what David had to say. "So, he was indicted for drug-related charges. Heroin. Now, I know you didn't have any information about this from the evidence you gathered, but I did a bit of digging and interestingly enough, those dealings he was involved with... I think they might have been with some pretty dangerous folks."

"What do you mean?" Chandler was the one who spoke, not me. I glanced at him for a moment. He looked very thoughtful, even though I knew he was in a lot of pain. He clearly wanted to be active in this investigation, and I appreciated it.

"This is going to be a little crazy, but bear with me—" David said, and how he phrased it made my stomach lurch. "I think this guy might have been getting the bulk of those drugs from mafia ties. And I'm not sure he was even aware of it, honestly. I barely figured out the connection myself. I just happen to be a bit of a history buff, so I made the little connection."

"The *mafia*?" I repeated, blinking. "I mean, my uncle has always been a pretty scumbag of a guy, but I feel like the mafia is a bit of a stretch—"

"Like I said, I doubt he's even aware of it. There's just a bit of history of some prior heroin trafficking in Nevada. There's a whole web of them actually, all over the country, all connected with this huge global heroin network post the second world war called The French Connection."

"Le Milieu." It took me a moment to realize Chandler had spoken instead of David. "The French mafia."

"Aha, another history buff with us, I see," David sounded pleased on the other end of the line. Meanwhile, I'd glanced at Chandler, who'd looked back at me. He shrugged, looking lost in thought, but I didn't focus on it too long, still wondering where David was going with all of this.

"The French Connection itself is pretty much a thing of the past at this point," David said. "At least unless you want to talk to the more conspiracy theorist history buffs like myself. You look up any records of it online, they'll tell you it was disbanded in the seventies. But there's plenty of little indications, if you look hard enough, that it's still very much in existence. Little threads woven all over the country. How they're doing it exactly beats the hell out of me. Le Milieu happens to be pretty damn good at hiding themselves."

There was a clatter, and when I looked over at Chandler, I noticed he'd dropped his phone. His eyes had gotten a little wide, a strange look on his face. It disappeared a second later, quickly retrieving the phone from the ground. "Sorry David, my hand slipped, and I dropped the phone. Anyway, you were saying..."

My eyes were still on Chandler for a few seconds again, but he seemed to have focused back on the conversation at hand. I didn't dwindle on it, turning my focus back on David. "So you think one of these 'threads' you're talking about is in Nevada? My uncle was getting drugs from them, and he didn't know?"

"Yeah, exactly," David replied. "And I think if I can find the right angle on it, we might be able to use it against him to keep the bastard put."

I had just been about to answer David, thrilled that he'd already figured out some way to potentially help me in my years of efforts in trying to bring justice to a man I hated beyond measure, but Chandler beat me to speaking. "David, I think you need to be really careful about what you're digging into here. There isn't anything else we can use? Cassandra sent over a lot of evidence. Surely there has to be something."

My attention shot straight to him, surprised, out of anything, that was what he'd said. David seemed in agreement with me. "I thought you'd be more enthusiastic that I had a lead at all, Chandler. This is pretty huge, and it was a big part thanks to your very vigilant girlfriend you have—all those records she kept helped a great deal in me being swift to figure any of this out. I'm pretty sure this is about as solid of a case against him as you're going to get. If we can connect him to some of these people I have records of being associated with Le Milieu—"

"I'm just a little concerned you're going to stir up something you shouldn't be," Chandler replied. I hadn't once stopped looking at him. "If what you're saying is true, if Peter Blackstone was somehow involved with the mafia in any capacity, and whoever he was involved with found out what you were doing... It could cause a lot of problems. Not even just for you. It could lead back to us, to Cassandra, too. I don't think that's a safe thing to be doing."

There was a long pause on the line. For a second, I wondered if David had hung up entirely. Chandler finally looked up at me, meeting my gaze. He must have noticed how absolutely baffled I was because he started to defend himself. "I'm trying to *protect* you all here. It's not like I don't want to see that son of a bitch taken down. Believe me... I'd probably kill the man if I ever saw him after all the things you've told me." He was still staring straight at me. After a pause, his attention dropped back to the phone. "I'm just saying, let's not be brash. Think about this a little before we make any sudden moves."

Chandler adjusted himself and abruptly let out a sharp cry of pain. He winced, taking deep breaths for a moment. After he'd stabilized, he wobbled to his feet and then handed his phone to me.

"I need to go get the brace," he said quietly, his eyes not meeting mine. Chandler's entire face was ghost white. It worried me, but I nodded, still wanting to talk to David. The second I took the phone from him, Chandler hobbled off away from me.

While I watched Chandler go, I took David off the speaker, putting the phone to my ear. The minute he was out of earshot, I spoke again. "I want to look into it anyway," I said, my attention still on Chandler, watching him as he had Abby help him off the stage. "See what you can find, and then just contact me when you do. I can handle it."

While I'd hated making that decision without Chandler, I wasn't about to let an opportunity to bring my uncle to justice get away from me. Not if I could help it. I'd take that risk. David said goodbye to me, and I hung up, bringing myself up off the floor. As I wandered back across the theater, I couldn't help but wonder if the fears Chandler had over the last few minutes were in any way related to his family. If he really did know what he was talking about and how dangerous it could be.

Briefly, I worried I had made the wrong decision. But my concerns about how much Chandler knew about his family, his involvement, and the danger he was so adamant about made me think otherwise.

CHAPTER 25

CASSANDRA

Drawing toward the end of the semester at Dreamers Academy, it was obvious the holiday spirit was in the air. Garlands and wreaths hung from the towering columns supporting the ceilings of Tremblay Hall. A Christmas tree had been set up in each of the four corners of the building. Perched on some of the window sills in front of the stained glass were large, intricate menorahs. The school had certainly spared no expense to be festive.

However beautiful and light everything was, with the students bustling through the hallways in relatively good moods despite finals looming around the corner, I had felt grumpy. Wanting to be anywhere but there in those moments.

It had been lightly snowing outside when I left the building, trekking across campus a short distance to the facility adjacent to Tremblay Hall. I had visited the building a lot in more recent times, on occasion to visit Professor Larson to get work from her classes to grade. But most of the time, it was for a different reason.

The moment I stepped through the doorway into Chandler Moreau's cramped little office at the far end of one hallway, I found him standing there waiting for me. He drew forward with a few simple steps, pushing the door closed with his hand beside my head before the gap between us dissipated.

His mouth crashed into mine, pressing us so tightly together I could feel the carved designs on the wood door behind me. My hands drew up into his hair, bundling it in my fists, kissing him back just as furiously.

In usual form, we were relentless until neither of us had much more air to breathe. When we broke away from one another, the cold air of the room was a welcomed thing to tame all the heat raging through my body. Chandler was grinning at me.

"Well, I wasn't expecting *that,*" I said, panting softly, unable to help myself from grinning at the beautiful man in front of me.

"I missed you," Chandler shrugged, also trying to catch his breath.

"I've been gone an hour," I noted. It occurred to me he'd been waiting by the door. "How long have you been standing there? You were like a dog sitting by the door waiting for its owner to return or something." I laughed, shaking my head.

Chandler motioned to the watch on his arm. "I figured you were on your way when I noticed the time. I hadn't been standing around *that* long."

"Whatever you say," I replied, winking at him. We both were quiet for a moment. I decided to wander further into the room, sitting down in the chair opposite his desk.

Across from me was a picture frame decorated with Christmas wrapping paper and adorned with a bow. The first time I'd come here, I had been a bit unsettled by all of the jarring pictures of clowns. I'd asked him about it and learned he was in agreement with me, but they had apparently been necessary for the room's structural integrity, unable to be removed for one reason or another.

Much to both of our relief, however, I'd been creative in disguising them from view in an attempt to make the room a little festive. Something told me the wrapping paper might not ever come down.

Chandler came to sit across from me at his desk. His playful expression had shifted, and I could tell he'd gotten a little concerned. "Is something bothering you?"

I sighed, sinking back into the chair. It wasn't the most comfortable thing ever. Everything in Chandler's office, which had been sparse in general, was old and barely touched, indicating how little he liked to be there. And the office looked nothing like the aesthetics he generally preferred.

"I absolutely *hate* Elizabeth Larson with a passion," I replied, frowning. "She spent our entire lesson trying to undo every single thing you've been showing me at rehearsals the last few months. Completely convinced it was all wrong. It was infuriating. I'm so tired of it. I really wish you were still teaching me."

"Well, while I certainly agree I am the all-knowing master of silks," Chandler grinned, and despite my soured mood, it made me laugh a little. "I still teach you, Cassandra. Just not here. Which is the way it needs to be. You know that."

My attention drew back to Chandler after he'd spoken. Our eyes met, and I tried to gauge his expression, which was perfectly in line with his usual as of late. Calm and collected. All things considered, it unnerved me a little.

After the bits of information Andre Morales had been telling me about the Moreaus confirmed some of the suspicions I'd had about Chandler's father, I'd felt rather unsettled. Couldn't understand, for the life of me, how Chandler wasn't more worried about everything—unless he was ignorant of it. Which is what I'd been clinging desperately to since I'd never found anything connecting him specifically. Only his father, maybe more of his family too, but I hadn't figured that out quite yet. As much as I knew about Chandler, after all the years I'd devoted my life to him, it was hard for me to fathom a world in which he'd be involved with anything Gabriel Moreau was, at any capacity.

"Yes, I realize we have to lie low because of your father," I replied to him, finally bringing my attention back to the room. Shortly after he'd gotten me the position at Cirque du Lys, Chandler had enlightened me on why everything had occurred the way it had. Gabriel had suspected our feelings for one another and had threatened to remove me from the program. It was to ensure, regardless of what happened, I still had an opportunity to learn from the man I'd waited half my life to mentor me.

It had all worked out, and I was grateful. This façade I had put on while working at this school, however, still left me a little unsettled. Mostly because if Gabriel ever figured us out, I wasn't quite sure what he was capable of.

"Cassandra," Chandler called me back to the room. I realized I'd drifted far away into my thoughts again. I shook my head, returning my focus to him.

"There you are." He smiled. "Don't let her get to you. Besides, the semester is almost over. You'll get a little break, and I'll have an opportunity to bestow my geniusness on you so that you can tell her how it is next year."

"You're ridiculous," I replied, smiling. His comment had me relaxing again, wrapped up in the sweet little words of affection he always had toward me. "But thank you. That makes me feel better. Even if you're going to turn me into a defiant, rebellious heathen."

I watched Chandler's facial expression shift yet again. But gratefully, it had been what I'd probably needed in those moments. A distraction, far away from all the other little thoughts plaguing me.

He got up from his seat, towering over me as I sat across from him. He planted his hands on his desk, drawing forward, closer to me. The man's face had gotten serious, but I'd known from the way it had looked playful seconds earlier that this was an act. One I was looking forward to seeing played out.

"We certainly don't need you turning into a rebellious heathen, Ms. Blackstone." The look he was giving me, the subtle shift in his tone, having grown deeper with his air of authority—I *lived* for moments like this.

I got up too. Leaned into the desk a bit, eyes locked on him. With one swift sweep of my hand, I sent the neatly stacked pile of papers I assumed were students' homework assignments flying off his desk.

The growl that came from the man seconds after I'd acted was the best thing that had happened all day. At least, I thought it was until the whole act continued.

"You know I don't like *messes,* Ms. Blackstone," he said, fiercely. He was ripping into me with his glare, and I ate every second of it up.

"That's unfortunate, Professor Moreau. Because I seemed to have made one." While I was speaking, I watched him move around his desk. In dangerous pursuit, like he was a lion on a hunt for the gazelle he'd spotted in the grass.

Instead of waiting for him to get to me like I would have normally done, I decided to surprise him. Swiftly, I turned, darting toward his office door like I'd been making an attempt to escape him. Which, I was pleasantly surprised, got the exact reaction I'd wanted.

His pace quickened behind me. By the time I'd reached the door and started to open it, he'd gotten to me, slamming himself into me and the door, pressing firmly into my body. I was trapped, locked in place between the door and the ravenous man behind me.

I felt his hands wrap around my wrists, drawing my arms above me. His mouth came to the side of my head, his voice growling low into my ear.

"*Ms. Blackstone.* Did you really think you were going to get away from me that easily?" He leaned down, and I felt his mouth on my neck, biting down roughly against me. It was actually a little painful, but I sunk into it, gasping and writhing beneath him helplessly. His mouth came back to my ear, "I believe you and I have some things to take care of first. Consequences for the little *act* of yours."

"Are you going to *punish* me?" I managed to reply, feeling his body tremble slightly behind me when I said it. The response got a little smirk from me. "Because I've been feeling *very* defiant lately, Professor Moreau. I think you might need to fix that."

My words must have ignited him because, in one swift motion, he released my hands, and I felt his fall to wrap around my hips. He swung us both around, nearly carrying me off the ground until I'd been pushed roughly up into his desk.

His hands released from me, only to press firmly into my upper back until he bent my upper torso forward. I planted straight into the cool wood of the top of his desk, gasping when I did. My hands fell on either side of me, and my head tilted to the side. In my peripheral vision, I saw his profile.

Only a few seconds had passed, and he had spent the entire time roughly drawing my pants down my legs. My entire lower half was lying naked in front of him in his office. I could see those intense green eyes of his drilling into me like usual. Waited, my heart thudding in my chest, for him to do anything at all.

It was an agonizingly long wait. Almost enough time that I'd started to inquire. But then I felt his fingers rake over the skin of my backside roughly. I gasped when he did, writhing on top of the desk.

"Are you going to apologize for your behavior, Ms. Blackstone?" He asked me. He sounded so fierce and authoritative, switching from the former lower tone he'd had.

"I don't know what you're talking about, Professor Moreau," I replied innocently as his fingers left me.

Before I had one solitary second to think, his hand came firmly down. The sound of it was so loud it reverberated around the room, followed by a loud gasp from me. It stung so intensely for those first few seconds my head spun.

"Care to try again?" He asked. I jumped in surprise when his fingers fell back onto my skin, gently drawing against where his hand had landed. Like he'd been soothing the injury.

Though it had hurt, the intensity of the heat shooting down my legs was absolutely surreal. I was trembling a little from it, finding myself suddenly addicted to this new little power-play game we were locked in. There wasn't any way in hell I was ending this. Not yet.

"No, thank you," I replied, swiftly. This time, the consequence of my words didn't happen immediately. He had removed his fingers from me. And I laid there, each second growing more and more agonizing.

It came from nowhere. When I had least expected it to. And again, the searing sting of it was teetering on the edge of being almost too much, but I sunk into it after. Enjoying the after-effects of it far too much to care. My entire body was absolutely wrecked with desire.

His fingers resumed again, attending to where he'd lashed out at me. I sunk into the feeling for a few seconds. He dropped his hands again, backing a few steps away from me. It took me a second to realize he had, and eventually, I looked over my head back at him, wondering what he was doing now.

"Get on your knees, Ms. Blackstone," he said, eyes on me again. "I want to watch you clean up the mess you made. Feel as dirty as you made my floor."

I almost died right then and there. Swallowed deeply at his words. Paused for a half-second before I got myself up from the desk. Turned around, kicking off my flats and my pants the remainder of the way off my legs. Eagerly, I drew down onto his floor, getting to my hands and knees like he'd asked me to.

When I looked up, he was right on top of me, looking as deliciously menacing as ever. He nodded to all the papers on his floor. "Get to it. I won't ask again."

The entire time I crawled around on his office floor, he was watching, trailing behind me. I picked up the pile, stacking it back on his desk. After I finished, I sat back on my knees, looking up at him again.

"I suppose that was adequate," he said matter-of-factly. "Get up off the floor, Ms. Blackstone. You're filthy enough as it is." My eyes flashed at him as I pulled myself up into a standing position. Once I had, I took a step forward toward him, so the small gap between us had almost completely vanished.

"Oh, I am *very filthy*, Professor Moreau," I drew out the words as low and sultry as I possibly could, still giving him that gaze I had been, my lip curled slightly.

"Fuck, Cassandra," Chandler gasped, and I realized I'd made him snap. He'd lost it, and it had been made apparent when he grabbed me by the waist, spinning me back around again. Thrusting me right back down on top of his desk.

I heard his pants unzipping and, seconds later, hit the floor. Didn't have to wait much longer until he came crashing into me with reckless abandon, making my head spin wildly.

The man was relentless, thrusting so hard, so fast, it was moving the desk slightly every time he did. We didn't stop, inching forward with it. He had reached up, wrapping my ponytail in his fist. My head yanked backward, so I was looking up at the beautiful tiled and arched ceiling of his office.

It hadn't been long, and I'd tumbled off the cliff he'd been dangling me on. Trying desperately to be as quiet as I could, still whimpering his name into the room as I writhed on the desk, completely lost in the overwhelming sensations. He fell against me, seconds behind, grunting and gasping my name in reply.

Once we'd both winded down a bit, which had lasted far longer than I had expected, we spent a minute or two catching our breaths before he removed himself from me. I spun around, finding him grinning as he pulled his pants back off the floor, dressing himself.

"Are you going to behave yourself now?" Chandler asked me, walking back around his desk as I picked up my clothes.

I looked up at him after I'd finished collecting myself and redressing, smiling back. "I guess for now, at least."

Chandler glanced at his watch, and I saw him frown. "I probably should go. There's another staff meeting this afternoon, as much as I hate them. This is why I don't want to teach..." He grumbled, getting to his feet again and collecting his bag off the floor.

I would have been paying more attention to what he was doing if I hadn't spotted something on his desk. Something which must have been buried underneath the papers I'd sent to the floor a short while prior. A small black journal with the Cirque du Lys emblem on the front.

My heart picked up again in my chest as I stared at it. Feeling incredibly panicked by the sight of it. I must have been staring too long because I heard Chandler speaking to me again, bringing me back to the room. "Cassandra? Did you hear what I said?"

As soon as he spoke, my head jerked back up. "What?"

Chandler looked down at where I'd been focused. I could tell by the sudden shift in his facial expression he realized what I'd been looking at. What made it worse was he looked slightly puzzled for a half-second, but it barely lasted before he returned his attention to me.

"I'll be home early today," he repeated himself, though there was a strange expression still on his face. I felt sick looking at him, hoping desperately I was seeing things. He was being absent-minded or on some different train of thought. "Does Indian sound good? I'll swing by and grab it. We hadn't had it in a while, and I was getting the itch."

"Chandler, we literally had it last week," I reminded him, and I couldn't help but smile. Hoped maybe my mild amusement with him would somehow deter whatever was happening. "That's fine. Just don't forget to get me naan like last time. I know you did it on purpose."

It was Chandler who finally smirked at me, much to my relief. He nodded, and once he did, I weaved my way back out of his office with Chandler seconds behind me. We stood right outside together.

I had expected us to start down the hall but was surprised when I watched him pull his keys from his pocket instead.

Not once, in the dozens of times I'd left with him from his office, did I see him do what he did in those next few seconds. It had never happened because, truthfully, the man had next to nothing inside of the office and never cared. Today, however, Chandler fumbled with his keys for a moment, finding the one he wanted. I watched him turn back to the door, briskly locking it behind him.

When he looked back at me, he took a step forward and leaned in, planting a kiss on my forehead. "See you in a few hours?"

"See you in a few hours," I managed to reply. Feeling an overwhelming tumbling of my stomach as I turned, watching as he wandered down the hallway. Hating I had absolutely no idea what he had been thinking the entire time.

CHAPTER 26

CHANDLER

Half hitch on the stem. Loop through the working ends. Over the stem. Behind the stem. Back through the loop. Excess around the stem... And—tighten.

Cassandra let out a long audible breath of air. I'd been lost in a sea of twists and turns of tossa jute, in various shades of green, while on my knees in front of her. It was probably my favorite color of rope to use. It paired well against her olive skin tone and the tossa was newer and still had a vibrant sheen from the oils used to condition it. Cassandra had enjoyed it because it still carried a distinct honey-like smell, and its coarseness made the entire bondage experience more heightened because of the feel.

I'd been about to finish with the chain stitch corset, which was a new tie I'd never attempted before. My mind had been a mess the last few days, so I opted for a distraction with something different and Cassandra hadn't seemed to mind. It had certainly done the trick for the last hour or so, keeping my thoughts at bay. Now that

I was getting close to finishing, however, I was starting to feel preoccupied again.

After I'd twisted the rope into another half-hitch, which this particular tie was full of, I glanced up at Cassandra. Her gaze was straight ahead but she seemed to have noticed I had my eyes on her and looked down. We stared at one another, my movements having paused. Her facial expression had shifted and she looked curious more than anything.

"Are you okay?" All at once I felt her hands draw up along my head, fingers lacing into my hair. I sighed the minute she did it, unable to help myself from closing my eyes and giving in to the sensation. This little act had been a habit of hers during these Shibari sessions, when she hadn't been bound and unable to do so. It captured me every time.

Which wasn't the worst thing, since my mind was such a mess. I let it take me away briefly, falling into the rhythm of her fingers running against my scalp, sending little shivers down the length of me.

I had absolutely no idea how long I sat there, lost in what she was doing, but I came back to my senses eventually. My eyes opened again, staring up. Cassandra's focus had left me, looking off into the room. I resumed my work, trying to finish.

For minutes, I fought myself from telling her what was on my mind. The thing which had been tormenting me for days now, since we'd been in my office together. When I saw her reaction upon seeing my grandmother's journal on my desk—the look on her face had been unmistakable. She'd known *exactly* what it was. And after everything that had happened between us, my curiosity was maddening as to how the hell she'd managed to throw me off her tracks as well as she had. How she'd convinced me my father had taken it, when it had been her all along...

There had been a dozen times since those moments in my office I'd fought myself to ask her. I had come close, but still hadn't managed to do so. After what had happened initially, when I'd gotten angry with her and it had done absolutely no good, I couldn't imagine it going any better this time around. Even if I knew for certain, whatever reasons she had for doing it hadn't been ill-intentioned. I knew her well enough by now.

However, I desperately wanted answers. I was about to ask her. Decided I was going to give in to temptation and do so, now that I was finished with what I'd been doing.

"And, *fini*," I said quietly, as I'd secured the last half-hitch completing the corset. While Cassandra admired the pattern in the mirrors behind me, I looked over her, checking my work. It seemed in perfect form, much to my satisfaction. The green jute looked beautiful against her. "That came out much better than I anticipated..."

When I glanced up, Cassandra had been smiling at me, her fingers running over the top portions of the jute woven over her chest. It was something she usually did, and would hold me hostage watching. She always got so wrapped up in the designs, as much as I did.

Eventually, her gaze came back. We lingered for a few seconds. It was now or never, I supposed. I needed to ask. Otherwise, I was probably going to lose my mind. There certainly had to be a reasonable explanation. I was convinced of it.

"I need to tell you something," Cassandra beat me. Her words had me sitting back on my legs, my attention focused on her. I wondered if she was about to admit it herself. It would have helped matters, since I hadn't been looking forward to interrogating her. I nodded.

"—I know you were worried and upset," she started, and I felt relief wash over me. It seemed as though it was exactly what she was doing. However, I was quickly corrected in the assumption. "I appreciate you caring so much, but I had to do it anyway. It was a great opportunity. This has been too big of a problem for far too long."

I blinked, utterly lost to what she'd been referring to. "What?"

Cassandra was staring dead at me, a strange look on her face. She continued a beat later. "I told David to look into the Le Milieu thing with my uncle anyway."

For a few moments, the words didn't register. I had already been on one train of thought as it was, now trying to backtrack to keep up with her. Then she'd gone tumbling in a different direction entirely and I was racing to keep everything straight.

Once it had repeated in my mind, I found my mouth dropping open. "You did *what*?"

"I told David Finch to keep looking into Peter's involvement with the mafia," Cassandra repeated, and I felt my ears starting to ring. "It was a good lead, Chandler. He called me earlier today and he's pretty sure he has all the evidence he needs to keep Peter put. Maybe take down a person or two he was associating with, too. There's going to be a lot of good that comes out of it. I know you were worried, but you need to trust me—"

"He called you?" I repeated again, feeling like I was being yanked off balance, unable to stay steady. I re-situated myself, sitting cross-legged. My attention had gone off in another direction, trying to process what she was saying. I looked back up at her. "He didn't call me. Why?"

Cassandra bit at her lip. I watched her drop to the ground, sitting across from me. "—I didn't want you to worry. You were so upset when we were talking about it at Thanksgiving... Chandler, this is a *good* thing. It's all going to turn out okay. David knows what he's doing. It's all working out."

My head was still spinning. I stared at her in disbelief. "David kept looking into Le Milieu?" I clarified yet again, and Cassandra nodded. All at once, my face twisted, finally registering what the hell she'd admitted to me. "After I *explicitly* told you both it was a *bad* idea? Warned you that it was dangerous?"

There was a strange expression on Cassandra's face. "Don't you think you're being a little overly paranoid right now? I don't get you. David's trying to keep the son-of-a-bitch where he belongs, and after everything, I thought *you'd* understand. I've told you more than I've told anyone, including Alex, and even she thinks this is the right thing to do."

"I'm trying to *protect* you," I argued back at her, feeling a whole slew of emotions hitting me like a brick wall, unsure of whether I was angry, or terrified or what the hell I felt. "This isn't a game. It wasn't a casual suggestion. This isn't me being overly paranoid. Those people are fucking dangerous, Cassandra. I know you're worried about your uncle, believe me. I am too. Don't think I'm not. But the difference is...your uncle is behind bars. Those individuals David's looking into *aren't,* and the minute they find out what he's up to—"

Cassandra's face flickered a little. "Chandler... Why the hell do you know so much about all of this? Why do I get the feeling your insane amount of concern about this situation is more than some 'history buff' knowledge like David was playing it off to be?" As the words came out of her, it sent a shiver ripping down my spine. "Does it have to do with your father? Why do I get the feeling this whole charade you've been having me put on by staying at Dreamers and acting like things are normal, has everything to do with how bad of a person he *actually* is?"

My ears were ringing so loudly, I could hardly hear. I knew my surprise had to be written all over my face. I was losing sight of reality. Of all of the people in the entire world I should never have been shocked to find she knew things about my family... I should have known better. The woman knew more about me than even *I* knew half the time.

"Cassandra," I started, trying to bring my voice to a calm, collected tone. "What *exactly* do you know about my father?"

Her gaze was steady. "Not as much as I want to." She'd spent so long afterwards not speaking, I'd started to reply, but when I did, she continued again, barrelling over me. "And I'm not sure now, after the way you've been acting. I knew for a very long time he was bad, but I didn't know *how* bad."

Cassandra situated herself a little, still staring me down. "Honestly, I didn't think he'd be the type to be in the mafia of all things. I still doubt it. I figured he was dealing with some shady people. I didn't like how nosy he got all those months ago about me. He seemed like the kind of person who might murder someone in the back alley if they crossed him the wrong way. And honestly, I've been worried about you. That's a huge reason I gave a shit about him in the first place. I wanted you safe, and I know for a fact he is not safe."

While the sentiment was flattering, it didn't make me any less concerned. "As far as I'm aware, my father has never killed anyone. He's not really the type." I replied, surprised I'd been bluntly honest with her. I hadn't liked where this conversation had gone, not any in the least. "And you're right, Cassandra. He *is* dangerous. It's why I was so concerned about you months ago, when he was so focused on you. And it's also why I'm going to ask you not to pry at me about him further. I promise you, I'm doing it for your own good."

She had opened her mouth to reply, but I beat her this time, not having finished my thought. "Yes. I know some things. Things you should trust my judgment about. Which includes my opinion about what David is doing, if he hasn't done damage already."

"Are you going to tell me what you know? Or is this going to be a 'your father' situation, too?" She didn't look the least bit pleased with me. I assumed it was because she knew what I was about to say.

"I'm not," I replied, and Cassandra's face twisted more than it already had. "You need to trust me. You should know well enough by now, I only want what's best for you. Everything I've done has been with the best intentions, and I *promise* you, I intend it to always be that way. I will do my best. But no, Cassandra. I'm not divulging information I want you *very* far away from. And I expect you to call David and tell him he needs to drop it with the mafia inquiries. That's not a suggestion, either. I mean it."

She didn't look happy with me in the least. A little pissed, if anything. This had certainly dampened the fun little distracting afternoon we'd been having. But I didn't care. It was something I wasn't going to budge on, and hopefully she'd understand. All I needed was confirmation that she understood what I had asked of her. Luckily, it came after a brief hesitation. "Fine. I'll talk to David."

"Thank you. I promise you, we'll figure out a way to take down your uncle. But we need to do it safely." I said it while trying to be as soft and kind as I could, grateful she'd agreed. Now she'd gotten that little bit of information out in the open, I still had my own questions. Questions which had been nagging at me for far too long. I needed to know about the journal. Especially since it was clear she knew information I didn't realize she did.

I'd been about to inquire, when I heard my phone begin ringing abruptly from across the room. There had been music playing before it had started. Sometimes I enjoyed the background noise while I practiced Shibari. It added to the meditative quality of the whole thing. The sound had me jerking my head and I glanced over to where it was coming from. I didn't get many phone calls, which was a good thing because I tried to avoid them more often than not.

As much as I'd wanted to inquire with her about the journal and ignore the call, I decided to ignore Cassandra instead. Thinking if I stopped the conversation all-together, tried to keep her far away from any thoughts about my family, maybe she'd drop it. Then I could figure out the damage David had caused, as soon as possible. Hopefully find some way to rectify the damage he might have done, to ensure everyone's safety.

Instead of asking questions, I got to my feet and walked across the room to fetch my phone. It had stopped ringing by the time I'd gotten to it, but it started again seconds later.

The moment I'd picked it up from the end table by the door, I regretted having walked over at all. I stared down at the number in disbelief. I never heard from this number. Ever. Whatever the hell Gabriel Moreau had been calling me about was something I didn't want *anything* to do with. I knew that much before I had even answered the phone.

And the fact it had been *him* calling, of all the times he possibly could have been, had a violent chill ripping through me that caused me to jerk in surprise. I shook my head. "What the absolute fuck does *he* want?" I muttered under my breath.

"Who?" Cassandra asked, apparently having heard me.

"My father," I said, not having cared I'd told her. As much as I didn't want to, I finally put the phone to my ear, growling. "*What?*"

Peace River ran along one side of Acrefort proper, and most of the area around it was suburban. A little more spread out the closer you got to the river, and condensed in the small downtown near the center. The Dreamers Academy and Cirque du Lys were adjacent to downtown, but off in their own little area.

The far opposite end of Acrefort, heading up further north into New York and into the large rolling hills and countryside that went in the direction of other cities, was more rural. A bunch of apple orchards, a couple of farms. My life had always been so wrapped up within the heart of the city, I never went out there. I never had a reason to.

Which was why the last place I expected to go immediately following the brief and uninformative conversation with my father, was in that direction. In the middle of fucking nowhere, for who knew what reason.

Instead of allowing me to get to where I was told to arrive myself, I was picked up by my father's town car. He wasn't in the vehicle when it arrived, thank God. But the idea he'd played it out this way, leaving me without an immediate option of escape and at his mercy, made me sick to my stomach the entire drive. If there was anything worse than things not being in *my* control, it was when they were in my *father's*.

The town car pulled onto a dirt road, leading up to a red and white farmhouse sitting on a large property. I was surprised it had been an apple orchard, which made me briefly think of my grandmother. I didn't stay in my thoughts long, because the car came to a halt and the driver told me, very curtly, to exit the vehicle.

Gabriel had been waiting immediately outside for me, along with two individuals I didn't know. All three of them had a terrifying air about them. My father was the one to speak. "I suppose this is how to get you to arrive for dinner more promptly. Having you escorted seems to do the trick quite nicely."

"I'll be taking my own transportation, thank you," I replied, curtly. "What the hell are we doing out here? Are—are you going to tell me anything, or do I get to be strung along, as usual?"

My father gave me a peculiar look I didn't understand, turning after and motioning for me to follow him. The two brawny men who accompanied him, at his side. I wasn't often intimidated by other men. Being nearly six and a half feet tall, with two decades of training with the silks relentlessly challenging nearly every single muscle in my body, there weren't many people who had any urge to fuck with me. And, despite loathing my genetics, I didn't mind that one particular fact in the least. Preferred it that way.

However, those two men following at Gabriel's heels, I did not like. And I wanted nothing to do with stirring up trouble with them, for certain.

We walked straight up to the farmhouse porch and my father went inside without so much as knocking first. I was last to enter, hesitantly trailing behind. The minute I got through the door, I noticed there was a man across the room, sitting at a table, a computer in front of him. He was leaning back in his seat, watching us as we entered.

Gabriel walked over, and I was a few paces behind. My father stepped out of the way, so the other man could come up to meet us. It wasn't until that moment I'd actually focused on him. And, like any other Moreau I'd ever met, it was absolutely clear as day whoever the hell this guy was, he was related to me.

The only thing different about him was the fact he had brown eyes, instead of the usual distinct green ones. That simple fact alone made the whole thing substantially more disconcerting, because the one person he had me thinking of in those seconds was—

"Chandler, I'd like you to meet Cedric," my father said, looking from the stranger, back to me. "Cedric Moreau. Lyam's and Charlotte's oldest son. Your cousin." If what he said was actually true, I had been exactly right. The guy looked strikingly similar to my younger cousin Samuel, with those brown eyes of his. The ones Samuel had gotten from his mother.

I stared at Gabriel, unsure if I had heard him correctly. "Excuse me?"

"Cedric is your cousin," my father repeated.

"How?" It was literally the only word I could speak for a few moments. "I would have known if I had another cousin... What the hell kind of joke is this, Dad? Did you bring me here to fuck with me? I don't have time for this." I'd reached into my pocket for my phone, deciding I'd call the town car to get me the hell out of there. Already tired of this bullshit, and I'd barely arrived.

"Put your phone away," Gabriel said, his voice so ominous it ripped a shiver through me. I immediately dropped it back into my coat pocket, taking my hand out. He looked satisfied and continued speaking. "Your aunt and uncle had what they deemed an *'unfortunate circumstance'* when they were in their early twenties, while your uncle was still in graduate school. As a result, they gave Cedric up when he was born."

Instead of my father continuing, it was Cedric who spoke. Unlike my father and me, who only had subtle hints of our French lineage in our voices, this man clearly had lived a substantial amount of time in the country like the rest of my estranged family. He had a slight accent, and it sounded similar in ways to my cousins.

"Oui," Cedric said, his brown eyes meeting mine. "They placed me for adoption. I knew nothing about them until I was almost in my forties. I made attempts to reach out to them recently, but it was in vain. Neither of them wanted anything to do with me. They acted as if they had no idea who I was. So, I decided to come here—looking for your father, and for you."

I studied the guy in front of me, who I knew absolutely nothing about. "I find it difficult to fathom my aunt and uncle would *ever* do such a thing. The man beside you, I wouldn't put it past." I shot a look at my father, who was unfazed. "But his brother is one of the nicest people I've ever known. Like hell he'd turn his back on you, if you really are his flesh and blood like you're having me believe." It was hard not to question it. He did look very similar to Samuel. But I still had serious doubts.

There was something off about this entire situation.

"If you are who you say you are, then there's something you're not telling me. Something more going on here. Honestly, outside the fact you do look strikingly like your *supposed* brother, I don't know you. You're a stranger. The fact you're, in any way, associating with *him*," I nodded at Gabriel again, "leads me to believe I don't want anything to do with you. Even if you do happen to be my cousin."

I reached for my phone, pulling it out of my pocket swiftly this time before my father could utter a word. While I clicked at it, I spoke. "I'm done with this. Whatever the hell is going on right now, I want nothing to do with it. I don't care. And for once in my life, I'm going to put my fucking foot down and tell you *no*." I'd quickly texted my town car driver to come get me and then pocketed my phone. The second I had, I spun around, intending to head back to the door.

By the time I'd taken one single solitary step, the two goons of my fathers, whoever they were, stepped right in front of me. I came to an abrupt halt, in time to hear my father speak. "I'm sending Cedric home to keep tabs on Samuel and the rest of the family for a little while. Conveniently enough, Sam got in touch, and wants to meet Cedric. Regardless if his parents aren't interested. It was the perfect opportunity."

In a flash, I'd spun back around. "Excuse me?"

My father didn't repeat himself, but continued his thought. "Your cousin has been...up to something. The last few years. Involved in things he *shouldn't*. Things which could get him in a situation much like Fredrick got himself—"

"Don't you *dare* say his name," I snarled loudly, taking a step forward. Hated the son-of-a-bitch had the audacity to bring up my late cousin. "Not ever. Do you understand me? You'll pay if you do, I swear. Don't test me, old man."

While Gabriel did pause after the loud and intense threat I'd made, he didn't stop all-together. "I need some information about what exactly he's been snooping around and doing. I almost thought about asking you to do it, but you've severed that tie unfortunately. Not to mention you seem to be *busy* as of late."

Those words snapped me to attention. I had guesses as to what he'd meant, and as much as I'd wanted answers about it, my father didn't seem to care. He had other things on his mind. "I've offered Cedric a job as my—ah—contractor, of sorts. He intended to come here to stay and needed work, so I offered him a substantial fee for...assisting with this."

My eyes flitted to Cedric, finding myself snarling again, this time at him. "If you are about to take my father's dirty money, to help him with things he has *no business* doing—" I trailed off for a second. Honestly, I sounded ridiculous threatening him, because I was the last person who should have been. I'd been taking money from my father too, for nearly my entire adult life. Tainted money

I should have stayed the hell away from and hadn't. I'd convinced myself, after all of this time, it had been for good reason, but I'd still done it, regardless.

I hated that I knew, by the look in my father's eyes, he was thinking the same thing.

A long roll of air left me before I spoke again. "I am going to say one thing. One thing, and then I am turning around and leaving." My gaze went to my father. "And you better tell those dipshits behind me to get the hell out of my way when I do." I took another long breath, and then looked back at Cedric.

"If I find you so much as *thought* about Samuel Moreau, if and when you go back home, I will make sure you spend the rest of your life regretting the decision. I will not hesitate. Stay the fuck away from my family." I was about to turn around, but spent one more second looking at my father. "And don't think I'm not warning all of them the second I leave."

"You can certainly try," my father replied, his eyes steady. Completely stoic.

I whipped around, charging straight up to the two buffoons behind me. Glaring as menacingly as I think I'd ever had.

"Move."

Their gazes went to my father. "Let him go," I heard Gabriel speak behind me. The minute they'd split apart, I moved as fast as I could across the length of the house, swiftly to the door. Before I'd shut it, my father called out again. Loud enough to ensure I heard him.

"You can run and hide all you want, Chandler. Be an oblivious fool. The world will keep turning, regardless. It'll all catch up to you, whether you like it or not."

I slammed the door behind me.

CHAPTER 27

CASSANDRA

A light layer of snow covered all the intricate stone details on the buildings of the Dreamer's Academy that evening. Even the gargoyles outside of Tremblay Hall were dusted in white. It was a cold day, and even more so now that the sun was gone. Right on the cusp of winter. I could see my breath as I walked along the sidewalk.

Chandler was beside me, noticing that I was shivering. Seconds later, I was surprised when I felt him wrap the wool coat he'd worn to his classes earlier that day around my shoulders.

"You don't need to do that..." I started, now worried that he was left without it.

"I'll be out of this weather soon enough," he reassured me, and I smiled graciously.

Despite what had transpired the other day between us during the Shibari session, things seemed to be okay. I tried to tell myself his concern had been for my safety, which had truthfully been mine, too. We cared about each other.

Even still, it wasn't *quite* as normal as I'd have liked it to be.

"Thank you. I was about to freeze to death," I replied. All the while, I worried why he'd been so nonchalant about the act in public. Then again, it had grown pretty late, almost nine in the evening at that point.

"We should consider investing in an actual *warm* coat or two for you," Chandler said, smiling back at me. "You've lived in Nevada far too long. Need some more time to acclimate to these brutal northern New York winters."

I nodded, wrapping the wool around me tighter. In addition to settling the disagreement we'd had the other day, I was also relieved that there hadn't been a mention of Chandler's grandmother's journal. My hope is that even if he'd figured me out, perhaps it hadn't fazed him as much as I worried it would.

"Are you sure you're going to be alright?" Chandler asked. He looked a little concerned, studying me over.

I offered him a sullen attempt at a smile before I replied. "I knew this was coming for years now. She's been planning this since our first year of undergrad. It's not a surprise or anything. I'm just a little sad, is all. Back then, I knew we would see each other here in Acrefort. Now, I don't know when I'm going to see her. I'm happy she's going to go to France and join her cousin's circus like she wants. I'm just sad about it, too. I'm really going to miss her."

Once again, Chandler seemed almost oblivious to the fact we'd been outside, where anyone could have had eyes on us. I felt him draw his arm around me, tugging me closer to plant a small kiss on top of my head. We broke away quickly after, however.

"Well, you can come and be sad at the condo after. I'll even get you that horrid pizza—" I watched his face twist in disgust, and for a moment, I felt a little lighter.

I laughed, shaking my head. "I wish I would have never forced it on you in the first place. I should have known better. Bread and sweet things together. No wonder you hate me now."

"I can absolutely do without ever tasting Hawaiian pizza ever again," Chandler agreed.

We finally made it to the edge of the campus, across the street from the diner where I'd met Henry for pie months ago. It had been a week or two since Henry and I had last seen one another. Between no longer assisting with Chandler's class, the end of the semester drawing to a close, all the Cirque du Lys rehearsals and now upcoming shows, and Henry's new girlfriend occupying a lot of his time, it had been difficult. We'd make time eventually. After today, he'd really be the only friend I'd have around outside of my Cirque du Lys colleagues.

Alex was waiting for me just up from where Chandler and I had been standing. I looked at him, letting out a soft sigh. "I guess I better go get this over with."

"Tell her safe travels for me," Chandler replied, offering me a small smile. I felt him reach out, wrapping his hand in mine to give it a small squeeze before I turned away from him and headed up the sidewalk toward my friend.

I was very grateful that Chandler had offered me his coat. It certainly helped. As I walked, I put it on more properly over my sling bag. The thing was monstrous, and I probably looked utterly ridiculous, but I hadn't cared. It was much needed, and even still my teeth were chattering a little.

"You're late!" Alex hollered at me as I approached. "Here I was thinking I wasn't going to have to wait around in this freezing weather..."

"This was *your* idea," I reminded her. The minute I reached her, we wrapped our arms around one another. "I've never been this fucking cold in my entire life. Only *you* would want to be out in the snow and the dark."

"It's the last time I'll get to enjoy New York snowfall," Alex replied, and her words saddened me all over again. She must have noticed the shift in my expression, despite my best efforts to hide it. "Oh, Cass, I didn't mean *indefinitely*. Just for a little while, you know? I'll come back and watch your shows, I promise. I wish I was going to be able to see the one this weekend."

"Next time," I replied before Alex linked her arm with mine, and the two of us set off down the sidewalk around the perimeter of the Dreamer's Academy campus. Both of us were silent, just admiring the views of the buildings and the snow-covered landscape. I was sure this was the reason Alex had wanted to subject me to the harsh outdoors.

Eventually, I couldn't stand the silence anymore. "Is Dana excited about France?"

The soft, complacent look that had been on Alex's face suddenly grew wide and excited. She turned to look at me, smiling brightly. "Oh, I swear I meant to call you last night and tell you, but I was freaking out about my final review this morning and got distracted." For a month now, Alex had been preparing for the school panel to watch her perform one last time for a final grade. She'd practiced relentlessly. I was certain she did wonderfully.

"What is it?" I asked her, raising a brow.

"I asked Dana to marry me last night. Over dinner." Alex said, grinning at me. "You know how you and I have been talking about it and all. I swear I was going to do something wildly more romantic, but—it just felt like the right moment, you know? We were talking about moving to France and starting this whole life together, and I just got all caught up in it."

"Oh my God, Alex!" I couldn't help but smile at her, squeezing her arm gently. "Please tell me that she told you yes, then."

"Are you kidding me? I mean, come on, Cassie. Who's going to turn *me* down?" I laughed, having stopped to hug her tightly, incredibly happy for her.

"That's seriously the best news I've heard in a while," I replied to her once we'd broken from one another. "I'm so happy for you, Alex. You really do deserve that, after everything. I know it's been a rough go for you, but it's working out in the end."

Alex looked a little choked up at my words, but she smiled regardless. "Yeah, it has. But you're right. Everything ends up working out. I mean, look at you. Got here to Acrefort, working with your childhood idol—I mean even better, *banging* your childhood idol."

"Oh dear God," I laughed, shaking my head. "Quit. You're making me sound terrible."

"All jokes aside," Alex said as we continued our walk together. "It all ended up working out in the end. There was a lot of shit we had to both get through, but we made it. We're better for it. And who knows, maybe the private investigator will have something on Peter here soon. Take that piece of shit down, and then you don't have to worry anymore."

When she said it, I felt a weird lurch in my stomach. While I had been grateful that things had seemed completely normal between Chandler and myself, despite the previous week at his office and our discussion in the Shibari room, I still felt rattled every now and then. And while I had told Alex some of my worries about Gabriel Moreau, she didn't know the full extent of it. Didn't even know some of the questions I had before I'd started digging more into Chandler's father. Questions I still wanted answers to, despite Chandler's every desire for me not to get them.

"I wish I had that private investigator to help me with other things," I said to her then, feeling the need to talk to her about it, at least a little.

Alex glanced at me again. "What do you mean by that? About Chandler's dad?"

How on earth she had guessed what I'd been thinking about, I had no idea. She had been my best friend for decades, so maybe she just knew me really well by now. I took a breath, very aware that I was about to start talking about things I likely shouldn't have been talking about walking around this campus, but part of me didn't care for whatever reason.

"I didn't tell you this before," I started, looking straight ahead then, trying to focus on the scenery around us as I got the words out. "I knew a little about Chandler's dad before I even got here. A little about Chandler's family in general, really. It just got a lot more unsettling once I had that conversation with Gabriel in his office. When he knew all that information about me, about my family..."

When I looked at Alex again, it appeared as if she was intently listening to me, so I continued. "I didn't say anything sooner for a good reason," I explained, suddenly finding I sounded a lot like Chandler had the other day, insisting keeping me out of everything was for my own good. "The whole thing is dangerous, probably even more than I can fathom. I needed to get a handle on it first and try to make sense of it. And I didn't really want to get you involved, but I kind of need your advice at this point..."

Alex stared at me, eyes wide, completely focused on me. I continued. "I am pretty sure that Chandler's dad is a very dangerous guy."

"What? What do you mean by that?" Alex said, and when I thought her eyes couldn't have gotten any wider, they did. "How bad?"

"Peter-level bad," I said, matter-of-factly. "Worse, maybe. I haven't even told Chandler this, so this has to stay between me and you, but before I got to Dreamers, I found this article about Elliott Moreau, Chandler's grandfather. It was on some weird conspiracy theorist website, and I thought it was a joke, but they were calling him some ominous nickname—*The Black Horse* or something. The article talked about how he might have been responsible for a lot of people's deaths... Alex, I think the guy was some sort of serial killer or mobster or something when he was alive. I have no idea. He was a bad guy. And knowing that, now I'm all kinds of concerned about Gabriel Moreau."

"Well, it's a good thing Elliott's dead, at least, right?" Alex replied, looking as completely in shock and confused as she'd been the minute I'd started talking. "—You don't think Gabriel is some psychopath serial killer or something, too, do you?"

I paused for a minute, studying her. Wondering if I should tell her the thoughts I'd been having the last few weeks or not. Tell her what had transpired between Chandler and me the other day. Wondered if I was betraying Chandler somehow by talking about it or if I really needed to talk to someone else about it to try to get to the bottom of it. Part of me wondered why the hell Chandler was so adamant I stayed out of it. It was making everything worse. "I honestly wasn't really sure," I admitted, staring at her. "But then back at Thanksgiving, when we first started talking to David Finch, that private detective Chandler hired, and he gave us all of that information about how Peter might have been involved with the mafia—"

Alex nodded. "I remember that. Have you heard anything about that?"

"Not yet," I shook my head. Not only was I breaking some sort of trust with Chandler by instilling the information I was going to, to Alex, but I also hadn't talked to David yet, like Chandler had asked me to. Still wasn't sure if I was going to either. "Not yet...However, the thing I failed to tell you was how adamantly Chandler argued against using that discovery to our advantage. David brought this awesome, compelling way to put Peter behind bars for good, and Chandler kept shooting him down."

"What the hell? Why?" Alex looked at a loss for words.

"He said getting involved with people from the mafia was dangerous. We didn't know what we were getting into and that someone could get hurt," I said. Despite the fact that I realized I'd been recklessly saying this information to my best friend in what could have potentially been a terrible place, I didn't care. I didn't have another opportunity to tell her, especially when I needed her advice. In a few minutes, she'd be leaving to go to France. It was now or never. I couldn't keep all of these thoughts to myself anymore.

"And he also, weirdly enough, knew about the mafia David thinks my uncle might have unknowingly had ties with. Le Milieu. The French mafia. It didn't faze me at first, but the more I thought about it, the more I kept wondering what the hell he knows and why he knows it. If it's something to do with his family. And honestly, I'm worried if he's involved with any of it."

"You actually think *Chandler* is involved with something like the mafia?" Alex asked me, sounding in sheer disbelief. When I looked back at her once we'd rounded the corner again, she was staring straight at me. "I mean, okay, Cass, I don't really know the guy like you do. You've literally followed him to the ends of the earth since you were a kid. But from my perspective, he's won himself a hell of a lot of points for everything he's done for you the last few months. And, I mean, he's a nice guy, at least every time I've been around him..."

Truthfully, there was no world in which I thought Chandler could have anything to do with something as horrifying as the mafia. Even still, after everything, I was feeling unsettled by it. Especially how he'd told me point-blank not to ask anything further about his father the other day. I wasn't sure what I was supposed to do after that and if doing anything might make the situation worse. "I honestly wanted to confront him about it. We were talking the other day, and he explicitly told me *not* to ask him about his father at all. That he was dangerous, and he was trying to protect me."

"Wait, really?" Alex said, looking genuinely surprised. "Well, that's not suspicious at all..."

"Right?" I trailed off for a second. "And then on top of what happened last week..."

"What happened last week?" Alex asked.

"Remember when I told you that story about going over to Chandler's house the first time when he did all the Shibari on me?" It had been more recently that I had enlightened my friend about this information, which had been a fun experience, to say the least. While I had made her swear not to tell Chandler I had said anything, she still teased me relentlessly.

"I still cannot believe Cassandra Blackstone is into all the kinky stuff now," Alex grinned at me, despite the seriousness of the situation at hand. "Still can't believe Maître ended up being Chandler, either. Thank you for not informing him or Dana about my wild amount of sex dreams involving Maître. As much of a disappointment as I am to gays everywhere. That show was hot as hell. I guess I will just live vicariously through you from now on."

I knew she'd been joking, and it made me laugh for a few seconds. Once I'd shaken my head and come back to my thoughts, I continued. "When I was over there that day, I was in Chandler's bedroom for a few minutes by myself—don't follow up with a joke now." Alex grinned again but nodded for me to continue. "I saw this journal on his nightstand. It had the Cirque du Lys logo on it, and it was pretty old. And as much as I knew it was the world's worst invasion of privacy, my curiosity got the best of me. It ended up being Lily Moreau's journal. Chandler's grandmother."

Alex was still watching me, listening intently. I knew we were getting close to being back where Dana had planned to meet us. I could see the end of the road approaching. "When I realized what it was, I was an idiot and decided to take it. I thought maybe I'd find out something about his grandparents, specifically Elliott Moreau. Even Lily, I guess, because Chandler always speaks so fondly of her, and I couldn't imagine her being married to someone like the person I saw on that conspiracy site... Basically, I was looking for something to prove my suspicions about how dangerous Chandler's family really is. And honestly, I'd done it since I'd been worried about Chandler. I should have just left it alone. Chandler knew I took it. At least he suspected."

"Jesus, Cassie," Alex said, shaking her head. "While I commend you on your relentless search for truth, yeah, I don't know how you didn't think that wouldn't end badly. Especially if you had all these reasons to believe his family was dangerous. God knows what Chandler could have done to you if he was somehow involved with any of it..."

"It was a stupid thing to do, but I needed to know." I agreed with her. "And honestly, Alex, I still can't see any situation in which

Chandler *is* involved. He just *knows* things, and I hate that he won't tell me anything. And the worst part is that the journal literally had nothing of use in it, either. Just sweet musings from what seemed like a very nice lady, exactly like Chandler speaks of her. And after I thought he knew I'd taken it, I even tried to pin it back on his dad to protect myself. I figured as much as he hates Gabriel, it might make more sense."

"How the hell did you manage to do that?" Alex looked at me again, wide-eyed.

"I left the journal outside of his dad's office shortly after I went and visited him. The day I called and told you about it. I figured he'd pick it up and do something with it, and it would be out of my hair at that point. There was no way in hell I wanted to try to explain to Chandler that I'd taken it or why. He was pretty pissed at me when he thought I did. You remember how upset I was with him that day. I mean, I wanted to give up working with him." Alex nodded. "And admittedly, I was a little concerned about everything at that point, but I feel differently now. I trust him too much to think he could ever be involved in anything his family might be."

"Okay, so Chandler's grandpa and dad are most likely dangerous dudes, and you recklessly stole his sweet grandma's journal and pissed him off. I'm following. What is it you're needing my help with, then? Besides me following up with warning you to be fucking careful, of course."

I paused for a second, having stopped walking entirely. We were getting too close to Dana at that point. I could see her car up ahead. "Something happened last week, and I'm pretty sure that Chandler knows I at least know *something* about that journal."

As much as I was certain Alex wanted context behind that statement, I wasn't about to indulge her about it. Too distracted. "He hasn't brought it up since it happened, but there's been this like—weird air, I don't know. I think I need to just confront him. Explain what's going on, try to get to the bottom of everything with him and get some answers instead of keeping it a secret. I need you to tell me whether or not I'm being rational or a complete nutcase."

Alex, who had stopped with me, pondered for a long while after I'd asked. I was getting anxious waiting, fidgeting in place while she did. Still feeling so ridiculously cold I could hardly stand it, but this conversation was far too important right then to care.

"Well, if I am going to tell you anything, it's going to be that you better be fucking careful with whatever you do." Alex stared at me, hard. "I am going to be pissed if something happens to you, and I have to go all cold-blooded killer on whoever was responsible to avenge your death. But yeah, probably coming clean about the journal would be a good idea."

I smiled at her then, shaking my head. Gracious, again, for those tiny bits of humor of hers. They were helpful, even if it was only minuscule. "I think I'm going to talk to him. I don't know. I'll figure it out. It's just been weighing on me, and I needed to tell you. Needed someone else to know in case something happens to me and you have to tell the police." The last bit was meant as a morbid joke, but it still wasn't inaccurate.

"Nothing is going to happen," Alex reminded firmly, and I nodded.

Suddenly, Alex was waving behind me. I spun, seeing Dana waving down the street from us. "Crap, I'm guessing she's freaking that we aren't on the way already. You know her, needing to get places three hours in advance. I'm going to hear it on the drive over there."

"Well, at least you aren't engaged to me. You'd also lose your mind being late to everything," I retorted, just as we started heading back toward Dana. By the time we reached her, my anxious mood had turned back to being very sullen again.

"Damn, I don't know how you both walked in this weather," Dana greeted, her teeth chattering. "Even growing up here, it's too cold for me. I could do without all this snow."

"Well, you'll have a very long plane ride to warm up," I reminded her.

Alex tugged my arm, drawing me into her arms. We hugged tightly, and I took in the last few moments with her and I together as best I could. Remembered how her hug felt, the way that she smelled. The sound of her breathing. I didn't want to forget her. Didn't want her to fade from my mind like a forgotten memory.

When we separated, I realized there were tears falling down my face, freezing in the chilly air and sticking to my skin.

"Aw babe, it's going to be okay," Alex reassured me, reaching up to try to wipe the tears off my face with the edge of her coat sleeve. "You're going to come visit, right? Maybe in the spring sometime? Get your rich-ass beau to take you on a trip. You deserve it."

I laughed, shaking my head. "I'm sure he would in a heartbeat."

"I think he's a good guy, Cass," Alex said, her facial expression having grown a little bit more serious. "And I think he really cares about you a lot. I think you're right. He would do a lot of things for you in a heartbeat. I feel pretty confident leaving you here with him. I think he really is trying to keep you safe more than anything. But if you need more than that, you need to tell him." We shared a soft look with one another for a minute, and I mouthed a gracious thank you to her.

Dana ended up nudging Alex gently, bringing both her and I back to reality. "I guess we better get going. Don't want to miss our flight, and Dana likes to be nerd early. Unlike my wonderful BFF."

"Shut it," I replied, smiling. "Get out of here then. Drive safe in the snow, Dana." Dana nodded to me, reaching out to squeeze my arm before she traveled back around to get in the car.

Meanwhile, Alex had reached over to cup my face and leaned in to plant a kiss on my cheek. "Be safe. I love you."

"Love you more," I replied, trying my best to maintain a smile on my face as I watched her leave and disappear into the car. A minute later, they'd taken off down the road, and I watched them until they turned the corner again a few blocks down. Suddenly, I felt so much colder and so much more alone.

CHAPTER 28

CASSANDRA

Standing in the center of the stage, I watched Chandler Moreau circle around me under the spotlight. Tonight, at The Crucible, he was his alter-ego, Maître, and I was his beautiful papillon. The one he'd trap for the audience in beautiful patterns of rope.

I'd been assisting him for over a month at these shows. We'd moved the day to later in the week to accommodate our schedules, but they'd resumed. They'd been a big part of the allure of Chandler's club, and he had insisted that he wouldn't perform another act with anyone else. So, we'd decided together that I'd help him. Even though I hadn't remotely minded.

Chandler had spent the last thirty minutes enveloping me in ropes, creating one of my favorite ties. A dragonfly tie was a bound tie. In some ways, it was similar to the tortoise-shell tie, but it made more triangular shapes across the body versus rhombus ones. It also fastened the arms together as one cohesive unit.

"And *fini!*" He'd said as he tied off the last bit of rope. Chandler wove me out into the front of the stage to show off the design to the mesmerized crowd. He spun me around in a circle to demonstrate how the backside had been tied.

All the while, I sunk into that all too familiar feeling of those ropes around me, my arms tightly woven to my sides. Enjoying Chandler's assertiveness over me in front of this crowd. After he'd finished putting me on display, the crowd applauded as we left the stage.

On any other night, Chandler and I would have excused ourselves to the wings behind the stage for him to unbind me. However, he surprised me that evening by walking me straight off the stage, still bound by the ropes and only in my underwear. Once we'd gotten down the stairs, he steered me through the crowd toward a familiar set of doors.

While I'd been to The Crucible quite a number of times since Chandler and I had gotten together, we had never been back through those doors he'd taken me to that night I'd shown back up after I'd been in his demonstration the first time. I knew, from a wide variety of people, that there was an entire other side of the club, but he had yet to take me there.

Tonight, clearly, he had other plans.

We passed through the doorway into the middle room again. This time, there was a small crowd gathered inside, checking in items at a desk. Chandler disregarded them, continuing to push me forward. People glanced at us as we walked by, staring at me woven into those ropes, and Chandler asserted his usual dominance over me as he pushed me along.

The individual guarding the doors on the opposite side of the room saw Chandler approaching. He offered a small smile and then immediately let Chandler through to the other side. The minute we'd crossed the threshold into the room beyond, I gasped.

A crowd was gathered mere yards from where we entered, sprawled out on a very luxurious set of leather couches. Mixed with people who were completely naked, some half naked, some completely clothed. And they were all wildly in the throws, all together in a cohesive unit of a half dozen people. I was witnessing some sort of orgy happening, and I stopped abruptly, mind-boggled.

"They're all having sex," I said, mostly to myself, but I realized that Chandler must have heard me, seeing him out of the corner of my eye.

Chandler drew up behind me then, pressing himself close. I stood completely motionless, unable to stop myself from watching the scene in front of me. Listening to all the moans and grunts, watching bodies thrusting together, fingers and mouths and appendages wrapped all around each other.

"If they didn't want an audience, they would have used one of the private rooms," Chandler explained to me.

"There's *private* rooms?" I spun, looking back at him. Chandler grinned before he tugged me along again, further inside. I'd never really inquired why the man had invested in a club like this, never imagined he'd do anything like it. But months ago, I'd been taken by surprise by his whole Shibari routine, too. So, I supposed everyone had their secrets.

I thought I'd been completely undone by the first set of people, but by the time we'd turned a corner into the main area of the other side of The Crucible, it had reached an entirely new level. The entire room, which was as big as a small movie theater, was flooded with people. It smelled and sounded and looked like nothing but sex every direction you turned. And not unlike anything else Chandler ever did, it was as luxurious and lavish as ever. Nothing like I'd ever imagine a place like this to be. Not that I'd spent that much time imagining.

We walked inward, straight through the middle aisle, which had been the only portion of this room that was clear. It was a wild sight to see, something I never imagined I would. There was leather furniture everywhere. Long mattress-looking pieces, couches, and big ottomans.

What stopped me abruptly was a scene toward the far end of the room. Interestingly enough, there was a naked man standing near the wall. I probably wouldn't have been so attentive about it if it hadn't been for the fact his torso was covered in an intricate and colorful design of ropes. Hemp rope, by the look of it. I'd gotten pretty good at knowing now.

"It's a Hishi Karada," I said aloud, recognizing the full torso Shibari tie almost instantly. Chandler had stopped directly behind me again, leaning inward so he could hear what I was saying. Out of the corner of my eye, I could see the side of his face, and he was smiling.

"The diamond tie harness," Chandler confirmed, nodding at me. "It looks like she's not finished, either." He was referring to the woman who was beside the man, holding on to another length of rope. Most of it was on the floor as she circled back around him to the front. Suddenly, I watched her drop to her knees in front of him, the man watching her as she did. Seconds later, Chandler entered my view again, staring at me for a moment. He'd distracted me from the Shibari scene, flashing me a playful look.

Before I could even comprehend what was happening, Chandler swiftly dropped, getting onto his knees directly in front of me. My attention shot downward, hyper aware that he'd done so in front of a room full of people, feeling my breath catch in my throat for a second.

"What are you doing?" I whispered to him, feeling horrendously distracted.

Chandler looked back up at me, that playful look still on his face. He nodded his head back in the direction of where the man in the Hishi Karada had been standing, the woman preparing to start on whatever she was planning to do next. A hip and waist tie, I presumed, perhaps followed by one with the legs and feet if she was going to be fancy.

"Tell me what she's doing, Cassandra," Chandler said, loudly enough for me to hear him through the wild noises going on throughout the room, but still in a soft way. I glanced back at him just sitting there, looking at me with that same gentle look on his face.

I looked back at the scene, watching as the woman started. Following along as she worked, deciding to humor him like he'd asked. "She's starting at his hips," I explained in the same tone of voice Chandler had used. Loud enough for him to hear me, yet still calm and steady. "Wrapped it three times, I think, like you usually do."

I was taken by surprise when I felt a gentle brush against my skin, right on the side of my hip. I realized he'd drawn his fingers across me. For whatever reason, I knew almost instantly what he was doing. "A little higher," I explained, and I felt him draw upward. Somehow I knew he was watching me, too, even though my entire focus had been on the Shibari routine in front of me.

I nodded and felt him draw an imaginary line where the rope would have gone. Kept telling myself to breathe, feeling a little overwhelmed by the sensation of it but enjoying it nonetheless. "Now she's making the first knot," I said, watching as she did so.

"What knot?" He asked, fingers lingering on me, having stopped right below my belly button. He clearly couldn't help himself, his fingers still dancing against me a little. I was surprised he'd asked. Though I'd been learning quite a bit, I wasn't quite sure if I'd be able to guess it. But after watching carefully as she finished, I realized.

"A double coin knot," I confirmed. The knot looked similar to an infinity symbol. He had used it on occasion with me. I felt him trace the same sort of shape against my skin where his fingers had been resting, and I shivered.

My eyes remained laser-focused on the scene in front of me, despite feeling simultaneously distracted by what was being done to me in tandem. "She's building out the harness some more," I explained, watching as the rope wrapped around the man in front of me. "Wrapped it around his thighs...Once...Twice...Three... Yeah, three more times." I was having trouble getting out words, feeling the same pattern being replicated on me in perfect form.

"Now she's looped it around again, taking it in between his legs now. Probably doing a half hitch in the back if I have to take a guess..." I found myself looking down at Chandler again, spreading my legs apart a bit without him even having to ask. He had been looking at me briefly with some sort of approving smile on his face, which I assumed might have been because of my guess of the knot being used. He returned his focus back to what he'd been doing, and I watched him draw his fingers right at the crease between my thigh and my pubic bone, wisping gently across me.

I let out a little gasp at the touch, even though I'd been expecting it. If I'd been able to reach out and grip Chandler's head at that point, I very well might have. But instead, I was brought back to the realization that I, too, was bound in those moments. Merciless, yet again, to whatever the man had wanted to do to me. It made my head spin a little.

Instead of continuing what he'd been doing by following along with the Shibari routine I'd been explaining to him, I felt his fingers drawing elsewhere. Gasped again, involuntarily, as he ran them against me gently and rhythmically, over top of the fabric between my legs. Felt my legs wobbling a little bit in surprise.

"*Chandler,*" I managed to say, trying to make it out as a coherent word, but it had ended up in another little gasp of surprise as he'd touched just the right spot, and I was sent spinning again. I felt his free hand reach up to hold my hip, steadying me.

"Tell me what you want, Cassandra," Chandler demanded. He still moved against me, but it was so gentle and wispy that it nearly felt like he hadn't been. He was making every effort to torture the fuck out of me, and it was agonizing.

Somehow, I managed to form a string of words to tell him. "Keep touching me."

Those minuscule strokes continued. I looked back down at Chandler, who was locked on me. He had a playful smirk on his face, clearly thoroughly pleased with himself. "You're going to need to be a bit more specific than *that...*" I felt him rake his fingers along the inside of my thigh.

"—Chandler…" I swallowed deeply and surprised myself that I continued speaking. *Demanding* him. Tired of his torments. "Put your fingers inside of me. Right now." My voice came out more authoritative than I had ever heard myself speak. I needed him to act, desperately.

Chandler's fingers had still been raking against my flesh, but they paused. That smirk on his face intensified. I felt him move swiftly, dipping between the fabric between my legs, and in seconds he'd done exactly as I had asked of him. A very satisfied gasp escaped me when it happened, my whole body writhing a little. Surprisingly, I couldn't have cared less he'd just done it in a room full of people. It had been the very least of my concerns at that moment. My entire body was on fire.

"Am I going to take you in front of all of these people, little papillon?" Chandler asked, having already started a little rhythm against me I was leaning into. My head was spinning wildly. Surprisingly, I nodded, and the second I had, he curled his fingers inside of me, and I moaned far louder than I expected into the room. There were definitely eyes on me at that point, but I hadn't even cared. All I wanted was for him to continue doing exactly what he was doing.

"You should know better than to think a simple little nod is a satisfactory answer, Cassandra." He halted abruptly, and I squirmed in place, quickly annoyed that he had. "I want to hear it. Tell all of these people who's on their knees for you right now, and beg me to give you what you want."

I bucked my hips against him, trying to get him to move, but he didn't. "You're such a control freak." My words had mostly meant to tease him out of frustration, and the second I said them, Chandler twisted his fingers again. There was no stopping the violent moan that shot out my mouth. "*Fuck.* Oh my God. Chandler, *please.* I'm begging you."

Our eyes met for a second, and he nodded back to the Shibari scene. "Keep explaining to me what she's doing. Every detail. I want to hear how well I've been teaching you. That is, until I've made it impossible for you to speak. And I'll know when that happens, so I expect you to do what you're told until then, Cassandra." I barely had time to enjoy the tantalizing commands he'd just given me. He started to quickly build a rapid rhythm against me with his fingers, sending me spinning wildly, barely able to hang onto the room as he did. "Now."

He dragged his fingers against me again, and I gasped. Tried to recover quickly, shaking my head, and then began explaining, as best I could, the scene in front of me. Finding it harder and harder to maintain my focus. I was so close it was agonizing and leaving me hardly able to stand upright with how violently my legs had started to tremble. My attention drifted downward again, and Chandler's green eyes latched in on mine.

"Show everyone what I did to you," Chandler demanded in a low growl. Then with one final motion of his fingers curling against me, my entire body trembled violently. Without any effort whatsoever, I gasped Chandler's name out into the room, over and over. Giving him exactly what he wanted. The pleasure he liked to derive from the fact that this was all his doing. He had wrecked me. And in those moments, I couldn't have given less of a shit if the entire world knew that fact. All I wanted was the sheer relief I got as a result.

When he finally drew his hand away from me, once my body had settled, he was smiling. I couldn't help but smile back at him, watching him as he got back to his feet.

I was still breathing lightly, trying to recover from my head spinning from the last few minutes that had occurred. Chandler leaned in, planting a kiss on my lips.

When he broke away from me, I couldn't help but say what had been on my mind, still seeing the Shibari scene behind me playing out. The woman had been working on some leg ties. "You should let me tie you up sometime."

Chandler raised a curious brow at me, looking surprised I'd said such a thing. He pondered on it for a moment. Then I watched his small smile widen substantially, and he shrugged. "I wouldn't be opposed to that."

"Really?" I asked him, surprised by his answer, given his constant need to be in control of literally everything. It had not been what I had expected him to say. He was still smiling when he weaved around me again. I heard his voice in my ear a few seconds later, whispering softly. "Come on. I haven't gotten you where I want you yet."

I couldn't imagine what Chandler had in store in those next few minutes, especially after what had just transpired, but I let him continue us onward through the room. My heart was racing, eyes darting every way imaginable, trying to take it all in.

Once we'd passed through another set of doors, we were in another hallway. There was an immediate left turn, which looked as if it led into another large room like the one we'd just been in. In front of us, however, were many doorways. Another attendant was lingering in the hallway and noticed Chandler's approach immediately.

"Is it still available?" Chandler asked her once we were in earshot. Meanwhile, I was still staring at random men and women passing around us, half naked and naked, still unable to believe where we were.

The attendant must have nodded because we continued our way down toward the end of the hallway. I watched as the door in front of us was unlocked, and then I was gently ushered inside the room. Once Chandler and I both made it inside, he closed the door behind us and then locked it again. I hadn't paid much attention, however, because I was too distracted by the room.

For whatever reason, it reminded me of Chandler's Shibari room in many ways. Lots of mirrors, a giant plush leather sofa.

There were various places where I imagined you could do all sorts of deviant sexual activities. I spun around, hearing Chandler doing something behind me. When I did, I noticed he was closing the blinds on a set of windows that had been open.

He must have noticed me watching, turning to look at me before he'd closed the second window. "I figured we didn't need an audience," he replied. While it made sense, I noticed the strange way his tone had shifted all of a sudden, and it made the hairs on my neck stand on end. I thought, perhaps, this was going to be another fun game like we'd had the previous week.

How unbelievably wrong I had been in that assumption.

Once Chandler was satisfied with the windows, I watched him approach me again. Had there not been such a strange look on his face, I would have found his approach very alluring. Instead, it just made my stomach churn, and my heart started to pick up pace again. Suddenly, I wasn't sure I wanted to be in private, having wished we were still outside amongst the crowd.

"Okay, Cassandra," Chandler said, drawing up close to me. He wasn't right on top of me, but he'd stepped close enough that I was a little intimidated by his frame towering over me. So much so that I took one small step back from him. "You and I are going to have a discussion, and I need you to be honest with me. And I'm saying please here because I assure you that it is important that you are."

The expression on his face was somewhat fierce, but at least his tone was relatively calm. Just incredibly serious. At that precise moment, I realized that I was still trapped in the tie he'd done on the stage a short while earlier. And immediately after I had, I knew, knowing Chandler, it had absolutely been on purpose. He wanted me trapped for whatever was about to go down.

I didn't like this one bit.

Shockingly, I didn't immediately give in and tell him the safe word. Whether it was in fear that he wouldn't even listen to me now, or that I was deciding to trust him first before I gave in to that temptation, or a mixture of both, I wasn't sure.

"Why did you take the journal?" Chandler asked me, his face steady.

My head spun, and I very nearly lost my balance standing there. I shouldn't have been remotely surprised. Should have expected this to happen, but yet I'd somehow decided to be naive. Why he had waited nearly a week to confront me about it, I was still confused, but he'd decided to do it. And I felt like an idiot for not having spoken up sooner.

I must have stood there for a very long time in silence, trying to figure out what to do. My heart was thudding so fast, and my breathing had gotten so erratic I was afraid I might just collapse on the floor from anxiety at any minute.

Surprisingly, it seemed as though Chandler had noticed. I watched his expression soften. His eyes tried to capture mine, and when they did, he spoke again.

"I'm not angry with you right now," he said, trying to hold my attention, which was very hard to do when I was so panicked about what to tell him. "Honestly, I'm pretty sure whatever reason you did it wasn't actually ill-intentioned, after all this time. I still trust you, Cassandra. I just need you to tell me what is going on for both of our sakes."

Out of everything I thought he would possibly say in those moments, I did not expect those words to come out of his mouth. After unraveling all the information I had on his father and grandfather, I had feared the absolute worst. Desperately, I had tried not to question his involvement in it all. Wanted so badly for him to not have anything to do with it, but I still had those tiny, lingering reservations. This certainly wasn't helping. But yet there he was, as steady and calm as he'd always been the last few months.

I hesitated for just a little bit longer. Still reeling on what exactly I wanted to say. Then I realized that if this was how he was acting, maybe my suspicions were right, and he was truly naive to it all. If he'd been acting this way and hadn't done something absolutely insane with the knowledge of what I had done, I had to believe that was the case.

So, I decided to be delicate instead. Didn't go the exact direction I had initially intended. "I was being stupid," I said, trying to keep looking at him, despite how difficult that was in those moments. "There was a picture of you on your nightstand when you were younger. That caught my eye first, honestly. It was such a cute picture, and I just wanted to look at it."

That part had been completely true. I loved that picture. He looked so happy and young. And I had wondered, even now, who those people he was with could have been. I didn't recognize them outside of the fact that they had those iconic Moreau features.

Chandler must have realized I was struggling to breathe. I felt tears welling up in my eyes, likely from the mass amount of guilt I was feeling. While he didn't approach me, his voice got softer when he spoke to me again. "Cassandra, keep breathing. I promise you everything isn't as bad as you're thinking right now. Just try to stay calm."

I hated how nice he was being. It felt so genuine and sincere. I didn't think there was any way I could doubt he didn't one hundred percent believe every word of it. And truthfully, it did make me feel a little bit better. Somehow, I managed to suck in a few deep breaths of air.

"I know how awful I must seem," I continued, this time having to look slightly away from him. "Invading your privacy like that. It was just that the journal looked so old. It even had the original Cirque du Lys logo, too. I knew it couldn't possibly have been yours. Otherwise, I wouldn't have dared. When I saw it was your grandmother's, I just really wanted to read it. I know how much you love your grandmother, and my curiosity got the best of me."

"Why didn't you just ask me if you could borrow it?" Chandler asked me.

I should have known that question was coming. It had been a very obvious one and one I didn't quite have a solid answer for. Not without divulging everything else.

"I don't know. A lapse in judgment, I guess," I admitted. "If I'm being honest, I knew you realized what I did in your office last week, and I was so panicked about it, I told Alex. And she said the exact same thing, that it was a stupid move. I think even then, I was just that same obsessive fan of yours that wanted every bit of information I could get. I don't really know that much about Lily, so I got curious. I'm so sorry."

Chandler nodded, but I couldn't tell what he was thinking. It made me a little sick to my stomach waiting for him to say anything. "My other question, I guess, is why you pinned it on my dad. I don't know how on earth you managed to do that, but that surprised me."

Again, I didn't really have an answer for that. Still, I managed to surprise myself, this time answering quicker than before. "I was panicking," I said, finally able to look him in the eyes again. Trapped in those green hues. "I knew I'd done something wrong. After you confronted me that day at class about it, how angry you were. The last thing I wanted was to upset you, and I felt horrible about it. And after I had that meeting with your dad about changing professors, I had such a bad feeling about it... I honestly had a suspicion he knew about my feelings for you. It was probably pretty obvious in hindsight. And when you disappeared completely from my life after that, I had a feeling he might have been responsible for that, too."

Mostly all of that had been true, despite the way I'd decided to twist the story. I had suspected Gabriel had done most of those things. Knew that, even if Chandler had been angry, that it had been so strange he'd just dissipated. I'd seen him so many times lingering around after the fact, checking on me, that I couldn't help but wonder.

"I guess I was angry at him," I admitted, which had also been true. "Even though I'd asked for that to happen, I just had this feeling he'd made the situation worse. And I wanted a reason for you to hate him more. Thought maybe if you did, you wouldn't have kept your distance. Forgive me. Maybe talk to me again, and we could have worked through it."

When I finally finished getting most of what I had wanted to say out, Chandler hovered in place for a long few minutes, lost in thought. I stood there patiently, letting him do what he needed to do. Eventually, he moved but didn't speak. He walked around behind me, and before I could ask what he was doing, I felt him undoing the ties on my back to release me from the ropes.

I breathed a very long sigh of relief, grateful that he was doing so, even if he'd been calm and collected during the whole ordeal. Without a shadow of a doubt, the fact that I had been so trapped in those moments had added to my anxiety. Had he gotten angry, I wasn't sure what I would have done, but I was glad I hadn't needed to find out.

"Thank you," I breathed as he continued undoing all of the ropes from me.

"You're right," Chandler said from behind me, and I glanced over my shoulder, curious as to what he meant by that. "I am definitely, one hundred percent, a control freak. I'm sorry I kept you like this when I knew what I was doing. The last thing I want is for you to not trust me when we do this, and I know this certainly didn't help matters."

For whatever reason, when he apologized, it made me smile. He'd been midway through untying me, but I turned around anyway. Waited until he met eyes with me again before I spoke. "The fact that you admitted it was wrong and apologized is what I needed," I said, the smile still on my face. "And that you admitted you are a control freak. Which you are, but it's an endearing quality most of the time. One of the many things I love about you."

I hadn't even realized what I'd said for several seconds after I had said it. It wasn't until Chandler's facial expression shifted from a very calm expression into a soft smile that it occurred to me. "Out of all the times I would have expected you to say that, it was definitely not after all of this happened."

Both of us were smiling. I wished I could have reached out and put my hands on his face at that moment, but I was still pinned down quite a bit. "To be fair, I've been wanting to say that for a while now. Probably since that night you brought me back to your condo after the first time going to Cirque du Lys and working alongside you. When you found my bag, practiced the Shibari and talked afterward. I was on such a high after all of that..."

Chandler's smile widened a little bit, shaking his head. "I had wanted to say it that night, too, actually. I thought it was a bit overeager, so I refrained. Then time just seemed to get away from me after that fact, and truthfully, Cassandra, I assumed you knew that after everything."

"I did, I think," I agreed. "But it's nice to have finally said it, regardless. Even if it was after a very humiliating admission of how clearly obsessed I am with you."

A very hearty laugh escaped Chandler then, one of those genuine full-belly laughs that was impossible not to warm someone from head to toe when they heard it. "Ah, Cassandra. As much as you say my control freak tendencies are an endearing trait of mine for you, it's the same for me with your constant need to know more about me than even I know. It's very cute. Giving me a bit of a complex, mind you, but cute nonetheless."

"Well, I'm glad you don't think I'm a freak show," I laughed, shaking my head.

We smiled at one another for a few seconds in silence. Then I watched Chandler take a step toward me, closing the gap between us. He reached up his hand to my cheek, holding it there, staring deeply at me. "I love you, too. More than I think I could love anyone, honestly. Sometimes it overwhelms me a little bit, but in a good way."

I felt my face sink into his hand, sighing a little at his words. Chandler continued. "Thank you for being honest with me about the journal. I told you that I wasn't mad because I knew you must have done it for a good reason. I know you better than that by now."

While I had been incredibly happy with those last few moments with him, riding the wave of emotions I had felt hearing the words he'd just spoken, I came down a little after he said the last few sentences. Felt a little guilty that he'd assumed I'd been so honest when I hadn't been entirely. But I reassured myself that, like Chandler said, it was with good reason. As much as Chandler trusted me, I trusted him too. And I desperately wanted to protect him.

In those moments, all I wanted was to stay here with him in this place we were in, far away from the rest of all those looming problems.

Chandler dropped his hand, and I watched him circle around again, resuming untying me. I waited patiently while he worked, both of us quiet the rest of the time. When the rope finally dropped off of me, hitting the floor, I felt him draw up against me. Moments later, his mouth was against my ear, breathing hot air against my flesh. I shivered.

"Let's go, little papillon." he said, his voice low and gravely. "I didn't just bring you back here for this. I have more plans in mind."

I raised a brow but didn't look back at him when I spoke. "Like what, exactly?"

Chandler paused for a few seconds, his breath still beating against me. I could feel the dampness of his lips brushing against my ear. Thought I might just melt through the floor in anticipation. "Let's just say I intend to continue to make a whole lot of people very envious of what I'm going to do to you while they watch me do it."

CHAPTER 29

CHANDLER

In the near-darkness, a crowd of twenty-three performers stood close together behind the fabric walls that marked the edges of the set on the stage. It had been so quiet for a few moments that I could hear breathing all around me. The nervous scuffling of feet. Fabrics of costumes rubbing together.

A very low string vibrato filled the room around us. It was ominous and brooding. All at once, I could feel the entire group of us gather to attention, including the woman nervously swaying in front of me.

"Breathe," I reminded Cassandra, my head against hers, barely able to say it before bright little pieces of piano scales came over the top of the strings. The moment they did, I interlaced Cassandra's hand with my own. Seconds later, the orchestra began the opening measures of the second movement of Berlioz's *Symphonie fantastique.*

The entire troupe took it as their cue, flowing onto the stage in a brilliant wave of bodies completely in sync.

As Cassandra and I weaved our way across the painted Cirque du Lys stage, beneath an array of colorful lights that illuminated it in its entirety, I admired the new coat of paint that had made it look as if we were walking under a marvelously old stone floor. The set around us had been created to resemble architecture reminiscent of the Dreamers Academy—that look of 16th century France.

High above us, Penelope Girard had been sent flying backward through a hoop, her body like an arrow as she twisted herself and landed on the other side. She was followed by another acrobat right behind her, who caught the edge of the hoop, spinning himself into it as it was flown upward from off-stage.

When Cassandra and I reached the silks together on the opposite side of the theater, we took our positions. She had chosen a beautiful set of emerald green silks to work with since she'd first started at rehearsals.

Sebastian had designed us a pair of striking skin-tight costumes to wear that reminded me somewhat of the masquerade mask that I'd given away at The Crucible. They were mostly black with hints of shimmering color that complimented our silks and had elaborate feathery necklines. While I often felt ridiculous in the outfits that Sebastian decided on every season, I always humored him.

Cassandra, despite my annoyance with the costumes, looked absolutely breathtaking standing across from me. Her honey brown hair was cascading into those black feathers around her neck. She'd worn it partially pinned up, but the majority hung down behind her.

I found myself watching her again as we stood at our positions, both of us wrapped around the silks. Staring out into what was a sold out theater for opening night of our winter season.

It was hard to make out the crowd through all the lighting, which was probably a good thing. Especially looking at Cassandra then, seeing the nerves on her face. It had been a while since I'd seen her as nervous as she looked. Likely since her audition.

The music still played behind us as I took a step closer to her. Our fellow performers were in the midst of our opening number to the show. In my peripheral vision, I could see Thomas and Abigail tossing fiery batons between one another across the stage. I found myself suddenly very grateful for the fabric I was holding onto.

"Remember, your only concern right now is our performance. Not your audience. Forget your audience. It's only us and the silks." I had drawn up close to her, leaning down to speak loudly enough in her ear that she could hear me.

Cassandra looked up for a minute, meeting my eyes and offering me a small smile. Unable to help myself, I kissed her forehead as the flute section began signaling our cue. I watched her instantly straighten, taking a long, deep breath in. Her attention was completely on the green silks in front of her. Following her cue, she took off into the air above me.

I watched as the song bellowed out into the room, waiting for the flutes to merge with the strings, and the second they did, I was following after Cassandra. She was already high above me, at least twenty or thirty feet.

"Ladies and Gentlemen! Good evening! *Bonjour!*" Many of the lights above us moved into the center of the stage, focused on the voice that was now below us. The one that introduced these shows on this stage for the entire time I'd been a performer there.

In his usual flair, Sebastian Taylor wore a very striking costume in many shades of whites and grays. Not unlike the rest of the designs he'd come up with for this show, they had the same streaks of bright colors running through the whites and feathers that lined around his collar and sleeves.

"It is my absolute *pleasure* to welcome you to the opening performance of the two hundredth season of *Cirque du Lys!*" The crowd erupted all around us, and it was the first time I was truly aware of how many people there were in the audience. I glanced up at Cassandra then, who had wrapped herself in the silks in such a way that she'd been more seated.

I was dangling just a half dozen feet below, waiting for Sebastian to finish his introduction. This opening number was mostly meant for theatrics. Our real performances were yet to come. It was just a fun few minutes for the entire group of us to be together on the stage.

Just as I was about to look back to Sebastian, Cassandra's attention drifted down to me for a second. Neither of us were able to stop smiling at one another, at least until Sebastian spoke again.

"Our very special milestone show this evening draws inspiration from a particularly wonderful French woman, who I was privileged to meet many years ago," Sebastian's voice echoed into the room, and the entire crowd went quiet again. My entire attention had turned to Sebastian. While we'd rehearsed this show top to bottom, I had never heard him say this opening introduction. Had no idea that it was what he had planned to do.

"Lilith Sabine Garnier Moreau grew up the daughter of apple farmers in Normandy, France. Many in France knew the Garnier's Orchard as a safe haven during the war, and Lily had told me a story or two about bringing hungry soldiers apples to eat. Including the man who would later become her husband, a French soldier at the time, Elliott Moreau."

For the first time in what may have been my entire life, or at least in as long as I could possibly remember, hearing my grandfather's name did not immediately fill me with fits of rage. Instead, I found myself as captivated by Sebastian's words as the whole audience appeared to be, as if I was hearing all of this for the first time.

"When the newlyweds came to the States shortly after the war ended, with hopes of a new life here, it was Lily who fell in love with our quaint little city of Acrefort. And I wouldn't need to tell you that it had everything to do with our abundance of apple orchards." I heard the crowd laughing over the music that had still been playing.

"Elliott Moreau purchased the nearby Le Rêveur Académie, as it was known many years ago. The Dreamers Academy. And, along with it, this very plot of land we are sitting on now. Some even say that Elliott had been so desperate to give Lily the dream that she wanted, of teaching circus students, he gave up his Croix de Guerre from the war just to ensure the sale. Supposedly, he'd had barely enough to make the purchase, but the military decoration sealed it."

At this point, I couldn't help but look up at Cassandra for a moment, feeling like, for whatever reason, she'd been watching me. Sure enough, I caught her hazel eyes reflecting in the lights around us, locked onto me. She was smiling brightly at me, though I couldn't understand why exactly. I barely was able to focus on her, however, since I was too wrapped up in Sebastian.

"But why a circus? What possibly could the daughter of apple farmers and a French soldier want with a life on this stage?" Sebastian was walking across the stage then, looking out into the audience. "I asked Lily this when I first met her. Horribly curious, as I'm sure anyone would have been. And she told me a little story about her going to her first circus when she was younger, with her father, not even a year before the war. Cirque Medrano, so it was called, in Paris. Still a traveling circus today, in fact. One of our acrobats was a former performer."

While I knew everything that Sebastian had been speaking about, most of it in great detail at this point, I was most surprised that he had too. He'd known my grandmother as long as I'd been performing with the show, but I hadn't realized they'd talked to one another as much as they apparently had. And I knew the story he was about to tell, as if she'd been standing there telling it herself.

"While Lily adored every portion of that circus show her father took her to, her fondest memories were of the silk aerialists. It comes in the family, I suppose, as that happens to be her grandson dangling precariously by those beautiful fabrics right behind me. Our ever spectacular Chandler Moreau!" I saw Sebastian turn to look over his shoulder in our direction. Instinctively, I waved to the audience and was greeted with a round of applause as a result.

Sebastian trailed across the stage in the opposite direction of us, the stage lights following him as he moved briskly. It was only him and the audience in those moments, but it was almost as if the rest of us didn't even need to be there. He had everyone so captivated. It was part of the reason Lily had snatched him up all those years ago. There wasn't a person I knew more suited to be a ringmaster for Cirque du Lys than Sebastian Taylor.

"Lily's dream, the one that had gotten her through the six years of the war, was that one day she could become an aerialist, too. Unfortunately, complications in her health made that impossible, but the dream still followed—all the way here, to Acrefort. For her to teach alongside her husband, who, too, came from a line of hardworking acrobatic performers. And while I never met Elliott Moreau myself, I know that the love story between the two was one for the ages. His very purchases in this town, love notes for his wife who had told him when they first met one another—

"—I want to live the rest of my life, the only things flying and dropping from the skies, acrobats and silks. Where dreams are only of possibilities and no longer of things that make us afraid. Nothing but sweet dreams." I had mouthed the next words he'd spoken. My grandmother had said them dozens of times in public appearances supporting the circus. They were as ingrained within me as my silk acts themselves.

Sebastian turned, having drawn back toward the center of the room. Every person in the audience, every performer on the stage, waiting. Including me.

"Which brings me back to our stage this evening. To a performance honoring the woman whose presence will now transcend the ages, trapped forever within these walls. Tonight, we honor you, Lily Moreau.

"—And now! Featuring two dozen of the most talented performers in the entire world. The spellbinding Cirque du Lys' Two Hundredth Season! Fais de beaux rêves! *Sweet Dreams.*"

In nearly perfect timing, which was something I could always expect and greatly appreciate from Sebastian, was the triumphant resuming of the orchestral piece that had been gently following along in the background. Every instrument bellowed into the room as the entire stage fell into a beautiful chaotic mess of performances. Every one of us in our own little world, yet somehow still connected.

As the last few measures of strings bellowed into the theater, Cassandra did her small drop, allowing me to catch her, so the two of us could weave our way together back down the silks. By the time we'd reached the ground, the song had faded out into the room. The entire stage of us had come together, bowing, including Cassandra and myself, whose hands were wrapped together.

Amidst a sea of cheering fans, we fled from the stage as the small bit of transitional music played between acts. First up would be Penelope Girard and the acrobats. As Cassandra and I made our way back under the cover of darkness of the backstage area, I watched Penny pass us. She gave a wave and a small smile.

"Good luck," I called out to her, returning the smile. Pleased to see that she looked happier than I'd seen her in a long time. The transition to being an acrobat clearly suited her. And after everything that had happened as a result, it seemed like it had been for the best.

From the wings, Cassandra and I got lost in the several acts that preceded us. We'd been moving out of the way for a trio of jugglers that had just been on the stage when I felt a hand stretch up awkwardly to ruffle my hair.

There was only one human in the entire universe who I knew would be so daring as to even attempt such a thing, and Thomas was grinning at me through his thick mess of facial hair when I spun around. "You were looking a bit too perfect there, Chandler. Had to rough you up a bit, give the rest of us a fighting chance."

Cassandra was audibly laughing while I attempted to fix the mess Thomas had made of my head. Abigail had been right beside him, reaching up to help me, but she was several inches too short to be of any use. I batted her away playfully.

"Way to get him riled up before we go on," Cassandra said, eyeing Thomas. I watched her turn, standing on her tiptoes to shove my hand away from my head. In a few gentle sweeps of her fingers, she'd worked her magic and tamed the mess my friend had made. "There you go. Almost as good as new." She kissed me gently on the cheek.

Thomas was grinning behind me still, holding onto a handful of batons and other random objects that I'm sure would all be on fire in a matter of minutes, given their act was next. Abigail had her giant mess of red curly hair pinned up in a similar fashion to Cassandra's and looked equally as stunning. She was still smiling at me for some reason.

"What? Did Cassandra do something with my hair?" I eyed her for a moment.

"I did no such thing," Cassandra retorted, eyes narrowing at me. "You look handsome as ever. Maybe a little grumpier than usual but—"

"Oh no, Cassandra, this is very usual," Thomas retorted, chuckling again.

My attention was still on Abigail. Clearly, she and I had decided to tune the other two disasters of humans out for a moment. "I was just thinking how proud Lily would be of you if she could see you now. After all this time. See this show still growing strong."

"Did you two know about that introduction?" I asked them, glancing at Abigail and then at Thomas, who had decided to settle down. Behind me, the acrobat performance was going, so I had to project my voice a bit for them to hear me.

Both my friends stared back at me, puzzled. It was then I felt a hand wrap around my wrist, and when I followed the direction that it had come from, I realized it had been Cassandra. Her beautiful hazel eyes were locked onto me the minute I focused on her.

"Sebastian and I did that together," she said, her face breaking into a small smile. "I heard him talking about wanting to pay a tribute to your grandmother somehow a few weeks ago. I thought I'd offer to help him a little, I guess. Seeing that I'm your biggest fan and all. She wrote some really pretty stories. I thought it was a shame for people not to know about them."

While finding out about Cassandra's strange need to steal my grandmother's journal from me a few days prior had certainly been an experience, what I hadn't expected was that she'd do anything like that. I stared at her, blinking, trying to wrap my head around it.

As nervous as it had initially made me when I'd figured out she had taken the journal after all, as panicked as I had felt that it might have come with information that Cassandra needed to be far away from, it had all worked out in the end. Her curiosity shouldn't have surprised me, especially in regard to me.

This, however, had been beyond anything I could have imagined her doing.

"Thank you," I said, wrapping my hand around her cheek to draw her in swiftly to kiss her. "That meant a lot."

"Lily would have loved you, Cassie," Thomas piped in from behind me. "I think if anyone would have beaten Chandler out as the most adored human to her, it would have been the female equivalent. And she *loved* your parents."

"I know," Cassandra said, looking back at Thomas for a moment. Then her attention returned to me before she spoke again. "That was kind of my way of telling her thank you."

A wild erratic string of notes cascaded across the building at that moment. The familiar song that accompanied the most dangerous act of the entire show.

"And now—please welcome two of the most valorous individuals in all of Acrefort. Thomas and Abigail Little. *Ceux de Feu!* Ones of Fire!" Sebastian's voice rang out into the theater again, and the audience cheered as they were introduced. Just before the two had slipped away off onto the stage, Cassandra and I both gave them a brief few silent motions of support.

As soon as they'd disappeared away from us, engulfed in stage lights, I heard Cassandra laughing beside me. When I turned, she was looking up at me, trying to get a hold of herself. "I don't think there will ever be a moment where knowing those two play with flaming objects all day doesn't completely shock me."

"I agree," I nodded in reply, unable to stop myself from grinning. "What's worse is if he doesn't stop letting that beard grow out, it's gonna become a fire hazard." Cassandra was still laughing, shaking her head, and her laughing had me laughing a bit, too, the two of us making our way over to watch our friends along the edge of the wings.

Even though I should have been terribly worried watching as Thomas dropped a flaming sword that his wife had handed him down his throat, I'd seen it enough times by now not to be completely paralyzed by it. Convinced myself that he had it under control, at least, I hoped so anyway. I was too distracted by the fact that Cassandra had reached up, running her fingers along my cheek.

I glanced down at her for a moment, catching our eyes together. She smiled softly. "How are you doing?" She asked me, completely as focused on me at that point as I was on her despite our friends making every attempt to murder themselves in front of a live audience.

While I had intended to answer her more quickly, I found myself pausing for a moment. Letting myself sink into the gentle touches of her fingers against my skin, right at the edge of my beard line. It was something she loved to do, which was a strange reminder of it even to me, but I assumed she was doing it to entertain herself.

"Let's do the drop tonight," I said suddenly. While I'd gotten lost in her touch for a few seconds, eventually, I found her eyes again. "The one we had been practicing. For 'The Flower Duet.' Right after you bow and arrow pose. You'll be in the perfect position to make that twist and—"

"Chandler," Cassandra said, her eyes narrowing at me a little, face having grown a little sterner than it had been before. "It's still a beautiful routine, even if we cut that part out. No one is going to think anything less of you just because we don't do one sequence..."

For several seconds, I was planning to argue with her. Because truthfully, the former athlete inside of me, the one she'd been watching from the audience all those years ago, was desperately clinging to any hope that those days weren't over. That I was still capable of everything I'd been able to do.

But it wasn't my injury that had been the problem, not in those moments. And I assumed she hadn't realized that fact either. "Cassandra, I need you to trust me."

I watched her hesitate for a few seconds, clearly thinking hard. Likely fighting herself as much as I myself had to not argue. Surprisingly, she eventually nodded to me. "Well then, let's go over it one more time before we go out. I could probably use the distraction from standing here worrying that one of my best friends is about to go up in flames."

Despite the fact that I knew she was worried, I still laughed. "Good idea."

Thomas and Abigail remained on the stage for a few more minutes with their act, allowing Cassandra and I time to walk ourselves through our own routine, which was to follow. By the time we'd finished, I could smell all the smoke in the theater from the ridiculous amount of fire that was involved in the last minute of their routine.

While the stage was still dark, and the stagehands were busy fixing the sets around for our act, Cassandra and I wove our way out into the theater. We passed Thomas and Abigail on the way, offering a round of enthusiastic congratulations while being swift about our trek across the stage. Unlike some of the other acts, the time we had to prepare ourselves was shorter.

Once I'd positioned myself beneath those towering purple silks I was using for tonight, I turned my attention to Cassandra for a moment. She steadied herself, focusing on what she was doing before looking over at me. I had expected her to still be looking at me worried, convinced that if I had been in her shoes, it would have been what I'd have done. Instead, she seemed relatively calm and focused. Convinced me to do the same.

"I can think of no better act to close out our show for you this evening than the man inspired by Lily Moreau herself. It is a pleasure for me to introduce to you two outstanding performers. Chandler Moreau and Cassandra Blackstone. *Ceux Avec Les Soies.* The Ones of the Silks!"

Before the song even started, there was a small flicker of light from off-stage. A very simple signal for Cassandra, who immediately began her ascent into the skies. I watched her in the darkness, moving so effortlessly, so completely in tune with everything that she was doing.

She'd gotten exactly where she needed to be as the lights on the stage gently illuminated again. In pastel colors that made everything around us feel like we were in a dream.

When the lights had started, so had the music of 'The Flower Duet.' Cassandra had drawn her body outward, like she was reaching into the audience, in a pose known as the falling star. I made my ascent, the first two measures before the beautiful French duet began. My eyes focused on Cassandra above me, spinning in a slow circle, completely locked in that pose, looking outward.

Below her, I began my sequence as the all-familiar French lyrics of the duet followed along. My parts meant to complement hers. Cassandra was certainly the star of this performance, hovering above me. Even still, I found myself moving effortlessly through things I'd done a thousand times. Things that were so familiar now it was like my body was moving entirely on its own.

I was just passing time in those moments, letting myself steady my attention on Cassandra high above me. She was balancing almost completely by way of her legs at that point, having released her hands from the silks. It required every ounce of focus, and she delivered every second of it.

When she fell into the next move, my focus came back to the room entirely. I took a few steady breaths before I looked back up again.

Cassandra had dropped into the bow and arrow movement. The audience clapped while she held herself in place for a few seconds. I watched her twist a fraction, looking down at me.

The moment we found each other, her hazel eyes locked so fiercely on mine, I was transported back to the theater for her audition. Those first moments we'd had together.

"Why do you want to be an aerialist?" Jeanne had asked her.

"Because of Chandler Moreau."

"I've got you, Cassandra," I called to her. Feeling a steady breath flow in and out of me. Around us, the singers had dropped for a second, becoming quieter. We had barely a few seconds now. She took another breath at the same time as I did.

Then the singers cried out into the room again in one harmonic string of notes. And I watched Cassandra, in one beautiful backward fall, come swiftly down from her perch above me. The entire room disappeared from view, in what was just an absolutely surreal experience of her tiny frame, enveloped in those green fabrics, as she transcended to an entirely different place and time toward me.

All of the paralyzing fears that had held me captive the last year of my life vanished the moment that our hands latched together.

Once she made it to me, I twisted us together so that her graceful fall had become something we shared together. A beautiful dance of drops and spins led us back to the stage as the song faded into the room.

We reached the ground, Cassandra still wrapped in my arms, legs wrapped around me, hands still holding onto the silks above her head. As she released them from her grip, they fell down along my face, and I couldn't help but kiss her. It only lasted for a few seconds, the sound of a roaring crowd interrupting us.

Cassandra and I drew apart again, wrapping our hands together. The two of us stared out into the massive crowd that filled the Cirque du Lys theater. We took a bow just as the rest of the troupe came back onto the stage. *Symphonie fantastique* played in the background, barely audible with the roar of the crowd around us.

When I looked over at Cassandra, she had already been looking at me. I absolutely adored the look on her face, that same sort of look she'd had the first time I'd brought her inside this building. Filled with so much excitement and joy. I remembered how that had felt when I was younger and standing in the same place, and it made me all the more happy for her. She certainly deserved it.

The cast went backstage again as the theater began to empty out. We chatted amongst ourselves until the noises of the crowd seemed to dwindle. Then, in usual fashion, the group of us went out onto the stage to assist the technical crew in cleaning.

As we wandered out, there were a handful of people still lingering around. Mostly family members and friends who had wanted to see their loved ones. Waiting on one of the steps to the stage was Cassandra's friend Henry and his girlfriend. She squeezed my hand gently before I watched her go over to speak with them.

Meanwhile, I found another familiar face amongst the crowd. Stella, too, had come to see the opening night, having taken a ticket I'd offered her weeks ago. I walked over to the edge of the stage, sat down and carefully hopped onto the floor below to meet her. She hugged me, kissing me on the cheek before we broke away from one another.

Stella was beaming at me. "Of all the shows of yours I've ever seen, this one was by far my favorite." She brought her hand up to cup my cheek. "You looked the happiest I've ever seen you." I smiled at her softly as she drew her hand away again. "And Cassandra was just lovely. A perfect partner for you, for certain. Clearly a protege of Chandler Moreau's."

"And since when did you become an expert at the silks?" I raised a brow at her, grinning.

"Since I've been sitting in these shows for the last decade," Stella reminded me playfully. "Now, I might not know all the fancy names and technical terms, but I'm pretty certain I could guess some of the things you do before you do them."

"You're saying I'm predictable now?" I teased her. Stella laughed, shaking her head at me.

I had just been about to continue my thought when I saw something out of the corner of my eye. It caused me to turn immediately. The air ceased to exist around me. Time slowed. Stella disappeared. All that existed was Gabriel Moreau, heading straight toward me. My mother, too, steps behind him. I tried desperately to breathe, all the while keeping a steady gaze on him. Fearing any subtle movement or gesture would prompt my father to think or do something he shouldn't in those moments. Not that he wasn't already thinking something already, knowing him.

Then, as if it hadn't already been bad enough, I felt a hand wrap into my own. My head jerked in the direction of where it had come from. The moment I saw Cassandra standing beside me, I ripped us apart, putting at least a foot of space between us as rapidly as I could. I barely even had enough time to see Cassandra's startled and confused expression on her face before my attention turned back to my father.

"The infamous Cassandra Blackstone," my father said as he drew up in front of us. When I glanced at Cassandra again, I saw her grow rigid as she turned her attention toward him, having finally realized he was there. "A pleasure to see you again." He held out his hand to her, offering what, to the casual observer, might have appeared to be a very pleasant smile. When I saw it, however, it made me immediately nauseous.

Cassandra hovered in place for a moment before I saw her reach out to shake my father's hand. When they broke away, she attempted the most polite smile she possibly could before she spoke. "You came to the show?"

"Ah, yes," Gabriel replied, glancing at me. I did my best to meet his eyes but found myself having to look away from him. Worried that the expression on my face was condemning me. "My wife Madelyn and I," he motioned to my mother beside him. "We come on occasion. I heard this season was honoring my late mother, so I assumed it would be appropriate to attend and see what all the fuss was about."

"Nice to meet you," Cassandra looked at my mother then, holding out her hand. They shook, my mother offering Cassandra a soft smile. Then Cassandra turned her attention back to Gabriel. "I hope it didn't disappoint you. It was a privilege to be able to honor her."

Gabriel studied her intently for a few seconds before he spoke again. "It certainly wasn't a disappointment. Enlightening, really. I'm sure Lily would have loved it."

Enlightening, really. My stomach was knotting so much I could barely stand it. "We're in the process of cleaning up the theater. Cassandra and I should probably get back to what we were doing. Thank you for coming. I'm glad you enjoyed the show."

"How does it feel to be the first student in, ah—decades, right Chandler? Maybe even since my mother ran this place. The first student in a long time to perform on this stage?" My father was staring at Cassandra again, an intense look on his face. "The board certainly seemed impressed by your talent with that resounding vote of approval. Quite impressive, really."

As if that wasn't evident by her performance, I thought to myself. "It was Thomas and Abigail Little's idea," I replied before Cassandra had a chance to. "They've been friends with Cassandra for years and knew how talented she was. When she auditioned, the rest of us just agreed."

"You could let the woman speak for herself, Chandler," my father said to me, his eyes shifting to mine. "I was surprised that you even convinced Jeanne, of all people. You must have had a pretty compelling argument."

I felt Cassandra's attention draw onto me for a moment, causing me to swallow deeply. That had been something I hadn't mentioned to her. The visit I'd made with Jeanne and Patrick that night she'd first arrived at Cirque du Lys. Hadn't really thought it had been necessary, but in those moments, I regretted that I hadn't.

"I'm sorry for interrupting you," I finally managed to say, glancing at Cassandra.

"Chandler's right," Cassandra replied, looking back at Gabriel. I couldn't get a read on her face in those moments. "Thomas and Abigail have been my friends for a long time. They seemed to have been a big reason why I got the position, which I'm very grateful for. I hope I made your mother proud tonight." It had been impressive how quick she'd been in replying to him, catching on to my attempts to weave him away from the truth.

"—Like I said, I think we should be getting back to it," I tried to interrupt again.

"We never really got to properly talk about your own parents," Gabriel noted, looking head-on at Cassandra again. "I recall telling you how fond our family was of them. I'd love to chat with you for a few minutes. That is if Chandler can spare you from your—cleaning duties..." He glanced at me, and I knew, despite my every effort, I must have looked overwhelmed with what he'd just asked her.

"We probably should be getting home," my mother interjected. I watched her attempt to wrap her arm around Gabriel's and realized that she might have said what she said, noticing how I'd suddenly gotten panicked. "It's getting late, and I'm getting tired, Gabriel."

"I'll only be a few minutes, Madelyn," Gabriel swatted her away. "One walk around the building, perhaps, Ms. Blackstone? What do you say? Humor an old adoring fan?"

"I don't think that's necessary—" I tried to reply again, but this time, I felt a hand wrap around my wrist. Surprised to see that it had been Cassandra that had done so.

I looked over at her, and while she was making every attempt at giving me a convincing smile, I could see it all over her face that she was also trying desperately to be brave. Just as much as she had the entire time I had known her. My papillon.

"It's okay, Chandler," Cassandra reassured me before pulling her hand away. She seemed to gather her wits about her, standing up taller before she turned her attention back to my father. "Okay. Let's take a walk. It's snowy out again, and I enjoy the view of the tent all dusted in white. It would be nice to stretch my legs a bit, too."

"I'd enjoy a walk—" my mother started to say, attempting to wrap her arm around my father's again. Once again, he jerked away from her, but his attention remained on Cassandra.

"I'd prefer it just the two of us," my father replied. "We'll be back shortly." He nodded to Cassandra, and I watched, horrified, as she walked over around the stage to go fetch the puffer coat we'd recently gotten her amongst the pile of things the troupe had left. The minute she was gone, I fought desperately to say anything at all to him. I wanted to threaten him, to even refuse him to be able to do what he was about to do. But I found that I couldn't.

When Cassandra returned, she glanced at me for a moment, looking as if she was trying to reassure me. Then her attention turned back to my father. "Okay, let's go."

I watched the two of them as they wandered up the aisle together. Felt myself as helpless as I'd felt in an extraordinarily long time. Prayed that my father's intentions had been as innocent as he'd claimed they were, but every part of me knew that they weren't. I had to trust Cassandra in those moments. That she knew what she was doing and that she'd keep herself safe. As much as I wanted to go after them, I knew I couldn't. Not without making it worse.

"It's just a walk," my mother assured me, clearly seeing that I was in a panic. "You know your father, always overly curious about everything." That was definitely one way to put it.

In my peripheral vision, I saw Stella had been chatting with Thomas and Abigail. It looked as though their conversation had wrapped up, and she'd turned to look at me. She gave me a wave and a smile before she, too, headed out of the theater.

"Can I help you all with cleaning?" My mother offered, breaking my train of thought. "I might as well make myself useful in the meantime."

Despite everything, I managed to offer a small smile and then my arm to her. She took it graciously as the two of us wove our way along the aisle, back up to the steps of the stage. Every step I took away from the direction Cassandra and my father had gone, feeling as though I was letting her slip through my grasp. Realizing how impossible it was to protect her in those moments. And it was one of the most horrible feelings I'd ever experienced in my life.

CHAPTER 30

CASSANDRA

The chilly winter air ripped against my skin as Gabriel Moreau and I made our way out onto the sidewalk outside of Cirque du Lys. I tugged the coat around me tighter, trying not to notice how much I could see my breath and that it was adding to the chill I was already feeling. The chill was worsened by the fact that I had to follow around this horrible man and make conversation with him, knowing the things I knew, however vague they still were.

"I remember when this building was first constructed," Gabriel said, and when I looked at him, he'd turned his attention toward the tent beside us. "My mother designed it herself. There had been a fabric tent that sat here for many, many years, but it was finally decided there needed to be something more permanent." I watched him turn his attention toward me then. "My father had it built for her as somewhat of a surprise over the summer one year. She'd been planning it, but he was the type to want to keep her on her toes. A romantic in that way, I suppose. At least he was for many years."

In those moments, I was somewhat grateful that Gabriel had decided to just start talking. That he hadn't been asking me questions or interrogating me at all. It was a relief, more than anything. One that I had hoped he would continue doing, but unfortunately, he didn't.

"I'm sure given your fascination with the school, the circus, even my son himself, you'd enjoy that bit of information," Gabriel said, his attention turning back to me then. Those green eyes, so much like Chandler's, honed in on me. I swallowed deeply.

"I find it fascinating what a vested interest you seem to have in our entire family, actually. My son, I understood, given your clear talent for his profession and desire to train under him. But I was surprised by all this *research* you seem to be doing."

We weaved around the corner. Abruptly, we were in the alley in between the buildings. I was hyper aware of the fact that we'd drifted away from any semblance of the public eye. We were alone, and it terrified the shit out of me, given the words that had just come out of the man's mouth.

Even still, I tried my best to be casual about my reply. "If you're meaning my help with the show, researching about Chandler's grandmother, I did that specifically to help—"

"Ah, Ms. Blackstone," Gabriel spoke right over me. "I'm certain you know what it is I'm referring to. I find it charming how alike you and my son seem to be, playing ignorant like you do. I suppose it makes sense for the two of you falling for one another, though I'll have you know I've been aware of this for months now. Neither of the two of you are subtle."

All the dominoes were tumbling. I was finding myself unable to stop them, feeling a massive amount of panic. Wishing desperately that I'd let Chandler jump to my defense after all, even let his mother attempt to help me. That I wasn't trapped in some alley with a man I knew was even more dangerous than I fathomed him to be.

Gabriel continued while I flailed, finding it impossible to find words to speak. "Does the name Andre Morales help clarify anything for you, Ms. Blackstone?" Hearing that shady guy's name I'd been working with for the last few years to bring down Peter made my heart start pounding so hard in my chest that I swore I was going to go into cardiac arrest and die. That may have been a better way to go, more so than what could have possibly been waiting for me at the end of this conversation. I regretted that I'd ever asked the piece of shit to look into Gabriel at all.

"I am assuming by that terrified look on your face, you have some idea of who I'm referring to. He was easy to get information out of, too, considering you were barely paying him anything at all. I'm assuming because you were doing this yourself, without my son's knowledge or finances. Which, while unfortunate for you, proved very useful to me."

Despite the fact that I was far more terrified than I probably had ever felt in my entire life, which was surprising given the years I'd been around Peter Blackstone, I managed to steady myself. Forced myself to stand up tall and turn to face the man. Gabriel stopped as well, turning his attention toward me.

"What the hell do you want from me, then?" I finally managed to ask him, though my voice was a little shaky. "Are you going to kill me or something? I suppose like father, like son, right? What did they call him on that website... *The Black Horse?* You probably know all about that, don't you?" I regretted the instant I'd finished speaking, but it came tumbling out of me.

Gabriel paused for a moment, eyes zeroed in on me, brow raised. For a matter of a few seconds, he looked surprised. Curious, even. I watched him take two steps toward me, closing the gap. Until he was right over the top of me, that same towering frame of Chandler's but far more ominous. Somehow, I managed to stay steady. Didn't move a muscle.

"You are a wealth of curiosity, aren't you, Ms. Blackstone?" I almost thought I saw a brief look of amusement on his face, but it barely lasted. "While certainly a fine quality in the right circumstances, I assure you, it can have dangerous consequences in others. Of course, you don't need to worry. I haven't come out here to *murder* you in some back alley. That would be quite reckless and completely unnecessary. I don't like getting my hands dirty. I never have."

I spoke before I could stop myself, and even as the words came barreling out of me, I felt my body growing so cold, it was like I'd fallen into an icy lake. "Chandler said you weren't the type to kill people, but I'm still not sure I actually believe that."

I could feel my own hands trembling, despite every attempt to get them not to. It should have been a relief hearing the words he said, but I felt just as terrified.

Gabriel spoke again, looking completely unfazed by my admission of what his son had told me. And I spent every second hating myself that I'd condemned Chandler like I had. "Let's not sit here digging any more holes for ourselves." He paused for a second, those sharp green eyes locked straight on me. He continued, nostrils flaring. "I'm being kind here, Ms. Blackstone. Consider this your one warning. Quit putting your nose where it doesn't belong, trying to quench your curiosity. Even though I'm sure the whole thing was some desperate endeavor to try and help my son, for whatever it is you think he actually needs protecting from."

I hated how easily he saw through me. I'd been so horribly obvious in everything I had done up to that point. "I've dealt with enough traitorous pieces of shit family members in my lifetime to let you do the same to him. He's done nothing but try to help me all this time. It was the least I could do for him in return."

"You're referring to your uncle, I'm assuming? Peter Blackstone?" I could feel the blood slowly draining from my face at my uncle's name being uttered out of Gabriel Moreau's mouth. Both surprised and worried that David's suspicions about his involvement with Le Milieu weren't entirely inaccurate, nor were my suspicions of this man.

"Cassandra." When he spoke my name, it made me cringe so deeply that it took a second to recover. I loathed it. "You couldn't possibly have believed you were the only one keeping tabs, could you? Did you not wonder why out of the thousands of applicants to receive one of only two full scholarships to Dreamers, you'd been one of them? Clearly, you are exceptionally talented, as evidenced by the show this evening... Comparatively to your peers, however, you were irrelevant in regards to your background. Yet, here you are."

"What the hell are you talking about?" I asked him, feeling my head spin at his words. "The letter said I got the scholarship based on the decision of the audition committee."

"Ah yes, Chandler came barging into my office the moment they got through that day, insisting upon that. But you'd already had that scholarship months before he thought he had anything to do with it. The minute we received your application, in fact. My son's ability to keep himself ignorant about things is sometimes very useful."

My mouth was hanging open, my heart still thudding, my body still trembling slightly and trying to force myself to keep breathing. "Why?"

Gabriel shrugged at me, looking rather unfazed by anything I'd been saying. "You've been a pawn on a chessboard this entire time. Whether you like it or not."

It had taken every single ounce of self-restraint not to spew a slew of words I'd been thinking about him in those moments. Somehow, I managed. I had been about to reply to him, but Gabriel beat me yet again.

"It's getting chilly out, Ms. Blackstone. I'll circle back to my point. Your warning. The only warning I will give you, and you can ask my son if you are questioning my sincerity on that statement. Keep that curiosity of yours in check. While you certainly don't have to fear me doing anything to you, I assure you I have the resources to make sure there are consequences if you decide otherwise."

"And what if I go to the police? I have enough information that I'm sure they'd look into it." After everything, I was surprised that I had the will to argue with him more. I knew better than to threaten that. It was a terrible idea, knowing what I knew about the man. They likely wouldn't be able to do anything at all.

Gabriel's face shifted in those next few moments, and I had never felt so cold and so nauseous in my entire life. Thought I'd turn into a sheet of ice yet again. He flashed a smile, his eyes trained on me. "You can certainly try, can't you?"

Before I could speak another word, he weaved around, heading back out of the alley and around the building. I stood motionless for a few seconds before I trotted after him, weaving around the corner to call out to him. "I'll tell your son everything—"

Even despite my threat, Gabriel kept walking. Didn't give me a second's attention. I watched him walk all the way back to the front doors of the theater, disappearing inside. Stood there, unable to do anything at all, despite how terribly cold I was.

Over a series of speakers that had been hung on lamposts lining the town square of Acrefort, an acoustic guitar played "Greensleeves." The entire few blocks that marked the center of downtown had been festively decorated with lights and garlands and a giant Christmas tree that towered in the center of it all.

Hand laced with my own, Chandler wandered beside me, admiring the scenery around us. I hadn't been able to help myself, looking at him as often as I did. Not only because I always had enjoyed admiring him, but more specifically because *somehow*, Abigail Little had gotten him into what was a *very* ugly Christmas sweater. It had been made to look like he was a Christmas tree, and every time I looked at him wearing it, I couldn't help but smile.

Unfortunately, Abby had spared no expense with me, with a sweater that looked like I was a giant present with a giant bow stretching across my chest. Chandler had made it slightly better, having whispered to me in private after seeing it that he'd be more than happy to unwrap it later. Regardless of our slight displeasure at the Littles' insistence upon torturing us, I was grateful for them. Grateful for the distraction.

"Ah, Chandler—you've been walking around all this time and haven't even been wearing this correctly," Thomas was standing beside Chandler on the opposite side I was on. He was staring intently at the sweater. In one swift motion of his hand, he fidgeted with the collar. All the while, Chandler scowled at him, and soon after, all the little lights on the Christmas tree lit up brightly.

I laughed so loudly that I'm sure people several blocks away heard me. Thomas looked pleased with himself, and even Abigail was restraining her own amusement. Meanwhile, Chandler had stopped in his tracks, looking as utterly annoyed as ever. "I swear to God..."

"I don't think I've been any happier than I am at this very moment," I stated, grinning. Chandler shot me a dirty look, but it was barely holding. I knew he was amused, too, despite everything. "You look so cute right now. I can't handle it."

Chandler rolled his eyes, leaning down to kiss me gently. "I thought you had the worst deal with that giant bow, but after this—Thomas, you're officially dead to me."

"Well, my friend, I go out with no regrets," Thomas shrugged at him. "However, I've been eyeing that beverage cart we keep passing, and I'm feeling a spiked hot chocolate. I believe I saw some sort of apple cider Moscow mule for the grumpy old anti-sugar heathen of ours. My treat, if that will win your forgiveness for 'brightening you' up a bit." He winked at Chandler, beaming.

"I'll take a hot chocolate," I said first.

"Bribery by alcohol," Chandler followed after me, scratching at his beard a bit. "I'll have a bit of Cassandra's drink. Don't worry about me. You're forgiven, Thomas. At least for now. Consider it your Christmas present."

Thomas and Abigail took off together to fetch our drinks. Meanwhile, my attention turned to Chandler. I couldn't help but laugh again when I saw all the colorful blinky lights strung across his chest. Chandler narrowed his eyes at me. "You better quit, or I won't unwrap you later like I promised."

"That was a good try, Chandler. But I'm one hundred percent sure that will be happening with how many times your eyes have been locked on my chest all evening. Don't think I haven't been noticing." I grinned at him, teasing him gently and squeezing his hand that was still wrapped around mine.

"That bow is fucking gigantic," Chandler argued, and I laughed again.

"And look at you, having hot chocolate. Color me surprised," I leaned into him, laying myself into the side of his arm. I felt him kiss the top of my head lightly. For whatever reason, despite how much I adored Chandler's little random bits of affection, it briefly made me feel anxious. My mind drifted back to my encounter with his father again, instantly feeling nauseous.

Chandler shrugged, his voice interrupting my wandering thoughts. "I might be feeling a little festive, I suppose. It's Christmas Eve."

I looked in front of us, admiring the large Christmas tree a dozen yards away. Watched the little flakes of snow falling all around us. Getting lost in the scenery for a few moments and all the happy people bustling around. Eventually, I looked back up at Chandler, surprised to find he'd already been looking at me.

Since I'd had the altercation with Gabriel two weeks ago, I'd been an absolute wreck. Worried at every turn, trying to decide what to do. Grateful that school had been over at least, so I wasn't stuck there with the man looming at every turn. There had been so many times I had wanted to tell Chandler what was going on. Thought that maybe if he knew, we'd be able to figure it out together. Maybe he'd actually tell me *something*. Anything at all. Any shred of knowledge to make me feel better. But then I'd convinced myself that somehow that might make it worse. If Gabriel knew I told Chandler anything, something could happen to him.

So, I'd held it in even though I desperately did not want to. I'd been so stressed out and at a loss of what to do that I didn't think I'd ever calm down again. So this evening together with our friends, doing something normal, was a welcomed distraction. Even if it only helped to a certain degree, and I was still lost in my own head.

"You know, you've seemed off these last few days," Chandler noted, and I felt him reach up to tuck some of my hair behind my ear, as he often did. He left his hand against my face for a little while after. "Are you okay? I actually wondered if maybe this was a hard time of year for you, given everything with your parents. I wasn't sure if I should ask or not."

Despite the question making me a bit down, I couldn't help but smile at him, however small. "It always is. I've luckily had Alex around many of the years since. But yeah, I always get a little sad." Chandler squeezed my hand softly, running his thumb along the backside. "But you know, ever since Thanksgiving, I realized how much that's changed for me this year."

Chandler raised a brow at me curiously, and I continued. "I just feel like I actually have family again," I admitted, shrugging. "All of those 'traditional' meanings of family are kind of irrelevant and bullshit, honestly. I like being able to choose how I define that. Being able to feel like Thomas and Abigail are like that fun, eccentric aunt and uncle I never had." My eyes drifted to Chandler again. "And you—"

I paused, feeling my face get warm despite the cold outside. My embarrassment immediately got a rise out of Chandler, who grinned and nudged me gently. "And me, what, Cassandra?"

"—Nevermind," I shook my head, trying to recover. "What I meant to say is, I'm just glad I am able to make my own family now. That's all. And that includes you."

When I finally had the nerve to look at Chandler again, he was still smiling. "I feel the same way, I hope you know. I understand that feeling very much. And as someone who stayed in a marriage for a *very* long time out of obligation. Watched my mother stay with my father for so many years. I hate that he's the only reason I can't enjoy things like going to visit them tomorrow... I can tell you that having a 'found family' is a very refreshing thing." He hadn't been looking at me, but his attention eventually came back. "And as far as what you were alluding to just then—"

"Oh God, please don't," I grumbled, shaking my head. I felt Chandler's hand drop from my own and draw under my chin, pulling my head up so I met eyes with him.

"It's been on my mind too. I just need it to be the right moment. I'm not planning to rush it or anything. My divorce, unfortunately, took a lot out of me in that regard. But rest assured, Cassandra, that is most certainly coming at some point or other. When you least expect it to." Chandler kissed me on my head again gently.

While I'd certainly been surprised by his admission and would have been even more overwhelmed by it, I had been more distracted by what he had said seconds into his speech. "You're going to your parents tomorrow?"

Chandler frowned, shaking his head. "Unfortunately, yes. Another obligation I'm annually forced into, just like the Thanksgiving dinner. If my mother wasn't involved, I wouldn't remotely bother. But I owe it to her to come visit at least sometimes. I feel bad enough as it is that I don't go over there more often than I do."

I completely understood his frustration in those moments. However, Chandler hadn't seen his father since the opening night at Cirque du Lys. We hadn't even really talked about that conversation and had mostly avoided it altogether. I hadn't wanted to say something I shouldn't, and I honestly didn't want to think about it. Now, it was coming crashing back at me.

"Piping hot chocolate, incoming!" Thomas interrupted my thoughts, handing over a large paper cup to me that smelled magically of chocolate and alcohol. I took a small, delicate sip, embracing the warmth to help break me from the cold. It was as delicious as I'd hoped.

Chandler took my drink from me carefully, pulling it to his mouth. While I had expected him to take a little sip like I had, he stood there for several seconds, drinking a good portion of it down. I swatted at him playfully. "What the hell. Are you going to share?" With coaxing, I managed to snatch it away from him. Sure enough, he'd downed half of it. "You're going to be a nightmare later. I have never witnessed a Chandler Moreau sugar-buzzed inebriation, but I am guessing that's going to happen, and I am going to be forced to settle you down."

Thomas grinned, sipping on his own drink. "First time for everything, eh?"

I felt Chandler lean down, his warm mouth against my ear. It caused me to shiver a little. "I'm sure you'll have no problem finding a way to settle me down, Cassandra." I turned just in time for him to plant his lips on mine. He'd done it more aggressively than I'd anticipated, and it took me by surprise. I pulled my hands up to plant them on the side of his face. For a moment, I kissed him, feeling my head spinning before I broke away.

"That sugar is already getting to his head," Abigail laughed, and I watched them start walking again in front of us, holding hands.

"Clearly," I laughed, grabbing hold of Chandler's hand. After I'd taken another drink, I handed the hot chocolate back to him. "I'm going to regret this, I'm sure, but you can have the rest." Chandler grinned before tossing it back in a matter of a few seconds. I shook my head, still laughing.

Abigail had gone up to some booth that had been selling candles and soaps, Thomas following along after her. Chandler and I had been a few steps behind when I felt him stop abruptly. He tossed the empty paper cup into a nearby garbage before he fished through his pockets, pulling out his phone. It had been vibrating.

"It's David Finch," Chandler said, studying the phone for a moment. It took me a few moments to recognize the name, but Chandler clarified quickly. "I haven't heard from him since Thanksgiving." He quickly answered the phone, putting it to his ear. "David? Hold on a second. I want Cassandra to be able to hear too."

I called out to Abigail and Thomas that we'd be a moment and then followed Chandler to a nearby alley that was quieter than the rest of the area. Chandler put the phone on speaker. "Okay, David. We're both here."

"Glad I caught you both," David said with that thick Boston accent of his. So far, despite his every effort to try and assist us with getting more information on Peter, he'd come up empty. Which was why the phone call completely caught me off guard. "I have a bit of an update. As much as I wish it was more good news after that huge win we had with the mafia stuff... Man, I still have feds calling me thanking me about a few of those bastards we pinned down, but anyway—"

The moment David uttered those last few sentences, I immediately felt Chandler's intense gaze drilling into me. I couldn't even look at him. I could only imagine the vast amount of emotions he had to be feeling in those moments. Likely furious with me that I hadn't done what he'd asked and stopped David from pursuing the mafia lead, and probably equally so for having kept it from him.

"Anyway, I'm afraid it's not great. And I'm sorry about that, given it's the holidays—"

While I was already cold from being outside in the snowy weather and from the paralyzing gaze Chandler had on me, it worsened a great deal with David's words. I looked up at Chandler finally, whose facial expression had shifted. He clearly had been livid, but all at once he looked very concerned. He spoke first. "What's going on, David?"

"I'm surprised Cassandra hasn't heard yet, all things considered," he started, and the moment he'd said that I prayed to every single entity that he wasn't going to say what I thought he might next. "Apparently, as of yesterday, Peter's been considered for a reduction in his jail sentence. A compassionate release."

I had to brace myself against the wall of the building beside us, fighting to breathe, my head spinning. "He what? How?"

"It's actually pretty bizarre, honestly," David said, and I was barely able to make out his words with how bad my ears had been ringing. "Does the name Anna Moulin ring a bell at all?"

The name wasn't familiar to me. I was about to reply when I felt a hand grip my shoulder tightly. When I looked over at Chandler, his eyes had grown wider, his mouth hanging slightly open, looking very much surprised. "Anna Moulin was the daughter of a neighbor of my Aunt and Uncle's growing up. She used to play with my cousins and with me when I visited France. For whatever reason, I thought I'd heard she'd died or something... What the hell?"

"Well, she's *going* to die," David explained. "Stage four liver cancer. Probably won't make it another year, from my understanding. Apparently, her family passed away not too long ago, though I haven't figured out what happened. All I know is that she's been alone the last year or two. That was until she married your uncle a few months ago."

"*What?*" My head was thudding. It was getting so hard to stand that I had to slide myself down along the wall and sit on the ground. Chandler came down beside me, still clutching the phone. "Peter *married* her? I don't understand."

"It was pretty ingenious on his part, actually. Why the court let him get away with it, I have no idea. And now I'm even more puzzled with the woman's connection to Chandler, of all things. I thought maybe you would know who she was, Cassandra. Not Chandler..." He faded off for a few seconds, then cleared his throat. "But anyway. One of the eligibility criteria for compassionate release is that if your spouse is suffering from a terminal illness and has no other way to take care of themselves, then you can be granted it in that case."

"What the fuck?" Chandler blinked, and when I looked at him, he was shaking in disbelief. "Clearly he married her with malintent. How was that not blatantly obvious?"

"No clue," David replied. "And it got way more bizarre now that I know the woman has some connection to you, too. I'll have to dig into it more. Anyway, he's scheduled for a hearing after the first of the year. I just wanted to prepare you. I know we'd hoped to have more information on him, and I assure you I'm doing the best I can, but I've been coming up dry at every turn. I'm going to do my best to knuckle down until then. See what I can do. Don't lose hope yet, but just be prepared."

"Thank you for letting us know," Chandler said. I hadn't been looking at him, staring off into space, completely lost. "Keep us posted if you find anything." I heard them exchange a goodbye, but I stopped paying attention. The minute Chandler had put his phone away, I felt him wrap his arm around my shoulders. "Jesus Christ," he sighed.

"Chandler, if he gets out of jail—" I was having trouble thinking straight. "I won't be able to stay here. He'll find me. I swear to God he will find a way to hunt me down and kill me. Probably kill you, too, if he knows what we've been doing. This is so bad. Oh my God."

"One thing at a time, Cassandra," his hand slipped away from my shoulder, and I felt him cup my chin, drawing my attention back to him. "He hasn't gotten to do that yet. We still have a little while to figure this out. David's working as best he can. And we don't know for sure he'll even be granted compassionate release, anyway. I have to believe that a judge will see straight through what he's trying to do. You need to try and see that, too."

I met his gaze then, staring into his beautiful green eyes that were trying so hard to be as comforting as he could in those moments, but nothing was going to save me. And I would have dwelled on it longer if Chandler's facial expression hadn't grown quickly darker.

"And while I realize this is inconvenient timing, to say the least, I'm going to ask you anyway..." I knew the next words coming out of his mouth. He hadn't needed to say them. "Why the *hell* did you not listen to me, Cassandra? I told you *exactly* what to do, and still—"

"Because *last I checked, Chandler...*" I sucked in a long breath of air before I continued, feeling entirely too wound up and on edge from the conversation with David to want to indulge him with this argument, too. "I'm a grown-ass woman and can make my own decisions. I realize you were concerned. You're entitled to your opinion..."

"It's not an *opinion,*" Chandler snapped back at me. "It's forty-one years of fucking living in it. I am trying to protect you. Jesus, I've spent my entire adult life trying to protect everyone I love from all of this... And I *knew* the moment I first saw you, the moment I realized how completely and utterly lost I was in you—" He tapered off for a second, shaking his head, looking immensely frustrated. "I knew better than to get you wrapped up in it. I'm still in a constant state of agonizing worry that something will happen to you because of it. And if something happened to you, Cassandra—"

Chandler's voice cracked a little, and he stopped speaking abruptly. He looked closer to the verge of tears than I had *ever* seen him. Ever. I stood there patiently, letting him take a few deep breaths before he finished his thought. "I don't want to talk about it here. This isn't the place. I'll tell you about it eventually. But—I lost someone. One of my favorite people to ever walk this Earth. I lost him because I couldn't protect him from the very thing I am trying so desperately to keep you safe from." He was shaking a little, staring at me hard. "And that *cannot* happen again. I won't survive it."

As chilled as his words had made me, and the terrifying look on his face, I didn't let it stop me. I rushed straight to him, wrapping myself around him as tightly as I could. Feeling like the only thing

I wanted in those moments was for him to know that I was still there. That I wasn't going anywhere, and he didn't need to worry. After everything, it was the last thing he needed.

I felt his arms wrap around me in return. He planted a soft kiss on top of my head, and I could still feel him trembling a little, clearly worked up about whatever it was he'd vaguely just admitted to me. Regardless, it didn't matter. I just wanted him to know I was there.

The two of us stood there a while in the alley, holding each other. Eventually, I felt Chandler's breaths steady again. He seemed to get his normal demeanor back. When I pulled away from him, he'd quickly swiped a few tears from his eyes nonchalantly. Which only worried me a little further, but I didn't press him about it.

Even still, I needed to say what I wanted to say to him. Regardless of what had just happened. I looked down, reaching for his hand, taking it with both of mine. Holding onto it as I looked back up at him. Waiting until those beautiful green eyes came back to me.

"I hope you know my maddening curiosity isn't just because of my overwhelming obsession with you," I said, trying to smile at him and lighten the mood a bit. Chandler looked slightly more lighthearted, a small smile lingering on his lips. He was still staring straight at me. "I worry about you too. And—" This time, it was me who had a very rapid surge of emotion, causing my voice to quiver for a few seconds. Even still, I managed to hold steady. "I've also lost two people who I loved more than anything, very tragically and unexpectedly. And," I couldn't help but laugh a little, despite still being on the verge of tears, shaking my head as I realized how alike the two of us were without having realized it. "I'm trying to protect everyone too. Trying to bring Peter down."

"Cassandra, I wasn't trying—" Chandler instantly looked concerned, noticing I was right on the edge of breaking and feeling guilty about it. I dropped one of my hands from his, reaching up to put my finger to his lips to stop him from speaking. He let out a long bit of air from his nose but didn't say another word.

"I'm trying to say that we're a lot alike," I replied to him, finding myself smiling as I looked back at him head-on. "I've been alone in those same kinds of feelings too. For years. Wanting to protect people, wanting to do everything I could to help... Maybe not quite as many years as you, obviously—"

Chandler had caught my playful age jab and shot me an equally playful dirty look in response. I laughed then, feeling relieved as I let my hand fall against his face, tracing that line between his cheek and his beard with my fingers. He closed his eyes for a minute, enjoying the affection. I let him get lost in it until he returned.

Then I spoke again. "Chandler, I don't think either of us should be alone in it anymore." I cupped his face with the side of my hand, still smiling. "You trust me when we're eighty feet dangling in those tiny pieces of fabrics. That could just as easily end your life, you know."

Finally, Chandler's shoulders dropped, and he let out a very amused laugh. "Okay, I suppose you may have a bit of a point." He reached up with his hand that I'd been holding, grabbing mine from the side of his face and kissing it softly. "We can talk about it. Make an evening of it. Tomorrow, maybe? After I get home from my parents?" I didn't think I had felt so much relief flood through me as it had in those moments he'd spoken those words to me. All I could do was nod in reply.

Chandler smiled softly at me, wrapping our hands together. Just as he had, a voice called out down the alleyway. Thomas had been waving wildly, clearly ecstatic about whatever it was. "Chandler! Abby found us a bonfire we can check out! Let's go! Chop chop!"

"Something burning. Ha. Why am I not surprised?" Chandler said, shaking his head, and I laughed, wrapping my arm around his. He paused instead of immediately walking, leaning down to speak to me quietly. "And Cassandra... We'll figure something out about Peter, too. I promise. You're right. Neither of us has to be alone anymore. Just keep being brave, little papillon. You're the bravest person I know." I felt him kiss the top of my head again before he started walking, tugging me along gently.

And, as worried as I still was about Peter, it was far less than I had ever been before—knowing that, no matter what, the man I cherished more than anything was beside me. He'd meant every single one of those words, just as sincerely as the first time he'd spoken that pet name to me as his alter ego at The Crucible. I believed every word.

CHAPTER 31

CHANDLER

My mind had been off in a far-away world with my cousins when I was younger. In Melun, a place I thought of often but only dreamt of on rare occasions. Beneath a beautiful cerulean sky, we'd run down the city's cobblestone streets. I could almost feel that warm summer breeze against me, hearing the birds chirping in the trees. It must have been happy memories I'd been lost in because I could still feel the warmth washing over me as it started to fade and I'd begun to stir, waking from a pleasant night's sleep.

When I opened my eyes, still in a sleepy haze and trying to come to, I realized I was engulfed in darkness. Darker than my bedroom should have been. Seconds later, I could feel something against my face. It was soft, resembling the feel of the silks. And it smelled very distinctly like the lemon-scented detergent I used.

The sudden realization I couldn't see, inhibited by whatever fabric wrapped around my eyes, had me immediately jerking my hand upward to rip it away. The moment my hand began to move upward, I felt something wrap around my wrist. It was gentle, and I instantly knew what it was, confirmed a second later by her voice whispering softly into my ear, raising the hairs on the back of my neck.

"You're going to spoil your Christmas present if you do that." Cassandra's hand had been the one to move mine away from my face. Meanwhile, the words continued, her warm breath beating into the side of my cheek. "I was a little excited and didn't want to wait until you woke up in the morning. Merry Christmas, by the way."

I laid there, my hand returning to my side, while Cassandra interlaced our fingers. I squeezed her gently before I replied. "Merry Christmas, Cassandra. What time is it, anyway?"

"Twelve-oh-one," she confirmed, swiftly.

Her admission made me laugh. "You were more than a *little* excited." I paused for a second, realizing that she'd said something about presents, which had been a surprise. We'd discussed it weeks ago, having both agreed we wouldn't exchange them with Cassandra's anxieties about money, deciding we'd just enjoy the holidays together, and that would be enough. Clearly, I'd been mistaken about something. "I thought we said no gifts?"

Cassandra's mouth had still been so close to my face that I swear I felt her smiling. "Okay, well, I lied. You get one gift."

I frowned, a little annoyed despite being curious too. "That's not exactly fair."

I felt her lips draw on my ear, kissing it softly. It sent a shiver ripping through me. "Trust me. It's for both of us." She lingered there, breathing against me but not speaking for a while. Eventually, she continued. "Do you want your present or not?"

Even though I nodded, I still argued. "I don't get to see it?"

The entire time since I'd woken, Cassandra's voice had taken on some very commanding, alluring quality that had my entire focus, but it went to a completely new level when she'd spoken again, her mouth tickling against my skin. "This isn't a gift you need to *see*, Chandler."

After Cassandra said the words, I felt her drawing up from where she'd been lying. Seconds later, she started to tug my hand, still wrapped in her own, I assumed in an attempt to get me up. As much as this entire situation was leaving me a nervous wreck that I had no idea what was going on, feeling somewhat out of control of what was happening, I still did what she asked. Let her tug me from the bed.

We hadn't even left the bedroom yet, and I knew where she was going. Which was the biggest reason I fought through all of my anxiety—I was far too curious about what she intended to do. Quite certain, whatever it was, I wasn't going to mind.

It was a curious experience, being led to the Shibari room without being able to see it. I hadn't realized how well I knew my home, which shouldn't have been a surprise with how long I'd lived there now. It was easy to guess about how many steps we needed to take and where the door likely was. When I heard the sound of Cassandra twisting at the knob, I knew we'd reached it. She'd paused us there for a moment.

Once again, her face was against my own, mouth up as close as she could be to my ear, having had to have been on her tiptoes. "Are you ready, Chandler?" That voice of hers was making my legs wobble a little. I swallowed deeply and nodded in reply. Cassandra clearly wasn't satisfied. "You should know a little head nod isn't a satisfactory answer."

I was smiling and laughing then, her words all too familiar. "Ah—I should have known that would come back to haunt me..."

"Tell me what you want then," Cassandra whispered, still lingering where she had been, her breaths beating against me. I had felt her smile yet again, and it only made my own smile widen.

"I want to know what the hell this Christmas present is," I said matter-of-factly. "If you'd be so kind as to oblige—"

Before I'd been able to finish my thought, I was yanked into the room by Cassandra. Once we were both inside, I heard the door close behind us, and then felt her lead me a dozen steps or so forward before she gently stopped me. If I had to guess, she was standing in front of me by the sound of her bare feet scuffling around on the hardwood floor. A moment later, I discovered I was right when she gently kissed me and whispered again. "Wait here."

Her footsteps trailed off, and I tried to discern where she could have been going. My best guess, if I knew the direction I'd been standing, was that she'd wandered off toward the wall of ropes. What on Earth the woman had in mind to do, I had no idea, but every second of waiting for her to enlighten me was torturous.

Subsequently, I heard her returning, along with the sound of what I could only assume were several bundles of ropes hitting the floor. It was the first time I had ever paid such blatant attention to the noise, and it sent a wild array of feelings through me.

I didn't have too long of an opportunity to reflect on the sound because all at once, I felt a scratchy line drawing across my cheek and right under my nose. When I breathed in, that very distinct, very pungent citrusy smell consumed me. Cassandra had grabbed jute rope, as evidenced by both the scent and its coarseness.

My curiosity was getting the best of me, and I had been seconds from asking her what she had intended to do when she decided to speak. "You know how I like to close my eyes when you're working?" I nodded in reply, and she continued. "Well... you were doing that one tie last week—when you were teasing me about it..."

"The Hishi Harness," I confirmed, remembering what she'd been speaking about. "I was only teasing you about it because I think it's very cute when you do. I like it when you get so wrapped up in everything. You seem to do that with everything you do—"

I hadn't quite been able to finish my thought because I felt Cassandra draw up right on top of me, her body nearly pressed into my own. She braced her hands on my shoulders, one of the bundles of rope still in them, lying against me. I realized she must have pulled herself up on her tiptoes again, getting as close as she could to my ear and putting our faces next to each other.

"Do you want to keep rambling, or do you want to know what your present is?" Her voice had gotten soft and low. My mouth immediately snapped shut, and I heard Cassandra let out a little laugh before she drew away from me, removing her hands from my shoulders. Seconds later, I felt her gently grasp my hand and place the rope she'd been holding onto into mine. "I want you to do the Hishi tie without seeing it this time. That's your present."

For a few seconds, I stood there trying to register what she'd said. I'd heard her, but it had taken me by surprise, to say the least. "How the hell am I supposed to know what I'm doing? I have to be able to see it to know where the ropes line up..."

Cassandra drew a step closer again. I felt her hands wrap around my own, holding the rope she'd given me. "Chandler, how many times have you practiced a Hishi tie? Like a hundred times?"

The question actually had me laughing again. "Probably more like several hundred, Cassandra. That's a simple one, and I've been doing this a while—"

"Do you ever close your eyes when you're practicing in the silks?" The question sent my mind reeling for a second. "Like, when you're transitioning from one movement to the next? I actually don't even think I know the answer to this question, which I'm surprised by, honestly..."

I laughed again, shaking my head. "I'm surprised too..." I paused for a second, thinking about it because I hadn't been quite sure. It occurred to me, rather quickly, that I couldn't recall a time in which I had. I was always far too concerned about what was happening at every single second to indulge in that behavior. "—Honestly, I'm not sure I ever have... I appreciate your need to point out my control freak tendencies."

Midway through what I'd said, I felt Cassandra's hands fall on either side of my face. A second later, she kissed me rather intently, causing me to let out a little sigh in response. It only lasted a few seconds before she pulled away again. Her hands still lingered, however. "Try it without seeing it, Chandler. Trust me. You'll understand what I mean. You've done it a thousand times.

You know what the hell you're doing, I promise you." I felt her lips linger on mine again, and then she stepped away.

Seconds later, I knew I heard fabric hitting the floor. Could only assume she was undressing steps in front of me. The idea I couldn't see, only taking in those very pronounced sounds the fabric made, made the act much more heightened. Before I could think on it long, I heard her take steps, assuming she'd drawn in closer to me again.

"Okay, I'm ready," Cassandra said, softly. "I'm right in front of you. Take a deep breath. In through your nose, out through your mouth. You know what you're doing." Before I did what she asked, I felt my lip curl a little and shook my head. "What?"

My face split into a smile again. "You're just a very good student," I replied, simply. After, I took a long breath, as Cassandra had instructed, fiddling with the rope in my hands. Most of it fell down to the ground at my feet, and again I heard it, much more pronounced than it normally was. A second later, I took a step forward, reaching my hand out to try and discern where she'd been standing.

When my fingers grazed what I had assumed had been the side of her arm, I paused for a second, getting my bearings, but then continued, letting them draw upward, toward her shoulder.

While I had thought I'd already be rattling off the steps of the Hishi, I instead was completely consumed by the feeling of her skin against my fingertips. Something I'd noticed before, many times, but not like I had then. The whole motion had been charged and electric. I could feel her skin, delicate and soft like cashmere, against the taut and smooth lines of years of muscles she'd trained as an athlete. I'd admired her often. She was certainly a very beautiful woman in every sense of the word, but feeling her like this now...

I swallowed deeply, shaking my head. Drawing my focus back to what I was doing, taking a few more seconds to savor those touches before I drew up on her shoulder and paused. At that point, my mind started to run through the steps of the tie.

Carefully, I wrapped the rope around Cassandra's neck, underneath her hair—I hadn't realized how soft it truly was until that moment. Continuing on, I brought it down onto her chest and adjusted it until I imagined it was centered enough for my liking. It was a constant battle to reel in my imagination, running wild with the imagery of her standing there naked, wanting nothing more than to indulge myself in touching her elsewhere instead of fiddling with the ropes. I managed to draw myself back. Took another breath and started on half hitches.

I had barely been completing the second one when I noticed the thudding of Cassandra's heart pulsating beneath my fingertips. So pronounced it felt like I could almost hear it in my mind. It had me pausing again, my head tilting as if in an attempt to look at her, though I couldn't. "Are you okay?" I found myself holding completely steady, focusing on how she'd been breathing. Despite her racing heart, it seemed as if her breaths were calm.

Even though I couldn't see her, I could hear it by the warmth in her tone when she replied. "I'm good, Chandler. Maybe a little excited, but I'm enjoying your present. Like you should be, too. Keep going."

For a few seconds longer, I listened to her breathe, feeling her heart with my fingertips. It felt like it may have steadied a little, to my relief. At that point, I continued onward with what I was doing, completing one more hitch for the harness.

While Cassandra's breathing had certainly been calm over the next few minutes I worked on a fairly simple tie, I couldn't help but notice that mine had become slightly more labored and shaky, wound up with far too many nerves.

"Tell me what you're doing," I heard Cassandra say softly, directly in front of me.

For a second, it didn't register what she'd asked me. My entire body paused in place. "What?"

"The rest of the steps to the Hishi tie," Cassandra explained to me, in that same gentle but commanding tone. She was driving me mad tonight. "Tell me as you do them this time."

"I never do that," I replied swiftly, confused why she'd ask me to.

"I know that," Cassandra said, and I felt her hand reach up to gently touch the side of my face, tracing her fingers right along my beard line. A little sigh escaped me. "Humor me anyway. Just this once. Consider it your Christmas present to me."

That got another laugh from me. Shaking my head, I squatted down and felt around for the remainder of the rope she'd dropped on the floor. It took me a second or two to find, but I got back to my feet once I did. Reached out to find Cassandra again, my fingers grazing against her collarbone this time. I heard her let out a soft little gasp at the touch, and I couldn't help but trace along it, completely engulfed in what it felt like and what something so simple was doing to my entire being.

I cleared my throat once I'd found the rope in the center of her chest. Let my fingers draw it down, tracing over the first half hitch I'd made. Memorizing where it was in the darkness in front of me before I unraveled the rope in my hand.

And then I did exactly as Cassandra had asked. "I'm building out the harness now," I explained. I wove the rope through the half hitch, finding it again relatively easily. Drew forward closer to her to take it around her backside. When I would usually work my way around her, I felt compelled to stay in place in those moments. Felt some wild desire to want to feel her warm, naked frame against me, even if I couldn't see it. Knowing it was there was enough.

As I'd been weaving the rope around her again, underneath her arm, explaining as I went and drawing it to the second hitch I'd made, I felt the very gentle but swift touch of Cassandra's hand slide against me. She'd done it so elegantly and effortlessly, I hadn't even really been aware of what she'd done at first. It had woven its way between the only fabric that separated us from one another.

The moment I felt her hand wrap around me, her grasp growing firmer the second she had, my movements halted, and I let out a sharp gasp of air.

"Keep going," Cassandra demanded, sounding completely unfazed by my reaction to what she'd done. Again, even though I couldn't see her, I felt my head tilt in the direction I assumed her face had been, the room spinning as her hand began moving against me in a steady rhythm. I was hardly able to take in breaths, which only worsened exponentially when the beautiful woman in front of me spoke again. "Tell me every step. Until I make it impossible for you to speak anymore."

As wildly as my entire body was raging in those moments, I found myself laughing again anyway. My voice was quivering with the reply, trying to hold steady. I'd had to brace myself on her shoulder for a second because she hadn't stopped since she started, and her touches were obliterating me. "—You're really giving me payback right now for that, aren't you?" I laughed until Cassandra shifted what she'd been doing slightly, the sensation sending me to a different plane of existence. I gasped again.

"You like it," Cassandra replied, laughing alongside me. Then her voice returned back to its soft but serious tone. "Keep going, Chandler. What's next?"

I swallowed deeply before I continued with what I'd been doing. Offering her explanations as I did my best to complete the tie. Struggling more and more every second that went by, my breaths growing more and more ragged. Thoughts becoming muddled. I was consumed by my imagination. Visualizing all the places I was touching her along with the texture of that rope on her soft skin. Her heart was beginning to race in her chest as much as mine had. That steady rhythm she had built against me...

Suddenly, just as Cassandra had so blatantly teased me about, I could no longer formulate words. I braced myself against her, falling into what she was doing, unable to do anything else but let myself be consumed by it all, a mess of quiet gasps, my entire body trembling against her.

And when I thought I couldn't have gone to a higher place than I'd been, Cassandra spoke again. More familiar words that were a million times more profound than they'd ever been coming out of me. "Show me what I did to—"

Cassandra didn't have time to finish. My hands, which had been on her shoulders, drew up to find her face in one swift motion, crashing her to me as she nearly brought me to my knees with what she'd been doing. Giving that mesmerizing woman exactly what she'd asked—showing her *exactly* what she'd done, my entire body trembling against her, gasping into her mouth.

Once I'd started to steady, and we had to break away to breathe, I heard Cassandra whisper softly, panting. *"And, fini."* Even while trying to catch my breath and recover, it had me laughing and smiling. I found her again, still in darkness, kissing her gently.

Cassandra finally removed what had been one of my silk ties from my eyes, letting it fall to the floor. I admired her for a second, a mostly-completed tie around her, and surprisingly in relatively good form, all things considered. Both of us were smiling at one another, still panting softly. "Remind me never to taunt you again," I laughed, shaking my head. Cassandra shrugged, looking equally as amused. "Although I'm a bit surprised. I could have sworn after that whole blindfold act you'd wanted to come in here and tie me up..."

There was a curious look on Cassandra's face, and that soft, gentle smile of hers had turned a little bit more mischievous. It sent a little shiver down my spine when I saw it, which only worsened when she replied to me. "Don't worry, Chandler. That's most certainly coming. When you least expect it to."

Despite my every desire not to leave her side, after everything that had transpired with Peter and all the uncertainty around it, I still found myself outside the steps of that familiar townhome on Christmas Day in the early evening hours.

My mother had decorated it with some string lights outside and a pretty wreath on the door, both of which made me think of Abby when I saw them. At least it gave me some comfort that Cassandra had gone to spend a few hours with her and Thomas that evening, both in an attempt to distract her but also to keep eyes on her for my own sanity. After the news from David, I hadn't wanted her to be alone.

I'd already knocked, wanting desperately to get out of the bitter cold air. Shortly after I had, my mother answered the door. She was dressed in one of her usual festive Christmas dresses, one she'd had for a long time. Purchased in a Paris boutique one visit to France when I was in high school, on one of our many visits over the years. Her light brown hair was pinned up around her face.

"You look lovely," I said, smiling at her as I made my way through the doorway. Once my mother had closed and locked the door behind me, and I hung my coat on the coat rack, we embraced. I hugged her longer than usual, feeling as if I needed those extra few seconds. My mother ran her fingers through my hair, and once we parted, she kissed my cheek.

"Merry Christmas, *mon rayon de soleil,*" my mother said, smiling. My ray of sunshine. I felt her reach up and gently run her fingers over my cheek, studying me. "How are you doing?"

That had been a loaded question, if there ever was one. Even still, I smiled at her. "As good as normal, I suppose. Keeping myself busy."

"How is Cassandra?" My mother asked me. Her fingers were resting against my cheek. I must have looked surprised by her question because her smile widened a little. "If words could tell you how wonderful it was to see you so happy at your show the other day. I missed that look in your eyes, like when you were young. It was such a nice thing to see."

I couldn't help but shake my head, my smile widening then, too. "I wish you could spend time together. You'd adore her. She's absolutely wonderful in every sense of the word."

"Clearly," my mother finally removed her hand from my cheek then.

It occurred to me then I'd meant to ask her. Likely better to inquire with her than my father since she seemed to be far more supportive than him. "I actually was wondering if you knew where Meme's ring was—"

Before I had a chance to finish, I saw the ominous presence lingering in the doorway. When I looked over, my father had been approaching us. By the expression on his face, I decided he hadn't been eavesdropping on our conversation. "You actually arrived at a decent hour," he said, staring me down. "Let's get this over with, Madelyn. I have things to take care of."

A small wave of annoyance washed over me. I wrapped my arm around my mother's, trying to keep her distracted from the rude tone my father had. The three of us made our way back down the hall to the dining room. Once again, my mother had already prepared everything on the table, ready for us to eat.

Like any other traditional Moreau Christmas dinner, my mother had assembled a poulet rôti, a French roasted chicken stuffed with a chestnut stuffing and adorned with roasted potatoes, chestnuts and cooked apples. As usual, it looked flawless in its presentation, like a photo from a magazine. In those moments, I wished that there had been some universe in which Cassandra would have been able to experience it.

Along with the chicken, my mother had prepared gratin dauphinois, another classic french potato dish, and green bean almondine, crisp green beans in brown butter with almonds and shallots. The green beans had always been at my request. And at the other end of the table, another French Christmas staple, a Bûche de Noël, or a rolled génoise cake frosted with chocolate buttercream. While it hadn't been one of my mother's lemon dishes from my childhood that I adored, it was still something I indulged in a little every year, regardless.

After we'd sat down, my mother leaned into me, whispering quietly. "I made an extra Bûche for you to take home with you to share." I looked at her, unable to help myself from smiling a little and kissing her cheek in gratitude. Cassandra would appreciate the gesture.

"It looks wonderful," I announced once I'd sat up and had a look at it again. My father had already been dishing himself food, and I followed suit.

Much to my surprise, to the point it felt a little unsettling, our dinner went over relatively well. While it was mostly my mother and me that made conversation, my father interjected every now and then, too. All things considered, he seemed to be in a strange mood. I couldn't really place it.

After we'd all had a slice of the Bûche de Noël, and I felt like I couldn't eat another bite, my father's attention drew to me. It was then that his very normal intense gaze reappeared. "I'd like it if you stayed for a few more minutes before rushing off like you normally tend to do." I stared at him, blinking. Eventually, I nodded, and my father slipped out of his chair, getting to his feet. He nodded for me to follow him. I gave my mother a curious glance, but she seemed as confused as me.

Gabriel wandered down the main hallway of the house and turned into his office. Once I'd followed him inside, he shut the door behind us. At that point, I started to feel unsettled. I watched him walk across the room, behind his desk, and take a seat. I followed, walking to the chair adjacent to him. By the time I'd sat down, he had already pulled out a cigar and a lighter from his desk.

"Must you really do that right now?" I asked him, feeling a wave of annoyance. "If you insist upon it, we could at least step outside instead of you trapping me in here with that foul stench. You know how much I hate it."

My father, in his usual form, looked completely unfazed. He lit the cigar, drew it to his mouth for a long few moments, and then let a long billow of smoke out. I felt my nostrils flaring in annoyance and was about to make another comment, but he interrupted me. "How much do you trust the Blackstone woman?"

I had to sit there for a very long time trying to process the words that had abruptly come out of his mouth. My mind had been hyper-focused on that God-awful cigar stench, and I hadn't quite heard him at first. Once I'd repeated what he said in my mind twice over, I finally answered. "Excuse me?"

"Cassandra Blackstone," my father repeated, taking another draw of his cigar. He leaned back into his seat, his green eyes honed in on me. "You two have been together for months now. She lives with you, yes? I assume you spend the majority of your time together. I'm asking you, Chandler. How much do you trust her?"

The words coming out of the man's mouth had my stomach rolling. While I had assumed he'd figured me out to some degree, the amount of information he knew rattled me regardless. As usual, he was always steps ahead, and equally as normal, I remained oblivious to it until it was too late. I decided to be candid with him for whatever reason. "I trust her. Far more than I trust anything that is about to come out of your mouth right now. I assure you."

Gabriel's nostrils flared a little bit in a similar way mine had a minute earlier. I watched him set the cigar down in a tray on his desk, grateful that he had. "Then I'm sure it won't surprise you to know she's spent the last few months sticking her nose where she shouldn't."

I raised a brow at him. "What do you mean by that?"

"She's been trying to incriminate more than just her uncle," my father replied. The fact that he had any idea about Cassandra's uncle made my head spin in surprise. I blinked at him again. "I'm fairly certain she's trying to take us all down, in fact. Including you, as much as I know you're trying to delude yourself into thinking otherwise. I had a conversation with that asinine human she'd had helping her with her uncle before you intervened. I'm sure you weren't aware she's still been using him?"

That had definitely been news to me. Surprising myself, I shook my head. He continued on. "Before you go blindly chasing after some fantasy you've concocted in your head, I suggest you think a little. *Mieux vaut plier que rompre.*" Adapt and survive.

"Fuck that stupid saying," I growled at him, feeling horrendously annoyed. "I don't know what you're trying to do right now. Turn me against her, fire me up. If she was looking into us, I'm sure it was with good reason. You must have given her one."

While I was doing my best to remain composed and confident, I felt sick with worry. Cassandra had woven herself far too deeply now, and without a shadow of a doubt, it had been my doing. Also, I felt a little bit rattled about what exactly she'd found out about. What information she'd chosen to keep from me. It left me concerned but not enough that I didn't trust her. I was certain if I spoke with her about it later this evening like we had planned to do, perhaps she'd give me answers.

"I also made it *very* clear to her that if she chose to continue, there would be consequences," my father said, matter-of-factly. The words sent me flying from the chair I'd been sitting, slamming my hands down on the desk, trying my best to tower over him. "If you think this little act is intimidating me in the least, you are more delusional than I thought you were. And that is highly disappointing, considering you are my son. I would hope you wouldn't be so moronic, but I suppose the apple fell further from the tree than I thought."

"And thank fucking God for that," I snarled at him in reply. "If you *dare* even look at her again, I swear to God I won't hesitate to make you pay for it. No matter the consequences. Do you understand me? I should have never let you go near her. No wonder she's been a wreck the last few weeks. I should have known better that you'd gotten into her head somehow."

"And yet still you're choosing not to even question her," my father shook his head, leaning back in his chair again. Completely unfazed by me and the conversation. "I'm ashamed of you right now, Chandler. Being as reckless as you're choosing to be. Refusing to think. But I suppose that's been your problem all along. At least your cousins and my brother cut themselves off entirely. They chose their path. I chose my path. Your grandfather chose his path."

I growled again, hating the mention of Elliott. Again, my father blatantly ignored me. " And then there's you. Leading this lie of a life, a fantasy, in which you've somehow convinced yourself that you can fall between the two worlds without consequence. You've deluded yourself into thinking that you've never taken a side, that you're so against everything that has given you the life you have, and yet here you still are. You still have it. Your career, your grandmother's beloved circus. Never once wanting for anything. A spoiled, privileged, ungrateful excuse for a man, who can't see the forest for the trees. You're a Moreau. That blood runs through your veins. Hide all you want, Chandler. Convince yourself you can play ignorant and get away with it. You know better, and it will catch up with you eventually."

"I don't have time for this fucking bullshit of yours," I shook my head, removing my hands from his desk, turning away from him and preparing to leave. But before I left, I swiftly turned around again, staring him down. "I meant what I said. Stay the fuck away from Cassandra Blackstone."

I had just about opened the door when I heard my father call out to me. *"Le Jour de La Poussière et du Sang.* Ask David Finch about that.

I'm sure it will be enlightening for you both." As much as I wanted to immediately storm out of the room, his words made me pause. I was completely stunned that he knew I'd hired a private detective. I desperately wanted to know why, but I'd been too furious in those moments to care. I wanted away from him as soon as humanly possible. So I left, deciding there'd be another time I could ask him about it, slamming the door behind me.

My mother was waiting for me in the foyer as I stormed back down the hall. "Sweetheart, is everything alright?" She looked worried, as she often did when my father and I were lost in these tailspins.

My coat flew off the coat rack, and my mother had to steady it to keep it from toppling over. I wrapped it around me, shaking my head at her. "I love you beyond measure, but I will never understand, for as long as I live, why the fuck you stay with him."

Madelyn reached for my hand, and I watched as she gave me a familiar red velvet box. It was so aged that it was torn apart, barely hanging on its hinges. She wrapped my hand around it. Then I felt her hand me another small paper bag, likely with the cake she'd promised for Cassandra. When she finished, and I looked back at her, she was smiling softly at me. "Sometimes we can't help loving the people we love."

The moment I'd made it out onto the streets outside my parents' townhome, I pulled my phone from my pocket. My plan had been to call the town car and head straight for Abigail and Thomas'. But the only thing I could imagine doing in those moments was ensuring that I had my own eyes on the woman I loved more than absolutely anything. We could finally have the conversation we'd promised one another.

Standing on the sidewalk, I looked at my phone and was instantly frozen in place. There was a text message. One single line. From a number I didn't have saved in my phone but had memorized decades ago. It hadn't changed since she'd gotten her first cellphone in college.

You need to come. Right now.

I went through the motions almost robotically, clicking the screen to immediately call the number. The phone barely rang once, and she answered.

"For the love of fucking *God,* Jeanne. I don't have time for this right now—" I couldn't contain the level of annoyance in my tone. It was the last thing I needed. More bullshit.

Then I heard her on the other end of the line, and it jerked me back to reality. She was sobbing. I heard Patrick trying to console her in the background without success. The sound was overwhelming me. Never in the history of our entire two-decade relationship had I *ever* heard Jeanne cry. Not once. On more than one occasion, it had been a joke that she must have been a robot because there had been no other explanation for her to have been so devoid of emotions all the time. I had even cried once or twice in front of her.

"Jeanne?" My voice calmed substantially, and I stood there trying to stay steady, pressing the phone closer to my ear. "Jeanne, take a breath. You're hyperventilating." She had been gasping for air between the horrible cries she'd been making. It was hard to listen to, mostly because it made me uncomfortable knowing whatever it was she was crying about had made her so upset that she was *actually* crying. I still couldn't believe it.

"Patrick, stop it!" I heard Jeanne fighting him on the other end of the line.

"Let him help you," I argued with her. "You need to calm down and talk to me."

There was silence for what felt like a very long time. All I could make out were trembling breaths as Jeanne tried to compose herself and the small muffled sounds of Patrick consoling her. Eventually, everything seemed to settle. At that precise moment, I realized it was horrendously cold out, and it was starting to hurt my ungloved hands.

"Okay," I said, taking a breath and pacing down the sidewalk. "What the hell is going on?"

"You need to come right this second," Jeanne said firmly, her voice still quivering a little.

"Jeanne, I can't do that—" I started.

She was very quick to interrupt me. "Consider this the strings, Chandler. I'm not asking you. I am fucking telling you. I don't care what you're doing. I need you—we need you here. Right now. And before you even ask me, I am not talking about it over the phone. You should know by now, after all this time and this nightmare we've lived through, that is a reckless thing to do. So just come. Now."

The phone immediately clicked. Jeanne hung up on me. I stood there blinking for a second. Still in shock, trying to process what was going on. Feeling as if I had no other option. Cassandra was still with Thomas and Abigail, which was safe enough in those moments. Jeanne and Patrick, on the other hand, I had no earthly idea what was going on, and if my ex-wife had gotten that hysterical, I knew it wasn't good.

I quickly called the town car to come get me, feeling if I stood out here much longer, I'd freeze to death. And there was absolutely no way in hell I was going back inside my parents' house to wait. Afterward, I texted Cassandra to let her know I'd be a little bit later than I'd anticipated but to stay with Abigail and Thomas until I came back for her.

On the snowy, dark drive over to the outskirts of Acrefort, I found my leg bouncing wildly. Tried to distract my wandering mess of thoughts in any way possible. Eventually, I searched on the internet for that random French phrase my father had said to me just before I left his office. It had something to do with a day of some sort, but otherwise, I was clueless. My French was rusty.

After a little bit of searching, I stumbled on the translation. *The Day of Dust and Blood.*

As luck would have it, we'd arrived at Jeanne and Patrick's just as I'd found the translation. We had pulled over alongside the white picket fence that lined Patrick and Jeanne's property.

Before I exited, I waved to my driver and let him know I wouldn't be long. Then, before I went inside, I closed the search I'd pulled up and clicked through my text messages. Cassandra had yet to answer me, but I assumed she was busy with Thomas and Abigail and didn't worry. I did, however, text David Finch.

Can you look into something for me? The Day of Dust and Blood. Le Jour de La Poussière et du Sang. Le Milieu. I need to know if there's any connection to the Blackstone family. And then I pocketed my phone, heading back up the path to that familiar house. Feeling even more uneasy than I had the first time I'd come here.

CHAPTER 32

CHANDLER

The wind was biting at me, standing on the porch of Jeanne and Patrick's house. I'd knocked the moment I was within reach of the door, desperately wanting to get out of the weather. Seconds later, it swung open. Once again, my former best friend was on the other side. For whatever reason, he was without his shirt, which sent my mind briefly spiraling to those moments I'd found him with Jeanne years ago.

It would have held me hostage for longer if I hadn't noticed that he was clinging tightly to a newborn infant in his arms. And that there were streaks of red all over his body. He was staring at me wide-eyed, and all the while, his child was crying loudly.

"Oh, thank God," he breathed, standing out of the way of the door to let me inside. I was still trying to process what I'd even been seeing with Patrick at that moment. Between the newborn and his clearly frazzled state, I wasn't sure what to think.

I didn't really have very long to. Seconds later, someone darted around the corner at the end of the hallway, and I found myself shouting in surprise when she did.

Jeanne Sophia Tremblay, a woman I had known since I was practically born, who was ingrained into every facet of my life for so long that it felt nearly impossible to scrub her away, looked as horrifying as I'd ever seen her. Unlike Patrick, she was still dressed, wearing a white nightgown. Or at least, what I had assumed had used to be white.

The entire length of her was covered in blood. It was unmistakable, having seen it several times too many in my life. And what made it all the more horrifying and hard for me to even process was that there was absolutely no way in hell it was all her own.

"What the—"

I watched her linger in the hallway, her usually commanding air having completely dissipated. Her blonde hair was in complete disarray, and it looked as if some of it had potentially been ripped out. Without a doubt, she was injured in several places. Stab wounds, by the look of it, but most of them weren't bleeding. Whatever injuries she sustained that had been worse seemed to have been attended to by Patrick and wrapped up. Whether or not he was successful, I had no idea.

Jeanne's eyes were wide and wild looking, staring at me more intently than she ever had before. She was breathing steadily, but I could see her shaking. "Come here," she demanded quietly, nodding at me.

While I had absolutely no earthly clue what the hell was going to happen in those next few moments, and in any other circumstance likely wouldn't have trusted her, somehow I forced myself to move. Walked to the end of the hallway, where she had been standing. As I had gotten closer to her, I noticed Jeanne had put up one hell of a fight. She was very much injured but clearly still standing.

My ex-wife nodded into the room adjacent to her, and I slowly turned in that direction, stumbling in surprise the second I had. Across the living room I had been in months earlier, on the rug that had been in this house since I'd been a teenager, was a very dead man, as evident by what I assumed was the rest of his blood that wasn't on Jeanne presently.

Beside his body was what appeared to be a boning knife from their kitchen, completely covered in blood. The longer I stared at the body, the more I realized that the guy, whoever he was, had had the shit stabbed out of him.

"What the fuck did you do?" I was hardly able to fathom words as I spun back around to face her, eyes wide. "Jesus Christ, Jeanne—"

"No!" Jeanne snapped at me, drawing up on me so fast that she looked like something out of a horror film in her state. " I didn't *'do'* anything. I *'did'* what had to be done. That piece of shit was in my *house,* Chandler. About to fucking murder my son, my husband—"

"Clearly you did *something* since you're standing here covered in a gallon of blood right now," I could barely keep my eyes on her. It was making me nauseous. "Jeanne, have you fucking lost your mind? You went and stabbed a guy to death. What the hell are you going to tell the police?"

"I am not calling the fucking police," Jeanne snarled at me. I hadn't been looking at her, staring wide-eyed at the dead guy in her living room again, trying to make sense of the absolute whirlwind that was the last twenty-four hours.

My head snapped back to her when she'd said it. I blinked. "You just told me that guy was trying to *kill* you all, Jeanne. You acted in self-defense. Why the hell wouldn't you go to the police with this?"

Between our livid bickering, I heard Patrick and Jeanne's son crying loudly behind me. Patrick was doing his best to soothe him, but the sound caused me to drop my voice a bit which I had realized got louder than I had anticipated.

Jeanne seemed to be on the same track as I had been, lowering her voice. "Because I'm *not,* Chandler." She was breathing heavily, pointing at the body. "And if you weren't such an oblivious fucking fool all the time, you'd stop making such asinine suggestions to me. After everything we've fucking been through, you should know better by now." I growled at her again, thinking I was going to have time to reply, but I saw her fish something out of her very bloody nightgown. When she handed it to me, it was half dripping.

I didn't care about the mess but for a half second. It was covered in blood and barely recognizable. Whatever words had been written across the metal, which appeared to be in the shape of a cross with swords running through it, was worn and illegible. The fabric piece on top, green and red, had nearly completely faded.

It was some sort of medal or something. Other than that, I was completely oblivious to why she'd handed it to me. "What the hell is this?"

My ex-wife stared at me for a few moments. I could see the air moving out of her nose, her body still shaking a little. "After all this time and how much you adored your grandmother and that circus, you don't know what that is?"

I blinked at her, utterly confused. She continued. "Chandler, that is the Croix de Guerre Elloitt Moreau traded my grandfather Elias for the Dreamer's Academy. The fucking medal he got for helping take down that brigade of Nazis in Normandy. The award my grandfather should have gotten, too, since they fought right beside one another and were in a fucking prison camp together. How do you not know what the fuck that is?"

I studied it in my hands again, flipping it over, looking at it intently. Mind-boggled that I was holding it in my hands. It had felt like something that had always been a rumor. Some made-up fantasy story about Elliott. Eventually, I turned my attention back to her. "Are you sure?"

Jeanne charged me, shoving me hard. I stumbled back, dazed. The sudden jarring motion made a very sharp stabbing pain run through my knee. It sent me spiraling a little bit with annoyance at her after everything. "Yes, I am fucking sure. Just shut up and listen to me." I snarled a little bit at her but stood steady, no longer speaking. Meanwhile, it seemed as though Patrick had settled the baby behind us. He'd wandered into another room.

"You asked me back in August when the semester started why the hell I just got up and left the school. Why did I inconvenience you so much? Well, I guess you get your answer now."

Jeanne started pacing, and I watched her trail down the hallway and then back toward me before she spoke.

"Back in August, the Croix de Guerre was stolen from my grandfather. He'd held onto it since Elliott first gave it to him. It hung in his office. And randomly, one day, someone broke into their house. Not a single thing was stolen, and you *know* my family. They have so many valuable things, far more so than some World War II military decoration which is even illegal to sell now. That fucking Croix de Guerre was the *only* thing missing. And whoever took it made it blatantly obvious, too. Smashed the frame it was in and left it on the floor. They wanted my grandfather, wanted Elias, to know it was stolen."

I stared at her, trying to process what she was saying. "My father immediately forced me to leave Dreamers. Forced me to abandon the career I'd devoted my entire life to. I can't even tell you how fucking pissed I was even then at your fucking father—hell, even you. After all this time, you traitorous Moreaus were still doing the same bullshit as always."

"Why the hell didn't you tell me this then?" I asked her, completely at a loss.

"Because I didn't fucking trust you," she replied, flatly. "I didn't trust any of you. None of us knew what the hell was going on. And I wasn't about to give you information just to have you turn around and tell your father everything."

"Jeanne," I stared at her, surprised by how calm my voice had gotten in those moments. "You must know me well enough by now to know that would be the last thing I would have done. You know how little I trust my father. You could have told me about this. I could have tried to help you."

I watched her stand there for a few seconds, seeming as if she was getting her wits about her again, not shaking as much, straightening herself. Her blue eyes weren't nearly as wild as they had been. Jeanne took a long breath before she spoke again.

"I trust you now," she said simply, voice steady, looking me head-on. "After what you did a few months ago for that student. I know the last place on the face of the earth you would have ever wanted to be was here, and yet you did it anyway. Truthfully, I initially helped you just because I hated your father so fucking much I would have probably done next to anything in spite of him." She let out an annoyed huff of air before she softened a bit, looking back up at me. "But I lost sight of that version of you that came here those months ago for a very long time. I didn't think it existed anymore."

There was a brief moment that I thought I'd ask her what she meant, but she continued before I needed to. "The Chandler Moreau I fell in love with was one of the most fiercely loyal people I've ever known. Even knowing your family, knowing everything I knew about your past... You were devoted to the people you loved. Would have moved heaven and earth for them. I absolutely adored that about you. It's why I stayed with you for so long, despite the fact both of us were miserable."

We stood there staring at each other, my ears ringing a little, in somewhat disbelief of what was coming out of her mouth. But clearly she hadn't finished her thought yet. "Chandler, I thought you'd just disappeared into that fucking nightmare our families drug us into. Something both of us had fought desperately to get the hell away from for so long. I thought you were a lost cause. But then you came here and did what you did, and I know better now."

She took the military decoration of my grandfather's from me, holding it up. "I know you have nothing to fucking do with this. That you were dealt the same shitty fucking hand I was. But I am pretty sure the person who stole this from my grandfather was the same person who intended on having all three of us murdered tonight and leaving it here to find."

"Why the hell would they do something like that?" I asked, completely lost.

"I think they were trying to lure you here," Jeanne said simply.

My head was spinning still, not really processing what she was saying. "Why do you think they were trying to lure *me* here?" I asked her dumbly.

There was another flash of annoyance on Jeanne's face. "Chandler, for the love of *God*. Your ignorance is endearing sometimes, but right now, I need you to stop. *Think* for a minute. My grandfather is convinced this whole performance was all orchestrated by your father. How that isn't blatantly obvious to you, I have no idea."

"My father?" I stared at her blankly. "Jeanne, you've lost your mind. My father would never do something so obvious. Elliott, maybe, but Gabriel—Gabriel's always been the puppeteer, holding the strings. He wouldn't dare risk the chance of garnering attention on himself. You know that as well as I do."

"You don't think that's exactly what's going on right now?" Jeanne shook her head, still looking beyond annoyed with me. "You don't see how this is a manipulative game your father is trying to play with my family? Trying to make us think Elliott is still alive? For what reason, I have no idea, but *that* part is *very* obvious."

"Jeanne," I stared at her, feeling a tiny painful pulsing in my temple from the massive amount of stress I had been feeling over the last few hours. It was just a flicker, but distracting, nonetheless. "I think you still might be too wound up from everything and not thinking clearly." Wound up was probably an understatement given what the hell my ex-wife had just done. "I still don't know why you think he'd be trying to lure *me* over here, of all people. Or why he's trying to mess with you. If that was really what he was doing."

"Because I'm willing to bet the son-of-a-bitch is up to something right now, Chandler," Jeanne said, those blue eyes drilling into mine. "And the fact that you don't see that clear as day, given you're his flesh and blood, both infuriates the fuck out of me, but is also a relief, honestly. If you're so ignorant to his bullshit, then clearly you're far more removed from it than I believed you were for a *very* long time."

I heard a door shut behind me and had so shaken in those moments, it made me jump off the ground in surprise. "Sorry," I heard Patrick say quietly behind me. How the fuck he remained so calm was beyond me. Seconds later, he'd come to join us. "Can we please do something about—that?" He eyed the mutilated body in their living room.

"Another reason I needed your help," Jeanne explained, looking at me again. She walked into the living room. "Between the three of us, I think we'll be able to get him the hell out of here."

For a moment, I'd watched her walk into the living room, Patrick following behind her. Meanwhile, I was trying to process the words they'd both just been exchanging. "Excuse me? What the hell are you doing with the body? You need to call the police. This was clearly out of self-defense. Anyone that sees the state you're in would gather as much."

Jeanne spun around again, staring me down. "It's mind-boggling to me that the grandson of one of the most dangerous Godfathers in the French mafia would be uttering those words right now."

"Elliott Moreau was no more dangerous than Elias Tremblay," I argued.

"That's my fucking point, Chandler," Jeanne shook her head. "They're fucking dangerous. And you know going to the police with this is going to do nothing but put us all in further danger. Especially since, like I said before, your father is *clearly* up to something."

I stood in the doorway of the living room, watching as Jeanne and Patrick started moving furniture around and rolling up the dead guy's body like they were making a fucking burrito. Feeling absolutely mortified. "Jeanne...You seem rather certain about this fact, but I still don't understand where this is coming from. There could be a variety of reasons this happened..." I said it, but I wasn't sure I believed myself when I did.

"I think you know better than that," Jeanne said, nodding to the rug the two of them had been working on. "Are you going to help us or not? I don't have the upper body strength I used to anymore, and that son of a bitch was huge."

I stared at her, shaking my head, trying to force myself to process what was going on. One thing at a time, I supposed. Instead of dwelling on my questions at that moment, I decided to do what she'd asked me to do. Even if I completely disagreed. And, minutes later, I found myself, along with my ex-best friend and my ex-wife, toting that large, blood-soaked rug with the dead guy inside, out their back door.

We walked straight down their wood patio, down the deck that went out to the Peace River behind their house. Given the trellis and the beautiful lights that were hanging out back, I would have admired their yard under different circumstances. Jeanne shut off the lights at the last minute, the three of us walking straight to the river in the bitter as fuck dark night.

And in one collective toss, we sent the stranger that Jeanne had just murdered into the dark and ominous-looking water. I stood there for a few moments, listening to the crash and the lapping of the water. In complete and utter disbelief.

None of us spoke again until we'd gotten back inside the house. I felt the most despicable I had ever felt in my entire life after having done what we'd just done. If it hadn't been for the fact that the guy had been trying to kill Jeanne and her family, I might not have been able to forgive myself for having done it. But I was taking solace in the fact that we had a good reason for what we were doing. At least, I was going to try to convince myself of that.

"Patrick and I are going to my parents in California," Jeanne said, looking at me. We'd gathered in their living room again. "If you don't mind helping him take care of this, I'm going to clean myself up and pack."

"You might want to go see a doctor first, Jeanne," I said, eyeing her over again. "You have fucking stab wounds. And they don't look good. I don't even want to know how bad the ones that Patrick seemed to help you with were."

"That's exactly why I'm *not* going to the doctor," Jeanne corrected me. "And if you would stop being a fucking idiot right now, you'd do the same thing we are. Get Cassandra and get the hell out of this city. Go anywhere else. Because I'm not joking, Chandler. Something is going on right now, and it's clearly not safe for any of us."

I wanted to ask how the hell she remembered Cassandra's name, but then I decided that I didn't even want to know. Instead, I waved her off. "Go, then. I'll help Patrick take care of this." Jeanne wasn't entirely wrong. After everything, I was starting to think that getting the hell out of Acrefort in those moments might have been the right decision.

Patrick and I had been in the middle of mopping up the blood off the hardwood floor of their living room when I felt my phone vibrating. I ignored it for a second, distracted by what I was doing, but then eventually fished it out of my jacket pocket. Wondered if it was Cassandra finally returning my call.

Instead, I was surprised to find that Abby had been calling me. I stared at the phone for a moment, a little surprised, but managed to answer it before it went to voicemail. Meanwhile, Jeanne reappeared in the doorway, looking a lot more collected. She had removed most of the blood off herself. She still looked pretty beat up, but I was pretty sure she could pass through the airport without question.

"Hello?" I answered the phone, standing up from the floor. My knee was throbbing. With every fiber of my being, I hated that there was fucking human blood all over my body. It made me so nauseous I could barely stand it.

"Chandler," Thomas was the one who spoke, not Abigail. I could hear all sorts of commotion on the other end of the line. For a man who was lighthearted and calm nearly every single time I'd ever been around him, he sounded like an entirely different person then. I had hardly recognized him when he spoke.

"What's going on?" I asked, taking steps away from Patrick, having helped him take care of most of the mess on the floor. Jeanne moved out of my way as I wandered into the hallway.

"Chandler, Abigail and I got here as fast as we could, I swear to you," Thomas said, his voice still sounding horribly off.

Every fiber of me was praying this had nothing to do with Cassandra. "Cassandra—"

"Cassandra's safe at the house," Thomas reassured me.

That relieved me until I realized that when he said it, he meant that he and Abigail weren't there with her. "Why the hell did you leave her alone when I explicitly asked you both to stay with her? It wasn't a casual suggestion, Thomas. I was serious. You two needed to have eyes on her—"

"Chandler, I'm standing here watching Cirque du Lys burn to the ground," Thomas interrupted me. He didn't need to say anything else. I'd already hung up at that point, racing down the hall, not even concerned that I was still covered in blood.

"Where the hell are you going, Chandler?" Jeanne called after me as I unlocked the front door, throwing it open.

I turned back to her at that moment, staring her down. In total disbelief that my ex-wife had been right all along. I still didn't give her the satisfaction of telling her that fact, however.

"Get the hell out of this city, all of you. As fast as you fucking can."

CHAPTER 33

Cassandra

A Hallmark Christmas movie was playing in the background on Abigail and Thomas' ridiculously large living room television. I hadn't been paying the least bit of attention, staring absentmindedly at the beautiful Christmas tree that was sitting beside it. The last time I'd seen Abigail's Christmas tree, I had been very young. My parents and I used to go over for their holiday parties when they'd still been living in Nevada.

One of the ornaments on the tree we had given them one year. The year they'd left for Acrefort to join Cirque du Lys. It was a beautiful hand-carved skyline of Las Vegas. I remembered it distinctly because I'd been the one to find it at a craft fair booth, and my parents had immediately snatched it up.

It was still strange to me at times how my entire world felt so incredibly different now, yet there were all these pieces that still remained the same. The fact that Abigail and Thomas had found their way back to my life again made me incredibly grateful. They were a small tether to a past that felt utterly lost at times.

Despite the movie playing, it felt eerily quiet in their house. Thomas and Abigail had left a short while earlier in a panic. Something to do with Cirque du Lys, from what I had understood.

I'd offered to go with them, but they'd insisted, very adamantly, that I had to stay where I was. And it annoyed the fuck out of me. I was halfway tempted to take a taxi ride over to the circus anyway because I hadn't liked that they'd left me with no explanation.

I'd stayed there regardless. However, it started to feel like so much time had passed that I was getting a little concerned. It was rattling around in my head so much that I walked over to the door to get my coat, deciding to throw caution to the wind and ignore what was asked of me after all. I didn't want to be left in the dark.

The second I'd reached the coat rack, my phone rang in my hand. I looked down to see it was Chandler who was calling me, much to my relief. I immediately answered.

"Cassandra, are you still at Abigail and Thomas'? Please tell me you are still there." Chandler hadn't even waited for me to speak, just barreled straight into what he had wanted to say. He sounded so frantic that it shot a cold chill straight through me.

"Yes, I'm still at their house—" I started to speak.

Once again, Chandler spoke right over me. "Good. Don't leave the house under any circumstances. I need you to call Henry right now. Call until he wakes the hell up, and tell him to come over there and stay with you until I can get back."

My mind was running in a thousand different directions. I managed to catch a thread of thought. "What is going on? Have you left your parents?"

"Cassandra, I need you to tell me that you heard me just now," Chandler said, ignoring my question. "Tell me that the minute you get off the phone with me, you're going to call Henry and tell him it's an emergency. He needs to come over there. Please."

"Chandler, what the fuck is going on?" I couldn't stand the way he was blatantly ignoring me. "Why can't you come get me? Why did Thomas and Abigail just leave? Why the hell do I have a feeling you know why, and you're just fucking ignoring me right now? Talk to me."

There was a long pause. For a few seconds, I thought he'd hung up on me. "Thomas and Abigail are at Cirque du Lys—"

"I *know* that," I said somewhat loudly. "Why the hell are you freaking out then? Is it like going up in flames right now or something, and you all are just neglecting to tell me this?"

Another pause. I was sick to my stomach waiting. "Cassandra, that's exactly what's going on." I sat there for a minute, trying to comprehend what he was saying. Blood running cold.

"It's also the reason I'm not coming to get you right this second, even though I am freaking the hell out about leaving you there by yourself. The last thing you need is to see something like that again. It's why I am telling you the minute we finish talking, you need to call Henry. I'll be there as soon as I possibly can, I promise you. But I am making myself very clear—you are not safe. No one is safe right now. And the less I have to worry about you right this second while I try to figure out what the hell is happening, the better I'll be able to do that."

I felt myself shaking despite trying to maintain my composure. "I'll call Henry right now. I promise."

"I'll be there as soon as I possibly can. I love you." Chandler sounded terrified.

"Chandler, please be safe," I begged him, feeling myself starting to cry as much as I was fighting it. Every part of me was scared shitless. "I love you, too."

It took me a few seconds after he hung up to calm myself enough to stop shaking and dial Henry once I'd found my way back to the couch. When I looked at the clock, it was almost midnight. I prayed that somehow he'd still be awake.

Sure enough, he answered on the second ring. "Hey, Cass! Merry Christmas! I just barely made it, I guess, given that it's like two minutes until it's over. But, hey."

I immediately broke into hysterics, unable to stop myself. Henry spent a good few minutes trying to calm me down. It was a gigantic waste of time, but I couldn't help it.

Once I'd managed to give him the address, and he'd finished having Elle take it down, he spoke again. "We're ten minutes away. Leaving right now. Just hang in there, okay? Do you need me to stay on the phone with you until we get there?"

My breaths were shaky, but I managed to calm myself again for the most part. "It's okay. I feel like if you stay on the phone with me, I'm just going to keep crying. I'll sit here and watch this stupid movie I had on and try to distract myself as best I can. Just please hurry."

"Be there soon," Henry promised me, and then I heard him hang up.

As much as I tried to keep my attention on the movie, it was impossible. Instead, I paced across the entire length of the house, feeling my heart thudding in my chest wildly. Tried to keep myself breathing despite feeling like I was going to collapse on the floor from anxiety at any second.

At least several minutes had passed since I'd spoken to Henry on the phone. Somewhere during that time, I'd decided that despite Chandler's demands of me, I was going to go over there anyway. I'd have Henry take me when he arrived. There was absolutely no way in hell I was going to let Chandler be alone during this. In truth, I was terrified that all the secrets I had been keeping from him had made this exponentially worse. I couldn't do this any longer. We needed to solve all of this together. I didn't want to be alone.

I had just bundled up in my coat when there was a knock at the door. A wave of relief washed over me, grateful that Henry had arrived. Desperate to actually do something instead of just flailing there helplessly.

"Henry, change of plans—" I'd started, throwing open Abigail and Thomas' blue door. Felt a rush of cold air, followed by something crashing hard into me. Everything happened in such a blur, I hadn't had time to think. A hand wrapped around my throat tightly, pulling me up off of the ground.

My head was spinning, trying to make sense of what was going on as I was slammed backward into the wall behind me. I couldn't speak, could hardly get anything at all out as much as I was desperate to scream. Instead, I tried to understand what was in front of me.

The minute I realized who had a hold of me in those moments, my eyes went wide. I recognized him immediately. The neighbor of mine from my apartment complex. The one that had reminded me so much of Peter. Who had stolen my bag from me. I had never found out what the hell happened to him.

Clearly not enough to keep him away. And clearly, he hadn't just been some freak mugger. Not if he was here now. I was so panicked my body was fighting to maintain consciousness, and I was futilely trying to breathe.

"Where is it?" The man demanded, his eyes drilling into me. I felt him release his grip a little. I was trying to kick him, my hands clawing at the one he had wrapped around me, fighting to get him to let me go.

I knew exactly what he was talking about, and as much as I had wanted to play naive in those moments, I decided at the last minute not to. Instead, I spat at him, trying my best to glare back at him even though I was terrified. "Go to hell, you piece of shit."

The man's grip tightened on me again, and I found myself gasping and choking, writhing in his grip. I wasn't going to last very much longer. "I'm going to ask you one more time. You can tell me, and I'll take it and be quick with killing you. Or you can not, and I'll kill your fucking friend first before I take care of you."

My entire body went cold, even amidst my attempts at trying to break free of him. I watched as another guy came around the corner. Watched Henry tumbling into the room with him, hands held behind his back. Fighting as hard as he could in the guy's grasp.

"Cassie!" Henry yelled, making an attempt to jump toward me. He was greeted with a forceful slam into his backside by the guy who had been dragging him, sending him tumbling straight to the floor.

I made a desperate attempt at screaming, flailing wildly in the other guy's grasp. Staring wide-eyed at Henry rolling around on the floor, groaning. Tried kicking at my attacker, but all it made him do was slam me back into the wall again. My head was thudding. Every part of my body was aching, and I was convinced my life was nearly over.

"Last time I'm asking," the guy repeated himself, eyes boring into me. He looked like a fucking psychopath. I felt him release his grip on me a little, allowing me the ability to speak.

"Please, for the love of God, let him go," I begged, feeling myself crying again. "I'll give it to you. Just please let him go." The man let me drop to the ground at that point, releasing his grip. I coughed and wheezed for several seconds, placing my hand against the wall to steady myself. As much as I wanted to check on Henry at that moment, I knew it would make things worse if I did. There was only one option at that point.

I wove my way around the foyer and into the living room. Across the room, sitting on the floor by the couch, was that bag that I'd carried around with me for years. So much evidence against my uncle inside. And while I had given Chandler and David Finch nearly all of it, there was a whole slew of things still inside that remained untouched. The singular copies I had because I didn't trust anyone with them. I didn't trust to put them on a computer. The only thing I trusted was that they were with me. And in those moments, as I wandered across the room to get it, I wished that I hadn't been so fucking stupid.

There was no doubt in my mind that the guy was just a step behind me as I reached down to grab the bag. The moment I had wrapped the strap into my hand, I was immediately startled by a whooshing sound and then blood-curdling screaming. The most horrifying shrieking sounds I had ever heard in my entire life.

Both the guy behind me and I spun around at the same exact moment. Standing in the foyer, a half dozen yards away, was Henry's girlfriend, Elle Green. The other guy that had been holding Henry hostage was in front of her. Engulfed in a sea of flames. Elle, holding a burning baton in her hand and a canister of lighter fluid they used to ignite them for shows, eyes wide and watching. Henry had been getting off the floor.

For a few seconds, I stood absolutely frozen in place, feeling myself losing sight of reality. Grateful, after all, that Chandler had deterred me from going to meet him at Cirque du Lys. Even the sight of the man in front of me made me unable to breathe. I was so panicked I couldn't see straight.

"CASSIE!" Henry yelled at me frantically, breaking me from my thoughts.

My body acted on instinct then. I saw the guy in front of me starting to turn back, and I immediately whipped the sling bag around me, using every ounce of upper body strength I had from years of athletic training with the silks, and slammed the bag right at his head.

It was full of papers, but I'd carried that fucking thing around for enough time, endured the way it cut into my shoulder every time I did, to know that it was heavy. And sure enough, I'd hit the guy hard enough that I heard a loud snap. He wobbled for a second and then crumbled to the ground.

The guy that had been set on fire was still screaming wildly, crashing into the walls. The entire house was going up in flames. I immediately locked on to Henry and Elle. "Get out!" I screamed at them, throwing my bag over my shoulder. Both of them took off back out of the front door. Meanwhile, I turned and frantically headed for the back of the house. Sucking in cold air as I stumbled onto their patio overlooking the Peace River.

I scrambled around the house, grateful to find that Henry and Elle had already gotten into Henry's car. The second I reached the back door and dove into the car, I screamed at Henry. "Fucking go, Henry!"

Henry slammed on the gas, barreling us down the road. All three of us were yelling expletives for minutes as my friend drove like a maniac trying to get us the hell out of there.

"We need to call the police, we need to call the police," Henry was freaking out. I could see him trembling, and his eyes looked panicked in the rearview mirror.

The three of us had gotten far enough away at that point, I could feel myself calming down a little bit. At least enough to think somewhat straight. "Henry, pull over. Right there. Now." Henry did exactly as I asked him, swerving into a parking space along the side of the nearly empty road. Once he'd parked, the three of us sat in silence, breathing heavily. All of us were still trying to wind ourselves down.

While my friends recovered, I decided to speak first. I looked at Elle, putting my hand on her shoulder. She turned her entire body back to look at me. "I don't even have the words to explain to you how grateful I am. If you hadn't done that, Henry and I would probably be dead." Elle nodded at me, her eyes wide.

"What the hell is going on, Cassandra?" Henry finally asked me. It was one of the only times I had ever heard him use my full name to me, and the sound of it coming from him was so jarring it immediately brought me to attention. "I would ask if we should be worried, but after that—"

"I'm so sorry," I said, feeling an overwhelming sense of guilt. Both for Henry and for his very sweet girlfriend, who had literally just murdered a guy in front of us in self-defense. "The last thing I ever wanted to do was to get everyone involved in this shit. I swear to God. This was never meant to happen."

"Okay, well, now that we're involved, can you clue us in? Especially since I just watched my girlfriend light someone on fire, and not for show."

"He was going to kill you both," Elle argued back, her eyes still wide, shifting between Henry and I. "Thomas has always told me at lessons we have to act on instinct sometimes. We can't overthink when we're in the moment because it just gets in the way."

Thank fucking God for Thomas Little. Another wave of guilt washed over me at the realization that his and Abigail's home was currently burning to the ground. I shook my head, returning my focus to my friends. "And I am so grateful you did what you did. Seriously." Then I made eye contact with Henry through the rearview mirror. "Can you drive us to Rochester?" It was the closest city I knew of that had an international airport, and I was already looking up tickets as I spoke. "I'll explain what I can on the way."

By the time Henry had pulled up to the curb leading to the front of Frederick Douglass International Airport, I'd explained a great deal about what was going on to them, at least the parts about my uncle. I decided to leave the Moreaus out of it for now. All the while, I'd booked a ticket on my phone, grateful for the money I'd been making at Cirque du Lys to be able to afford it. Both of them looked back at me once the car was parked.

"Henry, I know your family lives here, but Elle, do you have anywhere you two

could go? Preferably somewhere as far away from Acrefort as humanly possible. At least for a little while. Until this all settles down, hopefully."

"I've got a grandma who lives in Jacksonville," Elle confirmed. Florida. That was good enough. "We can go down there for a few weeks."

"Good," I replied, nodding. "Get out of here as soon as you can, okay? Promise me." Both of them nodded and promised. "Okay. I need to make a run for it if I'm going to make this fucking flight. And I have to make this flight. I have no other option."

"Alex knows you're coming?" Henry asked me, and I nodded. "Please stay safe, Cass."

I took turns hugging them both tightly. Kissed Henry on the cheek before I let him go. "You two stay safe too. And thank you. I swear to God I don't know how I will ever repay you—"

"Just don't die after all of that," Henry said, offering me a small smile.

It was hard not to smile back at him a little after that comment. "I'll do my best. I love you both. I will try to be in touch as soon as I possibly can. I'm sorry for everything." They both nodded as I slipped out the door. And then I took off as fast as my feet could possibly carry me. A whirlwind of emotions followed the realization that every single one of my dreams was coming crashing down around me. Once again, all because of my fucking traitorous piece of shit uncle. And, I was almost certain, Chandler's father, too.

I was coming to the realization that along with what I'd worked for most of my life, I was losing something that was equally as important to me, if not even more important. The man I loved more than anything, the one I had desperately been clinging to since I was a child. I knew that the only way I was going to keep him safe, keep everyone I loved safe, was by leaving them behind. As much as I almost couldn't bear to do so. It was so utterly devastating that I couldn't even think about it in those moments. All I could do was press onward. Run like fucking hell.

I was getting out of Acrefort. I was going to France.

CHAPTER 34

CHANDLER

From the back of the town car, dozens of blocks away in the darkness of the night, I could still see the giant billowing clouds of black smoke towering in the sky. It was like some horrifying nightmare as we made our approach. A dream that I thought, for certain, I would awake from at any moment.

The car turned onto the street where Lily Moreau's beautiful white circus tent had been standing mere hours ago. Still ablaze, most of it was gone at that point. What little was left was enveloped in fire and smoke or lying in ashes on the ground around it. A row of fire trucks and police cars were gathered around, blocking off most of the street. They were working hard at trying to get the remainder of the fire out.

Once we'd gotten as close as we could, I hopped from the car, running down the length of the sidewalk in search of my friends. I found Abigail, Thomas and Sebastian huddled together, having just finished talking with police officers. The moment they turned back around, I finished my run to them.

All three of them looked distraught beyond measure, but it was a sobbing Abigail who had my attention first. Thomas was holding onto her shoulder, but I immediately drew her into my arms the second I got close enough. She wrung her arms around my neck, hugging me tightly. I let her cry as I stared up at the remains of a place that I had known as home, even more than the condo in downtown Acrefort. My life for decades.

Thomas and Sebastian had been looking too. After a minute, Abigail seemed to calm down, and I let her go. The three of them turned to look at me. All at once, that completely lost expression on Thomas' face shifted. Followed shortly by Sebastian, and then lastly, Abigail, who had still been trying to catch her breath from crying.

Soon after, I realized that they were all three staring at me, wide-eyed and motionless. Eyes drawing down the length of me. When I glanced down, I realized that I was completely covered in blood still, a horrible mess.

It was Abigail who grabbed me by the wrist, dragging me down the sidewalk. The other two walked behind me as if all three were trying to shield me from the fact that we were surrounded by a whole brigade of police officers who could be asking me a lot of questions if they saw me in the state that I was in.

My friends seemed to follow when I darted in the direction of my town car, which had been waiting where I'd left it. The group of us slipped inside quickly, and I told the driver to take us around the block for a few minutes. Preferring not to sit there watching my grandmother's beloved circus burning into ash.

"Chandler, please tell me you just got back from slaughtering a pig for the first time or something," Thomas said as I laid back into the seat. My friends had all chosen to sit across from me, whether on purpose or it had just ended up that way, I wasn't certain. But I was also pretty sure they were all completely at a loss about what to think, which was highly understandable.

For once, instead of lying to a group of people who loved me beyond measure, who had been as close to a family as I had here in Acrefort, I decided to tell them the truth. Some of it, anyway.

Jeanne was probably long gone to the airport by now, so they likely wouldn't be able to interrogate her for the time being, regardless.

"Someone broke into Jeanne's home earlier this evening," I explained calmly, though I was anything but in those moments. "They tried to kill all three of them. Jeanne—ah—managed to take care of it before he did."

All three of them looked as though their eyes were going to fall out of their head, they'd gotten so wide. "What?!" Abigail gasped loudly.

"Oh my God," Thomas said, looking as though he was unable to fathom words. Sebastian also looked like he was trying desperately to say anything at all, but couldn't, as unusual of a thing that was for him.

I had been just about to continue, but Thomas spoke again instead. "Why was someone trying to kill them? Are they all okay? And why the hell, out of anyone, did she call you? I mean, Chandler, you'd be the first person I would call, for certain, but Jeanne—"

All three of them were still staring at me intently. I found my hand running through my hair. It was going a million different directions, and it was crunchy and tangled together in places. I didn't want to think about the fact that it was likely blood from that fucking guy Jeanne had stabbed to death. My stomach tumbled again, and I shook my head.

It was then I looked at Sebastian, of all people. Staring at him as steadily as he'd been looking at me. "When you mentioned at our shows about never having met my grandfather, there was a very good reason for it." Sebastian blinked at me, looking utterly confused. "And I thank God you never did meet him, truthfully, because most people who had ever gotten face-to-face with him since they came over here from France didn't live to talk about it afterward."

The car was so quiet I could hear everyone breathing loudly. I sat back in my seat, looking out the window. We were still driving around the block, and I still could see that horrifying black pillar of smoke towering in the sky. I jerked my head away again, focusing back on my friends.

"I can't explain everything right now, as much as I wish I could, truly. That tent going up in flames tonight wasn't an accident. As much as I know you're sitting there wanting to believe it, Abby. It was deliberate. I think it was some sort of act of war, likely against my father. And I don't even completely understand what the fuck is going on either, which terrifies me."

Abigail still was staring at me, trying to process what I was saying. None of them spoke still, which I was grateful for, so I could get everything out. I was about to open my mouth again when I saw Abigail's attention divert from me. She reached into her pocket, pulling out her phone.

"It's Theresa." She looked up at me, looking horrendously confused. "Our next-door neighbor. Why on earth—"

Thomas looked at me then, clarifying. "I always make fun of Theresa and her husband because they're in bed by eight. Early risers. Like you, I suppose." He was right, I typically didn't stay out too late, and I was definitely feeling it a little, masked by the raging adrenaline.

"Theresa?" Abigail put her phone to her ear just as we'd turned down another street. She sat there, and I watched her facial expression go from somewhat dazed and frazzled to horrified in a matter of seconds. I could tell she was fighting to breathe, and her face had gone ghost white.

We met eyes within a matter of a second. "Tell the driver to take us home. Right now."

I anxiously waited for Abigail to finish the very brief conversation with her neighbor. And it was in those moments I could feel myself, like a spool of thread, unraveling wildly, with no way of stopping. I could barely keep myself grounded in reality. All I could hear in my mind was *mieux vaut plier que rompre.* My father looming over me, taunting me with my grandfather's words. Moreaus weren't emotional creatures. But it was a lie in those moments. My emotions were consuming me alive.

The Littles' house, not unlike Cirque du Lys, was up in flames. And I would have sacrificed that circus in the blink of an eye, hell I would have sacrificed *anything* if I had known that Cassandra Blackstone's body wasn't ash in the middle of their house in those moments.

Thomas, Abigail and I all dialed our phones in a panic, trying to get a hold of her. I'd been ahead of them. Immediately, it went straight to voicemail. Thomas and Abigail got the same response. I dialed again. A third time. A fourth. Losing the ability to breathe every second I continued. Unable to think, unable to do absolutely anything at all.

"Fuck!" I threw my phone across the car, and it slammed into the door, shattering the screen. All three of my friends jumped upon me doing so. I sat shaking, forcing myself to take in air, regardless if I didn't give a shit about doing so anymore. For whatever reason, the single idea of ripping my traitorous piece of shit father into a thousand pieces was the only thing tethering me to reality. With every fiber of my being, I believed that he was the one solely responsible for this nightmare we were driving into.

It was Sebastian who was the one to move from his seat across from me and join me on my side. He reached down, settling his hand on my leg, which was shaking so badly that I was probably moving the entire car. When he did, I found myself gripping my hand on top of his.

I forced myself to look in his direction. Sebastian was staring at Abigail and Thomas for a second, and then he turned to me. "While I realize this situation is particularly dire, I'm going to do my best to bullshit a sense of composure right now." He smiled weakly. "Let's take this one step at a time. It's all we can do until we have any answers. And I'm afraid while I may seem to be a true champion of the performance arts, in my ability to seem put together and calm under pressure, I assure you it will only last so long."

When Sebastian squeezed my leg gently, I turned my attention to him. "Chandler, out of anyone, you by far have some of the most unbelievable self-control I have ever met. It's not perfect, mind you, but it's incredibly impressive. I'm not sure if it's from your work or what it is—but my point is I need you to take over. You clearly understand what the hell is going on right now, at least more so than the rest of us, and we're all terrified..."

Sebastian's voice drifted off as the car turned onto Thomas and Abigail's street. Once again, a building was engulfed in flames. The home that Thomas and Abigail had lived in since they'd moved to Acrefort all those years ago to join the circus. No longer remotely recognizable.

My heart was sinking so deeply inside of me as we approached, it was hard to accept the image I was seeing was real. Then I felt Sebastian squeeze my leg once more as the car slowed to a stop on the sidewalk. Whatever was left of the Acrefort fire department and police squad had gathered around the burning house.

"Don't assume the worst until we know it for certain," Sebastian reminded me.

Even while looking absolutely devastated beyond belief, Thomas met eyes with me. I watched him as he took off the coat he was wearing. He was a lot smaller than me, but the coat was still big. I was worried about him without the coat when he handed it to me, but I wasn't about to sit in the fucking car and do nothing.

"Thank you," I said graciously, throwing it on. I felt like I was sausage stuffed tight in casing, barely able to breathe in the fucking thing, but it sure as hell beat walking out in the state I was in and drawing unnecessary attention to myself. It would be good enough.

The group of us exited the car. Weaved our way through a sea of people gathered in the street. It looked like a lot of the nearby residents had come to see the commotion, and as soon as Abigail found who I assumed was Theresa and her husband, she and Thomas walked over to meet them.

Meanwhile, Sebastian had stuck by me as I frantically searched for the first firefighter I could find. There had been one suiting up by one of the two fire trucks that had arrived, and I halted in front of him.

"Was there anyone alive inside that house?" I asked, the words flying out of my mouth so fast I barely spoke them coherently.

The guy who had been throwing on his jacket, looking soot-covered, spun around to look at me. He blinked for a second, then nodded over my shoulder at the blaze behind me. "There were only two people in there. We're pretty certain," he explained to me, meeting me head-on with his brown eyes. "One of the bodies was burned almost beyond recognition, but he was an older male. They already took what was left of him away. And whoever else they just found, another casualty, is down at the other end of the street there with the pol—"

I didn't let him finish, spinning around and charging through the crowd as fast as I possibly could. Sebastian shouted and chased me. My body weaved in and out of people, all a blur. My ears were ringing. I tried desperately to cling to the words that Sebastian had told me in the town car. Don't assume the worst. Not until I knew for certain.

If that other dead body they'd pulled from Thomas and Abigail's house was Cassandra, I wouldn't make it. Swore to myself in those last minutes I spent with my cousin Frederick, dying in my arms, that if I ever had to go through something like that again, I'd be done. I wouldn't be able to handle it. It would break what was left of me.

The moment I swung around behind an ambulance, whose doors were wide open, I saw the gurney. Noticed the body on it, lying lifeless. Half burned up, bits and pieces beyond repair.

And I nearly collapsed right then and there in gratitude that it hadn't been Cassandra.

I likely would have fallen straight to the ground if it hadn't been for the fact, looking at the man's head, seeing that scraggly gray hair and absolutely distinguishable face of his that was forever burned into my mind after wanting to beat the ever living shit out of him.

It was the man that had stolen Cassandra's bag all those months ago.

A hand wrapped around my shoulder, and I spun around quickly to find Sebastian right behind me. And behind him, Thomas and Abigail. All three of them still looked completely in a haze. Even still, I breathed huge, unbelievably grateful sighs of relief in those moments. Despite everything that had happened.

"Cassandra's still alive," I breathed, hardly able to get it out audibly. Suddenly realizing that my knee was killing me. I leaned over, gripping hold of it, trying to steady myself and catch my breath. "Cassandra's alive."

All of them were still staring at me in disbelief. "I don't know what the hell happened, but she's still alive. She fought off those pieces of shit and got away."

I also realized in those moments that if the same guy that had stolen that bag from her months ago had appeared yet again, it must have had to do with her uncle. Cassandra would have come to the same conclusion, too, I was certain. Why the hell he'd gone after her now, after all this time, I still had no idea. Unless it had something to do with his potential release from jail. But the guy that had gone after her was as dead as dead could be, so I had no way of getting information out of him, one way or the other.

My mind was racing, trying to figure out what was going on. Trying to think what her next steps would have been. Where the hell she could possibly be. Wishing in those moments that I hadn't lost it in a fit of rage and destroyed my phone.

"Fuck. I need to get a hold of Alex," I growled mostly to myself, realizing that if she had contacted anyone in those moments, it would have been her. If she'd been avoiding me, it had likely been on purpose to protect me from this. After I had gotten David Finch involved, there were certainly eyes on me, too. Cassandra knew that.

"Cassandra's friend?" Sebastian inquired, having heard me. My head shot up, and I nodded in reply. Then I watched him fish his phone out of his pocket and click through several screens wordlessly. Feeling a tinge of annoyance that I had no earthly idea what he was doing. He handed me the phone, a number dialing. It was labeled Alex Ledger.

I took it from him, putting it to my ear, just as Sebastian explained, "I learned at Thanksgiving she and I both enjoy supernatural dramas and psychological thrillers." He shrugged at me. "Apparently that is something neither Cassandra nor her fiancee enjoy, so I assumed she'd be happy to have someone to talk to about them."

If I hadn't been such a wound up mess, I likely would have laughed. It was perhaps one of Sebastian's favorite things to talk about outside of Cirque du Lys. Instead, I was instantly alert when I heard Alex on the other end of the line answering.

"Chandler, I was given explicit instructions not to answer if you called," Alex said calmly, but I could tell she was just as wound up as everyone else seemed to be. How the hell she'd known it was me instead of Sebastian, I had no earthly clue, but I didn't ask. "But I'm going to take a guess you're calling to ask me—"

"She's going to France?" I asked, not even letting her finish.

"I think her plane is probably leaving right now," Alex replied. I was about to hang up the phone when I heard her call after me. "She didn't want you coming after her, you know. Cassandra was trying to protect you. Which, now that I know more about you after doing some digging around myself after all the things Cassandra told me, I think is absolutely bat-shit crazy."

"What?" I settled the phone back on my ear, trying to understand what she'd said.

Alex continued. "At least that's what I thought for a little while anyway. Why the hell would she need to protect some dude in the fucking mafia? I mean, it's the *mafia*." I felt my entire body going numb with her words, but Alex went plowing on. "Except the more I started looking into it, I realized that you had to have been in some sort of position where you were just drawn a shitty hand and put in a bad situation."

"Why do you say that?" I managed to ask, trying desperately not to drop the phone. Horrified that Alex knew what she did and now was equally concerned that she was drawing unnecessary attention to herself that could lead to all sorts of problems. Problems that, once again, I had brought on all of them. Part of me was concerned, too, why the hell Cassandra had been divulging information to her friend—and what information she had divulged. Suddenly, I felt myself slightly concerned that what my father had been saying a few hours earlier wasn't entirely inaccurate. I shoved the thoughts away.

"Because there is no fucking way, after everything you have done for that woman the last six months, that you could *ever* be a person that would just kill dozens of people without blinking like your fucking grandfather. No way in hell. I think you're in a very bad situation. And while I think it's pretty fucking shitty that you drug Cassandra into it, I know her well enough by now she probably would have run into it anyway. With how much her entire world has revolved around you since she was little, hell, you could have been a Godfather, and she might have still—"

Alex cut off for a second. I moved a little, thinking maybe it had been the phone, but then I realized she'd just gotten lost in thought. Again, my mind was racing about how she and Cassandra had known about Elliott Moreau. I didn't like this at all.

"I'm sure you're probably on the way to the airport as we speak. Which, despite everything, I think is the right decision. You need to get here, and you need to be straight with her and tell her everything. Because she's got enough to worry about with her uncle, Chandler. And I can't fucking protect her like you can. Put all that fucking family drug money to good use, and figure out how to solve this. I'm serious."

My mind was spinning so fast that I was hardly able to keep up with myself. Alex condemned Cassandra more and more with every word she spoke. I didn't know what to think. "I'm coming. We'll figure it out, I promise. I'm on my way. Keep her safe until I get there."

The phone disconnected before I got a response.

I turned to Thomas and Abigail, both of which were still hovering around me still. "I know this is absolutely impossible for me to ask right this second, and I swear to you if it were any other circumstance, I wouldn't. Can you all ride with me back to the condo for a bit? You can stay as long as you need to or even come back here after. I just need the time to try to explain as much as I can to you. Come up with some sort of plan. I don't want to leave without any explanation after everything."

And, much to my relief, my friends followed me to the town car without question. All the while, I couldn't believe they even still trusted me, but I was grateful they had.

After I'd gotten my friends to my condo and explained to some degree the details of the dangerous situation we were in, I left them again in the early morning hours before the sun had risen. Sebastian had decided to stay with Thomas and Abigail, and I had assumed it was because none of them had wanted to be left alone. I understood completely.

Regardless, I couldn't let time go by any longer. Not after everything that had happened. I needed answers, and I needed them now. So, I'd left as soon as possible, headed straight for the place I absolutely abhorred going to, feeling as murderous as I had ever felt in my entire life.

Unlike most occasions I arrived outside that townhouse, I immediately charged for the steps the minute I'd left the town car.

Rang the doorbell multiple times, followed by slamming my fists into the wooden door with reckless abandon.

I waited for several minutes, expecting an answer, and got nothing. Frustrated, I wove around the length of the building, around to the back. There was an alleyway leading to the back steps of the house. Despite my father's wishes, my mother had hidden a key without him knowing about it for emergencies. Specifically for me to use.

Hell, if this wasn't a fucking emergency. It was about to be for Gabriel Moreau. I knew that much.

Thankfully, the key was right where she had left it for years and years now, buried in the bushes under a fake rock. I snatched it out and proceeded up the back steps, unlocking the door swiftly and throwing it open. It slammed into the wall loudly. I wouldn't have been surprised if I nicked it with the doorknob, but I hadn't remotely cared.

"Gabriel!" I yelled into the house violently, surprised by how dark my tone had gotten. Feeling some minuscule guilt for potentially scaring the shit out of my mother, but at this point, I'd completely lost every shred of my mind.

The house was dead silent. I'd been so noisy, yelled so loudly, surely I would have heard something. He'd have moved, given some indication he'd been there. But I could have heard a pin drop on the floor had it not been for my rampant breathing.

"You better hope you aren't here, you piece of shit," I yelled again, storming through the house. It was pitch black, but I could still make my way out decently, and I knew the layout well enough by now not to get caught up by furniture. I weaved my way down the hall and then around to the stairwell. "Dad!"

Nothing. Silence.

He wasn't there. Which may have been lucky for him and perhaps lucky for me, too, since I didn't do something absolutely reckless. However, it was also concerning beyond belief because if he wasn't there at four in the morning, and neither was my mother, then God knew where the hell he was.

I steadied myself against the wall for a second, suddenly feeling dizzy. My mind had been racing, my body filled with so much adrenaline thinking I was going to come in and likely kill the man the second I saw him, that when I finally settled a bit, I felt like I'd hit a brick wall.

Sucking in a few breaths of air, I tried to figure out what the hell to do. If I hadn't destroyed my fucking phone, I could have attempted to call him, but I was screwed in that regard. He likely wouldn't have answered me anyway, knowing him.

Finally, when I'd gotten my wits about me, I made my way toward the front of the house. The back door was still wide open, but I didn't even care to go and close it. Let him worry about who the hell was in his house when he returned. He deserved as much. Instead, I started to make my way outside.

As I was about to leave, I saw something on the end table that stopped me momentarily. Plane tickets that had been printed out, by the look of it. I blinked, reaching down to snatch them up. Luckily, enough light poured in from the streetlamps outside so I could make it out.

There were two tickets. I assumed for my mother and father. Tickets to Paris, France. When I read the date and time, my blood went ice cold.

They were for tonight. A few hours ago. The same fucking flight Cassandra had been on. I prayed to God the fact that they'd been left here meant they weren't on that plane. That she hadn't been trapped with nowhere to escape, with how dangerous my father was.

A slew of curses flew out of me. Unable to help it, I sent the end table flying across the room, along with the coat rack beside it, suddenly spinning rapidly out of control all over again. I completely lost it for a few seconds, furious at myself that I hadn't gotten here sooner. Not that it would have mattered, but I was still angry that

I delayed anyway. Feeling guilty. If something happened to her, if he did something—I would never forgive myself.

As much of a waste of time as it had been, eventually, I managed to calm myself again, breathing heavily and bracing myself against the wall. My mind centered, and I looked up at the door. Once I did, I immediately left, racing quickly back out of the house to my town car.

I knew I was out of options. My friends would have to make do without me, without all the answers I needed to give them. It had hopefully been enough for now. I would have to explain later, and I certainly would. I owed them that much.

Right now, the only thing I needed to do was get to France.

"Vous devez vous présenter à la porte 30 minutes avant l'heure du départ. Merci."

Almost a day after my conversation with Alexandra, I was finally able to leave Acrefort behind for a place I hadn't been since I was in high school. Thomas and Abigail had taken up residence at my condo for the time being, which was far safer than anywhere else they could have been in Acrefort. Preferring to not have to explain my private practices to them, however, I ensured the back room with all of my Shibari equipment had been satisfactorily locked, explaining to my friends that it was simply storage space. They seemed to believe me.

While I hated leaving my home when everything was in such disarray, I absolutely had to get to Cassandra. There was no other option. So, I left as soon as I could on an early morning flight that had me arriving in Paris in the early evening.

I'd been weaving in and out of the masses of people in the very large airport, feeling anxious about the crowds. At least I blamed it on the flood of humans around me, but really I had been a wound up mess about everything. I was still trying to formulate a semblance of a plan. I knew it would be impossible to focus until I knew Cassandra was beside me again, so I tried and mostly failed to keep everything as far from my mind as I could until then.

Just as I'd arrived outside the main building, I noticed it was significantly warmer than Acrefort while still being cold. I was grateful for that, as I'd be waiting for a ride for a few minutes to take me across the city to where I would hopefully find Cassandra. After another brief conversation with Alex, I'd learned about her distant cousin's circus on the outskirts of Paris, where Alex had been working for the last few weeks since her arrival here. Cassandra had supposedly intended to join alongside her.

Cirque du Lune. It was a relatively new circus, only a few years old. I hadn't even recognized it when Alex had told me, and I knew quite a bit about the circus scene. Either way, it was where I was told to go, so that had been the plan. Afterward, I had other things to attend to, unrelated to finding Cassandra. After everything that had happened and that I had yet to get in contact with them, I had no choice. But given they were an hour outside of Paris proper, and God knew what would happen when I saw them again, they would have to wait a little longer.

I'd been standing outside waiting for the taxi, listening to all the French chatter around me, taking in the scenery of a place I hadn't been to in two decades. I almost missed my phone ringing in my pocket. Before I'd left for France, I had replaced the one I'd broken.

When I reached it, I was surprised to find it was David Finch calling me. I hadn't heard from him since our conversation on Christmas Eve regarding Peter Blackstone. I'd sent him a text message the following day but had yet to receive a response.

Curious, I answered quickly, putting the phone to my ear. "David?"

"—Hey, Chandler," David replied, and I could tell immediately by the tone of his voice and his hesitation that there was something wrong. "I'm glad you answered. Just wanted to give you a quick update on things."

For whatever reason, I found myself sitting down on the curb outside, ignoring the fact that, once again, my knee was aching a little. It bothered me the last few days. "Okay, go for it."

"Well, first, in regards to your text message," David started. There was a long pause on the other end of the line before he spoke again. "I don't know where the hell you got that information, or maybe I might, I don't know—" He trailed off again for a second, and I found myself very confused but waited regardless. "You're right. Apparently, Peter Blackstone was involved with that event. You didn't tell me that your family is affiliated with Le Milieu, however. I got to learn that bit all on my own."

I swallowed deeply, my eyes darting around at all the people wandering around. "I try not to throw that information around unless it's absolutely necessary." Even being distracted by his mention of my family's involvement with the mafia, I was more distracted by the news regarding Peter Blackstone. I was hardly able to comprehend the words he'd spoken.

"Right," David replied, his voice still off. He continued. "Anyway, Peter was in his twenties at the time. I guess he just became involved and worked with Elliott Moreau as some sort of right-hand man. From my understanding, he's always had that role. I didn't quite nail all of it down, and maybe you might find someone who could help you with that, but—"

I blinked, trying my best to follow what he'd been saying. My head spun so fast that I had almost missed what he'd said just before he finished. "What do you mean find someone else?"

"Chandler," David's tone had grown even more serious and strange than it had before. "I'm out of this, okay? I have two kids to think about. My own well-being. After all the information Cassandra sent over yesterday, this is getting way too deep, even for me. And, while I want to believe that you're a goodhearted and well-intentioned guy, and I sincerely hope you are... After all the shit I read and the stuff I dug up today after the fact—"

"David, what the hell are you talking about?" I saw the car I'd been waiting on finally approach and waved it down as I got back up to my feet again. The fact that Cassandra had sent over more information to him was news to me. I had assumed she'd given him everything months ago.

"I can't, Chandler. I'm sorry. I even thought to try and warn Cassandra after I happened upon information about you and that family in Acrefort a few years ago, thanks to the stuff she sent yesterday, but I don't even know how she fits into all of this now. For all I know, you're both dangerous, as much as I don't want to believe that to be true. I can't do it anymore."

My entire body went cold at the mention of that family. I knew exactly what he'd been talking about. Hadn't needed to clarify. I didn't think I'd ever hear about that again. At least I'd prayed I wouldn't have to. Clearly, I'd been mistaken.

The line went quiet, and I heard David cough and clear his throat. "I honestly have no idea what the hell is going on, and I don't really care. I'm planning on staying far away from this. And I hope you respect my wishes and keep me out of it from now on."

"David—"

"Good luck, Chandler," I heard David say before the line disconnected. Meanwhile, the car stopped in front of me. I swung open the back door, hopping inside. Directed the driver to the address for Cirque du Lune that I'd looked up while heading out of the airport. My French was rusty, but it seemed good enough for the driver to understand.

As we drove away from Paris Charles de Gaulle Airport, I watched it slowly disappear from the rearview mirror. Took in the beautiful French sights around me. Even still, all I could think about in those moments was Cassandra Blackstone. I was terrified that every fucking thing my father had warned me about days earlier was actually true after all.

A man I hated more than just about anyone had seemed to know me far better than I gave him credit for. My ex-wife, too, for that matter, had blatantly pointed out my ignorance to me on several occasions that night I'd helped her.

Cassandra had been lying to me this entire time. How much she actually knew, what the hell she was doing with the information she had, I had no idea.

But I was here. I knew exactly where she was. And I had every intention of finding out.

CHAPTER 35

CASSANDRA

In a beautiful downtown district of Paris, France, one of the world's most eclectic, modern circuses, Cirque du Lune existed. A show that featured radical and modern urban influences and electro-punk inspirations. It was one that fit my best friend Alex's unique tastes perfectly. She and her cousin Cecilia Blanchet, who owned and ran the place since its inception a decade prior, seemed to have that very much in common.

While I certainly had heard all about this place many times over the years from Alex, it had been the very last place I had ever imagined myself ending up. Years ago, after I'd first seen Chandler Moreau for the first time performing, my only desire had been to be able to learn from him one day and, if I had been lucky enough, work with Cirque du Lys.

Months ago, I'd thought I'd spend many years in Acrefort, attached to the circus I'd dreamed about for half my life. Perhaps, when I was ready to try new things, Chandler and I would go elsewhere. He'd teach, and I'd perform. Maybe we'd both even teach together.

I had been in France for only a day now, so it was still hard to wrap my mind around. Every single second, I had to continue to tether myself to my new reality. One in which nearly all the dreams, all the expectations I had, changed. Somehow, I'd have to accept and make sense of this new life I was forced to lead, however unexpected it had been. In a world in which I existed without a person who had been the entire reason I'd made it to where I was in the first place. A world without Chandler Moreau.

The only reason I was continuing to hang on to a reality like that, the only reason I hadn't given up entirely, was for the simple fact that, even if he would never know about it, I still desperately wanted to impress him. Still needed him to be proud of me and everything I accomplished in regard to my career. So, that singular thing kept me grounded the last few days, despite everything. I tried to convince myself that I was honoring him still, carrying on that duty as his protege.

If we couldn't be together, it was the least I could do after everything he'd done for me.

"What do you think?" Alex asked me after we'd wandered around the building. She'd been showing me backstage in the wings. We'd been looking at some of the old sets that were stored back there, all of them mesmerizing and intricate. Just as spectacular as anything at Cirque du Lys. The two of us wandered back onto the stage again and then down into the audience, sitting down in some plush blue seats.

When we settled, I turned my attention to my friend. Admittedly, the entire time I'd been there that evening, I'd been lost in my head. Even through their rehearsals. I was still in denial it was happening, as much as I was trying to force myself to accept there wasn't an alternative. After nearly dying from an altercation orchestrated by my uncle, fleeing had been my only option. Not only to protect myself, but Chandler too.

Whether I liked it or not, this was my reality now. "It's not what I saw myself doing," I admitted, looking back out at the stage, trying to take in the entire room. The place was smaller than Cirque du Lys, but I liked the intimacy of it. "But I mean, it's pretty great." I offered Alex a small smile then, shrugging. "Better than I could have imagined, given everything. I'm excited to get started."

That part had been true. As usual, if I could count on absolutely anything to distract me from the harsh realities of my life, it was when I got lost in the silks. They worked like magic every single time, without fail.

Alex looked down for a moment, and I watched her fish through her jacket pocket, pulling out her cellphone. She looked like she was reading something for a moment, then looked back up at me. "Dana just got off work. She needs my help for a few hours. Do you want to head back home?"

Home. God, it was so weird hearing her say it. The word didn't even register. Every time I had heard that word the last few months, it had been from Chandler or when I'd said it myself. I'd gotten so accustomed to thinking of his condo that way. It felt like such a natural thing. And yet, once again, I found myself completely at a loss with the word.

That little two-bedroom apartment I was now sharing with Alex and Dana was certainly a nice place to stay. They'd been gracious, and I appreciated it. But it wasn't home. Not really. That word had lost its meaning again, entirely. And it didn't really even have to do with the condo. Chandler had been my home. That apartment was just a place for me. Someplace safe with someone I loved dearly. It would be enough for now, I supposed.

"I actually was going to stay and practice for a little while," I admitted. "Cecile already told me I was welcome. She gave me the code to lock up after." The place had emptied out, outside of Alex and myself, and I had free reign of the aerial equipment. I thought I should probably use it to my advantage, and with the state of my mind over the last few days, I could certainly use it. I was going through withdrawal.

Alex nodded. "Okay, well, call me when you're on the way back, okay?" I could tell by the expression on her face that she was freaked out about me being by myself. I felt guilty because I'd become this fragile thing to her now, someone she was constantly worried about. Hated that my abrupt disappearance was probably consuming Chandler too.

It was an unfortunate reality, and I was doing my best at this point.

I waited until Alex had gathered up her things and left me. Once the entire theater was empty, the stage dimly lit and eerily quiet, I turned back. Made my way up the stairs and wandered around for a few minutes, taking everything in again. Still trying to force this new reality on myself. Still wishing, every single second, that it was just a dream.

But I was here. In France. At Cirque du Lune.

And if any singular thing would keep me here, where I needed to be now, where I had no choice in being—it was the long pieces of fabric dangling in front of me. There were several sets hanging, enough for three or four aerialists. At one point, Cecile told me a duo had been working there, but they had left for another show in Germany the previous week. It had left Cecile in a bit of a bind, so she'd been more than ecstatic to see me showing up to help.

For now, I'd get lost in those silks that always took my mind away. Just like they were meant to. I pulled the new phone I'd gotten myself a few days prior out of my pocket, searching for my music. Thumbed through a handful of playlists, finally deciding on some of the music from this very circus from seasons past. I wasn't really familiar with it, and it was all in French, but since I'd be immersing myself in it from now on, I might as well get started.

The music started to play, so I sat my phone down on the stage. Afterward, I returned my focus to the silks. They were around the same height as the ones at the Dreamers Academy, about seventy feet or so.

I took a long deep breath, steadying myself before I began to pull myself up from the stage and into the air. The world disappeared around me, and I fell captive to the music that was playing and the movements my body was making without even having to think about it. I got myself about two-thirds of the way up before I settled again, preparing to work.

Surprisingly, it had been a shooting star pose that I'd begun with, which had been one from the winter showcase at Cirque du Lys. I drew my hand outward toward the audience as I spun a little in the silks. Meanwhile, I closed my eyes for a moment, imagining Chandler a dozen feet below me in the silks adjacent to mine. Watching and waiting.

I lost myself in the movements that I made, deciding to go through with the routine I'd done for the showcase for whatever reason. It had been the last movements I'd done on the silks. It felt almost natural in a way, and as much as I thought it would make me feel devastated and sad, it was weirdly comforting.

Temporarily, my eyes closed as I fell down into that all-familiar bow and arrow pose. The pose I'd taken just before I dropped to Chandler in our routine when he'd made the call the opening night of the show to do it, and he'd executed it flawlessly. I hadn't recalled ever feeling so proud of him as I had in those moments.

My mind had been wandering briefly when I'd come back, paused in the pose I'd been in because I hadn't known what else to do. I just dangled there, upside down, eyes closed, trapped in those beautiful memories with him again. Grateful, after everything, that I would at least have those. Even if nothing else would ever happen again.

"I've got you, Cassandra."

That voice sounded like some ethereal whisper mixed in with the music playing in the background. It hadn't even fazed me at first, convinced I was too wrapped up in my head and those memories of the man I loved while doing the thing I had been convinced that he and I were meant to do for the rest of our lives together.

When my eyes fluttered back open, seconds after I'd heard his voice in my mind, I was grateful that I'd been wrapped up in the silks the way I had. That my brief few seconds of surprise hadn't sent me plummeting to my death.

I blinked a few times, completely convinced that I had to be dreaming.

Dangling a dozen feet or so below me, wrapped up in a set of brilliant gold silks that were alongside the royal purple ones I'd picked, staring straight up at me with those magnificent green eyes, was Chandler Moreau.

We stared at one another for what felt like an eternity, neither of us moving. Both of us seemed to have fallen in a similar rhythm of our breaths, as we usually tended to do when we were up here together, lost in the fabrics. Eventually, there was a tiny flicker on Chandler's face. A subtle thing I'd grown so accustomed to now that was meant just for me. In moments just like this. The minute I saw it, we both took another breath together, and then I released myself. Performing an effortless salto, straight down into his arms.

Though I'd still had a hold of my own silks, Chandler had wrapped us in his own the moment I'd arrived. I was caught so off-guard by his presence there in front of me and the fact that I was holding him again. I could hear him laughing softly into my ear as he clung onto me, too.

"You looked like a dream up here practicing," he said, face bright as ever. "I felt like I was in Soliei Theater all over again watching you." I pulled back from him a bit, so I could meet his gaze. My fingers drew gently along his beard line, getting lost in all those little flecks of grays interspersed with the dark browns. Convincing myself that I was actually touching him. That it was him here, holding me in his arms in those moments.

"You're here." I could barely speak the words at all. They came out in a breathy whisper, still completely dazed. "You found me."

"I did," Chandler was still smiling so broadly it stretched the entire length of his face. Every bit of it held me captive. He'd released one of his hands from the silks he'd been gripping onto, reaching out to swipe the hairs from alongside my face and tuck them behind my ear. The instant he had, I was smiling too. "I may have had some help from Alex."

So, it had been my best friend's doing, at least in part. While I imagined I could have been angry at her for her recklessness, instead, all I could feel was gratitude. There had been nothing I could have wanted more in those moments than this.

The two of us focused on each other, unable to stop smiling. Our breaths came in unison again, and after a little pause, we took off together. The music was still playing on my phone below us. And now, with Chandler here with me, I no longer cared so much about remembering that old routine of ours from Cirque du Lys.

Now, I just wanted it to be whatever it was. Whatever chose to exist for now, here, in these moments together. Chandler appeared to have the same idea, the two of us taking off side-by-side. He let me decide what I wanted to do, and the instant I'd made my first drop, he cascaded right alongside me. Lost in a routine that felt as absolutely perfect and natural as anything we'd ever done together.

Eventually, we transcended to the stage, both of us clearly satisfied with those moments that had transpired between us, the need for us to be together again with those silks we loved so dearly being satisfied, at least for now. By the time we'd reached the floor together, I was already back in Chandler's arms again. My body clung around him tightly. Wound up from a million different emotions all at once, between the thrill of performing with him and being mesmerized that he was there at all—and then, the instant we'd steadied back on solid ground, the most consuming thing of all. The feeling of being wrecked with desire for him.

"I thought I'd lost you," Chandler said to me in soft pants, our faces pressed together, bodies woven in fabrics. I was still trying to catch my breath too, but the moment he'd spoken those words to me, when those green eyes latched onto mine, I lost sight of everything else.

My mouth crashed into his, and I felt his hands draw around my face. Those entire next few minutes between us were nothing but a frantic mess. The moment I had started, I knew there wasn't any stopping it. Chandler had seemed equally as convinced, clearly as lost as I had felt.

Before I knew what had even been happening, he escaped from the silks. When we finally had to stop to catch our breaths, he slipped away momentarily. He moved as elegantly as when he'd done his Shibari ties on me, seeming to do it again. In some strange yet equally mesmerizing way, with the silks we'd been using minutes earlier.

Chandler bundled the fabric around me quickly. Nothing like all the times in his condo, all those thoughtful movements ensuring every little design, every knot, was in perfect form. This was some beautiful chaos. Some sort of strange, hurried mess. It wasn't art for him this time, my body that canvas he loved to lay those ropes on.

These were meant to bind. Meant to capture. In a beautiful mess of purple and gold.

As he yanked them frantically against me, I couldn't help but gasp in surprise. Forgetting the rush I always felt, completely helpless beneath every twist and turn and knot. It was no different then, perhaps even more surreal of an experience simply because he'd transformed something we both loved so dearly into something that was obliterating me.

I dangled there helplessly above the stage in those moments, feet barely dusting the ground, my entire upper body completely lost. I was quite literally one with the silks now.

Chandler had disappeared behind me in those moments after he'd finished wrapping me in the fabrics. I could hear sounds behind me. Knew nearly every single one of them as they began happening. His shoes clattering across the stage. Jeans, falling to the floor, his keys still rattling around inside them.

For a long few seconds, the room was eerily quiet, except for the sounds of our breathing. I had been seconds away from inquiring what he was doing, the wait agonizing. But then I felt Chandler's fingers dragging against me, roughly pulling down the leggings I'd been wearing to the floor. The moment he did, I found myself verbalizing some satisfied sound in reply, wanting this agonizing wait to be over. Though I knew Chandler well enough by now that he sometimes took a great deal of pleasure in tormenting me.

That hadn't seemed to be the case tonight. The moment I'd been relieved of the fabrics from the lower half of my body, I felt that familiar grasp around my hips. Oftentimes, he did it to steady me, but tonight he'd done it to lift me off the ground, legs dangling on either side of his own. Seconds later, he pushed into me, and I gasped into the room. He wasn't wasting a second of time, and it had been an utter relief.

The next few minutes of my life were beautiful chaos. I gave into every second of it, feeling the world spinning around me as Chandler sent me to another time and place, crashing into me with reckless abandon. Both of us filled that empty theater with the sounds of our gasps and moans, interspersed with our bodies impacting over and over again.

"Fuck, Cassandra," Chandler gasped behind me, and I lost myself in the way he'd said my name to me.

I lost all sense of time and place. It felt so eerily similar to those first moments on the stage of The Crucible with him when he'd bound me in jute for the first time. The entire room had disappeared. All I could think about, all I could hang on to, was the feelings. The experience.

Remember, little papillon. It's only you and this rope...

"Chandler," I found myself crying out, elongating his name. My entire body trembled beneath his hands that were tightly clenched

around my waist. The sound seemed to have sent him further spiraling than he already was. His pace quickened, slamming into me so mercilessly that I thought he'd knock my soul from my body.

The entire world disappeared. Every cell in my body ignited. I gave in. If I died right then, on that circus stage in Paris, I didn't care. Let my last memories be of Chandler Moreau fucking me into oblivion.

I'd already lost myself to every single second of the overwhelming relief I'd felt, pleasure beyond anything I could have imagined. I completely and utterly let it consume me. Chandler had been right beside me, calling out my name to me in gasps and moans as he continued on for what felt like forever. I savored every second of it.

He finally started to slow. The world came back into view again. When it had, the moment felt like it had barely lasted. I already wanted to be back there again. I missed it desperately.

Chandler eventually removed himself from me. Both of us were panting audibly. I dangled there, still tightly bound in the fabrics, feet barely able to touch the ground. Couldn't see him as he began to move around the stage, but I could hear him. He'd picked up his jeans. I knew by the sound of his keys again.

I waited patiently, assuming once he'd finished dressing himself, he'd come and ask if I was ready to be untied like he usually did. After, I could have those moments I wanted. To be able to touch him again. I needed to reassure myself that he was actually there with me, that this wasn't some wild dream I'd been having after I'd fallen asleep in the audience or something.

The wait for him was agonizing. It felt as if it drew on forever. After it had seemed as though he'd dressed himself, at least by the sound, I just dangled there. The room was silent outside of my breathing. I didn't even hear Chandler breathing for a little while.

I'd been seconds away from calling out to ask him what he was doing and if he could let me go when I felt a rapid, sudden jerk of the silks. I was shot upright, my body straight and tall. No longer was I able to touch the ground with my feet. I was completely suspended in the air.

Chandler had been the one to do it. The only reason I knew was because the second after it had happened, I felt his mouth press against my ear. He'd done it so many times before. The sensation was very distinct, along with that all-too-familiar graze of his beard tickling against me. The heat of his breath was pulsing against my skin, ripping a shiver down my spine.

"Okay, little papillon..."

That voice, the very distinctive tone of his, which would normally have me quivering in anticipation when he said the pet name to me, had completely shifted. It wasn't seductive. Didn't hint at anything remotely pleasant following after. Chandler Moreau was deathly serious. Far more than I had ever heard him in all the time I'd known him.

My breath hitched. My entire body went ice cold.

"No more games. No more secrets. You're going to tell me *everything*."

AND, FINI.

DISCIPLINE:

Book Two of the Ties That Bind series

Releasing **September 5th, 2023**

Discipline follows Chandler Moreau and Cassandra Blackstone to the beautiful and romantic city of Paris, France. You'll get to meet some of Chandler's estranged family he talked about in *Obedience*, as well as a variety of new characters... And maybe a few surprising ones, too! While this story still certainly has plenty of romance, it also is very much a mystery and suspense book too...it'll leave you guessing and on your toes until the very end.

Cassandra and Chandler must figure out a way to trust each other again, after everything that went down at the end of *Obedience,* and they have to figure out the way to the truth of things. All the while, the mystery between their two families and the secrets that have been looming start to come unraveled, all while the pair's beautiful romance story continues in the city of love.

Don't miss the second installment of the Ties That Bind Series, which in Liza and her Circus Crew's humble opinion, is even better than the first book!

A Note About the Audiobook: While the ebook and paperback are confirmed for this date, negotiations for the audiobook are still in the works, but I highly doubt Daniel will leave you (or Cass) hanging with that cliffhanger. I think he likes Chandler a little too much. If you listened to the audiobook, be sure to give the fabulous narrators a follow on social media, and a shout out if you want to tell them how awesome they are—and how much you want them back!

Follow Daniel Zbel
on Instagram

Follow Rapunzaroo
on Instagram and TikTok

About Liza Snow

Liza is pretty much your average thirty-something from Florida. She lives with her husband and her three animal children (Gideon — Labradoodle, Neelix — Collie, Vegeta — Siberian cat). When she hasn't been obsessing about *Obedience,* which pretty much was before October 2022, she loves binge-watching shows, reading scifi, fantasy and romance novels, playing video games and board games, and eating a wide variety of foods—especially Indian! Which is why Chandler's fav was Indian.

Liza would like to give a special thanks to her wing-woman throughout this entire series, Mads Arlow. While Liza did come up with the story and wrote most of it, it wouldn't be anything like it is now if it weren't for Mads. She is as much of a contributor to the book as Liza. Thank you so much for everything!

Follow Liza on Social Media

Newsletter Sign-Up
Facebook
Instagram

Printed in Great Britain
by Amazon